love con.

presenting with
DANIEL

a second chance
romance

Belinda E Edwards

Belinda Edwards

ISBN: 978-1-917169-12-7

Sparkling Creatives.

G7 Beverley Enterprise Centre, Beck View Road Beverley, UK. HU17 0JT

Dedication

This story took time to emerge. I am so grateful for the support I feel from my husband for what I decide I want to do. He always seems to understand what I want from life. Without his support and encouragement, this book would not have been written. This book is for him.

Prologue

Daniel Woods took a moment to watch what was happening. He stood with his back against the wall, watching the party going on around him. Something felt off. He was usually the centre of any party, but today felt very different. The pizza and beer were flowing, and everyone else seemed to be enjoying this post-training get-together. He studied carefully the way his teammate and host, Charlie Robertson moved with ease in the group. The guys, all members of the same county cricket team, were enjoying the atmosphere.

Daniel was most interested in the way Charlie behaved around India, his live-in girlfriend. He was pleased to see them finally together. There had been times when Daniel thought it would never happen. Tonight's question was, where did he fit in? He felt lost, and it sat like a lead weight in his stomach.

India was busy making more pizzas for them all, and he wandered over to help.

"What can I do? Want me to make a few of those now?"

"No thanks, Daniel." India's answer came a little too quickly. It would normally roll off him, but today, he wondered if she would ever trust him. *Does anyone take me seriously?*

The doorbell rang, and he strode over to open it. Anything to be useful. When he found Joe and Tilly Cookson, he smiled and bowed as he opened the door. Daniel secretly admired Joe. He came from a successful family, and he had married Tilly, despite all the objections. Now together, they had a growing business of their own. And Tilly? They all loved fiery Tilly.

Daniel's eyes followed Tilly as she breezed in, carrying a plant and gift-wrapped box. She made a beeline for India in the kitchen. Joe followed, hot on her heels, with a stack of cheesecake boxes. Charlie collected a fresh bottle of prosecco and joined them all at the island.

Joe and Tilly emptied their hands, and everyone exchanged hugs and handshakes. India was hugged and kissed so hard she nearly keeled over. Charlie grabbed her elbow, and then slipped his arm possessively around her waist, kissing her temple. Daniel felt his heart stop. He couldn't imagine that he would ever have that sort of relationship. He watched the four friends interact, not sure why it bothered him so much. Daniel felt like the audience today, watching everyone, not sure where he belonged.

There seemed to be some excitement in this group, so Daniel edged closer to listen.

"It's from my dad. Please open it," Tilly urged India. Inside the box, India found a bunch of keys and a sheet of paper. The keys to her new office.

"Thank you. You don't know how much this means to me." Daniel smiled, happy to see her settling into Leeds, but somewhere deep in his stomach was an empty feeling.

"Oh, I think we do. Anyway, when do you think you will have the office open?" Joe asked.

"A couple of weeks. Why?"

"We need to make an appointment to come and discuss a new project with you," Tilly gushed. "That is, if you are both up for it." Her eyes bounced between India and Charlie. India appeared to pick up on her excitement.

"So now you have to tell me more. What is it?"

"We are taking Gym Away to shopping TV. We have a meeting at the studio in three weeks. So, are you in?"

Although they answered in unison, India said "YES" as Charlie gave an emphatic "NO." Something about this exchange made Daniel's heart skip. *If Charlie is saying no, could this be an opportunity for me?*

Daniel quickly checked out the others in the room. He soon realised he wasn't the only one to hear. *Bloody Zach's ears are spinning. He's heard it, too. Damn the man.* Zach Mitchell was a hard man to hate, but Daniel was so jealous of the easy way he drifted through life; hate was almost the word for it. His older brother, Ben, seemed to have it all, except Daniel realised how hard Ben worked. His being so perfect made his own life harder, but he still loved his brother. Zach was a different matter.

Daniel plastered on a smile and grabbed a bottle of beer. He needed to think this through. That was a novelty for him. Mostly, he saved energy by not thinking at all. He took his beer outside, where he found the younger players. A broad grin broke out across his face as he recognised the game in progress. Once Daniel joined in, everyone was laughing at his antics, and now Daniel was in his element.

Someone passed him another beer, or was it two? It could have been three, Daniel wasn't counting. Who cares anyway? Daniel certainly didn't. He had trained hard and now he was going to play hard. Wandering back into the kitchen, he managed to trip on the step to the door. Tottering for several steps until he bumped into Tilly Cookson. He grabbed her arms to stop himself from falling and stood up again.

"Sorry about that. Are you OK?" Tilly looked shocked, and over her shoulder, Daniel saw Joe Cookson glaring at him.

"Sorry!" Daniel repeated as he let go of Tilly.

"Just slow down, mate," Joe sighed. It didn't help that Daniel had such long limbs. They seemed to be a big part of his problem. Joe held Tilly's arm.

"Are you OK, babe?"

"I'm fine."

"I just worry, even more now. What happened anyway?"

"I guess he tripped. I always think he is going to fall over."

"Look at him. I can't believe he is a professional athlete."

"Joe Cookson, I know you have a soft spot for Daniel Woods, so don't try to pretend otherwise."

"And you don't?"

"Oh yes, I do! I just don't understand why." A grin spread across her face as she leaned into her husband's shoulder.

Daniel shook his head and made his way to the kitchen, where his brother was saying his goodbyes. Daniel didn't hide his disappointment as he grabbed Ben's arm.

"You're going already?"

"Yes, I have to pick Amanda up and get back to let the babysitter go and now I'm taking you with me." Daniel stood back from his brother.

"Me? Go home with you? Now?"

"You can't drive home after all that beer, and Dad will expect your help tomorrow, so it's time to go."

"I could just stop drinking now and stay here, couldn't I?"

"Well, you still shouldn't drive! And don't look at me like I enjoy parenting you like this every day."

Daniel put down the bottle of beer he was about to open. He blew out a long breath and looked at the younger players still enjoying themselves. Annoyingly, his brother was right. *He's always bloody right. If I go home with Ben, I can see the rest of the family. I have to work on the farm tomorrow, so going now is a good idea.*

"I would like to see the kids, so OK, I'll come with you."

"Don't make it sound like you are doing me a favour, Dan. Face it, now I need to wake up early in the morning to get you off to the farm."

Getting ready to leave, Daniel hugged Tilly and apologised again for bumping into her and shook Joe's hand. The conversation about shopping TV still bounced around his head. It seemed a sensible idea to be nice to them. When it came to saying goodbye to India and Charlie, he decided he should say something about the TV opportunity.

"Charlie, thanks for inviting us all today. It's great for the team to be together."

"Ha, it's more India's way to see you all. She would adopt a few of you if I let her."

"Really? And you're stopping her?"

"I would rather we had our own kids."

"Well, I'm sure you'll enjoy some part of that happening."

"I'm working on it."

"I better go thank her now."

Lifting India into a hug, he thanked her and, as he lowered her again, he mumbled. "If Charlie won't do that TV thing, I would do it for you."

India swallowed before she answered. "That's a huge commitment, Daniel. Are you sure?"

"Maybe you need to tell me more about it, but yeah, I think I would enjoy it."

"Let me get moved into my office and we can talk after I know more myself." Daniel gave her one last little hug and left with Ben. He got the feeling that India wasn't as keen as he hoped she would be.

As they reached the door, Zach Mitchell shouted goodbye to the brothers as he set off upstairs, taking them two at a time. *I guess if Zach is living with Charlie and India, he's more likely to get this new job.* Sighing, he tried to figure out how everyone seemed to love Zach and take him seriously, yet still think he was fun at the same time.

Getting into Ben's car, the banter between them resumed.

"So, big brother, how do you get away with not helping on the farm these days?"

"I still help when he needs me, and you know it, but I'm not living there, paying no rent, and getting my meals cooked. I bet Rebecca is still doing your washing for you, too."

"Yes, but that's because I am doing other jobs." *Why didn't I even start this? I can't win, well, not with Ben anyway. I've known that since I was ten. Time to change the subject.*

"So, where are we picking Amanda up from?"

"Sally's house."

"And who is babysitting?

"Amy."

"Amy? As in Sally's daughter?"

"Yes."

"So, we are driving past your house to pick Amanda up, to go back to your house and pick Amy up, to take her back to where Amanda is?"

"Yes."

"Why?"

"Well, my kids are 4 and 2. I'm not leaving them on their own!"

"No, but now you have me, so if we go to your place. I can stay with the kids whilst you go to Sally's and swap Amy for Amanda."

Ben took a while to think about this, too long for Daniel. Inside, he was sifting through all the times Ben didn't trust him. He felt sure that his big brother resented him. But right now, he was getting so annoyed that his brother didn't think he could look after two children for half an hour.

"Oh, I see!" Daniel folded his arms over his chest and glared at his brother. "So, you leave your kids with a fourteen-year-old, but you won't leave them with me?"

"Fifteen."

"Fifteen?"

"Amy is fifteen, but no, you are right. It's just, well, that was the plan this morning, and I hadn't considered changing it. Then I was thinking about how to get back to the house from here."

"Go left down this next street and then left at the bottom. That brings you on to Cardigan Road." Ben stared briefly at his younger brother, then did as he suggested without speaking.

Ha! He actually listened. Ben took the next left, and soon they were pulling up outside the Victorian villa. From the outside, it looked like every other house on the street. Inside, the house had been so modernised it was hard to remember what it looked like when Ben bought it six years ago.

"Wait there, big brother. I'll go send Amy out." Not waiting for Ben to reply, Daniel bounded out of the car, striding up to the dark red front door. Punching in the key code, he continued into the sofa area, where he found Amy settled in front of the TV. Daniel's hands covered her eyes as he blew a raspberry on top of her head.

"Dan? Is that you? Stop messing!"

Daniel threw his legs over the back of the sofa and bounced down next to Amy. Pushing his bony elbow into her ribs with three bounces.

"So, when did you hit fifteen Amy One?"

"Eleven months ago! I'll be sixteen very soon."

"Wow, how did I miss that?"

"Well, judging by the smell, you were drinking beer for most of it. My mum says she has never seen you sober."

"And I thought she liked me. Go get your coat. Ben is taking you home. What have you done with the kids?"

"They're in bed. Amanda got them ready, and the boy-child was in bed by the time I got here. The girl-child was ready for a story. She is in bed, but I wouldn't be surprised if you see her. She's been asking for her daddy since I arrived." Amy put on her coat and started to collect her glass and plate from the table.

"Leave those, I'll sort them. Go save Ben coming in the house."

"Thanks, Dan. Goodnight."

"Goodnight, Amy One, and thanks for looking after the kids."

"Why do you call me that?"

"Amy One? I thought you liked it?"

"I did when I was twelve, but now…"

"Now, you are nearly sixteen, you want me to stop?"

Smiling at the dejected look on his face, she softened. "Well, not in front of other people."

"Ah, just between us, young Padawan, I see. I'll try to remember that. Now get off before Ben comes looking for you."

"Thanks, Dan."

Daniel followed her to the door and watched her get into the car with Ben. He waved as they left. Returning to the sofa, he picked up the glass and plate and took them to the island in Amanda's shiny new kitchen. He wandered over to the fridge and was about to help himself to a bottle of beer when the comments from today flowed back through his brain. He put the bottle back and went to switch on the kettle. Whilst it boiled, he washed the small number of pots on the side. Amy's comments were the ones that went mostly back through his brain. Had Sally truly never seen him sober? His coffee made, he dried the pots and put them away. *I can do this. Why not? I can show India and Ben and all the others in my life that I can be responsible.*

As he took his coffee back into the lounge, he heard a little voice at the top of the stairs. The girl-child stood looking down from the top step. "Daddy?"

"No, baby girl, just Uncle Dan." Martha made her way carefully down the stairs until halfway down, she sat on the step.

"NuncleDanDan, where is Daddy?"

"He's gone to get your mummy. They'll both be home soon. Now, why are you out of bed?" He put down his coffee, walked up the stairs, and sat down next to his niece.

"I like Daddy's stories."

"And you don't like mine?"

"I like the one with the lion that roars. Rwarar! But Daddy's stories make me sleepy." *I bet they do!*

"Would you like me to read you a story until Daddy gets home?"

"Will you read the one about the lion?"

"If you want me to." Taking her by the hand and leading her back upstairs, he forgot all about his coffee and went into full-on storytelling uncle mode, complete with funny voices.

The following day, Daniel found the drive home harder than usual. The effects of drinking at the party the night before reminded him of his need to change. Unusually, he hadn't been able to sleep. He had struggled to get comfortable, and he'd spent too much time thinking.

The drive back to Malton could take over an hour, but it was early, and the roads were clear. He enjoyed driving but today, it gave him too much time to think. Much as he loved the feeling of going home to the farm, it reminded him he was still living with his dad and sister. It was something else that made him less of an adult. Yes, he worked hard to help his dad, but he didn't need to do anything that involved making a real decision. He told himself he stayed because his dad needed him, and that was being grown-up. But deep down, he knew it also meant he didn't have to worry about any of the boring stuff, like paying electric bills or buying food.

He worked for his place on the farm but the wages he earned for playing cricket were his to spend how he liked, and he enjoyed having fun. He didn't even pause to think about going out when he was away with the team. He loved to splash out on holidays, but it was his constantly changing mood regarding cars that cost him the real money.

When he eventually pulled into the yard outside the farmhouse, he watched his sister Rebecca unloading groceries from the back of the old Land Rover. He paused for only a moment before jumping out of his shiny Range Rover to help her carry the shopping into the kitchen. He knew the drill. All the bags were placed on the scrubbed oak table in the centre of the room. Only when all the bags were in the house would Rebecca direct him where to take everything. Not that he didn't know, but he preferred to be told, just to be sure he got it right. As the youngest in the family, no one ever held back telling him when he got things wrong, no matter how hard he tried.

He did all this without a word, so before she started giving him instructions, Rebecca paused and gave her "little" brother a long look.

"OK, what have you done wrong this time?"

"Nothing!"

"Something is wrong. You're far too quiet. Did the party go well at Charlie's?"

"Yes."

"Oh! One-word answers! Now I know something's wrong." Daniel sank into a chair at the table. He looked at his sister, wondering how much he could say. Biting his lip, he tried something.

"Becca, you trust me, don't you?"

"With my life, little brother, but with my friend's hearts, my car or a pack of chocolate biscuits, not so much."

Daniel's head hit the table and Meg, his favourite dog from the pack his dad kept, slipped her nose onto his lap.

"Hey, look, Meg trusts you. What's brought this on?"

"Yesterday, India wouldn't let me help make the pizzas."

"Have you remembered you started a fire at their house making toast last year? And that wasn't your first kitchen fire."

"I just got distracted."

"So, you are this upset because India wouldn't let you make pizza? Did you actually want to make pizza? Or is this about something else?"

"I just wanted to help. I like India and she shouldn't have to cook for all of us so often."

"I have a feeling this is more than that, though. Isn't it?"

"I just don't like people treating me like a child anymore. I'm twenty-five."

"Why do people treat you like that? Did they treat Ben like that when he was twenty-five?"

"Come on Sis, you know Ben has been behaving like a mature adult since Mum left."

"And how have you behaved, Dan?"

"I like to have fun; I like to make people smile."

"Do you think acting the idiot is the only way to have fun and make people smile? Why can't you behave more like Ben?"

And there it was, comparing him to Ben again. When would it ever stop? When Daniel could not reply, Rebecca sank onto the chair on the other side of the large table. Seeing her face, he realised she regretted saying it, but it had been said. Maybe if he explained how he felt.

"Because I could never be as perfect as him. Dad would never talk about me with the same pride he talks about Ben. I'll always have to be the little brother, however old we get." Daniel stopped playing with the shopping bags on the table and dropped his hand to stroke Meg. Anything but look at his sister.

"Do you want to change that?" Her voice was still stern. Daniel suspected it was the only way she knew to speak to him.

"Yes." Again, with the one-word answers. He knew she would see through him.

"Good. Then, can I leave you to put this away while I just go up and change Dad's bed?" Without waiting for a reply, Rebecca got up to leave the room.

A last look at Daniel's panicked face said it all.

His eyes darted around the bags on the table, looking for anything strange she might have bought that he could get wrong.

"Look, just leave anything on the table you aren't sure about."

"But what if I get it wrong?" His voice was still quiet.

"Then you will do it better next time. And it probably isn't wrong as such, just not in the place it usually goes. Just give it a go. One little step at a time." Rebecca exited the room slowly and without saying anything more.

Left on his own, Daniel felt the sweat on his forehead. What had he done? Rebecca would make him do more jobs now. It was amazing how much he got out of because no one trusted him to do a simple job right. He was mainly supervised and did what someone else told him to do, which made his life simple. Now he had to decide whether to grow up or stay the fool. Something else he hadn't thought through.

As he set about putting things away, he tried to stay calm and be logical. *This wasn't really that hard. I did OK at university ... that was so you could play cricket and enjoy all the parties ... but I still passed my degree. I am not stupid; I can put the shopping away.*

He took his time and did the best job he could do. He knew Rebecca liked all the labels facing the front, so he made sure to put away the tins and jars in the pantry, just as he knew she would do it. When he came to a box of cleaning materials, he was bewildered. He remembered she had a place for the back stock of such things in the room his mother had called the 'back kitchen'. India called hers the utility room, so he took them there. As he lined them up, he tried to read the labels and work out what they were for. He knew hand soap, shampoo, and toothpaste. But this many laundry products? What did you use it all for?

When Rebecca came in carrying the sheets, she found him still trying to figure it all out.

"Can you show me what to do? Then I can bring in my stuff from the car and get it sorted."

Rebecca froze at first, and Daniel thought she would brush him off again. Then, after a second or two, she broke into a broad smile and agreed. Maybe he could do this. Rebecca seemed to be with him. Somehow, he didn't see his dad being so easy to convince.

Chapter 1

A smug Daniel Woods stood in the shower, congratulating himself on all he had achieved since deciding he wanted to change. Just this morning, he had managed to get up early and make a start in the yard before his dad and his sister had surfaced.

In a short but productive time, he let the chickens out into their new run. He made sure their water was clean and left the eggs on the kitchen table with a note saying what he had done. Daniel lingered in the barn with the horses, taking the time to talk to Debbie, his mother's mare. He turned out the two mares with older foals with their offspring. Watching them enjoy stretching their legs in the paddock.

He had left a pan of porridge on the warming plate of the range, just like his mother used to do. It felt good to have done those things. With no one there to remind him to be careful, he had relaxed and found the work easy.

Now it was time to get ready to charm India and Tilly about the job on shopping TV. If he wanted people to trust him and treat him as a grown-up, he still had a long way to go.

His father lifted his head from his porridge as Daniel walked into the kitchen carrying his shoes and his suit jacket. Much as he looked to be enjoying his breakfast, he didn't seem pleased to see his son. He grunted as Daniel found a cloth to polish his shoes.

"Where the heck are you off to now? It sure isn't the yard."

Daniel frowned, determined he would not let him burst his bubble today.

"I'm off to Leeds to see about a job. I should be back by the time you've finished your lunch, and I can help you with whatever you want then."

"Are you going to have some of this porridge Rebecca made before you go?"

Daniel didn't know how to answer that. The eggs were no longer on the table, so he presumed his sister had moved them. He stood staring down at the table, trying to find the words to talk to his dad. *I need to get going and where do I start to explain it all to Dad? He won't be listening, and I don't want to be late.* Daniel's upbeat mood slipped down with his shoulders as he let out a long breath.

"Dan, thanks for making the porridge today and for all the yard jobs you did. Now get off to Leeds before Meg gets all over that suit!" Rebecca's voice was curt. He knew she was trying to save him, but ... *But what? She can't change the way she speaks to you overnight. At least she is trying.*

"Thanks, Becca. Be back as soon as I can, Dad."

He hoped he did better at persuading India and Tilly he was capable of this. Joe would be harder to convince, but Joe liked him. Daniel looked at his watch as he unlocked his car, anxious about the time. A small tingle of nerves hit his stomach. He told himself it was just like pre-match nerves. *It's just a sign of the adrenalin you'll need for the challenge.*

He was relieved to at least be on the road. He should be there in plenty of time. One of the things he needed to prove to them was his timekeeping. His friends from the team often teased him about it, and yes, he was sometimes late, but that was usually due to him being mixed up about the time he should be there. He was pretty sure he managed to get to most things by the time he thought he should. But being late was not the way to get these two very beautiful ladies to trust him with a job.

Driving the familiar route back to Headingley, he rehearsed his arguments. Maybe he should start by asking them some questions about the job. He had never watched much shopping TV himself, so he had little idea what they expected of him.

As the scenery changed from the hills and fields of his home to the buildings and people that dominated the cities, his excitement grew, and his mind began to drift. Suddenly, on his ever-present film screen of a memory, he heard the replay of Charlie saying an abrupt NO! Perhaps he should have talked to Charlie first. Maybe he had a good reason not to do this. *Surely it can't be that bad, can it? But why would Charlie say no so emphatically? It's probably too late to think of that now.*

He parked his car on North Road near India's shiny new office. With his hand on the door to Topaz PR, he suddenly thought about locking his car and clicked his remote to do the job. Finding the office door locked, he checked the time. Early! Daniel's body didn't know what to do with this information. He couldn't remember being early before. What were his options?

Sit in my car? He was too wired for that.

Go buy a Racing Times? He already had one.

Go talk to Charlie? So maybe it isn't too late after all. Leaving his car parked and locked where it stood, he strode round the corner to Charlie's house. He couldn't see India's car parked in the drive. *I am sure it was today. Have I got that wrong?*

Charlie answered the door with a puzzled look. Daniel decided that wasn't unusual for Charlie.

"I thought you were meeting the girls at the office?"

"Yes, I am. I wanted a quick word with you first. If you have the time?"

"Sure. Come in Dan. India's gone to pick up Tilly. Tea?"

"Thanks."

Daniel said nothing whilst Charlie poured his tea into a mug.

"Two sugars?"

"Of course."

Passing the mug to him, Charlie perched on a stool at the breakfast bar opposite where Daniel had settled himself and waited for him to talk. Daniel swallowed his first gulp of tea and looked down into the mug.

"Why did you say no?"

"Sorry, what?"

"When Tilly mentioned the TV, you said no. Why?"

"How long have you got?" Charlie paused. "Look, I did the photos because India asked. I thought it would help her - I had bridges to build, you know - well, to be honest, I needed the cash for Mum." Charlie sipped his own tea. "And now, well, things have changed. I want to work on coaching and spending time with India." He grinned at the last comment and Daniel could still see the grin over Charlie's mug as he drank the last of his tea.

"I couldn't do that… The coaching, I mean, not spending time with India, not that I would do anything with India." Daniel shook his head. "I'm going to shut up now."

"Let me change this round. Why did you say yes? Why do you want to do this?"

"You don't think I can do it?"

"Oh no, I think you are very much the performer, Daniel. The question was, why?"

"The truth?"

"Of course!"

"I am sick of being treated as a child, well, you know, not a sensible adult, with the team and in the family." Daniel watched Charlie for a reaction, but he got nothing back from the stoic Scot. Frustrated, he carried on. "It's at the farm I most want to change things, you know. I was ten when Mum left, and Ben and Rebecca had to help look after me. They had to grow up fast, and well, I didn't. They don't give me any credit; Dad doesn't trust me to do anything."

"And you are ready to change that?" Charlie paused, but Daniel just looked into his tea. "Do you think this job will do that?"

"It is something different. It's not farming like Dad, who has been doing it all his life, and it's not cricket, where Ben is the golden child. I just can't compete. This is something I know I can do, and I can do it for myself."

"That's a big speech."

"At least you didn't ask why compete! It's who we are, isn't it?" Charlie grinned back at his friend. "Please don't tell anyone I said all this. I am trying alright, let's leave it at that. I don't want anyone throwing this in my face if I fail."

"Are you planning to fail?"

"Oh no, I want to do this for me, but I promise I won't let India and Tilly down."

"That's good then."

They heard India parking her car and the laughter as the girls walked around the corner to the office. Daniel stood up.

"I'd give them a minute to get in the office, sit down and finish that tea. Get your head on straight for the interview. It's not like they don't know you."

"That's the problem Charlie, they think they know me. How do I get them to see that I am serious about this?"

"I take it you don't want to tell them what you just told me?"

Daniel sighed, "Yes, and YOU can't tell them, Charlie." Charlie didn't respond.

"CHARLIE?"

"No, I get it. I won't tell anyone what you have just said."

"OK. Time to go do this."

Daniel picked up his jacket but didn't put it on until he got to the front door, where he paused to look at Charlie. As they stood looking at each other, Zach Mitchell came down the stairs. Charlie took Daniel's arm.

"I won't tell them. Just go."

As Charlie turned to go back into the house, Zach came down the stairs and shared a look with Charlie.

"You heard all that, you Australian Elephant, didn't you?"

Zach didn't reply, but Charlie had his answer. "You can't say anything."

"Don't know what you are talking about. Can you let India know I am not going over for the interview? I don't think I can do the job."

Daniel left his car and walked around the corner to India's stylish new office. He tried walking slowly and calmly, but it wasn't happening. The street door on North Road stood open, but he still knocked tentatively as he walked in.

"Hello?"

"Come through Daniel, we're in here."

As he made his way through to the inner office with India's large white desk, he could hear joyful laughter from the girls. *I'm going to enjoy working with these ladies.* He slowly pushed open the door to find India with her hands on Tilly's stomach. He stepped back.

"What did I just walk into?"

India looked questioningly at her friend. Tilly nodded.

"Tilly is having a baby. Isn't it fabulous?"

"Wow! Yes… Yes, of course. That's wonderful news."

The girls moved to sit on chairs at the far side of the desk. In front of them were three boxes, each containing a Gym Away set.

"Let's begin with the basics," Tilly started. "Obviously, we both know you. We met you last season when we started working with Charlie. We have both seen you play cricket. But this isn't about how fast you can bowl."

"Obviously!" Daniel bit his lip. *Let them speak, you fool.*

India smiled, "Can you tell us why you want this job?" And with that smile, he began to relax.

"When you were working with Charlie, I remember thinking, I can do that. Why haven't they chosen me? I think I even said so." India blushed, and Tilly flashed her green eyes at him.

"With your other commitments, can you fit this in?"

"I guess that depends on how often you expect to be doing this."

"We have some hurdles to cross first, but they told us one visit a month. That could be one, two or three shows. Joe is hoping we can start with two shows a month on the same day."

"Last year, I used the fixture list to sort out dates for Charlie. I can do the same for you, but what about the farm?"

"India, if you can work around the team, I guess I can manage one day a month."

"Would you be interested in doing some of the other work, such as the photoshoots and things?"

"Does that mean you aren't using Charlie this year? I don't want to take it away from him."

"But you would do it?"

Daniel flexed his biceps and smiled his best smile.

"If Nick can make old Romeo look good, I reckon I can do that, no problem."

"It might not be Nick. It could be India taking the photos."

"That's fine." Daniel looked from girl to girl. India blushed and pushed on with the list of questions they had written in front of them.

"Daniel, have you watched a lot of shopping TV?"

"I must admit, I hadn't watched much before you started talking about it the other day, just as I was flicking through the channels. But I made a point of watching some recently. I presume I would do a show with someone from the TV company."

"As I understand it, but the first thing that will happen is a screen test. That's a test for who we take to go in front of the camera and for the product. So, you would have to go through that before we could confirm the job."

"OK. Do I have to have someone talking in my ear?"

"No, I don't think so." Tilly looked at a thick document at her side as if it had the answer to his question. India looked at her list of questions. Neither looked at Daniel. He took the opportunity to re-arrange himself on the chair. India looked up, and with a smile, she threw out the part he had been waiting for.

"Imagine you are in the TV studio. Show us a couple of ways to use the Gym Away." Daniel stood up and smiled down at India and Tilly. He had been trying this in his bedroom in front of the mirror.

He started by talking through a couple of exercises, one for the arms and one for the legs. Daniel fiddled with the resistance bands, unable to tell what the girls were thinking. As he racked his brain for something else to impress them with, India's phone rang.

"Oh, hi, Zach, oh really?"

"Yes, I guess I understand."

As she put the phone away, she looked at Tilly and then back at Daniel.

"Daniel, could you go out and get us some milk?"

"You want some milk?"

"No, to be totally honest, I need to talk to Tilly. Can you give us about five minutes?"

"Yes, of course. Why didn't you just say that?"

"I don't fudging know. Maybe if I had realised, it would be this hard, I might have done. Now, can you just give us a couple of minutes?"

Daniel walked down the road from Topaz PR, wondering what had just happened and whether it had anything to do with the phone call from Zach. In his mind, he saw Zach on the stairs as he left Charlie's. *Did Zach hear me? Had he said something to India?*

A little lost, he wandered into the bakery. Cakes, maybe if I buy some? Can I get hired by buying food? Is that a bribe?

Daniel spent a long time studying all the baked goods lined up in neat rows. Deciding to buy the cakes had been one thing, but how did he decide which to buy? The time ticked by, and a small, freckled-faced girl waited to serve him.

"Can I help you?"

"Yes, can I have three cakes?"

"Certainly, which ones?" As Daniel pondered, a look of recognition hit the girl's face. "You play cricket, don't you?" Daniel smiled. "Yes, you're that Ben Woods, aren't you." Daniel's smile disappeared.

"Daniel."

"Pardon?"

"Daniel, I'm Daniel Woods. Ben is my brother."

"So, you don't play cricket, then?"

Daniel opened his mouth to correct her, then stopped. What is the point? I'll buy three different cakes, well four cakes then.

Eventually, Daniel left the bakery with three white square boxes balanced in a tower. Each box contained four cakes and was tied with red and white twine.

As he pushed open the door to India's empire, he called out.

"If I have cakes, can I come back in?"

Tilly answered first. "I'm eating for two, so come here."

"Three boxes?"

"I wanted to be sure to get ones you liked. Perhaps you could take some home."

"I'll put the kettle on, and you can let Tilly inspect how well you have done."

Tilly bounced with excitement. As Daniel put the tower of boxes down on the table, she reached for the scissors. Tossing her red hair over her shoulders as she opened the first box.

"Thank God! A vanilla slice. My favourite. The only thing better is a chocolate éclair."

"You're going to love the next box, then." Daniel grinned at his success.

India arrived with a tray of tea.

"Thank you, Daniel," she sighed as she scooped up a cake of her own, oozing with cream.

Daniel sat patiently, waiting for them to continue the interview, but both girls were too busy enjoying the pastries.

"Was that part of my interview? Did I pass?"

"Well, it wasn't, but if it was, then you passed." India managed between bites.

Tilly licked her lips. "If you promise to keep treating us like this, you can have the job."

"Really. This means so much. Thank you."

India gulped. "Tilly was teasing you there, Daniel. But we have decided to give you a try. If you do OK on the screen test, then we would like you to do three trips to the studios. So about three months' work."

"The screen test would be in London on Wednesday."

"No Problem."

"Our first show is pencilled in for two weeks later. For that, we thought we would all go down the day before on the train."

"You are asking me if I want to go away with you two, overnight, to a hotel in London. Does Charlie know?"

"Actually, we are planning to use my grandparent's flat."

"I guess I can do that."

"We'll be in touch then."

Chapter 2

Natasha took the time to meticulously press each of her dresses for work this weekend. She had agreed to do an extra day to cover for Alex, who said he needed time off. Much as she liked to think she was being a good friend, deep down, she knew she was doing it for herself.

The TV played to itself in the corner while she hummed along. She mentally listed everything she needed to take with her. She liked to stay with Emma when she went to London to make it easier for work. Another excuse, she told herself.

Matthew would be coming home for the weekend to work in the constituency. With a huge sigh, she acknowledged that their marriage was over and much as she wanted to remain friends with him, it had become harder now he had become involved with his new assistant.

She just didn't want to watch them together. As an image of them in each other's arms filled her head, she heard the news reporter say, "The Prime Minister has ruled out an election this year." Would this ever end? She dropped onto the sofa, struggling to sort more dates in her head. *How much longer can he ask me to wait? I know I promised, but honestly, I am not sure I can do this anymore.*

Her phone announced an incoming text. Natasha snatched up her phone in the hope of a subject change. No such luck.

MP: Coming home tonight. J's birthday. Can you make sure we have some Bollinger in the fridge and whatever else makes a birthday?

Natasha sat still, staring into her future. How had this happened to them? The changes had crept up on them gradually. Or had they always been there? Was it her realisation of the differences that had slowly come about? Matthew Poole's political career was important to him. Of course, she knew that, and she knew as his wife, she would play a part in that but over the years her own identity had been lost.

So, what did she do now? Staring down at the phone still in her hand. She made several decisions at once.

Tasha: Emma, any chance I can arrive tonight instead of tomorrow?

EM: I just saw the news. Are you OK?

Tasha: Yeah, but they are coming back tonight and it's J's birthday.

EM: Come when you are ready. Nick might be around, but he won't mind.

Tasha: If you are sure.

EM: Of course.

Natasha finished her ironing and put everything away. Only after she had checked that she had everything she needed ready to pack did she answer Matthew's text message.

The Mrs: Sure, I won't be here but will leave everything in the fridge. Mikey is at my dad's. If you are busy, he'll be glad to keep him.

MP: Thanks x

And there it was. X at the end of his message.

With a heavy heart, she picked up her keys and left to do the shopping. Wine, Champagne, a chocolate cake, and nibbles from the deli to pop in the fridge. A card and a present from herself to her husband's secretary, too. It was time to stop being the one to do their weekend shopping, but today wasn't the day to kick up a fuss and spoil a birthday.

Once she had left everything ready in the fridge so even Matthew couldn't mess it up, she carefully arranged her own card and gift on the island in her kitchen. Looking around the house they lived together in for so many years, she wondered what they would do about that when the time came to separate. She had enjoyed making the stone-built house a home when they married. Matthew had always been so busy, so that left Natasha to buy the extras. The cushions, the throws, and even the artwork. Most of the furniture had been her grandmother's, although Matt loved it, she had a history with it.

What to do about the house and everything in it kept her busy for the drive down to London. She made a mental note not to tell Emma she had taken the time to leave everything ready for the lovebirds and the birthday celebrations.

It was late when Natasha pulled up outside the Putney flat of Emma Mansfield, her producer and best friend. This little space, with the friend inside, was her sanctuary in the madness of her current life. Emma's flat was messy, and the rooms were full of clashing colours, but she felt safe here. The lights were on, and she could see Nick's car parked behind Emma's. She took a moment to centre herself before going inside. To be honest, it was longer than a moment. On the drive down, she had been thinking about the house and everything else that came with a divorce. She didn't want Emma to see how emotional she had become because she wasn't ready for another lecture.

Natasha knew Emma simply wanted to protect her friend from any more hurt, and she couldn't understand why she hadn't just divorced Matthew. She wasn't sure she understood herself. Matt had asked if they could wait until after an election that the whispers said was in the pipeline, and she had agreed, presuming it would be one more month.

Eventually, she stepped out of her Mini and retrieved her bags from the car. A deep breath helped her up the few steps to the door of the flat that was becoming her hideaway most weekends. Emma understood a lot of what was going on, even if she didn't like it. Nick opened the door and pulled Natasha into a swift, silent hug, then grabbed her bags. *Hmm, she told him*! She quickly realised that Emma would have needed to explain why their night was going to be interrupted.

As Nick took her bags to the spare room, Emma appeared with a large glass of red wine and another hug.

"I didn't want to spoil your night; you could have gone out. I wouldn't have minded."

"I thought you might need the company. It must be hard knowing they're enjoying a celebration back at your house. Besides, it's only Nick."

"Here! I heard that." Nick grabbed Emma from behind and tickled her. She collapsed in his arms as he kissed her, then picked her up and dumped her on the crumpled sofa.

"I'm going home now; I know when I'm not wanted."

Natasha opened her mouth to protest, but Emma stopped her.

"Don't go feeling sorry for him. He has an early shoot in the morning and planned on leaving earlier, but he wanted to be here to say hello when you got here."

"She's right, and I wanted a hug, too." Nick pulled Natasha into his arms and squeezed as if he wanted to put her back together. "I do have an early morning, and I know girls need to talk. But Tash, let me just say if I can help with anything, just ask, and if this one's messy flat gets to you, I have a spare room, too."

"Thanks, Nick."

"Any time."

As Nick left, Emma reached for the wine. Natasha hadn't started hers yet, so she sat down on the sofa and took a big gulp.

"Have you eaten?" Emma looked at Natasha over her shoulder as she opened the fridge.

"I'm not hungry."

"I'm going to have some cheese on toast. Want to join me?"

"You are joking! Four days of being in front of your cameras, and you want to feed me bread?"

"There is some fruit." While Emma switched on the grill and started cutting up cheese, Natasha picked up an apple and nibbled it slowly, chewing each tiny bite.

"What have we got tomorrow?"

"There's been a change; you're going to help with this month's screen tests."

"Did you do that? Are you scared I won't get you to your targets if I'm upset!" Natasha turned away, and Emma said nothing.

"Sorry, I know you aren't as motivated by targets as some, so I guess you did it for me?" She looked across at her friend toasting the bread. Emma still said nothing.

"God, I am sorry, Emma! Look at me biting the one friend I have in all this." Emma quietly got on with making her snack.

"Who have you told?"

At last, Emma turned around and faced her.

"I have only shared it with Nick and even then, I didn't give details. He has too many friends in the Press. He wouldn't mean to say anything, but stuff slips out. At work, I have told no one. I know how careful you want to be."

"Need to be Emma. It's how careful I NEED to be."

"I get it, well, I don't really understand the waiting bit. I know you want to keep your promise, but things have changed a bit since you made it. Have you talked to him about it again?"

"No." It was a soft no that was almost a whisper. Talking to him would mean seeing him, and Natasha had been doing an excellent job of avoiding him altogether for the last few weeks.

"And after today? The announcement about the election being delayed further? The way he expects you to help him with celebrating his bloody secretary's birthday. Which I hope you didn't do!"

One look at her friend's face gave away that she had indeed shopped for the birthday celebrations. "I bet you even bought a card, didn't you? Oh, Tasha, why are you doing all this? Just divorce the man already."

"I promised, and I don't like to break a promise. It's important to Matthew, so it's important to me. He was my friend for a long time before we ever went out. We met during the first week at university. We were just eighteen."

"It was more than that if you got married."

"I guess that was the same, though, all our friends got married. We went to so many weddings and when Matthew decided to go into politics, he proposed. I said yes. I had not really dated anyone else. Being with Matthew is all I have ever known."

"That doesn't mean you have to stay with him to be wheeled out when he needs a wife. You can't put your own life on hold with no idea how long for. Surely he cares for you, too. You aren't even looking at other men, Tasha. Have you got everything sorted for the divorce ready for when it can go ahead? What am I saying? You are the most organised woman I know. I bet you have it all planned out, don't you?"

"No." another whispered confession. Emma's shocked face made Natasha explain more. "I'm scared even to google divorce lawyers, let alone see one. If this gets out, then all this waiting has been for nothing."

"Tasha, you must be ready for this. Sort your money out at least, and the house."

"The house is still Dad's, and I have my own money." Natasha sipped her wine.

"There must be something you can do."

"Would you mind if we change the subject? There is not much I can do right now except protect my heart, box up my emotions and throw my energy into work."

Emma reluctantly agreed. "I can see tonight's not the time to push you on this. But seriously, Tasha, after today, I think you really need to rethink this promise business. It's time to start thinking about yourself. I still say, if he still cares for you, as much as you claim you care for him, then surely he'll listen."

They put the wine away and settled down on the sofa with a cup of tea and watched a film. Natasha realised that Emma would have more to say about this.

When she went to bed, Natasha went through her evening rituals as if she were walking through porridge. Working on TV and being an MP's wife meant she had to be always on display. She never felt she could just hang around in PJs or even leave her bra off for a day. No. Everything in her life had to look perfect, whatever the reality. As she brushed her hair for the required one hundred strokes, she allowed herself to look into her future, but other than still going to work at More.U TV, she didn't know what the future held for her. Even when she lay in bed staring at the yellow ceiling an hour later, she had no idea what she wanted.

Was she just a convenient wife? She had certainly played the part; she had been his partner at events and hosted dinners. Natasha had been his secretary, but then they drifted apart, and when her own career took off, Matt took on a secretary or personal assistant, as he liked to say.

Natasha had been so happy when he told her what he had done. It meant she could step back from the marriage a little more. It was all part of the plan to divorce when they could. Part of the promise he had made if she waited for the right time. Making that promise had not been hard. She knew more than anyone how hard he worked and how good he was at his job. Natasha still wanted him as her MP, and he had been a friend for so long. She didn't hate him. In some ways, she regretted the time it had taken them to realise the mistake, and now her body was not getting any younger.

The yellow ceiling was just too much, so she rolled over to her side and instead looked at the flowery curtains against the bright pink wall. Where did Emma get her decorating style from? If this were Natasha's flat, it would have a lot more neutral colour.

That was just the thought she needed, and she drifted off to sleep, designing her next home. The first home that would be just for her and not an appendage to her husband's job.

Chapter 3

Daniel was enjoying the drive down to the studio. He liked the idea of being able to mentally prepare on his own. On the long drive to London, Daniel had gone through every emotion. Sometimes full of confidence that he could do this but mostly wondering what the hell he had started. Talking to himself he tried out ways to describe the product he had been researching ready for today. Tilly had given him a Gym Away last year, and it went everywhere with him. He knew how to focus. This was where he excelled at university and how he had passed his exams.

Daniel pulled up at the metal gate guarding the studio, wiping his clammy hands as he pushed the button to lower his window. A large man, struggling to fit into the buttoned shirt of his uniform, stepped out of a gatehouse. His name badge announced his name was Richard.

"Can I see your pass, sir?"

"My pass?" Daniel's brain was blank.

"Yes sir, your pass. This is private property and access is restricted."

Daniel's left hand randomly patted the seat at his side as he searched in vain. Eventually, the mist of panic cleared when he remembered it was on the table in the kitchen back at the farm.

"I don't have it."

"Sir?"

"I left it at home."

"Well, I can't let you in without one."

"I have an email on my phone, just hang on." But Daniel's expensive phone was out of charge again. It was not an unusual situation.

"Just let me think."

"If you could move your car out of the way whilst you do that."

Daniel edged his car over to the side of the road and got out. As he paced up and down, trying to figure out what to do, he kicked at the grass, annoyed with himself for failing before he could get to the place he was meant to be. He could see the large modern building across the car park, but a single bar and Richard stopped him from going there. He lifted his head at the sound of a runner coming towards him. The sun shone behind her, and it flooded his eyes with light. He could make out very little other than it was a woman. A petite woman whose long ponytail swung with each stride she took towards him. Each step she took brought more detail into focus for him. The small but perfectly proportioned figure was dressed in a colourful Lycra top and matching leggings that hid nothing of her figure.

Her hair clung to her face, telling him the run had been a serious one. Daniel's brain finally started to function again as she stopped a few feet in front of him and pulled out her phone. *I wonder if she uses the same running app as me.*

As she walked towards him, he watched as her chest worked hard to recover. Bringing her breathing back to normal. Daniel was stunned and staring. A fine mist of perspiration covered her brow.

"You can't park there!" she huffed as she passed, staring at her phone. HER PHONE! Daniel's brain engaged with his mouth.

"Could I use your phone?"

The woman lifted her head from the screen, and only then did Daniel see her eyes. There was some sadness deep in those eyes, and Daniel felt an inexplicable urge to take that sadness away. She screwed up her face as she looked up at him. Daniel tried to explain his situation, the words tumbling out of his mouth faster than ever.

"I forgot my pass. I can't get in; my phone is out of charge. India will kill me, and after everything I promised, too."

It took a while for the woman to process what he was trying to say.

"Where do you want to call?" She was still scowling and seemed reluctant to hand over her phone. Daniel decided she was more likely from London, not Malton, given both her accent and her behaviour.

"India... not the country ...my boss."

"Do you know the number, and I'll call her for you...sorry, I am not handing over my phone." She was edging closer to the gate, and Dick came out of his box to watch. *What does he think I am going to do to her? Actually, I know what I would like to do... but I wouldn't.*

Realising how it must look, he stepped back. His shoulders dropped as he went back to kicking at the grass. He didn't know India's number.

"Forget it. I have the number in my phone, but it has no charge." And as if to explain that further, he waved the dead phone. Now Dick (as Daniel had decided he should be called) spoke to the newcomer.

"Are you OK Ms Poole? I told this gentleman I can't let him in without a pass."

The woman's face relaxed, then screwed up again. Turning towards the man in uniform. She spoke with an assertive voice that boomed from her tiny body.

"Richard, if this gentleman is due at the studio, he will be on your list, or you can phone reception. If he is late because of your stalling, you could be responsible for expensive studio time." Her soft voice changed to that of an annoyed teacher he used to know, and Daniel started to feel sorry for Richard, but not for long. Had Dick had the solution to his problem all along? Daniel stared at Richard and wondered if he should have done something different earlier.

"Sorry, Ms Poole. What is your name again?"

"Woods, Daniel Woods," these words were directed at the woman rather than the man in uniform. Softening his voice and face, he offered her a quiet "Thank you, Ms Poole." But she had turned away and was walking towards the main entrance, slipping her phone into the pocket on her thigh. As Daniel enjoyed the rear view, he hoped she had heard him. Yes, he was very much enjoying that view.

Richard cleared his throat. "OK, Mr Woods, if you would like to park your car in the area marked with yellow lines to the right of this gate. Then, if you go through that door, you'll be at the reception. They are waiting for you."

It took Daniel longer than it should have to register what had been said. Dragging his eyes away from the door that Ms Poole had disappeared behind, he returned to his car and approached the gate again. This time, the barrier lifted as Richard managed a smile. Daniel parked his car and hurried towards the door; he was halfway there before he remembered his bag. He opened his car boot to grab the bag, and as he lifted it onto his shoulder, a piece of paper fluttered to the floor. His Pass!

Chapter 4

Inside the modern reception, they were indeed waiting for him. Two beautiful girls in tight pencil skirts and uniform shirts looked up at him as he signed himself in on the list and entered his car details. India and a stunning brunette were also waiting.

Is everyone beautiful around here? This is going to be fun. Daniel hitched his bag further onto his shoulder and stepped over to India, who looked relieved to see him.

"Daniel, this is Emma." Compared with the women sitting behind the reception desk, Emma was dressed casually. In boyfriend jeans, a sunshine yellow shirt, and trainers, she had still caught his eye.

"Pleased to meet you, Daniel. I'm going to be in the control room for your screen test," she smiled. "Did you bring a change of clothes?"

Daniel pointed to his bag in response and offered her one of his best smiles. The word 'test' always made him feel nervous.

"Good! Someone from the production team can show you around and get you set up in studio two. I'll find Natasha, who is presenting with you today and we can go over what we would like you to do." Emma turned as a huge door swung open. "Here's Paul." Smiling at the newcomer, "Can you give India and Daniel the tour? See they have everything they need to set up?"

"My pleasure, come this way," he growled, staring up at Daniel. Paul swiped a pass at the side of the doorway and held the door open. India and Daniel stepped into a long corridor with doors on both sides. Paul kept smiling as the two followed him further into the building.

"Let's start with the green room, and you can leave your bags there. The stage crew have your product, and you can come through to studio two and see where you are going to do the test." That word again. Daniel gulped.

"When you come to do your shows, you can bring more props." Paul paused in front of a grey door; it was a corridor full of grey doors.

"Here's the green room." He opened the door to a large room painted white and filled with sofas and small tables. One wall had a row of four

TVs all showing different shows with no sound. In one corner was a kitchen are with brightly coloured mugs, a kettle, and a microwave.

"Down this side, there are a couple of changing rooms and the toilets. You can make yourself a drink and bring food when you come for longer." He opened the fridge to find a lone empty bottle of milk.

Paul sighed. "Every day the same!" Obviously annoyed, he pulled his radio from where it sat on his belt and called reception to stock up the kitchen and walked to the door. He turned to Daniel.

"Leave your bags and phones in here. Bring nothing but yourself into the studio."

As the door swung closed and they were alone, India punched Daniel on his arm. "Another conquest! How many is that today?"

"What?"

Before India could explain, three young women burst through the door and collapsed in a fit of giggles onto a large sofa.

"I can't believe you said that!" one managed to say through her laughter.

"It's your fault! You looked at him!"

"How do you think we did?" the third girl asked.

"Well, we won't know until the witch comes with the numbers!"

Paul came bustling through the door, "Well done, girls. Now, let's get those mics off you."

"Shit! I forgot we were mic-ed up." All the giggling had now stopped, and the girls exchanged worried glances.

"No worries, girls, we stitch up the mouths of all the sound guys so they can never tell your secrets."

Daniel watched as Paul helped the girls remove their mics. Something else to get his head around. With three mics safely retrieved, Paul looked to India and Dan.

"I'll be back for you." Sitting beside India on a bright green sofa, Daniel was hypnotised by these girls. They seemed over-excited after their show. He was trying to work out what had gone wrong so he could avoid it. *Why didn't I think this through? If things go wrong, someone I know will have recorded it.* Daniel thought his mouth had sealed shut.

"I can see why Charlie said no," India sighed. "How did I ever let Tilly talk me into all this?"

"Why didn't she come?"

"Tilly would be here in a heartbeat, but the doctor has ordered her to rest." India sounded sad, and it didn't help Daniel's mindset. "I understand it, but I do really wish she was here."

When Paul returned, he was ready to just get this over with.

"Ready for the next phase of the tour?" Daniel looked at India, who looked as lost as he felt. They both nodded to Paul.

"Leave everything here, especially your phones."

Nodding again, they followed him back into the never-ending corridor and round a corner towards an enormous red door. The door was covered in signs.

STUDIO TWO
NO PHONES
No Open Toe Shoes
SILENCE

Paul paused for them to read all the warnings. Then pushed his back against the heavy door, holding it open for them to step through. Inside, the space was huge. High ceilings and cables everywhere. The studio had five-room setups. Three had counters near the front. Dan spotted the Gym Away equipment laid out on a corner space with a small counter and what looked like a yoga mat on the floor. In the centre of the room were three cameras. Two were pointing at the corner set-up.

"We're showing something live from studio one right now and we are using studio two for screen tests today. This studio is mainly used to pre-record things. Anything from interlinks, previews and complete shows if we need to." India and Daniel didn't speak. They knew nothing was being recorded right now, but they still stayed quiet, just nodding to Paul.

"I'll let Emma know you are here."

Left alone with India, Daniel began to pick up the Gym Away pieces. Looking at the resistance bands and fastening them together. Testing them to see just how much he could pull. He smiled at India as her mouth twitched into a smile. She looked like she was about to burst out laughing at him. Daniel frowned, turning his focus back to the bands. Just as he had all of them attached to the handles, Emma walked into the studio, and with her was the tiny blonde woman Daniel had met at the gate. Ms Poole.

She had changed into a smart pair of blue trousers and a top with soft, splodgy roses across it. Instead of trainers, she now wore heels. She had showered and styled her hair since their first meeting. Daniel stood transfixed by the transformation. Earlier, she looked beautiful but now she was simply stunning. He held on to the bands, tightening his grip as he fought to find his voice. Emma introduced her friend.

"India, Daniel, this is Natasha Poole. She is going to be your presenter today. I don't want you to worry too much about the product at this point. We need you to relax and for this to look like two friends having a chat."

"Nice to meet you India. And Daniel I'm glad you got through the gate in the end." India raised an eyebrow at Daniel which he ignored and just spoke to Natasha. It was a nice name. Dropping the equipment and wiping his hands on his jeans, he reached out to shake her hand.

"Natasha, I'm looking forward to working with you. I hope you will look after me when this all starts."

From the corner of his eye, Daniel saw India standing back, letting the other three talk. She looked nervous about this whole thing. Daniel hoped he could stop her worrying.

"Right Daniel, if you and Natasha can stand behind the counter so we can see you together." Natasha led the way and Daniel followed. His eyes were drawn to the swing of her hips; he watched as the gentle curves moved away from him. Emma coughed, and he turned to grin at her, shrugging his shoulders.

When Natasha turned, Daniel stood next to her.

"Daniel, stand closer to Natasha, you need to be close, the viewer needs to see you as friends." Natasha smiled and put her arm around his waist, pulling him towards her. Daniel was sure his face was going to explode as he lost the power of speech once more. This was an unfamiliar experience for him.

"How are we going to introduce you? You are Ben Woods' brother, aren't you?" Her smile grew wider, but Daniel's smile disappeared.

"Do we need to mention that? Is it important?"

"No, of course not, how do we introduce you?" That smile was going to undo him, he thought for a moment.

"Daniel Woods, professional cricketer? Is that enough?" Daniel's eyes searched for India *Why is she being so quiet?* India nodded in reply to Daniel's hesitation. Natasha smiled.

"That sounds fine." Emma stepped up to the counter and explained.

"Then Tasha will ask you to tell us about the Gym Away. As I said earlier, just try to relax and think of Tasha as your new best friend." Dan's eyes sparkled as he looked down into Natasha's smiling face.

He had expected some pre-match nerves, but the emotions running through his body were so new to him. He picked up the resistance bands to distract himself from staring at Natasha.

Emma, India, and Paul were huddled to one side and looked to be talking about the set-up. India was busy taking notes on her phone. Natasha touched Daniel's hand. "Whilst they are busy, tell me about this product. It will help me ask you questions when they switch the cameras on." With one deep breath, Daniel started talking about the kit. He had been doing his homework and remembered what he had heard over the last year. His voice had lowered to something that had authority. The group chatting at the side stopped talking and watched. India didn't hide her surprise as she beamed a smile over to Daniel that helped to relax him. Emma looked pleased, too, as she got things moving.

"I think we should get started. Paul, can you get Dan a mic?"

"Sure." He pulled a microphone from his bag and approached Daniel, working out where to fix the battery pack.

"Great, you're wearing jeans. They have just the right sized pocket, turn around and let's get you sorted." Daniel was feeling nervous again, but Paul just kept talking. "These are long legs; however do you find trousers long enough?" Paul pushed the battery pack into his jeans pocket and then fed the wire under his T-shirt.

Daniel's smile returned.

Chapter 5

Emma's voice in Natasha's ear was a distraction she didn't need. As she looked up into the eyes of Daniel Woods, she realised she was lost again.

"Earth to Natasha Poole, are you receiving me? Have you fallen for a very tall cricketer?" Tasha tightened her smile, looking hard into the camera, glad this was a test and not a live show. Standing up straighter, she relaxed her style and asked Daniel a question.

"Is this just for men?"

"No," Daniel frowned, "It is so adjustable and adaptable. That is why it has sold so many times. All the cricket team have one, and most have bought an extra pack so their partners don't steal theirs."

"He is a natural, but let's just run a few more minutes, so he gets used to answering questions, something more than simply talking by himself. Get him to show you something you could do with it." Emma whispered into her ear.

"So, will you show me what someone like me could do with it?"

Daniel's smile exploded. "Of course." Adjusting the setup of the bands in his hands.

"I know you are an excellent runner," the smile was very mischievous now, and Natasha wondered if he was picturing her from earlier. "But after a good, hard run." Her stomach flipped at the way he said hard. It felt like a long pause before he continued. "You need to stretch."

"Oh, this is gold, Tash... Do it!!" Natasha touched her ear, hoping Emma would get the hint and back off.

"I am not really dressed to do much," she softly replied to Daniel.

"Ah, yes, sorry." Confident Daniel had disappeared, and he looked down at the bands he was adjusting. A silence fell over the studio and Natasha knew it was her job to fill it. Emma persisted in her ear.

"Tash, it will help the camera guys work on transitions."

"Well, Daniel, we should make the camera team work for their money today. So, what can you show me for after my run?"

"How are your hamstrings?" he asked, clearly checking out her legs.

"He's blushing. Oh, Tasha, you must do something with this guy. The chemistry is amazing."

"Well…" unusually lost for words on set, Natasha blushed, too.

"Never mind, come lie down for me." He took her hand and led her to the yoga mat.

"I bet he has said that before, and I am guessing they were usually quicker at responding to him. Tasha, just do this one exercise and I'll call it."

With Tasha lying down on the mat, he lifted her right leg and, holding her ankle, slipped off her shoe. She could feel the heat of his palm on the sole of her foot. *Why am I doing this again? Oh yes, because I don't want to be home watching my husband with his secretary. Is my life some long joke on me?*

"If you have a partner who can help you stretch, they can work with you on this, so you get a long gentle stretch all the way down your leg." His voice was softer now as he ran his other hand from her ankle along her leg and down to her thigh. "Here, pop your foot in here, like this. He gently slipped the strap over her foot and passed her the handle. The heat from his hands burned into the skin on Natasha's foot. That heat made its way through her body, finally reaching her face.

"Are you blushing?" Emma laughed so loud in Natasha's ear that she thought everyone would hear it. "I don't blame you."

Daniel was still talking, his hands dancing over her body. "Now relax your other leg," his hand ran along the leg on the floor until he reached her hip bone. Daniel now had two hands holding her pelvis. "Relax your hips into the ground, no twisting." The authority voice was back. Commanding her to do as he said. How could she ever relax with him touching her? *This is silly. I have only just met the man. I am at work, fully clothed, in view of two camera operators. Emma is at the control desk, too. Let's not forget Paul, who if I have read his body language correctly, rather liked Daniel himself. So why is my body reacting to him? Ah, it's just my body!*

Daniel's eyes held Natasha's for the briefest of moments. "Now, use the weight of your arms to create a steady pressure on your foot. You should feel the stretch from here to there, down your leg through your calves and thigh muscles." His hand stroked down her leg, emphasising his point. "Can you feel that?"

Natasha Poole didn't know what she was feeling. She wanted to melt into the floor and for this man to fall on top of her. She swallowed a tiny "yes."

Natasha hoped against hope that Emma would call a wrap to this test. Daniel had more than shown he could do this job. He held out his hand to help her up from the floor, and as she took it, her eyes found his, and the smile spread to his ears. *Perhaps I should be glad it's Emma and not creepy John in my ear.*

At last, Emma said, "Thank you, sweetie, we have enough."

On her feet, Natasha found the voice she needed to end the test.

"Well, thank you, Daniel. I can see we are all going to enjoy finding out more about Gym Away."

The cameras moved towards another set, the lights went out and Natasha was left with a suddenly noticeably quiet Daniel Woods. She was waiting for Emma, as the producer, to bring India through. It was just moments. When she did these things, she would always take the time to chat. She liked to help the person who had just done the test relax again. She would offer advice for next time, but what could she say to Daniel? He was simply perfect. She sighed and then covered the sigh with a cough in her embarrassment.

As they stood side by side so close, the temperature rose between them as his body radiated energy towards her. He smelt of mints and a cologne she didn't recognise. The time stretched, she was sure she could hear his heartbeat, or maybe it was her own. She knew she should say something reassuring, but all she could do was stand perfectly still and hold on to the counter in front of her.

The big studio door swung open as everyone joined them, their chatter shattering the couple's shared silence. Daniel stepped to one side and started to carefully and meticulously pack the Gym Away into the outer bottle.

Shaking her head to wake from her dream state, she walked around the counter to stand near Emma. Paul appeared from nowhere and was clearing the set.

"How was it for you?" Emma's eyes twinkled as she stared at Daniel but kept a squirming Natasha in her sights. *I'll get you later.*

Daniel and India were talking animatedly with Emma. India was gabbling about things they could do differently. She asked Emma about Daniel wearing clothes in the brand colours. Natasha was lost and found herself imagining a very different next time, which involved Daniel Woods showing her lots of moves with the Gym Away and no clothes.

Emma and India moved to the side of the studio and looked to be discussing how to dress the set. Daniel returned to packing the kit, and Natasha watched his large hands working. Everything about him seemed on a big scale. She glanced down at his feet and yes, they were big, too. Looking up into his face, she discovered he was watching her. Once again, their eyes locked, and Natasha forced herself to look away. She couldn't resist looking back and found Daniel still eyeing her, one eyebrow raised and a smirk on his face. *He's so smug. He must get this all the time.* Natasha fumbled with her microphone pack, and Paul rushed over to help.

"You did so well there. I would have been a pool of melted butter if he had me on the floor. Where do I sign up for your job?" Paul whispered in her ear, not too quietly. Natasha didn't reply.

Emma was busy chatting with India. "The buyer will be in touch if we are offering you some dates. Personally, I can't see why not. You have a fabulous… product." Emma seemed to be checking out Daniel. But Natasha was very aware it was her that Daniel was staring at. Without saying a word, she walked out of the studio, cross with herself for being so brusque.

She argued with herself with each step up the stairs to her dressing room. She sat down, picked up her phone, and looked into the mirror. That was not who she was. Natasha Poole was polite and encouraging to every guest she had ever met. Why had she been so rude to Daniel Woods? Did the why matter? She stood up and took one last look at herself.

Downstairs again, she paused with a hand ready to open the door to the green room. *This is silly. I can do this.* She pushed forward, and when she finally entered the room, she found Daniel alone. He looked as confused as when she had met him outside.

"Are you OK?"

"India is waiting for me, and I can't find my phone." Natasha watched as he searched through a long sports bag. Despite his happy-go-lucky approach, his bag was organised, but no phone. "I had it in my hand a minute ago. I just unplugged it from charging it. Here's the lead, but where is the bloody phone?"

"Do you want me to ring it?"

"Why didn't I think of that?" Natasha was touched by how relieved he looked. As he rattled off the numbers, she punched them into her phone. It seemed to take too long to dial out. "Is it turned on?"

"Oh, I don't know," the confused and dejected look had returned, and Natasha couldn't stop herself from reaching out to touch his arm. As she touched him, the back pocket of his jeans began to vibrate. As the smile broke out wide across his face, Natasha felt her heart snap to him. Like a magnet finding a magnetic field, powerless to do anything but be drawn to him.

"Better go find India."

"Goodbye, Daniel." She finally got to say as she reached the door. Her body shook inside, her heart dancing around her chest in celebration.

"Thank you, Natasha. Thanks for everything."

Chapter 6

EMMA: Where are you today?

TASHA: Just back from my run.

EMMA: Don't you ever rest?

TASHA: Do you want to swap roles and then you can stand in front of the camera?

EMMA: Anyway, Thanks for the gift basket. You didn't need to.

TASHA: I am grateful for you putting me up. Or should I say putting up with me?

EMMA: Are you OK now?

TASHA: I keep telling you I'm fine.

EMMA: Liking a guy isn't wrong.

TASHA: I was on set with two cameras and you in the gallery!

EMMA: Ha! You didn't say 'I'm a married woman'. That is a step forward.

TASHA: … …

EMMA: Are you still there?

TASHA: YES Just digesting that last comment.

EMMA: Even if it's not that fabulous cricketer. It's time to move on.

EMMA: I say this as your friend.

TASHA: You know my situation.

EMMA: I do, and I still say it's time.

TASHA: You could be right.

EMMA: Just talk to him.

TASHA: Got to go, salon time.

EMMA: You have a week off.

TASHA: No instead I am Mrs Matthew Poole. M.P.

EMMA: Only until you do something about it. Just think about what your life could be like Tash.

TASHA: OK.

EMMA: Please think about it.

Natasha sat down to take off her running shoes as another text bounced into her phone.

Unknown number: I wanted to thank you again. If it wasn't for you, I might not have made it into the building.

Her phone might not recognise the caller, but Natasha could still hear Daniel rattling out the numbers. It was imprinted in her brain. A small smile started, but she stopped herself. She was a married woman how could she even think...

Unknown number: It's me, Dan.

She couldn't help herself; she smiled all the way upstairs to her shower. But when she saw the smile on her face in the bathroom mirror, she stopped.

Maybe it is time to talk to Matthew about divorce again.

Chapter 7

Catching herself adjusting the clock on the mantle for the third time, Natasha realised she was carrying a lot of tension in her body. The uneasy feeling in her stomach said she was nervous as she waited for her husband and his secretary to arrive on the 7 o'clock train. When her phone beeped with a text, she was so worked up she felt sure it was terrible news that something had happened to Matt or them both.

MP: Trains delayed. Could be after midnight when I get home. Don't wait up.

As Natasha sank onto the sofa, the word 'home' echoed around her brain. Despite everything, his life in London, his new love, he still thought this was home. For so many years, Natasha had thought Matthew Poole was her home. That she would be happy as long as he was with her. Rich or Poor.

She still loved Matt, but she wasn't in love with him and looking back, she wasn't sure they had ever been 'in love'. There had been no fireworks, no special chemistry, they had been great friends. Theirs hadn't been a wild, impetuous affair, but it grew from their friendship. They were simply the two friends left when everyone else paired up. As their friends got married, it felt natural for them to do the same. And when their friends had children, well, it just never happened for them. *Perhaps that's a good thing.*

Feeling the limbo of needing to have 'the talk' with Matt, not knowing where to start and not knowing when he would arrive, she drifted upstairs and started her normal rituals. Brushing her hair took longer than usual as she tried out words to open the conversation.

Matt had been the one to broach the subject the first time. She had thought him cruel, now looking back, Natasha realised how hard it must have been for him. They had shared their dreams for so long. Theirs had been a much-planned future. It was still hard for her. She didn't hate him; she still cared for him and wanted what was best for him. What she was slowly realising after much pushing from Emma was she also had to love herself and want the best for herself, too.

She couldn't help but wonder why now. She had spent twenty minutes, thirty at the most, with some guy who was totally not the right person to move on with. As soon as she thought of him, without her wanting to, she was back lying on the studio floor looking up into his eyes. His hands holding her foot firmly but gently. She could feel the sensation of his touch even now. No man had ever had that effect on her, and she was at a loss to understand it. Still brushing her hair with long, even strokes, she looked into her mirror and saw how flushed her cheeks were. If simply remembering their encounter changed her face so much, no wonder Emma had made such a fuss.

As if to cover the blushing, she creamed her face using the techniques her mother had taught her. It had been five years since she died but her mother's voice still haunted her when she looked in a mirror.

Look after your looks Natasha, it is your ticket to your future.

No man will look at you if you don't look after your looks.

If you look the part, you will never have to work.

Natasha wanted to work; she loved her job. And that, she thought, was the problem with her marriage. Maybe if she had the children they planned, she would have been content to stay home. Whilst he said he was happy for her to have a job; Matthew Poole needed a full-time wife. So, when her job became a career that made demands on her time, he had to replace her.

Still watching the clock and checking her phone, Natasha tried to relax on her first weekend at home for some time. Matthew needed her to attend an event this weekend. He would be annoyed about the train delays, but that was nothing new.

She picked up the remote, hoping to find something to distract her on TV. An old film was playing, so she picked that. When the couple fell into each other's arms, she was once again reminded that Matthew's strong arms would be holding someone else. *The long arms of Daniel Woods would be stronger and his chest firmer.* She shook her head, annoyed with herself for thinking of him yet again.

Finally, a text bounced in just as there was a knock at the kitchen door.

MP: Stuck just south of Oxford.

God! He will be going crazy.

Slipping her phone into the pocket of her robe, she went to the door. The kitchen door was near the garage, so it was the door the family used. Everyone else came to the front door except her dad. Mikey was dancing excitedly around her feet, impatient for her to open the door which only made her more convinced this was her father.

"What have you forgotten today, Dad?"

But it wasn't George Webb standing in front of her. It was a bedraggled Jack Wilson gripping a backpack. Looking vastly different to his normal business-like self in pale jeans and a hooded top, he looked like he had been drinking. Sadly, he still had the capacity to stir Natasha's senses.

"Jack?" Shocked at what she saw, she stepped back a little too quickly for the small terrier at her feet. Ever the drama queen, he yelped and hopped between the two people he loved most, holding first one and then the other front paw up in the air. Still stunned, Natasha watched as Jack dropped his bag and scooped up the little dog.

"Oh! Mikey, are you OK? So sorry, Tasha, I know I am not supposed to be here, but I miss the grumpy bugger." Still talking, he bustled into the kitchen. "Put a light on, Tash. Let's check this one out." Mikey was busy licking his knight in shining armour. Natasha, still at a loss for words, did as he asked and then sat down at the breakfast bar, watching Jack. It was the first time she had seen her husband's secretary anything but immaculate if anything, the rumpled look made him even more attractive. She studied his face as he checked over Mikey.

"You old fraud." He pronounced to the dog. "You are just like your daddy. He always makes a fuss like this."

Jack Wilson lifted the dog down onto the floor. "Sorry for arriving like this. Matt is going to kill me. Where is the boss?"

"He hasn't got here yet. His last message said stuck outside Oxford." She shook her head. "How did you get here?"

"I grabbed a lift with Tom, an old flatmate. Best not mention that to Matt, he will be annoyed enough with the train delays." Jack was already filling the kettle and reached for two mugs. "Tea, I think, you don't want coffee at this time of night. I am loving that get-up lady, brings out those new highlights." Jack carried on talking and moving around her kitchen with ease. Natasha let him, happy to not be alone waiting for Matt.

When he finally stood a steaming mug of tea and a small plate of digestive biscuits in front of her, he stopped talking to take a sip of his tea.

"Why is Matt annoyed? Other than the trains?"

"The Prime Minister confided in him that the election is not likely to happen this summer. I probably shouldn't have said that, but Matt was, I mean is, going to say something about a long delay. Sadly, my dear, you have to stay Mrs Poole a little longer which means I'll have more dates for your diary. Matt wanted to talk to you alone, to explain. I couldn't understand why he thinks this is all his fault. The delay I mean. I guess it is him that has strayed AND him that is asking you to wait longer.

Natasha felt all her resolve from earlier draining away from her. She had already promised Matt she would wait. When she made that promise, she didn't know how long it would take, she didn't know how hard it would be to see Matt in love with someone else. And what surprised her most of all was what she would feel like when she too met someone new. If that is what this was. Could it be just her hormones coming out of hibernation? She sat quiet, struggling to process what Jack was saying and what she was feeling. He was still stunningly handsome despite tonight's journey. She sipped her tea, feeling the hot drink begin to warm and relax her. She reached for a biscuit and broke it in two. Nibbling slowly at one half thinking about what she would say to Matt. Would she still ask him to start the process?

"Do you ever eat a whole anything?" Jack scoffed at her, wriggling his eyebrows in a suggestive, comical way.

Natasha started to cough as the dry biscuit hit the back of her throat, and the image of a tall cricketer leaning over her flooded her brain. The blush was back, and Jack noticed.

"Mrs Poole! Are you blushing? Have you been having sex? Is it anyone I know?"

"Stop it, Jack! I know you are only playing, but Matt will be here soon." She wiped her mouth. "As you said, he is going to be cross that you are here, how is he going to feel about you telling me what he wants to say?"

Natasha sipped her tea, watching Jack over her cup. Had she done enough to put him off the scent?

"So, we won't tell him what we have been talking about. You won't mention Tom or that I told you his news. And I," Jack paused in his usual dramatic way. "Won't tell him you have been having sex."

"Well, that's good because I haven't been having sex yet."

"Ha! Not YET! That means there is someone."

"Jack, stop it. No, there isn't anyone."

They both stopped bickering because the door opened to reveal Matthew Poole. Clearly not impressed finding them together in his kitchen.

"What the hell are you doing here, Jack? You know why I wanted to come up alone this weekend."

Jack stood up defiantly swiped another biscuit, and moved to leave the room. With his hand on the door, he turned and smiled at Natasha.

"Natasha's met someone."

"Jack!"

"Sorry T but he would have known I had already told you, you are such a terrible actor, I had to use the diversion."

"Tasha?" Matt looked hurt as he dropped his case and ruffled the top of Mikey's head.

"That's just Jack being Jack. Where would I meet someone? All I ever do is work."

Jack came back into the room and sat opposite Natasha. Resting his chin in his hand, he stared at her. Mischief dancing in his eyes.

"So, you met someone at work? Really?"

"I have not met anyone. I promised." She turned to look squarely at Matt, anywhere but look at Jack. "I understand what would happen if I were seen out with someone."

"Tasha, you promised me you would wait." Matt sounded upset. "Have things changed? Have you met someone?"

"No, I haven't met someone." She narrowed her eyes at Jack. "But tell me, Matt, how long do you expect me to wait?"

"Yeah, Matt how long do you expect us to wait?" Jack chorused.

Matt looked drained. "I honestly thought this would be over now. I'm sorry I don't know what else to say." The room was quiet. Mikey looked from person to person and eventually put his paws on Natasha's leg. She mindlessly broke up the rest of her biscuit and fed it to him. For once, Matt didn't scold her for feeding him between meals. Jack noticed, too.

Taking charge, Jack picked up both his bag and Matt's case.

"Come on, Boss. I'm travelling light, so you'd better have packed my favourite shower gel."

"Jack!"

"OK. So, I packed it myself this morning. Come on, someone needs to sleep. We can talk tomorrow."

Chapter 8

Matthew and Jack had returned to the London flat and life for Natasha felt back to normal. She had walked in on them kissing the day before, and this time she didn't feel quite as sick. It was getting easier week by week. She still wasn't completely comfortable. But she'd survived.

That morning, she had shaved thirty seconds off her personal best time for her run. She had opened a fresh bottle of Basil and Neroli Shower gel and her hair was neatly plaited for the day ahead. Today, she was going shopping at the garden centre but first, she took the time to take Mikey for a walk in the park.

Once inside the ornate park gate, she slipped his lead and let him run. Natasha made her way to the opposite end of the park whilst Mikey replayed his puppy days. He ran and ran as fast as he could in large circles around her. When he spotted a young Labrador puppy playing with a ball, he rushed to join in.

Watching the two dogs sharing the ball and chasing each other brought a spot of joy to her heart. Life wasn't feeling so heavy today. She wasn't trapped watching the lovers and so she didn't have to think about the future. She could enjoy the sunshine on her face and the fun of sharing her life with a dog.

When the puppy left, Natasha and Mikey carried on out of the park and onto a footpath, making their way back home.

This is the life. The builder put in the path when they built the houses. Somehow, it looked like it had been there longer. Mature trees lined the path as it meandered gently back towards the shops, sitting between the farmland and the new estate. Something about walking along there sang to Natasha's heart. She loved living in this town, close enough to her father that he could come and help when she had an emergency. She liked to think she could talk to her dad about anything, but she hadn't shared about the problems with her marriage. How did she start that conversation?

When her phone vibrated in her pocket, she thought it must be her dad. But no, it was Matt,

"Tasha?"

"Hello?"

"Tasha?"

"I'm out with Mikey."

"I'll call back."

"I'm going out after this, those things from the garden centre."

"I'm sorry."

"What did you want, Matt?"

"I've just had Jack bending my ear. He says I'm not being fair to you."

"Well, I don't know what to say."

"I realise it must be hard, but you know why I want to wait?"

"I understand why you'd think after the election would be best for you."

"So why is Jack so adamant about you being upset?"

"Matt, just because I understand doesn't mean I like the situation."

"You do like Jack? You've always liked Jack?"

"That hasn't changed."

"I don't know what I can do. I know you want ... we should ... you know. We talked about it enough."

"Did you ever think this is unfair to him?"

"On whom?"

"Jack!"

"Unfair on Jack?"

"Well, yes."

"I'm the one stuck in the middle, torn between the two of you."

"I beg your pardon?"

"I am the one trying to keep both you and Jack happy."

"Explain what you are doing to keep me happy, Matthew."

"Well ... I'm ... well, you know, cleaning up on Sunday before we leave ... shit, I try, Tasha." He paused.

"It's just that things are getting tight. We are fighting for every vote."

"You can stop right there, Matthew Poole. Both Jack and I look after you. So you are in the middle, you are in the middle of two people who make your life easier."

"I'm sorry, it's just this morning, Jack…"

"As I said, Jack is probably the one upset."

"Do you think so?"

"Quite probably."

"OK."

"But Matt, this can't go on forever."

"I know, bye, Tash baby."

"Bye, Matt."

Damn! Damn him for disturbing me today.

With her phone still in her hand, Tasha flicked to the camera and took a photo of the walkway with Mikey looking back at her. She needed to remind herself of the good bits in life.

She hadn't gone fifty feet when her phone rang again. Emma Mansfield, at least this call would keep her upbeat.

"It's her!"

"I'm sorry?"

"India, from Gym Away, it's her?"

"What about her?"

"India from Gym Away is Nick's India." When Natasha didn't respond, Emma continued, "She is the girl in the photo in Nick's office, don't you remember?"

"Emma, I have been there once. As I remember it, Nick has a lot of photos on his wall."

"This one is bigger; it really stands out," Emma sighed.

"I asked him about it one day. I casually asked what agency she worked for; you know, being casual." Her voice was shaking.

"Nick said she wasn't a model and that she is the one that got away."

"But Nick has moved on, hasn't he? And she lives up in Leeds, doesn't she?"

"Yes, she's in Leeds, but she has booked him for some shoots."

"Has he said or done anything that makes you think he still has feelings for her?"

"He says they were only friends, and they are still friends."

"So why would he call her the one that got away?

"I guess he hasn't acted on his feelings yet, but if she is back in his life? What do I do?

"I don't see there is anything you can do. Probably the last thing you should do is make a fuss. I am fairly sure he won't respond well to any jealousy."

"I know, but it drives me mad. Knowing that every day he is working with those models. Changing clothes all the time."

"And yet, who does he come home to?"

"But not all the time, and he doesn't seem keen to move in. He claims that having somewhere to drop when he is working the late nights or early mornings makes sense."

"Well, it does make sense."

"Do you think it's because I am messy?"

"I don't know."

"What about the bright colours? Is my flat too bright?"

"Don't go painting everywhere, magnolia, for a man!"

"I wasn't planning to. His flat is white, though. Very minimal."

"It's close to his studio?"

"Yes, I guess it is. He walks home and leaves his car at work most of the time."

"Nick doesn't strike me as the sort of guy to mess with lots of different women."

"No, I thought that."

"And now you think differently?"

"I don't know. I guess it's me being paranoid, but you know what they say, being paranoid doesn't mean it isn't happening."

"Nick is not seeing other women."

"What do I do, Tasha?"

"You focus on you, on doing what you want to do, enjoy work, enjoy time off. Just decide to be happy. Nick is wonderful, and I am sure he is happy with you, but if he's not, I am sure there is someone else out there who is right for you."

"Do you mean Nick is not right for me?"

"That's for you to decide. If you can get past what he does for a job, the hours he works, the people he works with, they are all things that are impacting on you, well your relationship."

"I was going to go shopping, but you know what I am going to do? I'm going to clean the kitchen and then do some self-care before Nick comes over tonight."

"Emma, do something for you."

"Oh, I will. What are you doing?"

"I have been walking Mikey, and I am nearly home now."

"How did it go? Did you get sorted about … you know …"

"We talked about it, but for now, we're still in a holding pattern. Matt rang me just before you, actually. It seems Jack has been telling him he isn't being fair to me. I suspect Jack is fed up with the situation himself."

"Well, let's hope he gets the message soon."

"Thanks, now you go be happy. Enjoy your day."

"And you."

"I am."

Natasha ended the call, wondering how two quick phone calls could kill her mood. Finally, back at the house, determined to recapture her joy from earlier, she decided to fit in one more job before she went garden shopping. She took a tape measure down to the bottom of the garden and measured up for that arbour. It was time to make her own choices and not sit waiting for someone else to make her dreams happen.

Chapter 9

Daniel closed his mouth and eyes in ecstasy. Tasting the food and enjoying new flavours. When Tilly spoke, he opened his eyes to survey his dinner companions. India looked tired but her cousin Stella was bouncing with energy. Tilly was just being Tilly.

"I thought in first class they would feed us on the train, well, more than those sandwiches." Tilly looked like she would take the pattern off the plate.

"How come you had time to cook, Stella? Mum said your new job was keeping you busy?"

"Oh, don't get me started about the job. However, this was easy. I just shoved this in the slow cooker this morning."

"But the job's OK?" India examined her younger cousin with concern. She was all too aware of how the dream job in London could be more a nightmare than a dream.

"It's more than OK. It's exactly what I wanted. The budgets are mind-blowing and there always seems to be a new project to work on."

"Joe and I have one of those," Tilly said between mouthfuls. "Slow cooker," she explained as she slowly licked her lips. "Wedding present. Not sure we have used it."

Daniel smiled to himself; he was pretty sure cooking would never be Tilly Cookson's calling. She was great but "daddy's money" had affected her even if she tried to deny it. He was enjoying this time with the ladies. He hung out mainly with the boys from the team. This was new.

"So, this is your granddad's place?" He looked at India and then around at his surroundings. The tall ceilings and large windows had great proportions. It had been decorated in a traditional style, but he suspected that had been done recently.

"Yes." India was enjoying the dinner, too.

"And you live downstairs?" Daniel turned his trademark smile onto Stella.

"Yes, and so did India before she ran off to play house in Yorkshire."

Daniel took another mouthful. He was in full flirt mode.

"If you cook like this, you would be very welcome to come 'play house' in my part of Yorkshire anytime."

"Fudging heck, Daniel Woods! Do you ever stop flirting?" India kicked at his shins. "Leave my little cousin alone, you serial flirt."

Stella stood up next to her cousin. "Not everyone can be as tall as you, India."

"Wow, you are tiny!" Daniel stood next to Stella. With his long limbs, he towered above them all. He threw his arm around her shoulders. "Don't worry Stella—we are all the same height lying down."

Stella's natural energy lit up the room. Her short-cropped black hair and sparkling blue eyes would have usually put her on his radar, but today, he was only teasing. Somehow, all he could picture was a certain presenter. Daniel wondered if he would be working with her for either of the two shows tomorrow.

"Daniel Woods, are you still using that line? I told you about that last summer."

Tilly put down her fork. She scowled at Daniel.

"Hey, Dan? How come you never flirt with me?"

"That is simple, Tilly Cookson. You are a married woman!" and he touched the very tip of her nose. "Just like India here."

"I'm not married!"

"Only because you keep saying no to Charlie!" Tilly spat out.

"So, you think of me as 'married', but you still flirt with me?"

"Only when Charlie is there, though."

"It does rather wind him up."

"Now, why can't I flirt with your cousin?"

India looked embarrassed and focused on finishing the stew on her plate. Daniel was enjoying himself.

"And why do you keep saying no?" He was growing curious.

Tilly grinned and wriggled in her seat. This was her favourite subject. "How many times has he asked you now?" She had been trying to get India together with Charlie since the day she met him. Now, she couldn't wait to see them married. Daniel himself had watched them and couldn't understand why they had fought the relationship for so long. The entire team thought of India as Charlie's girl from the start.

"It's not because I don't love him. I do, I really do. Maybe I am not ready to be a wife."

Stella snorted; her wine went up her nose as she laughed. "I think it's more likely you aren't ready to have a Barrington Jones Wedding."

"You could be right. Dad says my mum has been planning mine since the day I was born."

"She definitely had her opinion on every wedding we were bridesmaids at. Your brother's was hard because she did most of it, but all the time, you could see the cogs working on how it will be better at yours. And at my dad's wedding to the latest one, she was amazing. Certainly, kept me entertained."

"So that's the problem. Does Charlie know?"

"I don't think I realised myself."

Stella came to her rescue. As she stood up to clear the plates, she asked. "Dessert, anyone?"

"Not for me, Stella. I've got to think of my figure. I have my TV debut tomorrow."

Stella smiled warmly at her new friend. "Are you nervous? I would be terrified."

"It's something new. It's exciting. I am looking forward to it."

"Really?" India looked hard at Daniel.

"Tell me India, do you know anyone else who has done this before?"

"No. No, I don't think I have."

"And neither have I." Daniel drained his beer and bounced his glass down onto the table with a flourish. Tilly, India, and Stella watched Daniel as his face lit up.

"See, all my life, I have been trying to be as good at stuff that someone else was already great at. The farm, cricket." He looked away, then pulling himself together, he carried on. "So, tomorrow, when I do this, I'll be the best at that out of everyone I know." He beamed at the ladies. "I am SO ready for this, and right now, I am going to bed to look my best for those cameras tomorrow."

"Is it just the cameras you want to look good for?" India teased. "You made a few conquests when you went for your screen test." Daniel smiled; he was used to making conquests, but one stood out.

"All I did was turn up and do a good job." He stood tall, happy this was something he could shine at. "Can I help it if everyone LIKED me?"

"Especially Paul?" India was enjoying this.

Daniel would happily spar with India. He enjoyed teasing her, but she looked tired, and he had promised Charlie he would look after her and Tilly. So, he refused when Stella offered him another drink. Neither Tilly nor India seemed to be drinking.

"Time for my bed." But once he had left the room, he started to go back to check what time they had to leave in the morning. Daniel wished he had just kept walking. With the door ajar, he could hear the girls talking about the next day.

"He was amazing last time. I admit I wasn't sure, but Charlie said he was a performer, and he was right. He seemed to come alive." Daniel didn't want to listen, but India kept talking. "I hope he is as relaxed as he was for the test. If we don't sell enough units, they won't want us back." India sighed.

"Hopefully, he is as good as he thinks he is. Joe and I had to have a lot of units made for this, and I'm not sure how we'll sell them if this falls flat."

"Oh, Tilly, I am sure we can do this."

"Well, it's my fault if we don't. Joe wasn't keen, cash flow and all that. It was me who pushed. If it doesn't end well tomorrow, India, we need a Plan B."

Stella laughed, "If there is ever anyone good at Plan B, it's a Barrington Jones."

Daniel decided to go to bed and leave them to talk. Safely in his room, he sat on the single bed and looked at his phone. He checked his text messages and scrolled down to the reply he got from Natasha. He had interpreted her message differently every time he opened it.

NP: My pleasure. All part of my job. Good luck with your first show.

'My pleasure' Daniel let the words roll around his mind. He had a stock of photos of her in his memory bank, but the one that had her running toward him was the one he replayed over and over. Only now, as she got closer, he opened his arms and lifted her in a kiss. It was a long, slow kiss, a lingering kiss, that tingled on his lips as he imagined it. Suddenly, his jeans were too tight. He stripped down and slipped between the sheets. He picked up his phone again and sent a message to NP.

DAN: I have my first show tomorrow. Any tips?

NP: Let your presenter guide you. That is what our job is.

DAN: Thank you, Natasha. I hope it's you. Someone I know.

In his head, he added the words I know and love.

Love? When did Daniel ever love anyone? He loved his sister, of course, and he cared about his dad and his brother. He was very fond of his teammates. He had lots of girlfriends, but he hadn't ever thought he loved a girl or a woman. Natasha was definitely a woman. Why did he feel so drawn to her? *She was kind to you, she's attractive, and she was kind to you, it's nothing more.*

Daniel turned over in bed. Leaving his phone on the side table, he had turned his back on it. His dreams proved he hadn't stopped thinking about Natasha Poole.

Chapter 10

Daniel was pleased to be arriving at the studio gate with Tilly and India. Between them, they had everything covered. They had the clothes they wanted him to wear, the Gym Away, and the props all delivered to the studio. No problems with remembering his pass this time.

A girl from reception escorted them to the green room, which was full of mature models for the show after theirs. Daniel found himself having to squeeze into a tiny pink changing room to get ready. It wasn't easy. He banged both his elbows and his left knee twice. *Why is it always my left knee?*

Paul discovered him and began to set up his microphone pack.

"No jeans today? What did I tell you about battery packs?"

"Can I just make it clear; I didn't choose these shorts!"

"I won't be responsible if these fall down."

"Would you mind telling the boss that?"

"Oh! Which one is the boss? Is it that stunning tall one? Or the fiery redhead?"

"I think as far as clothes are concerned, you need to convince them both."

"Leave that with me. Now, let's get you into the studio." Paul led the way down the dark corridor. This time to an orange door with the same signs.

"You left your phone, didn't you? I'll be in so much trouble if it rings on air."

"And where do you think I've hidden a phone in this outfit?"

"You have a point."

As they entered studio one, there was a live show going out from a set close to the door. Tilly and India were busy arranging props on a set to his left. They were trying to decide on the exact angle to have the packaging on the shelving at the back of the set. Swapping in fresh bottles and items from the kit. All this without saying a word. They had been fussing since breakfast, talking so fast he couldn't keep up. Often finishing each other's sentences.

Daniel hadn't been nervous last night, but since they arrived, he could feel those pre-match nerves rolling up from his toes.

Tilly and India kept stressing how important today was. He got the feeling Tilly and Joe had stretched themselves financially to buy the extra units.

They could fuss all they liked with the set; it was down to him to sell all those products today. He had just two shows. Each an hour. That was it. Sell the Gym Away.

He went over and over the features and benefits throughout the journey down on the train, last night in that tiny bed they had given him in the flat. And then, all the way here in the taxi.

Now, with so much happening since they arrived at More.U TV, it had all left his head. Every single fact.

He swallowed hard as Paul adjusted the mic on his t-shirt. The cameras were moving in and out on the other side of the studio. The two women selling nutrition supplements appeared to be enjoying themselves. They looked like old friends enjoying a good chat. *Is it me or is it hot in here?* Daniel blinked.

The heavy studio door silently swung open and lit up from behind the tiny silhouette of Natasha Poole. Somewhere deep inside Daniel Woods, he knew that today was going to turn out just fine.

As she picked her path through the cables on the floor, Daniel was struck by how different she was from him. So beautifully proportioned. He attracted attention easily but nothing that lasted. Once the girls saw him properly, they realised how weird his body was. How his long arms and legs always seemed to be in the way.

Tilly and India left the studio and Natasha took her place next to him. She stood so close to Daniel that her perfume filled his nose and then his brain. He gripped the counter in front of him and tried to take steady deep breaths. At his side was Natasha wearing Lycra today. *She's ready for action.*

Daniel was surprised to see her out of the immaculate clothes he had seen her wear in the studio before and then he saw her hair. She had it in some sort of intricate plait that Daniel just couldn't work out. It was nothing like his niece wore. Realising she was dressed for exercise, Daniel searched his brain for something he could show her how to do.

Paul was standing next to a camera with a large number two on it, using his fingers to count down from five.

5   This is it! First of two shows.

4   At least it's Natasha … It is hot in here.

3   Maybe she just wants good sales figures.

2   I wanted this! I need to prove to them that I can do it.

1   So here we go.

"I am so excited to be here today with the cricketer Daniel Woods, who is here to show us a fabulous new product, the Gym Away. I have had the pleasure of seeing all this before and I can tell you it is so versatile." She smiled at him. Daniel could feel the sweat on his hands.

Lifting a kit, she looked at the camera. "If you want to get your hands on your own Gym Away, there are three ways to buy. Online at MoreU.TV, on the phone at 0800 888700 or just tap the app on your phone."

"Press record now if you don't want to miss out on what you do with this." That professional smile was now turned towards Daniel.

"Daniel, can you start by telling us what is included in this amazing kit?"

That smile, the cameras or something else, flicked a performance switch in Daniel's brain. He put on his own megawatt smile, the one he used when reporters caught him away from the cricket ground. Even his voice had changed.

"Good morning Natasha," his voice now like a great coffee, rich and dark, full of depth. "The Gym Away may look small - indeed it is designed to fit in your suitcase."

He took the kit from Natasha's hand with a softer smile that said thank you. "But it consists of a set of resistance bands, handles, a wheel, and this container that fills with water to work as dumbbells.

Holding up the empty container with a firm, steady hand to the camera, he continued. "There is a scale on the side here, which helps you fill it to specific weights. Of course, you can use any amount of water, meaning you can have any size dumbbell up to three kilos."

"Ha, so I don't need to move from one kilo straight up to two kilos, I can do say one and a half?"

"Exactly you can have any weight that works for you in your suitcase."

"That's wonderful!" She sounded pleasantly surprised, and Daniel wasn't sure if that was real or part of being the "presenter".

"Of course, this kit is not just for your suitcase?"

"Not at all. It was designed for that, the businessperson working away from home a lot. It was great for us as a cricket team. Everyone I know has one." Daniel smiled at her and laughed. "Most probably because India gave them one, but the thing is they use it. And that I think is the most telling thing. How many of us have some sort of exercise equipment languishing away and we don't use it? This is not one of those things."

"So, professionals, as well as someone like me, can use it too."

"Yes. I am struggling to think of anyone who couldn't get some benefit from using the resistance bands. They are great to improve the way you stretch, and we all should stretch more. Warm up before we do something physical." Daniel's eyes trailed down Natasha's body. He swallowed hard and his voice changed again. "Cool down afterwards, it's the way to prevent injury."

Natasha broke eye contact with him as she looked into the camera. "Let me give you those numbers again. This is one unit, there is nothing to choose and no extras to buy. So, 981 751 is the number you need. Online, on the phone or on the app."

Now she was looking back at him, and he was searching to find that voice. The one that said I know what I am talking about. Look and listen to me. The voice that had served him so well at university.

"I want to show you the dumbbells. I filled this one up to the two-kilo mark with water. Now let's try some movements that will work your triceps and biceps."

"Hold your hand out and let your other arm hang loosely by your side. Keep your hips square and facing forward." He stood behind her, his hands holding her hips to correct her stance. Then he took her arm. "Holding your arm out to the side at shoulder level and palm facing forward." He was trying to use the words, but something made him touch her to reinforce what he wanted her to do. He tried to tell himself it was so she was clear what he meant, but he couldn't resist the urge to touch her. His hand held her wrist out and then ran slowly up her arm to her shoulders. "We want to work the arms, not the shoulders so let go up here. Relax these muscles and hold your arm out." His hands slipped back down to her hips. Now, pull your arm to the front. And hold that for just a couple of seconds before you turn your palm to face the back and push your arm backwards in a nice flowing movement." Natasha followed his instructions. Looking to him for the next one.

"You are already doing work on your arms, but now take the dumbbell and do that same set of movements." He handed the half-filled container to her and then put his hands back on her hips. "You must keep your hips facing forward and those shoulders relaxed." His hands now on her shoulders he stroked down her arms. "Can you feel the muscles working and now by using the weights you are working them harder?" The word harder seemed to resonate in his brain, and he felt his body react to touching her skin. Soft and firm. Still standing behind her he took a small step back so that she wouldn't feel it too.

"That's brilliant Daniel, I can certainly feel that up here." As she stroked her arm, Daniel fought hard not to react. It was time for him to think of anything but Natasha Poole in Lycra. To push her perfume from his brain. To stop remembering what it felt like to touch her.

"Let's look at doing something for your legs. A stretch for after those runs you are so fond of."

Daniel had her lie down and do the movement they had worked on during his screen test. They had been pleased with that.

With Natasha lying down beneath him, he moved to pick up the resistance bands from the floor. As he bent forward, he felt the battery pack slip along with his waistband further down. He used the hand away from the camera to hitch the shorts back up. Natasha was watching him from her place on the floor. Daniel thought she was trying to suppress a giggle. That didn't help him at all! Normally he loved to make a woman laugh, that was him, Daniel Woods, the clown. Today he needed to do something to stop those giggles.

He took hold of her foot a little more firmly than he meant but it did the trick it stopped the giggle before it escaped as Natasha too fought to remember she was at work. As he held her foot he tried with all he could to look at her face and communicate that this was serious.

"This will stretch out your hamstrings; and is for after your run."

As he pulled her foot towards him, it slipped and hit him in the groin. Daniel now knew for sure that Natasha Poole would be in no doubt what he was feeling at the moment. And just in case she didn't, the blood rushed to ensure what he was trying so hard to hide would be brutally obvious.

The Lycra outfit might cover most of her body, but it did nothing to hide her curves. The softness that made her a woman. Daniel paused as he held her foot. Natasha blushed.

Daniel swallowed hard. Natasha flexed her foot and finally, there was no way she couldn't know the effect she was having on him. The normal Daniel would have enjoyed this. Why not let a good-looking woman see that she excited you? Perhaps this wasn't one of those times.

As Natasha started the exercise they had done on the screen test, Daniel straightened. The shorts slipped further and there was a scurrying off to his right as Paul came into view.

Natasha sat up and said, "Let me tell you again how you can buy your own Gym Away kit. 981 751 is the number you need. Online, on the phone or on the app. Your kit will be with you in three or four working days. And remember you have a 30-day money-back guarantee whenever you buy from More.U TV."

On the monitor, Daniel could see they were showing a still image of Gym Away and all the product details. He felt he could breathe again. He still felt too hot. Paul pulled him by the arm until he was off to the side of the set.

"I warned you about those shorts, but to be honest, I was just worrying about the battery pack." He was carrying a roll of duct tape and a pair of scissors. He turned Daniel around and pulled his T-shirt out of his shorts and used the tape to stick the shorts to Daniel's back.

"Pull your T-shirt out at the front too. I don't think I want to use the tape on your other problem."

Daniel didn't say a word through all this. He worried his mic was live.

"Now, for the rest of the show, it is probably best if you stay behind the counter. But don't worry, there is not much that tape doesn't fix. As I always say, if tape doesn't fix it, you aren't using enough."

Daniel looked bewildered at Paul. "Go on, get back behind the counter, go sell your stuff with the lovely Natasha."

When he took up his place next to Natasha, the thought of Paul wanting to sort out his other problem with tape was enough to deal with the issue.

He wasn't sure how he got through the rest of that first show but before long he was back in the green room and sat down in between India and Tilly on the sofa.

"How did I do?"

"You were brilliant, I don't think I could have done it. Tilly and I have been making notes on how we can tweak the staging for next time."

"Did we sell enough for there to be 'a next time'?"

"I don't know we are waiting for the buyer to tell us."

"Can I get a shower, or do I need to be here for that?"

"Sure. Put on the green T-shirt for the next one. Someone from one of the other shows said blue and green work best on camera."

"I guess it is worth a try," he said thoughtfully. "And girls, I am sorry, but I can't wear the shorts this time."

"Oh?"

"It was a problem with the battery pack."

First Tilly and then India burst into uncontrollable laughter.

"Sorry Dan! Yes, I think that all needs a rethink for next time."

When he finally squeezed into the tiny shower, Daniel was wishing he hadn't bothered. The water was dribbling out of a tiny shower head that was low for an average person. They certainly hadn't planned to accommodate someone as tall as him. His elbows were getting a bashing.

After several minutes of attempting to wash all the essential bits, he gave up and climbed out and, in the process, Daniel grazed his elbow again. His skin was cut, and it started to bleed.

Once he was dressed and back in the green room, it was still bleeding. Both girls made a fuss, but it was India who went to reception and came back with a dressing. It took both Tilly and India to apply it to Daniel's arm.

They had just decided to make a cup of tea and try to relax before show two when the buyer arrived. Daniel tried to read her face but there was nothing to see, so he took over making the tea whilst the buyer talked to Tilly.

"Well, that was OK for a first visit. We sold 10% of the loaded stock. Hopefully, we can sell more in this next one. They all seemed to enjoy it. Lots of people were watching and maybe a few more sales will come through between the shows."

Daniel had no problem reading the look on Tilly's face. He was pretty sure they wanted to hear bigger numbers, certainly more than ten per cent.

Chapter 11

Damn!

Daniel Woods was standing behind the counter waiting for her. With him in the studio, Natasha was holding back, planning to go in at the last possible moment. Paul, the floor manager, had somehow made her think she was late, so she had rushed downstairs from her dressing room. Instead, she had arrived with time to spare.

Well, the first show went well. Emma seemed pleased as did the business owner. Maybe we can actually sell some kits this time.

As the presenter, she usually had no problem putting the guest at ease and teasing the best out of them. Those few minutes before the show started were so valuable for getting them to relax and creating that bond. So why was she avoiding this particular five minutes?

Emma was already in her ear. "Welcome to show two, Tasha. I hope you are prepared to rock this one like that first hour."

Natasha plastered on her professional smile. "Hello, Daniel. Are you ready for this show?" He smiled his reply.

"Good heavens, Daniel, what happened to your elbow?"

"I foolishly attempted a shower in that pink changing room."

"Goodness, they are tiny in there."

"Yeah, I'm not exactly built for tiny things, though."

Natasha found herself looking from his toes to the top of his head. She was relieved he wasn't wearing shorts this time. "I can see that!"

She softened her smile, "Next time you come to do a show, talk nicely to the presenter, we have a much better set-up."

"Next time? I need to survive this time. I don't think they will have me back."

Natasha laughed. "I'm pretty sure they will have you back!"

Daniel looked surprised, but she had no time to explain because Paul had started the countdown again. Natasha spoke softly to Daniel as he counted.

5   "Come on Daniel, just follow me."

4   Natasha squeezed his hand, "You've got this."

3   She pulled him closer, "Stand close. Remember."

2   She squeezed his hand again.

1   "Smile."

"Welcome to our second-ever show with Gym Away." Natasha sparkled into the camera. "I have with me, professional cricketer Daniel Woods, who is going to help me tell you about the gym you can take with you."

"Daniel, can you start by telling us exactly what we get in the kit?"

"I certainly can, Natasha." As Daniel started to list each of the items, in her ear, Emma was talking again.

"Tasha, I'm a little worried we don't have enough stock for this show. It looks like the sales rolled in after the last one finished. I'm trying to get the buyer now to see if we can load some more." Her frustration was clear, and Natasha tried not to show anything on her own face.

"I want you to focus on the product for now."

Natasha's eyes were focused on Daniel's hands as he moved the resistance bands on and off the handles. His strong fingers fascinated her. His dexterity was hypnotising.

"I can't find this buyer. I'm going to the head of the department. Stick with what you can do with it. I'll tell you when to push. The viewing numbers are great, and plenty are looking on the website. I just need you to get them ready to buy. I'm on this."

Natasha smiled sweetly at Daniel. "Can you demonstrate to us a few of the ways we can exercise using these bands, Daniel?"

When Daniel showed a simple stretch to work both biceps and triceps, Natasha couldn't stop herself from touching his arm. She found herself stroking down towards his elbow. A small panic began to rise through her. *What am I doing? What is it about this man?*

"It's OK Tasha to sell out and we are ready to load some advance order stock. I'll give you details as we get to that."

Phew! Now she had a reason for holding his arm.

"I'm going to have to stop you there, to tell people, this is so popular we already have limited stock.

Daniel looked at her. She couldn't read the emotion in his green eyes. She pulled his arm. Taking his hand in hers behind the counter. *God! He looks lost.*

"Camera one is on you, Tasha. Give them the numbers."

"If you want to make sure you get yours, check out your basket now." She reluctantly let go of his hand. "The fastest way to get yours is to use the app."

From the corner of her eye, Natasha saw Paul take Daniel to the side of the set and over to the yoga mats.

"We are down to the last few. Please don't miss out. Check out now." Daniel was now lying down on the floor. His long jean-clad legs stretched out towards the cameras.

"And they are gone. Go do some magic over there with that gorgeous man whilst we load the delayed delivery stock."

"Daniel, what else can we do with Gym Away?"

"I thought I would show you the wheel." He was sitting upright on the floor. Natasha watched his powerful hands screw the handles on the wheel.

"Nearly there, Tash … go with him on this. Let him do the exercise this time, so you can tell them about advanced orders."

"That looks simple Daniel, now can you show us what you can do with that?"

"Good Tasha. I've got camera two on him, and you on camera one. I'll switch between them as we need to."

Daniel was on all fours. The wheel in his hands.

"This will strengthen your core." Away he went, rolling the wheel forward, stretching out his torso.

"I have good news for those who missed out. We have secured a limited amount of stock on advanced orders." Daniel seemed to relax, well his face did. His body carried on rolling forward and back.

"Delivery is ten days, Tasha have you got that? Ten days."

"If you order your Gym Away today on advanced order, it will be with you in just ten days."

Across the studio, she could see Paul prepping the next set. On the floor at her feet, Daniel Woods was rolling in and out. Then, just in the corner of her eye, she caught an image of herself on the monitor of camera one, as she stood open-mouthed watching the rhythmic movement of the guest.

"Ha-ha, yes, close your mouth, Tasha. Let them know the numbers." Natasha found her presenter smile and began to sparkle down the lens of camera one. On automatic pilot, giving out all the details of how to order.

"So, 981 751 is the number you need. Online, on the phone or on the app. Just remember, these will be with you in ten working days, only that little longer to wait. And just like everything you buy from More.U TV, your Gym Away is covered with our 30-day money-back guarantee.

"Tash, we'll not last the hour, even with the extra stock. We need to start the next show when we hit the double sell-out."

"Ladies and gentlemen, I am told we are running out of those advanced orders, so let me tell you once again how you can make sure you get yours."

Paul talked to Daniel again as he jumped up from the floor. It took all of Natasha's willpower to focus on what she should be doing. Daniel stood behind the counter, just a tantalising distance away, breathing heavily, perspiration on his face.

"Tasha, I can't get you both in one shot. One or two steps closer to him." Paul stood behind camera two, waving at Daniel to move closer to Natasha. They both took that sideways step closer together and suddenly they collided. Daniel's arm shot around her shoulders to steady her. She steadied herself with a hand on his chest.

"After me today?" His smile was so infectious.

Emma's voice in her ear sounded excited, too.

"Just five left, Tasha. Get ready to hand over to Judith. We are going to run extra inter-mercials."

"There are just five Gym Away kits left. If you want one, you need to buy it now." She squeezed Daniel's arm. "Daniel, just two gym Aways left of those advanced orders. Can you show the viewers who have been lucky enough to get one just how easy it is to put away?"

"Of course, I can, Natasha. This is how I pack mine away. I start by laying out all the bands. I roll them up around the handles. The wheel screws onto the bottom and everything else stores inside the tube." His strong fingers still hypnotising her.

"That's it, Tasha, Double Sell out. Well done. Wrap it up."

Natasha gripped Daniel's arm to stop him. Her fingers flexed around the muscles and sinews. "Daniel, thank you. I'm afraid we have sold out so we can't continue. We are going to move over to Judith, who has some amazing More.U TV's very own supplements." She tightened her grip on his arm to keep him in the shot next to her.

"I've loved it!" Every inch of Daniel Woods looked like he meant it.

"Well, thank you again, Daniel. I look forward to your next visit to More.U TV.

"And we're out." Paul pulled the cameras over the studio towards another set. Daniel threw his arms around Natasha.

"God, you are wonderful. I love you." He pulled her close, her face held hard into his chest.

"Daniel shush. Your mic might still be live."

"I heard him." Paul rushed forward to retrieve his mic pack.

"I was just doing my job. But congratulations on selling out so fast." Natasha said in hushed tones, even though they were playing pre-records.

"That was brilliant. The second hour went so fast."

"Ah, it was only forty minutes. We sold out so fast."

"You weren't just saying that?"

"No. We aren't allowed to do that."

"Clear the studio," Paul hissed at them both. Natasha moved Daniel towards the door.

On the other side of the orange door of studio one, they found India and Tilly waiting for them. Big smiles on each of their faces. Natasha squeezed his arm one last time.

"Thank you, Daniel. Congratulations, ladies on a wonderful product. It's ideal for TV.

As she left them talking excitedly, she made her way to meet up with Emma.

"Hey Emma, thanks for a great show."

"The numbers were there in the end. Seems they mainly bought at the end of show one. We sold 85% of the original stock in the fifteen minutes after it finished."

"That good?"

"The boss stuck his head in. I think he'd heard about the sales. He commented on the chemistry. He loved that you had gone for Lycra, but he wants you to wear some we sell, so expect an email about that. And" she paused, looking at her friend. "He also would like you to take a Gym Away home as he thinks you need to do your homework."

"What does that mean?"

"I am guessing here, but I think he might be considering you doing some inter-mercial reels with you. Could even be thinking about pre-records for those shows we have to pull."

"Without Daniel?"

"Yep, without Daniel."

Chapter 12

Daniel stood alone in the empty corridor filled with grey doors. A rather excited buyer had spirited away Tilly and India, eager to talk about more stock. They had left him with one instruction: get clean and ready for their train, which wasn't for another two hours. He was sweaty again from working out under the hot studio lights. He rubbed his elbow as he pictured the shower in that pink hell. Natasha's words echoed through his head 'sweet-talk a presenter'. Was that an invitation? One thing Daniel enjoyed was sweet-talking a beautiful woman and Natasha Poole was certainly a beautiful woman.

Still on a high from the live tv shows, he threw his bag over his shoulder and bounced up the stairs two steps at a time. The upstairs corridor was empty and lined on both sides with simple blue doors. Each door held a nameplate. The third door on his right bore her name. Natasha Poole.

Now he had found it, he hesitated for the first time. He rocked on his heels and took a deep breath. Rocking forward on his toes, he knocked just once on her door. His heart pounded wildly in his chest as he waited for his answer.

When she opened the door, he stepped back. Each time he saw her, she had that same physical effect on him. It felt like a hard punch to his solar plexus. It took a beat for him to open his mouth.

"Hi Natasha, I'd like to thank you for looking after me today." He produced a teasing smile as he went on. "Someone with experience helping a TV virgin. It was kind of you. I want you to know how grateful I am." Daniel let his eyes travel down her body to her bare feet. Her toes sparkled with the same neat polish matching perfectly with her fingertips. Her robe was tied tightly at her waist. The soft satin draped around her curves in a way that made Daniel swallow hard as he waited for her reply. His eyes were drawn to the deep V at the front of her robe as it covered her breasts. She took her time to answer him.

"Oh, you are welcome, really just doing my job, you know." Her eyes glanced uncertainly down the corridor as she gripped the belt of her robe.

Daniel looked into her room. No windows, but a large mirror dominated the wall in front of him. He stopped himself from staring at her rear reflected towards him.

"So, this is where you get ready, a lot more space than the pink dungeon downstairs." Natasha stepped back, still holding her door but giving him a clearer view of the entire room. Daniel moved forward, one step looking around, a second step, he could see it all.

"Wow, what a lot of clothes." On his left, a long rail holding two dozen hangers of assorted outfits, each protected by translucent plastic bags. Natasha didn't reply, she held the door firmly in her hand.

"Oh, and last but not least, a proper shower. What do you have to do to get one like this?" He dropped his bag and walked straight into the bathroom, rubbing his elbow again.

"Well? I guess all the rooms are the same up here."

"Are there any empty ones I could borrow?"

"Sorry, we each have our own key. I can only access this room up here."

"Right ...," he said slowly, thinking as he spoke. "So, the only way I can use one is to use yours?" He looked longingly at the shower. "I don't suppose ... I mean, I am clean ... just hot and sweaty."

"I don't know, it's not usual."

"I'd rather not travel home on the train like this." Natasha started to smile. He pushed again. "Think about poor Tilly and India."

"Do you want to be responsible for more bruises on my delicate body?" he pouted, showing her his bashed elbow from earlier. Natasha burst into laughter at the suggestion of Daniel squeezing into that tiny cubicle. She seemed to be shifting, so Daniel pushed on. "I promise I'll be quick." The smile was out in full force, and as he looked her square in the eyes, he could see she was wavering. "I would be very grateful." Natasha laughed louder. "Did I go too far? Shit, I really just want a decent shower."

"My Boss is pleased with me for a double sell-out, so what the hell? Knock yourself out."

Daniel didn't wait for her to change his mind. He grabbed his bag and shut himself in the bathroom.

"And I'm only doing this for Tilly and India!" she shouted through the door."

"Me too."

In the bathroom, Daniel closed his eyes. This felt bold, yet it was nothing like how cheeky he could be, had been, in fact. He had once talked three girls into a hot tub, naked. Why did this feel so different, so forbidden, and why did that excite him? He undressed thoughtfully, folding the clothes that India had given him. *Who washes these? If it's me, I think I better get Becca to help.*

He stood up, naked and ready for the shower. Another huge mirror dominated the bathroom. Daniel examined his body, turning slowly to take in as much as he could. For this time in the season, he was happy with his training and the Gym Away was making a difference.

He turned on the water and then searched in his bag for shower gel. As he put it on the niche in the shower, he was conscious of how neatly the bottles were arranged and how many bottles there were.

Chapter 13

Natasha Poole was in a great mood. She had avoided the situation at home again. She had a double sell-out under her belt at the start of the weekend and now she was getting ready for a girlie night out with Emma.

Emma had been moaning about Nick again. But he had his own business and Natasha knew why he felt he needed to take work when it came along. She also understood Emma's frustration when it always seemed to change any arrangements he made with her. Of course, it didn't help when Nick worked with some exquisite women.

As she settled in front of the mirror to dry her hair, she was thinking about the weekend at Emma's multicoloured flat. Natasha was trying to work out how she could fit in more exercise than just her morning run which Emma had finally agreed was non-negotiable. Maybe having a Gym Away wasn't such a bad idea.

From her bathroom, the sounds of a man enjoying his shower filled her side of the room. It was an age since she had heard that, and it made her stop. She couldn't remember the last time she felt like this. Life was looking much brighter than just a week ago.

Still, she made the decision to not risk getting dressed when Daniel could come out at any moment. No, better to sit tight until he left. She tightened her robe and pulled her hair out over her shoulders. Flicking out her hands, she knocked a jar of face cream onto the floor. As she leant down, the jar rolled away. She reached out to pick it up just as Daniel burst into the room from the shower.

She looked up at Daniel Woods, trying to hide behind a tiny towel. Judging by his face, he clearly saw something more of her than he had before.

"Fuck I'm sorry. Shit, and now I can't pretend I didn't see anything," he cursed. Natasha blushed, replacing the cream in the neat row of others to her right, and refastening her robe.

Daniel Woods suddenly had her full attention, and it was Natasha who was staring. He stood dripping on her rug with the smallest of towels he was trying to use to cover himself.

"I think I left my towel in the pink hell downstairs. All I had was this cloth for …"

Daniel stopped talking and swallowed as his eyes fell on Natasha. From her spot in front of the mirror, she had a magnificent view of the effect looking at her was having on him. That towel was hiding nothing. She squirmed as her own body responded to him. She had forgotten that feeling, and her hand wanted to touch herself. To hold that part of her tight as if to stop the sensation that was creeping upward and taking over. As she pulled her eyes away from his body to his face, she saw desire.

Natasha couldn't remember the last time she had seen that. Matthew had made love to her, but there was none of the fire she was feeling now or the fire she saw in Daniel's face today. Her hand reached out towards him, the need to touch him so strong. As she did, Daniel's face relaxed, and he step forward until he was a tantalising distance away from her. He dropped his pathetic towel and revealed himself to her. Erect and bouncing against his tight body.

"See something you like, Natasha?" the cocky Yorkshire man smiled. Natasha relaxed too, a man showing that she was attractive.

"Did I do that?" she swallowed hard.

"I don't see anyone else in the room."

"Can I …" Her hand reached out again. In response, Daniel stepped forward. As her hand closed around his crown, Daniel stroked her hair. Sitting sideways to her mirror, she could see them reflecting back at her. His long legs meant he stood proud in front of her eyes. Her hand caressing the silken skin produced noises from him.

"Daniel, this is … you are so big … I just want to …"

"You want to what Natasha?" he said her name so slowly it lingered on his tongue and made her own tongue tingle. The smell of mint filled her head.

"Mint?" she raised her eyes in question."

"My shower gel. Want a taste?" He was so bold she could not stop her tongue from coming out and licking her bottom lip. Daniel's hands now framed her face as he bent down to kiss her. It was a slow, tentative kiss. A kiss that sought permission for more. Her response was immediate and without thought as she opened her lips to admit his searching tongue. Together, their tongues danced as Natasha's hands explored him further. Her hands roamed over his torso; his tight skin stretched over very defined muscles. She pulled away from the kiss to breathe and look at the body her hands were feeling.

"I guess you are liking what you are seeing as much as I am." His confidence was something she wasn't used to; Matthew had been careful how often she saw him. Daniel clearly had no trouble showing her his body, all of it. Natasha couldn't find the words to speak to him, but her body responded for her as her face flushed and her hand wrapped around his cock. She pulled it downwards towards her mouth and as she fixed her eyes on his, her lips covered his crown.

Her hand securely on the root of his cock, she tasted the mint, and then she could taste him. Her lips were firmly around his tip as her tongue swirled and reached for more. She slid him further into her mouth and Daniel's hands stroked her hair, slowly at first. And as he stroked confidently and with more speed, she matched his pace as she worked her hands and tongue. Exploring and enjoying this expression of his attraction to her. His hands slipped into her robe and found her breasts. His fingers caressed the roundness. Pulling gently on her nipples, Daniel seemed to have surrendered to the sensation, and he moaned as his hips pushed forward. Natasha dropped one hand to hold his thigh, to give her some control as his thrusts became more urgent.

His muscles tightened under her touch as he pulled back.

"Tasha I'm going to…" It was too late. Natasha swallowed hard as he filled her mouth with his saltiness.

As they stopped to gaze at each other, Natasha couldn't contain her smile. It felt amazing to have someone be so attracted to her that her own body responded too. She couldn't remember being speechless like this. Before either of them could find the words to say anything, there was a loud pounding on her door.

"Natasha, Natasha." It was Paul banging on her door.

"I'm not dressed sweetie, what is it?"

"Your husband is trying to contact you. Matt says your dad took little Mikey to the park, and he ran out in front of a car. They are operating. Can you call your husband, not your dad?"

The silence echoed around the room as neither of them spoke.

"Natasha, did you get that?"

Natasha closed her eyes as her hand covered her mouth. "Not Mikey."

Daniel stood in front of her, looking down, his eyes empty.

"You're married." He said nothing more. He didn't look at her, he just dressed and left. Natasha wanted to explain of course she did, but how. And right at that moment, her thoughts were in the Cotswolds, not with Daniel Woods.

Chapter 14

The journey home was not one Natasha ever wanted to repeat. At the top of her voice, she berated herself.

"What was I thinking?"

"At work, of all places?"

"What will Matt say?"

"After all my promises?"

"Please let Mikey be OK?"

"My dad will be upset; it's not his fault, Mikey can have a mind of his own and this time it got him in trouble."

The image of Daniel's face and his words 'you're married?' haunted her. How could she explain what was happening in her life?

"Which motorway should I take?"

"You know whichever one you pick will be the one with hold-ups!"

"Poor Mikey, please be OK Mikey. I need you right now."

As she hit slower traffic, she started to reminisce about the day Matthew bought Mikey for her. He was spending more time each week in London, leaving her at home in the Cotswolds. Her dad had been scathing about the 'designer dog'. In his head, it was another sign that there was something not quite right about Matthew. He was always careful about what he said, but his body language gave him away.

Natasha was beginning to see more of the ways George Webb disliked his son-in-law. Maybe because all the DIY was left to him. Matt was not at home with tools. It was George who unblocked the sink and fixed the guttering. Natasha loved decorating and had spent many hours painting their house, but it was her father who put up a set of shelves near the kettle for her coffee station.

Without trying, Natasha had a vision of Daniel Woods stripped to the waist, building the arbour she had dreamed of having over the bench at the bottom of her garden. In her version, his body was dripping with sweat, and she was carrying out a tray of exotic drinks. Then the picture of Daniel with a cocktail glass, complete with an umbrella. That made her smile. She was sure Daniel would never order a drink like that. *Stop thinking about that man, you stupid girl. He was right! You are a married woman.*

But as hard as she tried, she couldn't shake the image of Daniel coming out of her shower, struggling to cover himself with that impossibly small towel. But that wasn't going to help Mikey.

By the time Natasha Poole parked her car, she had no idea how she'd driven home. She was so relieved to see Matthew was already there. Of course, he had the news first and a secretary to arrange things. She had been avoiding seeing him for weeks, but right now, she needed him.

Pulling out just her handbag, she rushed inside in search of her best friend. All the way home, she had been praying that Mikey was OK. Having his warm body curled up against her own had become so much more important since Matt had found his new love.

She couldn't stop thinking that somehow she had caused this by turning off her phone when she had been so busy enjoying herself. Mikey was hurt because she had been distracted by a long streak of cricketer. His muscles still damp from the shower. Shaking her head to rid her of the image, she shouted for her husband.

"Matt! I'm home. What's the news? Tell me he is going to be OK."

"We are in the lounge. Come in. I'll get you a drink."

"A drink? Is it bad news?"

"I spoke to the vet. Mikey hasn't come around yet, but it's early." Natasha stood in the doorway, holding on to the frame.

Matt continued, "The vet is there all night. Come in, sit down, get your bearings, and we can call for an update."

Natasha finally sank down. Her shame hung heavily in her stomach.

"Oh, Matt. I'm sorry, I forgot to turn my phone back on when I came out of the studio. I had one more show and needed the shower. I'm so sorry." Her guilt was more than that, but she couldn't find the words to tell him exactly how she felt. Natasha didn't think she would ever share that experience with another soul. That was her moment with Daniel Woods, and she would never forget it.

"Tash baby, it's not your fault. It's no one's fault." Matt moved to sit beside her.

"But I …" Natasha sighed, "I feel so … This is so difficult."

"Tasha, you need to be ready. For unwelcome news, I mean." He took her hand in his. "It sounds like his pelvis is smashed and there are a lot of organs around there."

Jack sat on her other side and put his arm around her shoulders. They sat together for several minutes, the clock on the mantel ticking loudly to itself. Eventually, Natasha asked Matthew to call for an update.

Matt stood up and pulled out his phone just as it rang. Natasha knew instantly this wasn't another annoying work call, this was the sad news she had been dreading all the way home.

"Yes, this is Matthew Poole."

"Yes, I understand."

"No, I'm sure you did everything you could." Jack's arm tightened around Natasha.

When Matt ended the call, he took his seat next to Natasha. Jack made his excuses and left them to console each other. He silently took her keys and fetched her bags from the car. And just as quietly, took the bags up to her room.

As Matthew held her in his arms, she felt cold. Guilt froze her emotions and although Matthew held her she felt no comfort. She could hear Jack working in the kitchen. *Always the professional assistant, making our lives smoother. Is there anything he can't do? Save Mikey!*

When Jack eventually returned, he carried a tray with sandwiches, hot chocolate, and a pile of biscuits. Natasha looked at the carbs piled on carbs. Her face must have given her away.

"Natasha Poole you need to eat. Just relax." Jack's scolding was well meant, and she loved him for it,

Matt reached for a plate, put two small sandwiches on it, and then passed them to Natasha.

"He's right. He's always bloody right, don't you hate him." Matt smiled getting three sandwiches for himself. She had to agree.

Biting into her first sandwich, a small smile twitched across Natasha's face. "If you don't want him, can I have him? I'll look after him and walk him and everything."

"You certainly can have me, sweetie. You are much cleaner than him and I wouldn't have to sleep with you. "

"Oh, that's not an option?" She looked hurt, and then a small laugh escaped her. She was desperate for some light relief from the heaviness that had settled inside her.

"Not even for you, Tash baby."

With a soft groan, she came back to the situation they had to face. Natasha turned to her husband, "What do we do now?"

"We can have him home, or they can send him to be cremated and send us the ashes. We don't have to decide today."

"My dad, Matt? How do I tell my dad?"

"I'll do it now." Matt walked out of the room with his phone and closed the door. Jack sat next to Natasha and held her hand.

"Tasha, sweetie, please don't let this be something that drags you down even more."

"Even more?"

"I worry about you; I came along to help, and I stole your gorgeous husband."

"I had lost him long before you came along, Jack."

"But now, Mikey isn't here to cuddle you. Shall we get a puppy?"

"No, Jack, now is not the time to get another dog."

"I guess not."

"Any idea when this election will be now?"

"No, I did hear …" Matt walked back into the room and Jack stopped short of what he was going to say. Instead, he squeezed her hand and looked pleadingly at Natasha not to ask him to finish.

Jack once again made his excuses and left them together; Mikey was their dog, a child substitute in so many ways. He was certainly there to fill some gap in their lives.

Matt and Natasha talked into the morning. Remembering Mikey and looking through photos and videos.

When finally, she went to bed, Jack took her a cup of hot chocolate. He found Natasha asleep on the covers of her bed. She clutched a photo of Mikey and for some reason, her radio was playing a cricket commentary from Australia.

Chapter 15

Daniel was up early on the farm; it was becoming a habit. He did the yard jobs, fed the chickens, and let them out into the sunshine.

He didn't wait around to make the porridge his dad ate every morning, no matter the weather. Instead, he toasted a slice of bread as thick as a doorstep on the top of the coal-fired range. He smothered the toast with butter and a good portion of his sister's homemade damson jam. The phone in his jeans pocket buzzed with a text. He knew it was from her and just like all her other messages, he would not answer it. That didn't stop him from looking, though.

TASHA: I'd like to explain

He slipped the phone back into his pocket and bit into his toast. He could still hear his phone. More texts, this time from India.

INDIA: I have the dates for More.U TV.

DAN: I don't think I can make it.

INDIA: I haven't given you the dates yet.

DAN: Maybe you should ask Zach.

Still eating his toast, he collected Meg, who happily jumped in the back of the farm's old Land Rover. He threw in some fencing tools and set off to the north corner of the farm. This area was the nearest to the coast, and up there, you could smell the salt in the air.

They didn't use the field he was working in for horses, so the need for good fences was to keep the deer out rather than the horses in.

It was a hay meadow sprinkled with wildflowers starting to grow higher. His dad would want to cut the hay soon. Daniel parked up and Meg bounced over his knee and out his door as soon as it opened a crack. Together, they inspected the boundary. He tugged at posts and wires whilst Meg sniffed and mumbled along behind Daniel, happy to be spending time with her best friend.

"I'm not sure why Dad was complaining about this fence Meg, it's not so bad." A puzzled black and white face looked back at him. "But I guess we can improve it a bit."

Meg sat down; her eyes still trained on Daniel.

"I think if we sort these five posts, it will make a difference. What do you say, Meg?"

Meg barked just once, then dropped her nose down onto her paws. Daniel's phone beeped with a text. *Another text!* He knew he would have to talk to India at some point. The idea of bumping into Natasha was not something he was ready to face. Still, he looked at his phone.

TASHA: Daniel I need to talk to you.

He pushed the phone firmly into his pocket, unanswered. He couldn't think about her without feelings overtaking his body. His heart was beating faster just seeing her name in the text. He needed to keep busy. Daniel started on the first fence post. Meg sniffed around and wandered over into the next field.

"Come back here Meg. You don't live there."

Daniel worked on keeping his head down most of the time. He was focusing hard on the second post, which was proving far more difficult than the first one. It was taking all his attention, so he took no notice when Meg let out a little bark. He only reacted when two paws hit him firmly on his thigh.

As he looked up, a horse and rider appeared, heading towards him. Daniel knew he couldn't ignore his sister. He would have to talk to her now that she had found him.

"India rang for you."

"I got a text."

"So, why are you being so weird with her?"

"Weird?"

"She said you couldn't do dates she hasn't even given you,"

"I can't spare the time. There is so much to do here and with Ben tied up with the World Cup, well, it's down to me."

Rebecca slipped off Cisco's back and walked over to Daniel. She was tall, but not as tall as her brother. She looked at him closely, studying his face as she spoke.

"So, what happened?"

"Nothing happened. It's the cricket season and there is always something to do on the farm. Ben is going to be busy this year. What about the World Cup and stuff? It's time for me to step up."

"When you started this, you seemed so focused. You wanted to show how mature you could be. Or so you said." Daniel didn't reply, he kept steadily knocking in the fence post. He wanted to look composed, but inside his heart quickened again.

"Look at me, Daniel Woods. Do you want to tell me what the problem is?"

"There isn't a problem," he snapped. "Meg! Come back here."

"Is India adding more dates? I know there is so much cricket this year, Ben seemed stretched."

"I am not the golden child; the World Cup and the ashes won't hit my playing calendar."

"So?"

"So, nothing, Becca. Just leave it."

Rebecca laid down on the sunny side of his truck. Pulling a piece of grass through her teeth. She had stopped asking questions, but Daniel knew she was simply waiting, and she had not given up on wanting to know what the issue was. Meg curled up at her side, and he went back to working on the fence.

Well, his hands might be working on the fence, but his head was still struggling with the same problem he had brought home from London. It just wouldn't go away. So, what, she was married, he didn't know and now he did, well... that was the end, as far as he was concerned.

But it wasn't the end. His mind chewed on this long and slow like Rebecca's horses did on some good grass. He couldn't understand it. He had avoided married women until now. Even girlfriends of someone else. If a woman was in a relationship, Daniel wasn't interested, not since Sarah. Just the thought of her name made him feel sick.

As far as Daniel could see, there didn't seem to be a lack of single girls. They were everywhere he looked. He didn't have to try. There was always another single girl or two to enjoy when he went out. But these women came and went. He enjoyed being with women, and he definitely enjoyed sex.

Ben had married his girlfriend from school. He hadn't gone out with anyone else. Daniel's school days had been quite different. Things didn't work out as he expected.

In school, Daniel was fine and had plenty of friends, both girls and boys. Then in the summer between year eight and year nine, he had grown, boy had he grown. The next year was tough in so many ways, all arms and legs and he was suddenly rubbish at games too. That is when Sarah started to be nice to him.

The long summer before university, a combination of cricket and working on the farm, had seen him grow into that shape, filling out with muscles that meant he then had no problem attracting women. It was when Sarah made her move. But that was a hard lesson to learn and one he wasn't ready to repeat.

Why was Natasha sticking in his brain? They had sex. Great Sex. But as a married mother- who lived 150 miles away- that was it. He'd made a mistake.

This was a subject he had strong feelings about. He had a very low opinion of married women who didn't stay faithful. He expected men to be faithful, too. But there was something about married women with children. *How could she?*

Of course, he should have known she was married if he had only stopped to look. It was there in her bio on the More.U TV website. Hell, he had even found photos of her with her husband Matthew. *What have I done? Why does she keep messaging me? Can't she see it was a mistake?*

Rebecca was still there. Eyes closed, waiting.

Daniel finally let it out, "She's married."

Becca sat up with a jolt. Her eyes wide open. She looked curiously at her brother. "Who? India?"

"Natasha Poole."

"Well, yes, she's married to that MP. Isn't he Minister for Education or something?"

Daniel turned away from her and back to his work. Putting his energy into the physical effort. He should have known that wouldn't be enough for his sister.

"So, tell me, brother, why does your co-presenter being married matter? How does that stop you from answering India's calls?"

"I don't go with married women." It was a quiet reply, still not looking at Rebecca.

"I should hope not. But you are only doing a TV show with her, that's all."

"I touched her." He pushed his head into the back of his Land Rover to find a hammer, anything not to make eye contact.

"We all saw that, Daniel," Rebecca laughed, "you seemed rather excited by it, too." Daniel frowned at his sister and bounced the hammer in his hand, walking slowly back to the fence.

"I didn't know she was married."

"Daniel, she is an extremely attractive woman. I am pretty sure men get aroused by married women all the time."

"I don't."

"You don't?"

"No."

"Maybe you have before, and you didn't know they were married." Daniel hadn't considered that. It set his mind wandering through a string of faces. Had one been married?

"Relax, little brother. It says a lot about you if you don't chase after married women. I guess it's the thought that they are married that stops you … getting … you know. Perhaps you should talk to Ben about this rather than me."

"I am not talking to Ben about this!" Daniel's face reddened, and he hit the pins holding the wire in place faster and harder.

"Daniel, just call India. If you don't want to do this, she needs to know so she can find someone else."

"I will."

"Oh, and ring Charlie."

"God, was he upset about me avoiding India?"

"No, I don't think so because he said not to tell India about it."

Chapter 16

Daniel had agreed to do two more shows and a photo shoot the following week. India had arranged for them to stay at the flat with Stella again. He only had to speak to Charlie now.

The opportunity came after a training session. Everyone was in the first team changing room. Daniel got the impression Charlie wanted him to hang back so they could talk.

"Right lads, I want this place left clean." Ben Woods, the captain, and Daniel's elder brother, was making sure his voice was heard over the bubbling chatter from the team.

"The match is in two days, so I don't want you drinking too much on your day off. That means you, Daniel, have a rest."

"I have jobs to do for Dad, so no chance of a rest."

"I meant the drink."

"And how much drink do you think there will be on the farm? Have you forgotten what it's like living in a Methodist family?"

"Well, that hasn't stopped you in the past."

"OK brother, I get it, so no drinking."

"I'll believe it when I see it." Ben left without a smile and Daniel sank down onto the bench next to Charlie. The others had slowly filed out of the room, leaving just Charlie and Daniel. Charlie continued to pack his bag with the usual care.

"So, what did you want to talk about? Is it my guarding? I've been listening to what you told me."

"No, I saw you in the nets earlier. I can see the improvement." He smiled at Daniel. "No. This next trip to London." *Shit, does he know? Does he know what I did with Tasha?*

"Yes?" Act normal, whatever is normal.

"I want you to drive India down there."

"Of course, I can, that's not a problem."

"Daniel, I need you to do this for me."

"Romeo, I already said yes."

"But Dan, I want you to ask, she can't know I asked you."

"OK? I presume you have a good reason?"

"I would rather she stayed home, but she won't hear of it."

"So just tell me what you want me to do."

"She keeps throwing up, but I don't … I … you can't say that."

"What can I say? I prefer to drive, travel sick and all that?"

"Would that sound like you were criticising her driving?"

"Why would she think that?"

"Because she seems to believe I do it."

"We are staying at the flat again, so going in two cars is hard. There is so little parking. Could I just say it makes sense to take one car? What about Tilly?"

"Tilly isn't coming. I think India believes that as she is employing you, she should be the one to drive."

"So, I have to drive because you are worried she is ill, but I can't tell India that?"

"No. Don't you know anything about women?"

"Well, now you mention it, no, I don't. Maybe you should tell me how you do it."

"Do what?"

"Build a relationship with a woman? Living with them 24/7. What is it like?"

"I don't know. I think India does the hard work. I am still living in the same house; it's just she is there when I get home from a match. I love her, so anything she does that would be annoying in someone else is just her. Like when I see the mess she leaves in the bathroom, it simply reminds me she is there."

"So, you are happy being half of a couple?"

"Are you serious, mate?"

"No, I see you are happy, when we go to your house, you two, well you fit together. It's hard to think of her not being there."

"It felt like that the moment I met her, but she was so young."

"But come on, we called you Romeo for a reason, you didn't hang back with other women, did you?"

"Yeah, I have thought about that. Thinking back, I guess I was trying to prove she wasn't the only one. Who knows? I'm just happy she is here now. If I could only get her to marry me."

"Is it true you keep asking her?"

"Yes, but don't be telling the world, not until she says yes."

"Sure. You know SHE talks about it?"

"Who to?"

"Tilly and Stella."

"Did she say why she hasn't said yes?"

"Not really. Something about not being ready to be a wife, whatever that means."

"So, she didn't say anything else?" Daniel shook his head and looked at the ground between his feet.

"Charlie, can I ask you something?"

"I guess you will, anyway."

"How did you know?"

"Know what?"

"That India was the one?"

"Hey, that's serious talk from you, Dan. Is this part of that being seen to be mature you were talking about? Because if it is, then you don't have to get into a relationship to show that brother of yours that you grew up." Daniel looked puzzled.

"Why did you mention Ben? This isn't just about him."

"I guess not, but you must admit it's a big part of it. I saw your face when he had a go earlier."

"You need to remember Ben only remembers me at home. Before I went to university, and well, I think at Uni I got away from the life Dad wanted for us, so I might have gone a bit overboard. But I don't know. I guess I was always happy when I met a new girl, but I never felt the need to make it a full-time thing. I am usually just as happy when they decide they don't like my lifestyle and move on."

"Do you think that is why India won't marry me, the lifestyle?"

"No mate, she loves the entire team. Look at the way she is always inviting us around."

"You don't think she does that, so I am not out drinking in the pub with you, a bunch of randy cricketers?"

"I don't know."

"It's just she can't give me a reason."

"Maybe you should try thinking about it from India's side."

"You mean she doesn't want to give up her freedom?"

"No, she is happy with you. I am sure she isn't looking elsewhere."

"Then what?"

"Well, if she says yes, what would you have to do?"

"What do you mean?"

"Well, you need a best man and your kilt, and India. And well, India needs to choose a dress, and all that stuff that goes with it, a head thingy, flowers, shoes, bridesmaids…"

Daniel looked at his crestfallen friend and continued. "When Ben got married, it went on and on. Amanda asked his opinion, but really, it was down to her to make all those decisions."

"I would be happy to do whatever she wanted if she said yes."

"And what about her family? Listening to the girls at Stella's it sounds like India's mother would expect to be in charge. I got the impression India wouldn't enjoy that."

"So, are you saying it's the wedding she doesn't want?"

"How should I know, mate?"

"Well, you seemed to know a lot just then."

They both sat back and leaned against the wall, gazing out into a future they didn't understand.

When they finally stood up to leave, His phone beeped a text.

INDIA: Dan, would you drive down on Friday?

Daniel showed Charlie his phone.

"Thank Fuck for that!"

Chapter 17

Daniel felt heavy driving to the studios. This was a first. He wasn't excited or apprehensive. He wasn't nervous or confident he was just heavy. He felt like he was carrying three Gym Away dumbbells in his shirt pocket.

Tomorrow was his first photo shoot with Nick. He wasn't sure how he felt about that either but that was tomorrow's problem. India was with him, and she too, wasn't her normal bouncy self. They stopped twice on the drive down for her to be sick. She blamed Charlie's cooking, but Daniel wasn't sure. To him, she looked a lot like Tilly did.

India was talking but Daniel was still trying to work out how he felt about seeing Natasha again. Maybe he wouldn't see her. He didn't know how the shifts worked or if they even had 'shifts'. Then he realised that the idea of not seeing her felt physically worse than the idea of seeing her.

Daniel frowned. How could this show be as good as last time? In the seat beside him, India was looking through sheets of paper she had pulled out of a large envelope.

"And we are unlikely to sell out because they have lots more units available now for the show repeats."

"India," he asked slowly, "how important is it for me to listen to all this numbers bit?"

"Well …"

"It's just I have a lot to think about doing this …"

"Yes?"

"… and if I'm worrying about Joe and Tilly and money … surely my bit is going into the studio and showing people why they should buy Gym Away? The presenter is the professional. They tell people how to buy and they prompt me with their questions."

"Yes," she agreed.

"They are listening to whoever is in their ear."

"Yes."

"So, when you interviewed me, you asked whether I could talk about Gym Away for an hour and I said I could." He glanced over at her. "Now you want me to do a couple of photoshoots." He looked firmly at the road as he continued. "So how important is it for me to have to think about the numbers?"

"OK, Daniel, I get it."

"So today, I do two shows and show people what they can do."

"Well, yes."

"And tomorrow, I do what Nick says."

"That works for me."

"Will it work for Joe and Tilly?"

"Yes."

They drove in silence for a short time, and Daniel wriggled in his seat, he wasn't used to India being quiet. He wondered if he had said too much. To his relief, she began to talk again.

"How did you get on with Charlie and Joe?"

"We watched a lot of YouTube!" He laughed clearly they had seen more than they expected. "But I have written ideas down. One exercise on one card. Like revision cards, you know. I thought it might be something to discuss with the director person, you know, before the show." She was watching him closely, he wasn't sure why, but he kept talking. "Joe liked it. He is thinking about it as another product, maybe something to add to the website." He shrugged his shoulders.

"And there you are talking about sales!" she laughed. Daniel drew his eyebrows together.

"I guess I am but today … I am not sure I want to know the numbers. All the ups and downs emotionally last time … it was too much."

"I'm not sure how much we'll get to know today without Tilly with us. The last time was a bit weird though. You didn't help." Before Daniel could ask why she explained.

"After the first show when we thought we had sold so few and yet you were so high, then after the double sell out. Well, Daniel. You hardly spoke on the train home."

"Sorry." He couldn't look at her, instead, he focused on the road.

"No need to be sorry. It's just not the Daniel I know."

"I just thought I'd let you girls talk about babies and stuff." If he was honest, he had other things on his mind but once they got talking, he was happy to listen.

"So, you were listening?"

"I have sooo much to learn." He offered her his fabulous grin.

"I thought farmers knew all that stuff?"

"Biology is something I've had a handle on for a long time. Relationships, I have so much to learn."

"I didn't think 'relationships' was something that interested you.?"

"They're not!" came his emphatic reply. "I honestly don't understand them at all."

They pulled up to the entrance and India passed him the paperwork to show the man in uniform at the gate. Richard waved them in with a smile today.

As they got out of the car, India handed him a bag.

"To replace the shorts, I hope they are long enough."

Thankfully, the new shorts were much better. Something that Paul was quick to point out.

"Well, the sensible side of my brain says well done on the new shorts but there is a part of me that is disappointed. That was quite a show last time."

Daniel said nothing but Paul just kept talking. "It certainly brought the colour to Ms Poole's face! I have never seen her feathers ruffled like that. She has been pretty quiet ever since. Mind that was the day of the accident so no wonder she has been quiet. Poor Mikey."

If Daniel was quiet before his jaw was welded shut now. What could he say? Should he pretend he didn't know what Paul was talking about? Should he ask how Mikey was? He was regretting not answering Natasha's messages. He had searched the web for news. Daniel felt sure that if Matthew Poole was such a big noise in the cabinet, they would mention his son being killed. But there was nothing. Nothing about an accident anyway. There had been plenty of mentions of him in the news.

With his microphone in place on the new shorts, Daniel followed Paul through the orange door with all its notices and into studio one.

India was arranging boxes at the back of the stand, and Paul excused himself to help her. Daniel was left behind the counter, wondering how things were going to go with Natasha today.

When a guy walked into the studio and quietly introduced himself to Daniel as Alex Dunn, his presenter for the show. It hadn't occurred to him that he wouldn't be doing the show with Natasha. He couldn't hide his surprise.

"I usually work with Natasha."

"I thought this was only your second visit?" Alex said in hush tones that reminded Daniel where he was.

"It is, but she did my screen test too."

"Well sorry to disappoint you, she is on this afternoon. You might have her for the next show. We had to do a bit of juggling today to fit in a doctor's appointment." Alex wandered off to talk to Paul, which left Daniel far too much time to think about the words Natasha and doctor's appointment. *God! I hope she isn't ill, what if she's pregnant? Don't be silly that is NOT how you get pregnant. Maybe it's Mikey.*

He was relieved to see Emma arrive and racked his brains, wondering how he could ask about Natasha. He knew he needed to ask something, but how?

"Morning Daniel, I see you have met Alex. He is pretty good at this job, been doing it for years. He makes it look effortless, which can be scary for you. Don't worry, I'll be talking to him, and he will move you to where we need to be. Paul can nip in and let you know if we need a longer demo or a closeup."

Emma was using her normal voice, and it confused Daniel. She smiled and reassured him.

"We are showing a pre-recorded show just now. Yours will be the first live show today. We had to do some juggling, and that's why Tasha is coming in later."

"Alex said something about a doctor's appointment, is she OK?" Emma rolled her eyes and looked menacingly at Alex Dunn.

"It's Alex that has the appointment," she hissed, "and Tasha, who is too nice to say no."

"But what about Mikey? Is he OK?" It came out in a rush. He wasn't sure why, but he wanted to know, no it was more than that. He needed to know.

Emma looked puzzled, then sad.

"Mikey didn't make it." His heart sank. But Daniel was puzzled by the matter-of-fact way Emma shared this news until she continued. "I like dogs, but I have never had one myself. It's hit Natasha hard. Mikey was a bit of a child substitute." Emma smiled before she continued.

Her Dog! Child Substitute!

"Don't worry about today, Daniel, Alex can be a pain in the neck to work with, but he is a complete professional in front of the camera," Emma reassured him as Alex walked over to join them.

"Alex, I want to start with introductions and the product, then quickly into numbers, then demo, numbers followed by features and benefits, numbers, a final demo, and numbers. If we have time, Daniel did a lovely packing away bit last time with Tasha." Her hand reached out to Daniel's arm to reassure him. "Don't worry, Alex will be following my direction and he'll lead you into each section."

Paul reached around him to turn on his mic and then took his place by camera two.

The countdown began.

5   *Thank God! She's OK.*

4   *Why do I care?*

3   *I can do this.*

2   *Hell!*

1   *I wish she were here.*

The 55 minutes of the show flashed by. Daniel's face ached with smiling. He realised that this time he had to remember to smile, working with Natasha, the smiles just came.

Each of the minutes had been dream-like. He was saying and doing things he had been trying out at home in the mirror. He just hoped it had been enough.

Chapter 18

"Nat, get into position."

Natasha fought the urge to roll her eyes – she hated being called Nat.

Tony Richford was the senior producer, and he wasn't pleased with today's schedule changes. He normally worked with Alex Dunn, and he made it quite clear on many occasions that he considered working with the newer presenters beneath him. And today, he was making no effort to disguise his frustrations.

Daniel wasn't helping, he was standing as far away from her as possible. Emma had said he had been rather wooden in his first show.

"Lovely, now can you get the guest under control? My God! How tall is he?" This was her job, she was good at this, hell Daniel is good at this. I just need to give out the numbers and keep him on track.

"Daniel, sorry, you need to come closer." She was sorry for a lot of things, but mainly she was sorry she couldn't explain.

Natasha knew how important every show was for the companies behind them. Whatever had happened between Daniel and her, she had to do her best for the Gym Away people. This job was all about sales. If your sales were down, you ended up with the graveyard shifts and the dead-end products. It was the same for the companies. If they wanted the good time slots, they had to sell when they were on air.

At last, Paul started the countdown.

5 SMILE a relaxed friendly smile.

4 You do this EVERY DAY it's work.

3 I've never done this with someone I've been naked with

2 It's just 55 minutes.

1 God, he smells amazing.

"Daniel, welcome back to More.U TV. I'm pleased to see you back. We have so much more to learn about Gym Away."

"Give them the numbers early Nat." Damn, he is going to drive me mad keep calling me Nat.

"Now last time you came, we sold out of all the stock. I hope you have brought some more this time."

"I'm just here to show you how it works, but there is more stock this time."

"You'll be lucky to sell out this time, lady. There's a ton of it," grumbled Tony in her ear.

"They tell me there is plenty of stock, but if you know you want to buy yours today whilst Daniel gets ready to show you some ideas to use Gym Away, let me tell you just how you can do that."

She reeled off the buying options, all the time very aware of Daniel laying down on the mat to one side. Her heart seemed to have a mind of its own and kept speeding up.

"He's on two, you're on one. Nat, look at the camera. I have had to switch to the product card." *Have I missed sex that much?*

Natasha tried to tell herself she had been through a lot worse doing this job, with terrible products and obnoxious guests. *But he isn't obnoxious, he is the opposite, why I am I so attracted to this one man?* It made little sense.

"I can see you are ready for me," she smiled down at him, then blushed. Her face warm from her reaction to him. "Can you show me what this can do? The Gym Away. What can the Gym Away do?"

"For Christ's sake, Nat, stop acting like a schoolgirl with a crush." Tony was so loud in her ear that she thought her mic would pick him up.

She need not have worried. Daniel had taken his cue and had gone into demonstrator mode. Carefully showing a different exercise from previous shows. He didn't seem to want or need her help.

That was how the show progressed, rather like the textbook show he had done in the morning. He produced three demonstrations and showed how to pack away all the parts into the container. Natasha told people how to buy and gave him his next cue.

Daniel avoided her eyes and could have been a hundred feet away from her rather than three. He seemed cold, he did smile, but it appeared forced, like her own. But once he was pushed to stand next to her for the end of the show, she reached out to touch him. No matter how hard she resisted touching Daniel, her hands always seemed to reach for him. It was then she knew it would not be easy to walk away. That spark. The excitement that ran through her body just from standing close to him was too much.

As the cameras pulled away at the end of the show, she swallowed, trying to find the words to explain. She took too long, and Paul bounced in to remove his microphone. They walked out of the studio together, leaving Natasha alone. Being alone seemed to be all she could manage these days, but somehow Daniel, walking away, ripped a piece out of her.

Chapter 19

Emma threw her bags at Natasha.

"Hold these! I'm bursting!"

"I'll wait here then."

"Come in, Nick won't mind. We can scrounge a cup of coffee."

"Won't he be working?" Natasha called to Emma's back as she disappeared through the purple door to Nick West Photography Studios. If Emma replied, Natasha didn't hear it. Nick never seemed bothered about seeing her, but she couldn't help wondering what he thought of Natasha as his girlfriend's needy friend. So, she collected the bags from their 'Cheer Tasha up shopping trip' and followed her producer into Nick's studio.

The doorway opened up into a large room, the main studio, that was in darkness. Nick had a small work light by his side as he spoke quietly to the tall woman dressed in jeans with her back to Natasha. He was showing her an image on the back of his camera and Natasha was instantly jealous of this model, whose slim form was accented by her long legs.

Lifting his camera, Nick spoke to someone else. "The lights are going to flash now, and I want you to repeat that movement again. Just keep repeating it until I say stop."

As three large spotlights flashed, they revealed Daniel Woods in a pair of blue shorts and nothing else. His taut body was covered in a fine mist of perspiration. As he repeated the movements under the strobing lights, the muscles in his arms and back flexed. His head was bowed, focused on his biceps as they worked the resistance bands she had seen him use at work.

Natasha froze and immediately started to lose control of the shopping she had been struggling to hold. The bags fell to the ground, one by one, in what felt to Natasha like slow motion in contrast to Daniel's rhythmic pumping of his arm. Nick and his companion turned to look at her. The lights continued to flash, but Daniel had stopped and was frozen too. Staring back into her eyes.

Natasha looked away, first towards the door and the traitor who had brought her here. Emma knew! She bloody knew! Was this whole 'let's cheer you up' adventure simply designed to bring her here to confront Daniel? Didn't she get it? *It wasn't me who had backed off, it was him!* The minute he discovered I was married.

When she at last looked down at her shopping, he was there, almost naked, picking it up for her. Crouched down at her feet. Picking up first the bags of shoes and then her new dress. Finally, coming to the candy-striped bag from Pastels Lingerie. Daniel was now staring into her face. Confusion etched deep in his furrowed brow. Not looking, he stretched his arm out to reach for that final bag as he stood up. He had the bottom of the bag, not the top. And as he eventually stood, just inches in front of her, their eyes locked. Natasha fought herself to look away, to look for Emma. But it was useless. *Why? Why him? Why couldn't I have just walked on by that morning in the car park? Why can't I walk away now?*

"I sent you a text, well, several." Finally, she was able to break his gaze.

"I know, Tash, I could explain but … not here." He began to pass her the shopping until, of course, the lingerie bag. It emptied its contents at their feet, piece after piece of tiny satin and lace hitting the floor. Why had she listened to Emma? This was not the neat but delicate white underwear that she usually chose. Or the discrete, no-frills nude basics that wouldn't show when the Press followed her and Matt. No, today, Emma had pushed her to be daring and buy underwear that was perhaps too bold but matched the blood-red lipstick Emma had also persuaded her to buy. The lipstick that had been instantly hidden in her handbag amongst the sea of coral lip glosses.

Emma still hadn't emerged, and Nick had taken India into the office. Natasha wasn't sure which was worse, having an audience or being left alone with Daniel Woods.

Daniel was again at her feet, picking up the clothes he had dropped. Desperate to save face, she scrambled to pick up the lace and ribboned pieces before he did. And as their hands reached for the same piece, the last piece, Daniel looked again into her eyes. She wanted to fall into the depths of his green eyes.

"I'm so sorry." Natasha blurted as she grabbed the striped bag and left in search of Emma or anywhere that didn't contain HIM!

She reached the toilet just as Emma opened the door. Pushing past her friend she slammed the door shut firmly behind her.

"YOU KNEW!" She screamed.

"Sorry what?"

"You knew he was here!"

"Nick?"

"Not Nick... HIM." Realising the others could probably hear her, Natasha finally lowered her voice. "Daniel Woods," she hissed through the closed door.

"Shit, honestly Tash, I didn't know he was here. I never listen to what Nick is doing. I haven't even seen him since Monday. You know, you've been at my place." Emma sounded upset and Natasha came out of hiding to face her friend.

"Is she with him?" The look of horror on Emma's face helped Natasha see just how much this India thing was getting to her friend.

"Yes, she's there. Now don't go thinking he didn't tell you for a reason. Or did you actually know, and that's why we are here?"

"Tash honest. I just wanted to take you out shopping and maybe get you to see the possibilities."

"Possibilities?"

"What life could be like if you weren't Mrs Matthew Poole MP. He's moved on with his life, Natasha."

"Have you any idea what the Press will be like if they sniff this? I not only care for Matt, but I also know he is bloody good at his job. His job is his life, Emma. I can't take that away from him. I can wait."

"But how long will you wait? You said April."

"They can't put the election off forever. I'm in no rush."

"So, there is nothing between you and Mr Woods?"

"NO!" Natasha turned to look in the mirror. And when she did, the memory of what they did was there again.

"So, why are you hiding in the toilet?"

"Well…" still looking at her reflection, Natasha witnessed her face blushing, and so did Emma.

"Oh, my God. Something did happen! When?"

"IF! And I do mean if, I was looking for a new love interest, I don't think I'll be looking at a professional sports star who is in the media more than Matt." Despite the serious tone of her voice, Emma didn't believe her, and Natasha knew it. "Oh Emma, I must have looked such a fool. He was lit up by these flashing lights, all slick and toned and so sexy."

"Sometimes you don't go looking. Sometimes, the universe just sends you what you need when you need it. Daniel Woods might not be your long-term future, but he might help you get back on the horse."

"Emma!"

"Look, if India is out there with Nick, well, we need to go back out there. Are you ready?" Natasha looked back into the mirror; she had left her handbag outside, so all she could do was smooth her hand over her hair. "I'm not ready. I don't think I'll ever be ready, but you're right. Let's do this."

As the two walked back into the room, Nick looked at his diary.

"I don't have anything booked, but it's Em's birthday."

"That is brilliant. Why don't you all come? Tilly would love to have you there, Natasha. Inviting you was on my job list for when I get back to the office." When the girls looked blankly back at India, she explained.

"Gym Away are launching a new product at a corporate event at a cricket match next month. There will be some meet and greet type stuff, but with Daniel and Charlie playing, it's good to have a celebrity who isn't part of the team."

There was no sign of Daniel as Natasha's eyes scanned the room for him. She didn't know if she wanted to go to Leeds or how Daniel would feel if she did. Emma answered for them both.

"We would love to come. Nick is bound to be working on my birthday, anyway. This way, we get a weekend away. So, thanks, we would love it, wouldn't we, Natasha? Say Yes, Natasha. Come to Leeds for my birthday. We could go shopping again."

With all eyes on her, Natasha offered a weak agreement, hoping to decide when she was away from the others. Perhaps she could find an excuse later. Her friend's jealousy of anyone close to Nick was a powerful reason why Emma to want to go. Would her friend understand why she wanted to back out?

As she collected her bags to leave, she saw Daniel watching her as he slowly buttoned his shirt. Once their eyes met, he looked away. Damn him. There must be more people in Leeds other than Daniel Woods.

Chapter 20

Natasha Poole boarded the final train for the journey to Leeds. Emma was driving up from London with Nick much later. Not for the first time, she wondered if she should have cried off or even said no in the first place, but Emma had been most persuasive. She wasn't happy about Nick going alone. From what she understood, India was living with her boyfriend and another cricketer somewhere near the cricket ground. To Emma, that suggested that they all just shared a house, and it wasn't a steady relationship. Natasha worried about how healthy Emma's jealousy was. Even without the 'one that got away' comment, Emma would fixate over whatever model he was working with this week and how thin she was.

This is a job. That is how she explained it to Matthew. She could have said she was busy; it wasn't a lie. Without Mikey, the house felt empty. And how did she say no to a weekend in Leeds to celebrate her best friend's birthday without making an even bigger issue out of Daniel? She might not actually see him. Surely, he would be playing at the match, and Leeds is a big place. She was pretty sure she wouldn't bump into him shopping with Emma.

As Leeds got ever closer, the knot in her stomach got tighter. This is silly. Stop ruminating. This is a weekend away. You're getting paid for it too.

Her brain wouldn't stop. The event sounded simple enough. Just a meet and greet and her first cricket match. The weather forecast was good, although she wished it weren't quite as warm today. She felt like she could melt. This last train had no air conditioning. She was hot, and she was searching her bag for another drink when her phone buzzed and made her jump.

EMMA: We're going to be late. I am at Nick's studio, and he has equipment everywhere. Putting stuff in bags, then taking it out again. I have never seen him this nervous.

TASHA: I'm getting picked up at the station. I'll be OK.

EMMA: He claims it's this set of families. The parents are all 'important people'.

TASHA: I heard that some high-powered names would be there.

EMMA: Yes, but why is he nervous about meeting HER parents?

TASHA: Didn't he say nothing happened between him and India? I heard him myself explain she was the model that got away, not his great love.

EMMA: But why her?

TASHA: Stop this Birthday girl. Where are we going shopping tomorrow?

TASHA: Did you Google a map?

EMMA: Nick gave me an envelope of cash saying he knows I love shopping.

TASHA: That's nice.

EMMA: Is it?

TASHA: He wants you to enjoy this weekend.

EMMA: He looks too stressed for that.

TASHA: He just has the event to shoot at, doesn't he?

EMMA: Yes

TASHA: Maybe we can have a quiet drink tonight if you get up in time?

EMMA: There is a party. Didn't you know?

TASHA: Party?

EMMA: Damn, perhaps I was supposed to tell you.

EMMA: Sorry. It's someone else's birthday, so we're invited to their house.

TASHA: I might just stay at the hotel. It's been a long week.

EMMA: You can't let me go alone. Nick is excited about that bit.

TASHA: Nick excited?

EMMA: When he talks about the 'team' he gets animated.

EMMA: Got to go, he's ready. Now we need to go get his clothes. Bye.

TASHA: Bye x

Natasha was growing more annoyed about the temperature inside the train. Being sticky was something she hated. It made it harder to stay clean. To add to her bad mood, now she had a party to think about. The thought that this might be an event for members of the cricket team brought her body to high alert. Her butterflies were trying out for the Olympics, turning somersaults at her core. Maybe Daniel wouldn't be there. He lived out towards the coast, didn't he?

She closed her eyes. She had to get over the fact she was likely to see him. If she could see him at work in the close confines of a studio set, surely she could cope with seeing him in a bigger space. Eyes still firmly shut, she tried to relax, but the movement of the train, the sounds and smells wouldn't let her forget where she was.

When the refreshment trolley came trundling towards her, she chose a bottle of water. The coffee she had last time was warm and vaguely smelt of coffee but was otherwise disgusting.

She sipped the water, trying to use it to quell those persistent butterflies. Sadly, the water was warmer than the coffee, and all sense of calm had evaded her. The temperature inside the train was rising, and she wiped her hands once again as she pictured the shower she would have as soon as she landed at the hotel. Now there is a party. What sort of party? She had packed a dress for tonight, thinking they would be having drinks at the hotel. She had trousers and a pretty top with sensible shoes for the shopping trip tomorrow. The butterflies had stopped as she started to feel annoyed. She hadn't been 'out' for a drink in so long, and a quiet drink with Emma and Nick had been something to look forward to.

And now that quiet drink was some sort of party. *Could I cry off and just stay in my room?* It surprised her to realise she didn't want to do that. She'd had enough staying in. Emma would want her there anyway, this jealousy of hers was taking over. Natasha hoped it was as unfounded as all the other times Emma had got it into her head about someone. It was her mission to try and watch for herself this weekend. Then hopefully, she could reassure Emma that Nick and India were, just as he claimed, friends.

And if I stick by Emma's side then Daniel – Well Daniel couldn't – would you stop thinking about Daniel Woods.

It was too late. In her head she pictured Daniel talking to her, in a low sultry voice, his eyes glued to her own as she watched him over the top of a martini glass complete with olive. That was silly. She never drank Martinis, and she guessed Daniel didn't spend much time in the sort of three-piece suit she had just imagined. That was more something Matt would wear.

Natasha gulped more of the tepid water. Whatever happened with Daniel, she was pretty sure it would be nothing like her life with Matthew. As she emptied the last of the bottle, she had no idea how that thought made her feel.

The scenery outside of the window was changing fast and with the way her travelling companions were collecting their belongings, she assumed they were close to their destination. She didn't understand the haste, but she wiped her hands once more. With a mirror from her bag, she combed her hair and re-applied her lip gloss. Natasha sat still until the train came to a complete stop. Only then did she stand and slip on her blazer.

As she cleared the platform, India was easy to spot, waiting for her in exactly the place they had arranged to meet. India gave her one quick hug and grabbed the handle of Natasha's case, talking fast as she led the way to the pick-up point.

"It's ridiculously hot. We aren't used to this heat. Charlie will be here soon. I am sorry we have to make a quick stop on the way to your hotel. You could have stayed with us, but Zach has a lot of friends over for the World Cup. There are bodies everywhere. I'm considering camping out at my office until they all go back. You haven't met Zach. You'll like him, everyone does. You'll meet him tonight at the party."

"Party?"

"Oh. You knew, didn't you? Didn't Nick say? I guess not." India was searching the traffic. "So, tonight there is a party. You are invited, of course. It will give you a chance to meet the rest of the team. They will all be playing on Saturday." Natasha took a breath to speak, but there was no pause. Then she realised she couldn't say 'I'll just go straight to the hotel, thank you.' So, with another deep breath, she closed her mouth.

"Here's Charlie now. You get in the front, Natasha. I'll climb in the back." India was still talking as she pushed Natasha's case into the boot. It felt strange sitting next to Charlie in the front seat of a sleek black car. It smelt of new leather and cologne. He looked as gorgeous in person as in the photos she had seen littering the pages of the newspapers for some time. His dark blonde hair was on the long side, and his eyes sparkled out beneath it, as it fell across his forehead.

"Hello, Natasha, lovely to meet you, at last. I've heard so much about you." Natasha shot him a puzzled look. *Who from? India? Or Daniel? Why would he mention her to this stranger?* The gentle smile on Charlie's face made Natasha decide India was probably the source. She certainly talked a great deal.

Charlie moved the sports car through the city centre traffic with ease. In no time at all, they were pulling up in front of a large, traditionally built house on a long road.

"We just need to drop off some ice cream and juice. With two parties in one day, Amanda didn't have enough freezer space. So, we've been holding spare ice cream. With this heat, she called us to do an emergency run now instead of waiting until tonight." India was getting out of the car as was Charlie. Natasha sat still. She would just wait where she was, in her post-journey stickiness. But Charlie had other ideas.

"Come on Natasha, I want to give the birthday girl her present, and well, I might need to show her what to do with it. I can't expect Ben to do it properly." When she still hesitated, he leaned back into the car. "Come on Natasha, come and meet Amanda and Ben before we come back tonight."

"Charlie Robertson, calm down. This wouldn't have anything to do with jelly and ice cream and you wanting to hit the kid's food before the big kids get here?"

"What do you think? You've had that ice cream at our place all week and wouldn't let me near it." Natasha remained sat in her seat. India opened her door, but she was looking at Charlie. "Did you tell Zach about this?"

"No," he flashed a grin and lifted his shoulders, "and don't you be telling him." And he walked off holding tight to a pink sparkly gift bag.

"Come on Natasha, we can't let Charlie have all the jelly. I love a kid's party, don't you? And Martha is a darling. Ben is going to be mad when he sees what Charlie has bought her."

Charlie had disappeared towards the house.

India leaned into the back of the car, pulling out insulated bags. Then she too headed to the house and Natasha felt she had no choice but to follow too. As they disappeared behind the house, Natasha could hear the excited voices of children. Having not been to a children's party in years, she wondered if she was dressed appropriately and if she should have brought a gift. Worrying slowed her steps. She didn't know what to do or say. She just wasn't prepared.

"India! Wait. I don't have a gift … I'm not dressed." Her hand lifted her damp hair. India stopped and offered a soft smile.

"I'm sorry, I would have said had I realised the pull a kid's party would have on Charlie. Come on, Ben's lovely and so are his family. If it's terrible, we can drink wine with the mums."

Natasha relaxed. Of course, there would be parents as well as children. That was until she started to worry she wasn't dressed for this.

"I don't know what to say to children," Natasha confessed. India stopped and waited for her to catch up, and then together, they followed Charlie.

"Gwoar!"

As they rounded the corner of the house, they walked straight into Daniel Woods in full-on uncle mode. She had expected to see him at the match on Saturday, but he would be playing and not doing lion impressions three inches from her face. She screamed and reached out to grab India, who laughed. Daniel ran on, chasing a young girl that Natasha was about to discover was the birthday girl, Martha.

Charlie scooped the small girl up into his arms.

"I'll save you, Martha." The small girl clung to Charlie's neck, eyeing the pink gift bag.

"Charlie, put her down so she can open her present."

"A present? For me?"

"I'll open it for her," Daniel said, still in his roaring voice.

A group of small children all grabbed hold of Daniel and steered him back towards an inflatable castle. Natasha stood frozen on the spot. India had disappeared inside the house with the food bags. Charlie stood Martha down on the ground, the young girl's eye still fixed on the bag.

"Shall we open your present?" The young girl nodded her head and led Charlie towards a large table surrounded by a dozen assorted chairs. The debris of party food was strewn across a brightly coloured plastic tablecloth. Charlie sat down and lifted Martha onto his knee as he offered her the gift bag. Martha plunged her hands into the tissue paper and squealed when she pulled out a scaled-down rugby ball.

Charlie showed Martha how to hold the ball, and she threw it past him. The other children were still pulling and pushing Daniel around on the bouncy castle. Natasha looked for India, but before she had time to think, a man came out of the house carrying a pile of plastic bowls.

"Everyone sit down at the table if you like jelly, ice cream or cake." The commanding voice came from a mature version of Daniel Woods. This one wasn't as tall but had a strong athletic build. He looked stunning with a wonderful smile. Despite being dressed casually in jeans and a polo shirt, he looked smart. In contrast, Daniel and Charlie looked much more relaxed in their jeans. Daniel's jeans were worn and ripped at one hem.

Daniel ran up the steps into the house, flashing her a smile as he went. Then, as if he had remembered something, he dropped the smile. Natasha's heart froze. This was going to be hard if she couldn't get Daniel to listen to an explanation. As he disappeared through the door, Natasha caught a flash of another rip just below the ripe curve at the top of his leg. This was indeed going to be very hard.

That image of him standing naked before her in her dressing room was still etched into her brain. Fully clothed he looked out of proportion. Naked, he was perfect.

Once the children were settled with bowls of jelly and ice cream, India appeared with two bowls and passed one to her. Natasha looked at the bowl and took the spoon from India. How could she eat this? *This is going to be much harder than I thought.*

Natasha ate a little and played with the rest. She was feeling sticky and uncomfortable. It had been a long journey, and she was ready to get to the hotel. She was about to ask India how far it was and if she could get a taxi when Daniel reappeared. He was holding a tall castle-shaped cake with four candles, one in each turret. His wonderful smile plastered back on his face. He placed the cake in front of the birthday girl. In one smooth move, he scooped a smaller child, a boy, and lifted him onto his shoulders. Watching Daniel with these children, she could see how comfortable he was with them. India noticed her watching him.

"They all look so at home. When I see Charlie around our friends' kids, I feel so guilty. It's not that I don't want kids. To be honest, I'm not sure. But I know I'm not ready right now." Natasha just shared a sad smile with her. When she married Matt, she wanted children so badly. It simply didn't happen for them. Now she was glad they didn't even have a dog to sort out in the split. But today, watching Daniel, she thought about it all again. What if she couldn't have children? How would Daniel feel? *He's going to have to talk to me first. Maybe now is the time to speak to him.*

When Daniel went back into the house with some bowls, she picked up the rest of the dishes and followed him into the kitchen.

"Daniel, could I just have a quick word?"

Daniel spun around. He looked shocked to be alone with her. He opened his mouth to speak as an older woman walked in through the front door with a pile of presents. Daniel stared first at the newcomer and then back at Natasha, then without saying a word to either, he ran upstairs. Natasha was stunned.

"Don't worry dear, that was because of me," she reassured Natasha. "I'm his mother. Something he would rather forget. He hasn't spoken to me since he was ten."

Natasha was still holding the bowls. Putting them down on the side, she held out her hand.

"I'm Natasha. I'm pleased to meet you."

Chapter 21

Ben started to play the music he asked Daniel to put together for him. The louder volume left Daniel in no doubt that this was the adult party. Their parents had collected the children. The boy-child and the birthday girl had been whisked away for a sleepover with Amanda's parents so that Ben could enjoy his own birthday party with his teammates. He found Ben at the bottom of the garden, lighting some logs in the fire pit.

"So, big brother, why are you having your party at home this year?"

"Not sure. It was Amanda's idea."

"Ha."

"And no, I am not under the thumb."

"OK." Daniel looked back up the garden towards the house. "So, how many are we expecting?"

"Well, the team and the other halves."

"Any single women?"

"I haven't invited any, but some of Mandy's friends are coming."

"Anyone else?" *Just ask him. It'll be much easier to just ask him.*

"I left all that to Mandy." Ben nodded to his wife as she picked her way down the garden towards them.

"Ben! Can you get the beer out of the garage?"

"I organised the beer, though. Come on brother, make yourself useful for a change." Amanda nudged her husband with her elbow.

"Ben, you know as well as I do, Daniel has been a great help today."

"Well, he was until he disappeared as soon as Mum arrived."

Daniel didn't know what to say. He examined his feet as he shuffled them. It had been hard, but the fact that Natasha witnessed it, was upsetting him more. Fortunately, he was saved by the arrival of the first guests. Ben and Amanda became busy, and Daniel worked on fading into the background. Seeing Natasha had been difficult, but seeing his mother was a million times harder.

Each time he saw his mother, he felt the hurt of her leaving him all over again. Surely it should get easier. He didn't see how Rebecca and Ben managed to talk to her. They had been the ones to pick up more responsibility when she left.

Rebecca had tried to explain to him only last week. But he still felt the pain of her abandoning them to be with another man. The new relationship hadn't lasted long. But his mum didn't come back.

Rebecca explained it was not about the other man, it was about her not being happy on the farm. *How could anyone not be content living there?* He just didn't understand it.

Once all the team had arrived, Daniel was finding it easier to fade into the background. Zach had brought his friends who were over for the World Cup. They were a great bunch, but they seemed to make a lot of noise.

Zach Mitchell and Garry Bayliss, the two Australians that he had been playing with for the last couple of years, seemed to enjoy having the other guys here. They were all laughing when Nick arrived with Emma. When Zach and Garry spotted Nick, they started shouting over at him.

"Nick mate, come and meet my buddies. You can tell them how we caught the bad guys."

"Shhh, Charlie might hear you. That was the night he slept in India's room." Garry was laughing.

Daniel saw Emma's face drop. Sometimes the joking went too far. He was about to speak to her, but Natasha walked up to her, so instead he wandered over to the fire. From the shadows, he watched as Natasha appeared to talk to Emma. Nick must have noticed because he joined them and took Emma's hand. They exchanged a few words, and Emma's smile was back. They walked into the kitchen, leaving Natasha standing apart from the group. His heart leapt. He watched as she turned and when she saw him alone, she walked towards him.

Panic rose inside him. Maybe he should just get it over with. He didn't have to do what Rebecca had said, tell her about his mum. But then she had seen his mum today. Maybe his mum had said something.

He couldn't help but smile as he watched her get closer.

She looked nervous, and he realised he had done that to her. The smile left his face as sadness filled his chest. He hadn't been fair; he had a shock that day, but she had to face much worse.

"Hello Daniel." She looked awkward as she waited for him to respond.

"Welcome to Yorkshire. I'm sorry about this afternoon."

"Are you?" she sounded as sad as she looked.

"I wasn't expecting…"

"That makes two of us. I was picked up at the station and the next thing I know I am at a children's party and there was a Daniel-shaped lion."

"Sorry."

"I'd like to explain. I can see how it looks, but I need you to know it's not what you think."

"I think you are married. Are you telling me that isn't true?"

"Sadly, no. But it's not that straightforward. Daniel, I know I said I wanted to explain, but there is so much of this I can't tell you."

Daniel shook his head. He wasn't sure he was ready to listen to her, and now she wouldn't say anything more. So, they were no further forward. Except they were. She was talking, and he was listening. He couldn't help the smile coming back to his face as he realised he wanted to spend more time with her.

"Daniel, I wish you could trust me. I hope you know I wouldn't lie to you." She looked at him, trying to get him to see she was being truthful.

"I'm sorry, but I promised Matt. Daniel, I can't be seen with you. With anyone."

"Are you seeing someone?"

"No Daniel, I'm not seeing anyone. You are … were …"

Daniel hated seeing her so sad. He knew when he saw her face that he trusted her. It was just that simple.

"Let's go get you a drink." He stood up and held out his hand. She stood up but didn't take his hand.

"Sorry" It was a quiet word, nevertheless it broke Daniel. He led the way to the kitchen. They stood talking with Emma and Nick. After a couple more drinks, Daniel suddenly asked Emma to dance.

"Would the birthday girl have a dance with me?"

"Just you be careful with my girl!" Nick shouted as Daniel dragged her away.

"So, Daniel Woods, why are you dancing with me and not my beautiful friend?"

"Natasha tells me she can't be seen with me."

"I guess that's true."

"But if I dance with you and maybe a couple more of the lovely ladies here, then just maybe I could have one dance with Natasha without anything being said."

"Clever. I like your style."

"Can I ask you a question?"

"Sure, big boy."

"This thing that Tasha can't tell me, do you know what it is?"

"I do."

"So, can you tell me?"

"Sorry, Daniel. I promised. I haven't even told Nick."

"OK. I have another question. Am I being stupid, trusting her?"

"No. No, Daniel, you aren't. If you can trust her, it will all become clear soon."

"How soon? Should I wait?"

"I honestly don't know. But I can tell you, Natasha desperately needs good friends right now. If you are just playing at this, walk away. She could really use someone she can rely on in her life."

That shook Daniel more than he expected. He was worried Natasha was toying with him and now Emma was suggesting that he was playing with her.

"Daniel, I mean it, don't mess with her. I am not sure she can take any more."

"OK. I heard you."

The music changed, and the dancing became faster. They danced together, laughing, but the talking was over.

When the music stopped, Daniel excused himself and disappeared into the kitchen. He needed time to think. When he found Amanda talking to Amy's mum, he sobered up immediately. Amy's words still bouncing around his head, 'My mum says she has never seen you sober'. He poured himself a coke and went to talk to Charlie.

"Hey mate, how's it going?"

"Great. Charlie, is it OK if I dance with India?"

"Dan, you need to ask India. Not me."

"Really? You don't mind?"

"Of course, I mind, but India would kill me if I tried to make decisions for her. Just don't stand on her."

So, Daniel danced with India and then Amanda. He danced with Tilly despite warnings from Joe. He knew this playlist backwards. Daniel knew what was coming, and he waited.

He knew exactly what he was waiting for. When the first bars started, his stomach turned over. This was it. It had a fast beat, and he thought it would help Natasha say yes. His normal confidence had left him, but he played the part of the old young and foolish Daniel. He tried to hide the nervous energy that was building within him.

"Mrs Poole, I do believe it is your turn to dance with me. Come along." He took her hand and pulled her to the patio where most of the dancing was happening. Daniel had spent the last 74 minutes planning for this moment.

"Daniel, I shouldn't. I'm married."

"And so are Tilly and Amanda. India might as well be if she would just say yes to the poor boy. If you were the only one I didn't dance with, that would look suspicious." Natasha didn't respond. She moved to the music a small distance away from him. The dance was fast, and Daniel was throwing himself into it with plenty of enthusiasm. "Come on Natasha, you are at a party. Are you afraid someone is going to see you enjoying yourself?"

The last comment seemed to change her mind, and she danced like she wanted to be there.

With the last note, Daniel picked her up and hugged her. "I know you can't tell me what is happening, but surely you are allowed to enjoy a party with friends."

"I guess so."

"Thank god for that." He wrapped his arms around her, and the next tune started to play. A slow dance of love. Daniel sang softly to her. Me and Mrs Jones. Just those few minutes of having her in his arms had been worth it. Worth the time he had danced with everyone else at the party, just so that when this one song played, she would be in his arms. And as he sang quietly in her ear, he felt her relax in his arms. Her head fell onto his chest and all protests were forgotten. He didn't understand how dancing with someone could feel so different. His whole body was responding, and he was sure she felt it, too. As the last notes played, Daniel pulled her into his body, holding her, hugging her.

He knew it couldn't last, but he had hoped for a second dance. Sadly, it wasn't to be. Natasha could see Emma and Nick saying their goodbyes and she rushed off to join them. Daniel reluctantly followed her, not ready to say goodbye.

Nick shook his hand, and Emma gave him a huge hug as Natasha smiled weakly next to her.

"Well done Daniel, you did a lot of dancing for that one dance at the end. Thank you for making her smile again. At one point, I thought you wouldn't get there. And then when you picked such a fast song … I think you had inside information."

"You think I might have organised the music for my tone-deaf brother? I really don't know what you mean." Emma laughed but Natasha looked puzzled.

Daniel dipped his head and kissed her cheek, but close to her ear. "I'll see you soon," he whispered.

"Right, I am dragging her away. We have a big day shopping tomorrow."

"Goodnight, Daniel." Her voice lingered in his brain. He didn't respond and yet he watched her walk away. He stood watching as the taxi disappeared into the distance.

Chapter 22

Friday 1 a.m.

DW: Thank you for dancing with me.

It was good to see you away from the studio.

TASHA: I enjoyed it.

DW: Can I see you tomorrow? Or do I mean today now?

TASHA: Not a good idea.

TASHA: I'm taking the birthday girl shopping in Leeds.

I have a feeling it's going to take all day.

DW: OK.

DW: When do you go home?

TASHA: Sunday 9 a.m. train

DW: Did you run today?

TASHA: Yes. This morning.

DW: Goodnight Tasha.

TASHA: Goodnight Dan.

Sat on the edge of her bed, Natasha looked at the messages from Dan, trying to commit them to memory before she deleted them and went back to brushing her hair. With her nightly rituals completed Natasha picked up her phone and going into her contacts, she looked hard at what it said next to Daniel's name. She had just put DW work. She hoped it was enough.

Friday 8 a.m.

DW: Good morning, Have a good day shopping.

TASHA: Thanks. What are you doing?

DW: Physio for my knee.

TASHA: Too much dancing?

DW: It didn't help dancing with everyone before I dare ask you.

TASHA: Sorry.

Friday 5 p.m.

DW: Did you buy much?

TASHA: New running kit.

DW: Nice.

DW: Can I see you?

TASHA: We're meeting Tilly and Joe. Italian I think.

DW: Are you excited about your first cricket match?

TASHA: Worried I won't understand it. I hear it can be a difficult crowd.

DW: They will all love you so don't worry.

TASHA: Dan, please understand this when I say texting isn't perhaps a clever idea.

There was no response.

TASHA: I hope it won't be long before this is over, and we can talk.

Natasha needed to get ready to meet Emma and Nick downstairs. It didn't stop her from rechecking her phone. Still no response from Daniel. She tossed her phone onto her bed and didn't see it bounce onto the floor.

She was still drying her hair when Emma knocked on her door.

"Tash, have you got any earrings to go with this dress."

"Oh, Hi Em, come in let's see." She opened the door and let her friend into her room.

Emma was clutching the strappy dress she had bought that day. Natasha had been expecting this request and went to find her handbag. Emma's style was not hers, in fact, Natasha had a challenging time deciding what Emma's style was.

As Natasha was pulling her bag out of the neatly arranged wardrobe, Emma picked up her phone.

"Why is Denise from work texting you?" Emma started reading the text.

"Oh!" She sat down on the bed and looked at Natasha. "This isn't from Denise is it?" Natasha shook her head.

"This says, Dan. How long has he been texting you?" Natasha didn't answer, she didn't even look at Emma.

"Sorry Tash, It's none of my business. I'm sorry I asked."

Natasha sat next to her friend and handed her the small neatly packaged box she had retrieved from her handbag.

"It's OK Em. You're the only person I can talk to about this. Am I being stupid?"

"No, I think this is just what you needed. I know you think you aren't ready, but you are Tash, you are ready. A year ago, you wouldn't even have noticed him." Natasha shook her head as Emma opened the parcel.

"I think I would …"

"Come on, remember that guy who was selling vitamins, everyone at the studio noticed him but when he asked you to help check his microphone, you got Paul to do it." Emma's face lit up as she found the contents of the box. "When did you …"

"I bought them whilst you were trying on trousers. Happy Birthday, Emma. I hope you're having a fabulous time."

"It felt weird leaving him with India this morning. I felt like saying here's my boyfriend, I want him back at the end of the day. Talking to Charlie helped, he says he thought there was something there when he saw them together, but now he knows it was more friendship than anything else. It helped me stop thinking I was being paranoid. I'm not sure what scared me most, that he might be interested in someone else or that I was unhinged." Emma stood up and looked squarely at her friend.

"Anyway, back to Daniel Woods. Are you sure you don't want him to join us tonight?"

"Would I like to see Daniel? Yes. Do I want him to come with us? NO!"

"If you want to see him, you don't have to come tonight. No one will mind."

"Is that really a good idea? On Sunday morning, I must go home and play the dutiful wife to Matthew, and I don't know how long that is going to be."

"Does it have to be more than tonight?"

Natasha walked back to the mirror and brushed her hair. Long, slow strokes of the brush calmed her as she thought about what Emma had said.

"Natasha Poole, look at me. I know I said this is just what you needed but really, you aren't thinking about leaving Matthew and moving in with a farmer instead?" Natasha didn't do as Emma asked; she didn't look at her. She was thinking about what Emma had just said. It was only in the last two years that her own career had begun to flourish. Once she was more than Matthew's wife. Once they decided that having children wasn't happening for them. Was she ready to give that up? For what?

"Emma, I get what you are saying. I seriously do, but perhaps now you see why I don't think it's a good idea to see him again. Outside of work, of course."

"I better go get ready before I make us late. I bet the saintly India was never late."

"Emma!"

But Emma had gone, leaving Natasha to get ready and try to enjoy tonight even though her brain was working overtime.

As she put her phone in her bag, she checked for something from Daniel. Nothing. That is what she asked for, that is what she wanted. Wasn't it?

Chapter 23

Natasha couldn't help herself. She didn't hear what India was saying. Instead, she was staring at the tall figure replacing his brother at the crease. She was trying to decide if he was confident or nervous as he swung the bat around and around in large circles. First with his left hand and then his right, as his long legs carried him to the centre of the ground.

People thought live TV was scary, but this was something else. The stands weren't full and yet thousands of eyes watched him. Still, as he got closer, he stopped, his bat in both hands, he lowered it to the ground, stretching even more. When he finally stood in front of the wicket opposite Charlie, he took more time to find his place.

Natasha swallowed hard as she studied each movement. Her heart stuttered when she realised India had stopped talking. Instead, she was watching Natasha with a knowing look on her face. How did she explain this? She didn't have to, as India leaned in and said quietly.

"I know. It's complicated. It always is."

"Oh. No, it's not that, it's ..."

"I hope it works out because Daniel's heart ... well, it's a big heart ... he could do with someone who really loves him, no matter what else is happening in their life."

Natasha looked down into her drink, she understood every word that India was saying. It was clear how hurt Daniel was feeling. She offered India a small smile as her only reply. What could she say?

India was looking out at Charlie and Daniel, so she felt safe doing the same. As she stared through the glass, her heart clenched. It felt like her own heart was out there. As the bowler steamed towards the man that held her heart, she silently prayed that it could all work out.

"Is that ball hard?"

"Hey, don't worry, they know what they're doing. Is this your first time watching him?"

Looking behind her, Natasha cringed. Had anyone heard?

"Yes, India, this is my first cricket match. My husband isn't into sports."

India seemed to get the message.

"Have you met Tilly's dad yet?" Natasha shook her head.

"Come, let me introduce you," India led her towards a group of three men. She paused to whisper a warning, "and ignore anything Mr Wilde says." India rolled her eyes to emphasise her dislike of the man.

"I think we've met." Natasha racked her brain for the details of Jackson Wilde.

The men stopped talking and watched the two women approach. A shiver slid down Natasha's back.

"Max, this is Natasha Poole. We have been working with her at More.U TV."

"Ah, Natasha! Pleased to meet you. Is this is your first match."

"Yes, it is. Tilly was kind to include me." She offered the men her professional smile. They were all dressed impeccably but one man stood out. From his diamond cuff links to his overpowering cologne, he was Jackson Wilde. He slid his arm around her. "Oh Natasha, at last, I get you without that husband of yours." The sickly tone of his voice made Natasha feel like she needed to shower. She could see India's horrified face and with her earlier comment, she could tell they felt the same about this hideous man.

Maxwell Sykes seemed to know, too.

"Natasha, I'd like to introduce you to a few people. Come with me." He took her arm and pulled her gently across the room. As he led her away, he leaned in to speak quietly to her.

"I seem to spend too much of my life rescuing ladies from that man. I sincerely hope that one day, a husband or a father will put him in his place – on his arse."

Natasha couldn't help but smile at his comment and the way he used the word 'arse'.

"Now, who can I introduce you to? Have you met Zach yet?"

"Yes, we met last night." Maxwell Sykes stopped and looked down at her. He raised an eyebrow.

"Is that good or bad? I can't tell. I must be slipping."

"It's neither. You asked if we'd met. I said yes."

"Ah, you're in love with your husband!" Max studied her face. "Oh, I see you are in love, but not with your husband." He looked pleased, but the smile didn't last. "I'm sorry. I'll just shut up now." He offered a small smile. "I hope it works out for you." Something in the way he spoke made her think he believed it couldn't possibly go well.

By now, they had reached another group of men. They were standing by the window, looking out at the cricket, and discussing the match.

"Gentlemen, can I introduce Natasha Poole? She is the TV professional that India's working with." The three men stopped talking and turned to stare silently at her.

"Natasha, meet India's family. Her brother Andrew, her father William, and her grandfather Henry." These men were striking. The older man had a shock of strong white hair. The younger two had black hair and the same intense blue eyes that made Emma so jealous of India. Andrew spoke as the others continued to eye her suspiciously.

"Hello Natasha, so what do you think of the play today? Do you think Yorkshire can turn this around?" The older two men grunted as if such a thing was impossible.

Natasha gulped as she explained, "I think you're asking the wrong person. I haven't watched cricket before." Max smiled, but she was sure the other three men were confused. They each turned away from her and returned to watching the action. Natasha steeled herself for watching Daniel out there with Charlie, who seemed to be doing most of the batting.

"Why the hell have they put young Woods in at number 5?"

Natasha's stomach fizzed at this description. Max tried to help.

"It's unusual, I'll grant you that, but I am sure there is a good reason."

"He's not doing so bad for a bowler, Grandfather."

He's a bowler? How did I not know that? I thought they all did everything. This didn't seem like the time or place to admit that. Instead, she watched the group from the corner of her eye, whilst her heart stuttered as it became Daniel's turn to bat. Andrew looked quite a few years older than India. Like the other men there, they were all immaculately dressed. And so frosty. Not like India at all.

"The man's a bungling idiot, can hardly string two words together." Natasha's eyes hit this old man. She opened her mouth to object but stopped herself. How could she defend him? Maxwell Sykes had seen her face and his eyes softened. Then, in the same dismissive tone as the old man had used, he spoke up for Daniel.

"Have you watched him on TV with the beautiful Natasha. He is pretty eloquent then. I think he just isn't keen on gatherings like this."

The old man's nose twitched and moved his glasses across his face and back.

"Still a farm boy if you ask me. Not sure how his brother made captain."

"Four! At least he is putting some runs on the scoreboard today. When we saw him last year, he didn't score one."

"Charlie has been working with him." Natasha needed to say something but she was shocked at the response.,All three of the Barrington Jones men stared at her when she mentioned Charlie's name. Andrew's face showed sympathy, but India's father looked visibly annoyed.

"Damn it, William. Haven't you got over it yet? The man has stood by her as she creates her own business. That is more than you've done."

Uncomfortable in this company, Natasha tried to focus on watching the match. She was grateful when Zach came over to drag her away.

"You're too beautiful for a frown like that."

"I don't know what I was expecting, but it all feels so …"

"You got that right. I don't get all this family stuff. Max is nicer than people think but he picks who he is nice to. He clearly loves Tilly yet somehow I think he couldn't tell her that." He smiled down at her. "Come on Nick wants to take some pictures."

Natasha spent the next twenty minutes with Zach, Emma, and Nick going through various setups. This part she was enjoying. Zach was amazing to work with and seemed to feel the need to cheer her up today.

Tilly came gushing over and grabbed her arm. "Thank you," Natasha raised an eyebrow, "and thank you Zach, for rescuing her."

She threw her arm around Natasha's shoulder and whispered. "I wouldn't invite half these people if I had my way."

"That's fine, Tilly. Where's Joe?" Tilly nodded to a group of four men who stood laughing near the bar.

"He's over there with the brothers. When I met Joe, I had one brother, and I thought that was a challenge. Now I have three. Heart breakers the lot of them. Stay away."

A cheer from the crowd made their heads turn. The screens were showing Daniel skying a ball that was cleanly caught. He was out, having scored 25 runs.

"Bloody well done, Danno!" Zach applauded wildly and a small round of applause rippled through the room.

Natasha knew little about cricket, but she thought one hundred runs was something they got excited about. She tried to focus on what Nick needed because everything else confused her. She was glad Daniel wasn't having balls thrown at him, although she worried he would be upset. Daniel held up his bat and waved to the crowd as he walked off the field. The crowd seemed pleased. As he left the field, Garry Bayliss took his place amid more cheering.

Nick went off to change his lens, as Emma gave her shoulder a hug.

"Thank you. Are you glad you came now?"

"I'm glad I got to speak to him at the party. Shopping was fun." Natasha paused, her eyes scanning the room, "I'm not sure how I feel today."

"You knew it would be a tough crowd."

"I like Tilly's dad," she offered as Nick joined them again.

"You must be one of the chosen." It wasn't like Nick to be negative.

"Excuse me?"

"Watch him, he's a pussy with Tilly and India but watch him with me or Joe even."

"Joe? Tilly's husband Joe?"

"Yep, watch, make your own mind up."

"Come on Nick, no father ever thinks anyone is good enough for their daughter."

"Em sweetheart, they are married and having a kid. It's time for him to realise Joe is here to stay."

India joined them and the conversation.

"It doesn't help that most of Joe's family are not keen on Max. However, they are all in business together."

Nick put his arm around India's shoulders and pulled her into his side. "I see your family hasn't softened towards Charlie."

Emma stiffened. Natasha's thoughts went to her own father.

"My dad's not keen on Matt. Says he's away too much, but I think it's more down to the fact Dad's still doing all those little jobs. Being bad at DIY doesn't make him a bad husband."

Emma's eyes were fixed on her face, and Natasha had to look away. And as she did, her eyes landed on the TV screens in the corner of the room. They were showing a close-up of Daniel talking to Ben. Natasha couldn't help but remember her dream of Daniel building her that arbour and what her dad would think of him.

Tilly broke up the group and took Natasha on a tour of the room. India and Nick seemed to be busy working on lists, and now he was showing her something on his camera. Emma was standing to one side watching, looking increasingly upset.

Tilly stopped to see what had caught her attention.

"Emma's a good friend. Should she be worried?"

"Of India? Have you seen her with Charlie?" Tilly pulled her over to one side to talk more privately. They stood, picking up Gym Away from the table. "India has known Nick for a couple of years. She met him through her last job. It's how we met her, too. She was basically running around fetching and carrying and taking things to drop off at Nick's, who was their main photographer. Nick could see she had more talent than that. It was probably his faith in her that helped her leave and set up on her own. He helped her through a rough patch, but India is all in as far as Charlie is concerned." Natasha was starting to relax, but Tilly hadn't finished.

"I knew the first time I saw them in the same room they belonged together. I had my theories before then, too. They're both lovely people who were made for each other. Nick, well, he's like the big brother she would have chosen for herself." Tilly looked from Nick, busy still showing India things on his camera, to Andrew Barrington Jones.

"I'm sure Andrew would be OK if," Tilly leaned into whisper, "he got that stick out of his arse. He doesn't seem to get to relax. It makes India feel guilty that she escaped, and he didn't."

Natasha couldn't imagine wanting to escape your family, but she only had her dad now. She did wonder how her life would be if her mother were still alive. She didn't know how to explain the things that were happening in her life to her father, but her mother would have been a much harder challenge. Daniel hadn't replied to her text, so possibly there was nothing to explain, anyway. With no sign of the promised election, it looked like she would be in this limbo for a while.

When Yorkshire took the field to bowl, Zach took Natasha out onto the terrace to watch.

"This is when you get to see Danno put those long limbs to good use." Zach's cheerful tone made Natasha smile.

"Danno was born to do this." Natasha's smiling face turned to one of confusion, and Zach continued.

"Play cricket for Yorkshire ... this is his happy place ... when all that baggage he carries gets forgotten."

"Baggage?"

"Me & my big mouth."

"Zach?"

"It's for him to say, not me. I guess that's why he is like he is."

Natasha was desperate to know more, but Zach wasn't sharing. Well, not about Daniel anyway. Instead, for the next half an hour or so, they stayed on the terrace watching Daniel and the team. Zach was explaining so much her brain ached. He was a wonderful companion and had her laughing in varying degrees until her sides ached.

Emma came to find her and together, they escaped to the toilets.

"Are you OK?" Emma asked, searching her face for the truth.

"I'm fine," she smiled at her friend's concern. "Watching him batting earlier was hard, but as my new friend 'Zacho' tells me,

'Danno' was born to do this'." She shook her head. "I must admit there is more to this cricket lark than I thought. But I'm learning."

"Listen, dinner tonight, Nick wants to take me somewhere he knows, some place he's been with India. But I don't want to leave you alone, and neither does Nick. Do you want to invite Dan?" Emma watched her friend's face. "Or Zach?"

"Oh! Gosh no. Certainly not Zach and Daniel … well I couldn't, you know, even if he was talking to me."

"I thought you talked last night. And those texts?"

"I did but then this morning I sent him a text and he hasn't replied."

"Oh, I thought … from what he said last night. I guess I was wrong."

"Look, Emma, you and Nick have looked after me enough. It's your birthday trip. Go spend some time with him." She smiled at her friend. "I have to be up early anyway for this damn show with Matthew."

"Are you sure?"

"I'm very sure. In fact, I am going to say my goodbyes and head off back to the hotel. I need to run this tension out of my legs."

Natasha found India sitting with Tilly, talking quietly in a corner. They both looked exhausted.

"We have been told to sit down by the men folk who insist on doing the packing up. We've decided not to argue." India raised her eyebrows, suggesting that it had been hard to make the pregnant Tilly sit down. Tilly frowned.

"But we're watching them closely to ensure they know what they are doing."

"Of course. I just wanted to say thank you for inviting me. I had a wonderful time. I must be off early in the morning to catch a train back. I'm needed at an event with Matthew."

"Oh!" India looked sad, but she recovered quickly and smiled. "Thank you for being here, and I am sorry about that creep Wilde. At least he's gone now. Do you want a lift to the station tomorrow?"

"No to the lift but thank you. And sadly, I'm used to the Jackson Wildes of this world.

As Natasha headed across the car park towards the hotel, she felt sad that her time in Leeds was over. Last week, she was dreading coming and now she was sad to be going home. It made little sense. And then it did. A tall figure in a Yorkshire kit was just disappearing in a door at the side of the block that held her hotel. *Will I ever be able to make him understand? Will I ever understand it myself?*

Her walking slowed. She was so fixed on watching that door, hoping he would come back out, that she didn't see Jackson Wilde swooping in from her right until he was standing over her.

"Alone at last, Natasha. Now, can I whisk you away to a wonderful dinner and you can tell me why that husband of yours keeps leaving you alone?"

Natasha staggered back. "Mr Wilde I ... "

"Jackson," came the syrupy voice. "Please call me Jackson."

"Mr Wilde, I really can't. I have plans and I leave in the morning." Jackson Wilde gripped her elbow and dragged her over to the side of a green Jaguar car. Natasha struggled to pull away from him.

"Stop struggling, you silly girl. You know Matthew would want you to be nice to me. I am an extremely useful man to be nice to, Natasha." He rolled her name around his tongue as he hissed into her ear.

"Well, I hate to inform you, Mr Wilde, but I do not, I repeat, do NOT do favours to advance my husband's career. You've picked on the wrong woman." Jackson Wilde hung on to her elbow and leered at her.

"Really?"

Without blinking, Natasha stamped down hard on his foot and pulled herself away at the same time.

"Yes! Really!"

As she looked up, Daniel Woods was racing towards her, a look of panic on his face. Natasha shook her head, warning him to stay back. If Jackson Wilde got a sniff of this, then everything she had been trying to do for Matthew these last few months would be lost.

She straightened up and walked towards the entrance of the hotel, leaving a puzzled and confused Daniel Woods watching her leave him once again.

Chapter 24

DW: U OK?

TASHA: Yes. Fine Thanks.

DW: Who was that man?

DW: Was that your husband?

DW: I'm sure I've seen him before.

DW: TASHA?

TASHA: Sorry. Just getting into my room.

DW: Are you sure you are OK?

TASHA: Yes. Come up if you want to talk.

Daniel paused. What did he do? She said she was OK, and she had asked him not to text, so why was he even thinking about going up to her bedroom? Daniel knew he would not want to stop at talking, not to mention he had a physiotherapist waiting for him. No, not a clever idea.

DW: Sorry on my way to Physio.

TASHA: Thanks for caring. I should go for my run, anyway.

DW: In that new kit?

TASHA: Yes

Daniel turned from watching the doorway to the hotel and back into the physio's room. The jeans he had gone to get out of his car, totally forgotten.

An hour later, a moody Daniel Woods threw a kit bag into the boot of his car, cursing himself for not taking his jeans to the physio appointment. In the corner of his eye, a flash of bright colours. His head jerked up as he saw her. Her hair neatly plaited down her back. This was Natasha in running mode. It took him back to their first encounter and made his body tingle. Their conversation at the party had suggested that if he believed her, they had a future, but not yet. He couldn't understand what there could be that she wouldn't share with him.

As he locked his car and bent down to tighten his laces, he pondered what that meant. A week, a month, a year? Waiting for anything, let alone a woman was an alien concept for Daniel. He was used to having what he wanted, a new car, a new watch, a new woman. He didn't want to wait, and for some reason, he didn't understand, no other woman was attracting his attention. At Ben's party, there had been other women, ones without the complication of being married. Ben dared to suggest he only wanted Tasha because she was unavailable, but was she? Was he being stupid? She was married, and he didn't have many rules in his life. *It's not like she has kids. Why? Why am I even thinking about this?*

He had seen her laughing with Zach today, God that was hard. He wanted to be the one who made her smile, made her laugh. The smug grin on that bastard's face when he saw me watching them today. It should have been me smiling at making her laugh.

Daniel's hands flexed at his side as he pictured her in Zach's arms. Zach wouldn't care if she was married. *Was she flirting with Zach? Is Zach just doing it to torment me?*

A million and one possibilities surged through Daniel's head. As he reached the footpath, he broke into an easy jog. Slow, steady, rhythmic paces as he looked for her. Hopefully, he would meet her soon. He didn't think Ian, the physio he just left, would be happy with him trying to catch up with her. He smiled to himself, 'catch her'.

Holding back on his speed, guarding his knee, he had too much time to think. She's lost weight and still looks tired. I think she has been running more since she lost the dog. She's hiding it well, but I don't like those dark circles below her eyes. She claimed her husband was not to blame for them. His smile faded at the thought that anyone would hurt her.

His pace slowed. If I find her, what am I going to say? Something else I didn't think through. Typical, Rebecca is right I am just too impulsive. Well, I'm running now. If I see her, I can let her make the first move.

Even in his head, it didn't sound like a very good plan, but it was all he had. He focused his attention back on his run. Thinking about his stride length and trying to relax into a pattern. Ian's comments from this morning's warm-up were fresh in his mind. Today's match had left him in more pain. One Day cricket wasn't something he liked anymore. The faster pace used to appeal, but not today. Left right left right. It was his left knee that was complaining the most, so when he reached a small park on the corner of the next road, he stopped to stretch. He folded his arms, bending forward, using the weight of his arms to release the back of his legs. He stayed like that, feeling the steady pull.

"Daniel?"

Natasha's voice reached his ears and set off a train reaction. He hadn't expected to find her so soon. He remained bent forward, not knowing how to react. A panic began deep inside him making him want to run on and pretend he didn't hear her. *That's what the old Daniel would do. I thought you wanted to be a grown-up. I thought you did this to see her. What is wrong with me? This is silly.*

Daniel straightened up and once his eyes found the source of her voice, a smile hit his face. How could he not want to be with her?

"Hello Tasha, I didn't expect to see you tonight."

Natasha didn't speak. She sat still on a bench inside the park, but she looked at him. She didn't need to speak. Her eyes said she was hungry for him. As Daniel walked purposely toward her, she moved to make room for him to sit beside her. He sat down next to her, and his hand covered hers on the seat between them. He stared straight ahead and waited for her to speak. But he couldn't keep it inside. Within seconds he squeezed her hand and, still afraid to look at her, blurted out.

"Who am I kidding? I saw you setting off and followed you."

"You did?"

Daniel nodded, "I didn't get as far as working out what I was going to say, though."

"Does that mean I have to be honest too?" Daniel nodded.

"I knew what time your appointment ended."

Daniel put his arm across her shoulders and pulled her to his side in a hug.

"But you said…"

"I know, and I meant it. This is not a good idea. We can't be seen, but Emma is right. I need someone for me."

"I guess that means we both want to do this, then." They sat close together on the same bench. His hand gently covered hers. Daniel closed his eyes and took in the moment. The sun on his face, Natasha by his side, her perfume filling his head. All the uncertainty of just minutes earlier, gone.

"Will anyone see us sitting here?"

"I doubt it but come on." Standing up, he took her hand and pulled her with him. He led her further into the park to another bench tucked behind a large shrub. Daniel sat down and pulled her towards him. To his surprise, she sat on his knee, her legs astride his, her lips tantalisingly close to his.

He kissed her. A teasing, exploring kiss. It was a beginning. A kiss. One he wanted her to remember. Natasha sat still, letting him explore her mouth but she wasn't joining in. He stopped and searched her face for an answer. Had he gone too far again?

He got his answer when her two hands held his jaw, and she kissed him. Daniel returned the kiss. Each kiss more passionate than the last. Like a conversation, getting to know each other. Daniel used his hands to explore her breasts, tugging gently at her neckline. She squirmed on his knee, pushing herself further into his hardness.

When one breast broke free from her top, he bent his head to kiss her nipple, licking in circles. Her body was responding to him, and it filled him with a new warmth. He wanted to stay in this moment forever, but Natasha finally pulled back. She turned her face away from him and bit her lip.

Daniel held her chin and gently turned her face towards his.

"Hey, we don't have to rush. I'm sorry if I got carried away."

"Daniel, no, I... You did nothing I didn't want you to do."

"I keep expecting someone to shout, 'get a room'."

"I've got a room." Her voice was soft but the light in her eyes said everything Daniel needed to know.

Chapter 25

I've got a room; I've got a room. Those words echoed around Natasha's head. Who had said them? She was sure it wasn't her. What the hell was she doing? She looked down at her breast, thrust forward towards him, nipples tight as bullets. Daniel sheepishly pulled up the neckline of her top, covering her again and kissed the tip of her nose. It was such a simple thing, but it made her heart soar. It made her realise how dead her relationship with Matthew was.

She had loved Matthew. That wasn't in doubt. But there had never been the passion she felt in just that simple kiss from Daniel. The idea of doing what they had just done in a park was certainly not something that would have happened with Matthew.

"You better go first." His low and rich voice vibrated through her.

"Oh?"

"To get the key?"

"Of course."

"I'll run around the block and come from the other direction."

Natasha looked into Daniel's eyes, trying to decide if this was something he did often. Hook up with someone staying at the hotel. *Am I just another challenge to him?*

"Daniel Woods, I'm not going to have sex with you." Daniel didn't hide his disappointment from her, but he took both her hands in his and kissed her nose again.

"Yet!"

"Yet?"

"You are not going to have sex with me, YET." His thumbs stroked the back of her hands, and a soft smile licked his lips. How was she ever going to resist him? She was going to resist him because she was married. Matthew had agreed she could divorce him when he fell in love with his assistant. They just needed to wait for this damn election.

She realised she hadn't answered Daniel.

"It's a good word. Yet. So yes, I can go with that. I am not going to have sex with you yet."

"So, when will you have sex with me?" His eyes sparkled as he teased her, and that wicked grin was back. Natasha's stomach turned a somersault as she tried to remain calm, but the excitement of the possibilities with this man seemed so tempting.

"Not whilst I am a married woman."

"Oh! That long? We are talking about a long time, aren't we?" Daniel looked down at her small hands in his. Not looking at her, but she could still see the disappointment on his face.

"Daniel, I can't talk about this. I want to, but I can't tell you."

"Yet?"

"Believe me, I will tell you as soon as I can."

"OK, I ..." He didn't look convinced, and the hesitation in his voice scared Natasha. She knew she was asking him to trust her.

"I know I am not being fair, Daniel, so I am going to leave you to think about this. I am in room 108. If you don't come, then I understand. I hope you can trust me," she paused to watch his face, "but I get it." And although she continued to look into his green eyes, Daniel didn't answer her. She stood up and walked quietly out of the park and turned back towards the hotel.

It took a long time for Natasha to break into a run. She ran not because she was in a hurry but because running helped her process her thoughts. Right now, there was so much to work through.

The manager was on duty as she collected her key from the desk. She went through the motions of ordering an early breakfast tray and a taxi ahead of her train home in the morning. She still did not know if she wanted Daniel to knock on her door later or not.

There was a heaviness in her steps as she climbed the stairs to her floor. Each step seemed steeper than the last. In her room, she turned on the TV news and lay spread-eagled on the bed, one arm hung over the side. Resigned to her fate. She had to wait for Daniel to decide. Natasha hoped she'd said enough to help him decide to wait for her, but in her chest, it felt like she was asking him too much. Watching him dancing, chatting, and laughing with all the other women at Ben's party had not been something she enjoyed. The ease with which he did it, should have been ringing alarm bells. Emma insisted he only danced with them so he could have that brief dance with her. Was she being a fool? Would he come to her room still expecting to have sex with her? Or would he think she was too much trouble?

As she pulled her phone from the holder on her arm, a text bounced in from Jack.

JW: Just checking you have your ticket for tomorrow. I'll pick you up from the station. MP got an online meeting.

MRS: All OK here.

Who was she fooling? She was far from OK. And now, what did she do? Did she wait for Daniel to join her? She stared at the blue door as if she was able to will him to come through and scoop her into his arms like a conquering hero. *There you go again. Putting a man on a pedestal, as if he can save you.* Natasha hated how her mother's voice would echo through her head. Criticising her relationships. *Save me from what, Mother?*

Anastasia Webb had adored Matt and thought he could do no wrong. To her, he was the perfect husband for her only child. To be fair, he wasn't a terrible man, far from it. That's what made all this so difficult.

Sitting up, it horrified her to see her face in the mirror. She was going to need a lot of makeup tomorrow or a lot of sleep. She was pretty sure that seeing Daniel in the park would not cure her poor sleep.

Shaking her hair, she surveyed her already immaculate room. She swept away the one stray lipstick still out before checking the room door was unlocked and then slipped into the bathroom. *I'm doing this for myself, not for a man. Who am I kidding? I want him to come and yet I don't. A shower and a good night's sleep. That is what I need.*

Natasha took her time in the shower. She told herself she was indulging in self-care, but only a tiny speck of her brain believed that. Through her mind danced images of Daniel emerging from the shower in her dressing room, clutching that ridiculously small towel. A new image of Daniel bursting through the bathroom door this time and walking straight into the shower to join her, clothes and all. All this fantasising was new to Natasha. She had always tried to be the realist that living with her parents had prepared her for. She thought about her ever-practical parents meeting for the first time. They had never talked much about that. George Webb was a well-built man even now, and she knew from the photographs she had seen that they were a stunning couple in their younger years. Anastasia Webb always looked wonderful, but Natasha never saw her show affection to anyone.

After carefully washing and conditioning her hair, Natasha stood longer in the shower. She tried to imagine the water washing away all her worries. Her fear of having this new relationship splashed across the internet as some sordid affair, that this was going to be over before it had even begun. She tried to find images that told a different story. She tried to picture a time with Daniel when they could walk hand in hand. A time when they could stand next to each other at a party. When she dared to look at him without giving away her secret.

Natasha wasn't sure how long she had stood under the rain head of the shower, but the hard, driving water was now cold and prickling her skin. She reluctantly stepped out and wrapped herself in a towel and returned to the main room of her suite. The green of the cricket pitch filled one side of the room. Once again she found herself lost in picturing a future where she could be happy with Daniel.

By the time she had finished drying her hair, she knew in her heart that he wasn't coming. She had expected too much from him. He obviously wasn't interested. Natasha was both disappointed and relieved. Now she didn't have to navigate spending time alone, in a bedroom with Daniel Woods. She felt sure now that she wouldn't have been able to resist any persuasion from him to take things further.

Natasha tidied away the towels, and when her room was again in perfect order, she made herself comfortable on the bed with a cup of black coffee and her book. She glanced at the door, knowing it was still unlocked, but somehow she wasn't quite ready to lock it. Still hoping against hope that he would turn up.

The TV news channel was playing to itself as Natasha tried to focus on her romance novel. This chapter was getting steamy, and she wondered if it would have been safer to bring something less stimulating. As darkness fell, she snuggled down the bed and onto her side. She turned off the TV and reached to turn on her bedside lamp, only then did she realise she had left the light on in the bathroom. Pulling down the large t-shirt she was wearing to cover herself, she got up to turn it off. Just as she flicked the switch, the door to her room burst open.

Chapter 26

Daniel watched Natasha walking away, only when she finally broke into a jog did he turn and start to run in the opposite direction. *YET! She won't have sex with me, YET! She can't tell me yet!* The smile on his face was broad, and even Daniel was aware of how hard he was grinning. He shook his head.

Was that enough? Was that all he needed to know? He picked up the pace as he ran, his heart rate rising. The memory of those kisses in that tiny park stayed with him, dancing and tingling on his lips. The feel of her skin under his fingers was still there. He kicked up a gear as the road rose up the hill in front of him. Pushing himself harder now, wanting to feel his body respond. As he ran, the blood flooded to his cock. It had happened more than once. Getting aroused as he ran. The guys teased him about it. He tried to avoid it, but it still happened often when he was remembering a night before.

As he rounded the corner at the top of the hill, he was aware of the tendons around his knee pulling. Reluctantly, he slowed and then slowed some more until, at last, he was walking. Time to think about what he was going to do. That was what she said, 'think about it, Daniel'. At that moment, with her sitting astride his lap, her soft blue eyes focused on him, Daniel had no thought but to follow her to the waiting hotel room. He knew she wanted him to do that, and he wasn't going to disappoint her, was he? *I can behave myself just like I promised. Who am I kidding? Look at what happened already. Am I so weak? I am telling everyone that I want to be treated differently and then what am I doing? Sneaking into hotel rooms with a married woman. Where has all my resolve gone? No, I am not going to go like some lovesick adolescent panting after someone else's wife.*

Daniel pulled back his stiff shoulders and rotated his long arms, stretching, and going through his regular routine. Stretching his neck, pushing each ear in turn down to his broad shoulders. So now what? He walked slowly up North Road past Zinc PR. The office where he had promised India and Tilly he was going to do this. No, he had to be sensible. He had done enough wild things in pursuit of sex. His energy slumped, taking his shoulders down, and his smile was gone.

As he rounded the corner onto Ash Road, Charlie's house came into view. Maybe he could call in and see the gang there. He did have a few questions about the next set of shows for Gym Away. *You keep telling yourself that, Daniel, my boy.*

Charlie opened the door and seemed overly pleased to see him.

"Daniel, come on in, just the man I want."

"Me?"

"Yes! Come and see India."

Charlie led him through to the lounge area of the great room. India was curled up on the sofa, her eyes closed. "Ah! Maybe not just yet." Daniel looked to Charlie, who gestured for him to go on.

"Tea?" The question had taken him by surprise. It was then that Daniel realised he didn't know why he had come to Charlie's house, other than he didn't think he should go to the hotel, and he wasn't ready to go home.

"If I am in the way, I can just go …" Daniel turned to leave again, but Charlie grabbed his arm and turned him back.

"Not just yet, Dan, I want a word." Daniel could see the ordinarily cheerful Charlie was looking worried.

Daniel lowered his voice. "Is it about India? Is she OK?"

"I wish I knew. She is shattered after today's event. She's been stressing about it all week. Her dad being here didn't help." Charlie admitted, and then he repeated his first question. "Tea?"

"Thanks, Charlie yeah, I'll have a drink."

"Have you been jogging after your physio?" Charlie narrowed his eyes, taking in Daniel.

"Not far, just to stretch out, you know." Daniel wasn't sure Charlie was convinced but he didn't ask again, just made himself busy making the drinks.

As he handed Daniel a mug, Charlie again gestured for Daniel to follow him out of the kitchen and into the other room at the front of the house. It housed some gym equipment and the gear that came with having two pro cricketers living there. Charlie sat down on a black weights bench and motioned for Daniel to sit on a second one.

"Daniel, you remember when I asked you to drive last time you went to the studio?"

"Yes, of course. I can do that again if you like. We didn't have to use the excuse last time."

"This is a bigger ask, mate. Could you go to the studio without India next week?"

Daniel didn't reply. He had no problem getting to the studio on his own and doing the shows was becoming easier, but he wasn't sure he was up to all the jobs that India did. "I don't know Charlie. I have no idea all the things she does. What about Tilly?"

"Joe tells me she is constantly tired. Tilly says she is expecting a fresh burst of energy any day, but I can see Joe is not happy about her going."

"What about Joe?"

"Hang on." Charlie left him sipping his tea and came back with his phone in his hand and smiling.

"Joe says thank you. Can't believe we didn't think of that before."

"Probably because those two have been all over this from the start. So, Joe is going to come and do all the talking to the buyer and sticking all the kits over the set?"

"Doing what?"

"Tilly and India. They like to tweak all the shelves and things. Paul usually has everything out for them."

"Paul?"

"A guy at the studio who does all those jobs. I think he is the Floor manager. Of course, it might not be him this time?"

"So, how do we find out more about that? And Dan," Charlie paused and looked hard at Daniel, "without stressing Tilly and India out?"

Daniel shrugged his shoulders.

"Could you ask Tash?"

Daniel sighed and looked away. "God, Dan! What have you done now?"

"Nothing."

"Nothing? Really? Our friend Tilly seems to think that there is something between you two. And she isn't letting it go. She's a bloodhound where romance is concerned."

"Charlie, Natasha is a married woman. And you know my thoughts on that." Daniel was looking into his tea. He refused to look at his friend.

"Dan mate, not all women are your mother."

"Is that why you think I don't…" Daniel didn't finish what he was going to say, he couldn't. No one knew about Sarah, and he intended to keep it that way.

"My reasons are my own."

"But you know her well enough to ask her about all this, right?"

"I guess I could."

"Thanks, mate."

Daniel checked his watch; he could go and talk to her about it now. She needed to know he wasn't going to her room. It was wrong to leave her not knowing if he was going or not. He pulled out his phone to text her.

As he opened the screen, the app showed his run. Seeing his pause at the park and Daniel realised he couldn't do this in a text. She was more than that. He would go speak to her and explain everything. Well, maybe not quite everything.

Chapter 27

As Daniel took the last step of the stairs onto the first floor, his heart was beating faster than ever. He had walked as calmly as he could from Charlie's house on Ash Road down the hill to the hotel where Natasha was waiting for him. He checked his watch again. She would have given up waiting by now, surely. It was getting dark. Perhaps he should send a text after all. He certainly didn't think he could make a phone call.

No, be a man. Speak to the woman. She doesn't bite. Maybe it would be nice if she did. Daniel opened the stairwell door as quietly as he could and walked down toward the door that said 108. He stood outside, looking at the light spilling out around the frame. *She is still up then. I'm not sure I can do this.*

But Daniel couldn't debate the subject any longer. His heart rate increased again as soon as he realised that the lift doors were about to open. He couldn't be seen outside her room, so he dived in. He would explain.

As he stepped in, the lights went out and the only light came from a small blue lamp at the side of the bed. Natasha was standing immediately behind the door and shrieked with surprise as his body bounced into hers.

Daniel grabbed at her, putting his hand across her mouth.

"Shh, someone is coming."

Looking down, he realised he had startled her, and he let go but held his finger up to his lips.

"Daniel?" she hissed quietly.

"Shh," he was speaking in hushed tones. "Sorry, I was going to knock. I didn't know if you would be asleep. Then, someone started to come down the corridor, and I just dived in to avoid being seen. I did the right thing, didn't I?" Daniel's green eyes rapidly searched her face.

"I waited too long, didn't I? I can go as soon as the coast is clear," and he turned to open the door again.

"Don't go. Not yet anyway."

"I'm sorry. I can go any time you tell me to go. Well, when the coast is clear."

"Would it be hard for you… to be seen leaving my room?"

"Oh no, Natasha, I thought we couldn't be seen. You said… I mean, what would your husband say?"

"He knows."

"He knows? About me?"

"Well, not you, in particular. I didn't tell him anything. They guessed."

"They?" Daniel searched her face. Just how much was she not telling him?

Natasha opened her mouth to speak, but someone began pounding on her door.

"NATASHA! NATASHA! ARE YOU STILL AWAKE?"

"Emma!" she hissed to Daniel. Daniel looked at her for a split second and opened the door.

Emma stumbled in, followed by a very apologetic Nick.

"Daniel, you came. Did you know it's my birthday? I am so glad we found you. For Natasha, I mean." Nick was holding on to her elbow and trying to steer her back to the door. Emma kept moving forward, lurching towards Daniel. *How the hell do I deal with this?*

"Happy Birthday Emma." He smiled as she fell forward, her head hitting his chest. Daniel hugged her and kissed the top of her head before standing her upright again. Natasha looked scared as she edged her way back to the bed. Daniel tried to keep it all light and friendly.

"Daniel, thank you for looking after Tasha…" She grabbed at his arm. "She's my friend, you know, and I have been telling her."

Nick tried again. "Emma, come on, sweetheart. You can talk to Tash tomorrow."

Emma pulled her arm away from Nick and sat down on the bed.

"I can't 'cos she is going back to her cheating husband tomorrow." From the shocked expression on his face, Daniel thought this was the first time Nick had heard this news. But when Daniel looked at Natasha, he could see her struggling.

Her voice was breaking as she said, "Emma, sweetie, go back with Nick. I'll call you in the morning. We can chat whilst I'm on the train."

"I'm glad you've got Daniel now. He hasn't got a secretary to have sex with. You haven't? Have you, Daniel?"

Natasha looked away from him as a silent tear fell from her cheek. She wasn't looking at anyone in the room anymore. Daniel's heart broke for her. Is that it? A cheating husband? If so, why couldn't she explain?

He was lost. He wanted to go to her, to hold her close and stroke her hair, to wipe away her tears. Somehow, the room seemed too crowded for that. He froze.

Nick broke the silence.

"Shit, Tash, I knew it was bad, but she hadn't said why. Come on, Emma. Time to go."

"No! I'm too tired." She laughed as she collapsed backwards, laying across Natasha's bed.

"Come on, sleepy head." Nick scooped her up and carried her towards the door.

"I need to take the birthday girl back to her room." Daniel opened the door for them. Nick stopped in the doorway and looked back at Natasha. "I'm sorry Tash. Sorry for the interruption and sorry about... well, just sorry for everything."

Daniel closed the door behind them. He stood with his back to her and his hand on the handle of the door. Every inch of him wanted to follow Nick out of the room and keep going. He had stuff to process. But first, he needed to make sure Natasha was going to be all right.

His decision made, he turned around and walked back into the room. He crossed the room swiftly, stopping only when he reached the kettle.

"Tea, I think." He said nothing else, just busied himself making the drinks. Daniel kept his back towards Natasha. He couldn't watch her cry. He hoped that giving her space was the right thing to do. Maybe this wasn't the time, but he felt sure there was more he should know.

Daniel produced two cups of tea and passed one to Natasha as she sat up in her bed.

"Well! I guess now everyone knows!"

"Everyone?"

"Well, they know about you, and you and Nick now know about them?

"So, is that what you couldn't tell me?"

"Yes.

"And they know about me?"

"God! I've said too much already."

"I'm sorry, Natasha, I'm confused. Maybe this is why I don't go out with married women." Daniel put down his tea and walked towards the door.

"NO! Daniel, I'm the one who needs to apologise. If you want to walk away from this, I totally understand. I can see why you wouldn't want to get involved with me. I'm not even sure I should be interested in someone who would go out with a married woman. How silly is that?"

"I don't know, but then I don't know what is going on in your life. And, of course, you keep saying you can't tell me."

Sitting up in the bed now, her professional smile firmly in place, she smoothed down the cover and tried again. Daniel could see how hard this was for her, so he walked back and sat down next to her on the bed.

"My husband, Matthew is an MP."

"I know that, well, I know that now."

"Anything happening in our lives can be used against him. Let's just say there are plenty of people who would use anything to get him moved from his job."

"Is what Emma said true? Is your husband having an affair with his secretary?"

"God, yes!" more tears escaped, and Daniel slid his arm across her shoulders.

"I'm sorry Tasha."

"It's OK." Daniel wasn't sure he believed her, but she kept talking.

"It's true. Honestly, Daniel, our marriage had drifted so far. I think I was filling my time at work and trying to still be the good MP's wife. We started to talk about splitting up 'when the time was right' but the time is never right. When he fell in love with someone else, it hurt, but it was no surprise. He agreed to divorce but asked me to wait until after the election and, well, that keeps getting pushed back."

Daniel squeezed her shoulder as they sat in silence, staring at the wall. Questions were forming in Daniel's head. He waited until he felt she was ready. Then he put down his mug. Turning to her to take both her hands in his.

"I've got some questions." Daniel looked for a response. "If you'll let me ask them?" Tasha nodded. "And if you don't feel you can tell me, then that's just fine."

"Daniel, it's not fine, but thank you for saying it is." Daniel was still watching her closely.

"Your husband, Matthew? Are you still in love with him?"

"Matthew and I have been friends for a long time. I guess I will always love him." Daniel dropped her hands and swallowed. "But Daniel, I am not in love with him, and I am not sure we ever were in love. When I see him now, in love with someone else, I don't remember it ever being like that with us."

"You are planning on getting divorced, but it's a timing thing, so how far have you got with that?" Natasha grabbed Daniel's forearm, her eyes pleading with him to understand.

"It's the Press, you see."

"Oh, I know about the Press."

"So, you understand if I even google divorce, they will sniff it out. So no, Matthew has said I can divorce him on the grounds of adultery, but the only person I have talked to is Emma. Even my dad doesn't know."

"My dad would be the last person I would tell."

"I am close to Dad, so it's weird I haven't told him. I think he'll be more upset I haven't confided in him than he'll be about the actual divorce."

"I can see we have different relationships with our dads! But even so, I understand, Natasha. It must be hard watching each person's reaction. They will all be different. I guess the important question is, how do you feel about all this?"

"Sorry?"

"Tasha, this is your life. Forget your dad, the Press, Matthew. How do you feel about this? When that divorce comes through, how will you feel?"

"Well, we all have to do what we have to do, don't we? We sometimes must do things we don't like." She was using her work face. The professional smile.

"Look, I understand if you don't want to tell me, you can say that, but at the moment, you haven't answered the question. I guess I want to know if this," he pointed between them, "if you and me, is just a fling. Is it something for you to feel better about yourself?"

"Oh, Daniel no. You and me, I wish I knew how I felt. I guess I have turned off my emotions over the last few years. Matthew and I had drifted apart long before this affair. I was just getting on with my life and building up my career. I wasn't looking for someone else."

"And now?"

"We said earlier about being honest, didn't we?"

"Yes, I need you to be honest. I get that there might be things you can't tell me. But please, Tasha, the last thing I want you to do is to lie to me."

Daniel watched her swallow hard and then look away. Her fingers were rolling the edge of the duvet. "Sorry, that is a stupid question. I don't even know how I feel. Perhaps I am putting pressure on you to give the answers because this doesn't make sense to me. I should have just kept on running."

"Why didn't you?" Daniel bit the side of his mouth. *Because Charlie asked me a favour. Don't tell her that. I wouldn't be here if I didn't want to.*

"That's a fair question. The answer is lost to me, though. It's hard to explain. This attraction to you is not something I have felt before. It's definitely very physical. And then something more than the physical. That day outside the studio, I saw sadness in your eyes, and I wanted to change that. No more than that, I wanted to be the one who made you smile again. A real smile, not that one you use at work."

"Oh!" She looked down at her hands and smoothed out the duvet she had been gripping so tightly. "I think I know what you mean. It's an attraction but it's more. But I hardly know you. And how do we get to know each other like this?"

"Would you come up to the farm? It's in the middle of nowhere. We could spend some time together. Just the two of us.".

"I don't know Daniel."

"Well, will you think about it?"

"That I can do."

"Now what?"

"If you make more tea, there are biscuits in the cupboard, and we could try just spending time together?"

"We could try."

Daniel took off his shoes, made tea, and they settled down on the bed. Natasha was under the covers, and they sat side by side watching the TV. Drinking tea and enjoying biscuits, although Daniel ate most of them. It was all very normal until he accidentally put his hand down over hers.

For a split second, he thought to lift it again, but it felt too good, and she hadn't moved away. So, he stroked the back of her hand with his thumb. Gently enjoying the smoothness of her skin under his.

She turned to smile at him and, without stopping to think, he dipped his head and softly kissed her lips. Natasha's hand turned under his, palm to palm. She interlocked her delicate fingers into his powerful hand.

Daniel pushed on with the kiss, nibbling at her lower lip as he gently caressed her ear under her hair. Natasha responded to the kiss. Opening her lips, her tongue reached out. Daniel pulled her face to his, deepening the kiss, and devouring her mouth.

When the kiss ended, Natasha rested her head on his chest. His arm went around her shoulders, protectively holding her to him. It felt good. *Is it just me?*

"It feels right, doesn't it? Or did I go too far?"

"It feels right, Daniel. I can't believe how right it feels."

"Did you want me to go?"

"I must leave early in the morning. I've got a train to catch. So actually… Damn, what am I saying? I don't want you to go, Daniel. Can you stay?"

"Good." It was just one word, but it said all he wanted to say and with that one word, he pulled her closer. Feeling her resting against him felt wonderful. He wanted to hold her there and protect her from this man who had not just stopped loving her. He had been sleeping with someone else and she knew about it. Daniel wasn't sure he could be as patient as she seemed to be. Natasha was curled into his side, and her hands started to explore him. Daniel held his breath as her hand moved lower until it was cupping him through his clothes. Despite his efforts, his body was responding to her being so close, remembering what it felt like when her lips had held him.

"Natasha, you said no sex. If you've changed your mind, you will have to tell me. I heard you, but bits of me might not have got the message."

"Sorry." She sat up and pulled away. *What did I say that for?*

"It's hard for me. I just don't want to get this wrong."

"I know what you mean, but Daniel, I can't remember a time when Matthew wasn't in my life. I haven't done this with anyone but him."

"I see."

"I'm sure you have been with a few more girls than one."

"You could say that. But this is new ground for me, too."

"I don't understand."

"I've never set out to have a relationship with a married woman. It's always been a hard no for me."

They sat in silence, holding hands, not looking at each other. Natasha stood up and walked to the window. The T-shirt she was wearing barely reached her legs. Daniel watched her. He wanted to make this easy for her. He didn't know what that meant.

When his phone buzzed with a text, he took the opportunity to be distracted.

Romeo: Don't worry about asking Tasha. All sorted.

"Now he bloody tells me."

"Sorry?"

"Charlie, he wanted me to ask you something, and now he says it's all sorted."

"Is that why you came?" Daniel looked at her, but he didn't answer. "Daniel?"

"No, well yes, it was just …" He stopped talking. He could see the hurt in her eyes.

"I didn't trust myself to be with you in a bedroom and not want to … I wasn't sure how … you said no sex … but things were pretty heated in the park. I thought a bedroom might be even harder." Natasha turned back to look out of the window. Daniel stood up and went to stand behind her. He threw his arms around her waist and kissed the top of her head.

"Natasha, I'm sorry I'm rubbish at this. I'd decided not to come to the hotel. I knew I had to let you know that. Then Charlie asked me a question about our next shows, and he asked me to ask you. Next thing I knew, I was outside your door, and someone was coming out of the lift."

He kissed her head again and hugged her.

"Then, well, Emma happened. And I thought we probably needed to talk after that."

"I'm sorry. Am I asking too much?" Natasha turned in his arms and wrapped her own arms around his waist. Her head buried into his hard body.

"I know you might not be happy that Emma let your secret out. But I'm fairly sure Nick is not the sort to say anything."

"Nick knows a lot of people in the Press. He works with them all the time. You'd be surprised what can slip out."

"He had plenty of opportunity to throw Charlie under the bus last year, but he didn't. Nick is one of the good guys."

"I know. See I promised Matthew and he won't be pleased."

"From what Emma said, he has someone to talk to. Why shouldn't you have someone in your corner? And you said they know about me?"

"They don't know who. They just guessed there is someone."

"This is your husband and his secretary. And they are having sex?"

"Yes."

"But you and I can't have sex?"

"I'm daft, right? It's just I feel if I am divorcing him for adultery, then I shouldn't be committing adultery myself." Daniel hugged her and kissed her crown.

"One day, Tasha, this country will catch up with places like Australia and we will have no-fault divorce. It's on its way."

"But you understand?"

"I understand you have to behave to your own rule book. Would it be easier if I just go?"

"It might be easier, but I know it's not what I want." She hugged him tighter. "When are you back at the studio?"

"A couple of weeks, but I'm guessing that's one place we have to be careful?"

"God, yes."

"Will you think about coming to the farm?"

"I'll think about it."

"And maybe another cricket match?"

"I don't know?"

"Do you still want me to stop texting?"

"NO!"

"Really?"

"Just be careful about what you say."

"So, no sexting?" he grinned. It made Natasha laugh. That warmed Daniel. He wanted to be the person who made her laugh. *Is that why I play the clown? Is it about hearing the laughter?*

"OK. Before I go, can I kiss you?"

"I guess so."

"Come here." Daniel took her hand and led her back to the bed. He sat down and looked up at her. She seemed to understand because she sat astride his knee again, just like in the park. Daniel let a soft smile sit on his lips as his hands held her face.

"Now, where were we? Oh yes, I remember." His lips gently touched her mouth, soft and exploring. Natasha fell into the kiss, opening her mouth and letting her tongue explore his. Their tongues danced together. It was a fun kiss. Daniel loved the way she played with him. Kissing this woman lit up his body. He dropped one hand to her leg, feeling the soft skin on her thigh. His heart beat strong and loud in his chest.

Daniel pulled out of the kiss and ended with one more kiss on her tiny nose.

"I think it's time for me to get going. If I don't go now, well, I just better go."

Natasha stood up and pulled her T-shirt down. Daniel stood up and hugged her.

"I'm going to leave you, but this is not the end for you and me, Tasha."

Chapter 28

DW: Did you get home OK?

Tasha: Train was delayed. A bit of a panic getting to the event.

DW: When are you working this week?

Tasha: Wednesday to Sunday. Going to Emma's tomorrow.

DW: Take care.

DW: I'm sitting here watching the replay of our last show. It feels weird.

Tasha: That is not always a good idea.

DW: I like that I can see you.

DW: I'm not happy that I can be that close to you and not touch you.

Tasha: Are you missing me then?

DW: Missing you? I wouldn't say that.

Tasha: You can go off people you know.

DW: If I said I was missing you, would it help you decide to come up for a visit?

Tasha: I'm still thinking about it.

The following day, she found a link to Google Maps in a text from Daniel. He was trying to show her just how isolated the farm was. It certainly seemed to be a possibility looking at the satellite images. There was plenty of land around the house which looked to be half a mile from the road. A quiet road at that. It was outside the town and towards the coast.

Daniel had told her they kept horses. His sister bred them. Most of the land, though was used to grow speciality crops for feeding some of the top-quality horse stock in the area. It did look tempting. There was clearly lots of space and HR at work were pushing her to take her holidays or lose them.

DW: New team when I come down next week. Joe is coming instead of Tilly.

Tasha: Is Tilly OK?

DW: Yes, but Joe wants her to rest more. If you ask me he is wasting his time. She'll only find something else to do whilst he is down here.

Tasha: So, You, Joe, and India?

DW: Nope India isn't coming either. She is sick more often than Tilly.

Tasha: Is she OK?

DW: Going for more tests. We are bringing Stella instead. She's India's cousin.

Tasha: I am working, so hopefully we will get time to talk.

DW: Hopefully?

Tasha: Yes if I end up on the shows opposite yours…it would be hard.

DW: I'm guessing a shower is out of the question?

Tasha: Sadly, it's a bit risky.

DW: I guess anything other than talking is going to be hard.

Tasha: It's not forever Daniel.

DW: It would be easier if I knew when I was going to see you somewhere I can touch you.

DW: Sorry I guess I shouldn't have sent that … …

DW: I'll behave.

DW: Tasha?

Tasha: Sorry couldn't answer for a while. They were here.

DW: He brings her there?

Tasha: It's not like that.

DW: Shit and I thought it was hard not seeing you.

The next day, Daniel sent her a series of photos. A grey horse was looking over a gate. A group of five black and white border collie dogs. A single pretty black and white dog that Daniel said was called Meg,

DW: Meg is waiting to meet you.

The next day he sent a series of views, including open grassland, paddocks with grazing horses, views out to sea and another photo of Meg. They all made Natasha smile. *I'm guessing he knows better than to send me a photo of him.*

She didn't need photos of Daniel Woods; she had found plenty on the internet. There was one of the whole county team and she was using it to learn their names and as much about them all as she could.

DW: We're setting off this afternoon. See you in the morning.

Tasha: Where are you staying,

DW: At Stella's. We usually stay there. Before you panic, we are staying in India's old flat. It's still empty.

Tasha: See you tomorrow then.

Chapter 29

Tasha: If you are my producer today, can you come and help with wardrobe choices?

EM:? You don't usually need my advice. Is this because of who the guest is?

Tasha: This is because I must pick something we sell.

EM: On my way.

Natasha got up and unlocked the door for her friend. Emma flicked dispassionately through the things hanging on Natasha's rail.

"I see what you mean." Screwing her face up, she looked at Natasha. "Which do you like?"

"I don't know."

"Excuse me? You usually have outfits picked out for the week."

"I know but…"

"Are you OK? You seem nervous. Is this about working with him?"

"Are you going to help?"

"Sure. I'm just glad you're speaking to me, after my drunken outburst when I gave away the family secrets." Emma went back to browsing the outfits they expected Natasha to wear.

"I can't believe I was asking him to trust me, but I didn't trust him. But Emma you told him. You trusted him."

"You were just protecting Matt. And I was drunk." Emma pulled out a blue set with an all-over flower print. "This one. Wear this one."

"Really?"

"Daniel will be in blue and green. Wear this one."

"Thanks, Emma."

"Are you that bothered about today?"

"Just nervous for some reason. India isn't coming, by the way."

"She's not?"

"Tilly's husband is coming, and they're bringing India's cousin Stella. From what he said, they stayed at her place last night."

"Any reason?"

"Tilly is pregnant, and India is throwing up. Daniel thinks she may be pregnant, too."

"I met Joe in Leeds, he seemed OK. I better get down and meet him. See you in the studio."

"I might come down early."

"I bet you will!"

When Natasha pushed open the heavy orange door to studio one, she froze at the sight in front of her. Daniel Woods was dressed in blue shorts and a cut-away green vest. In his arms was a smaller version of India. He was lifting her in the air so she could adjust the Gym Away packaging on top of the display. Natasha felt sick.

This was a new feeling. Suddenly, she understood Emma's jealousy of India. Why can't he just move the box for her? Why does he have to pick her up? How old is she?

Behind her, Paul cleared his throat.

"Sorry." She whispered.

"It's OK. We are showing a prerecord. The guest is stuck on a train coming down from Newcastle."

"OK, then."

"You're early Ms Poole. Then I guess this is your favourite guest."

"I beg your pardon?"

"You know what I mean, so don't be coy with me."

"Paul I…"

"Don't worry, my lips are, as always, sealed."

Before Natasha could respond, Daniel turned. He probably heard her voice. He said nothing, but the smile he gave her said everything she needed to know. Joe was standing at the work surface, playing with the product, and sifting through a set of cards. Daniel stood looking straight at her whilst the girl was still re-adjusting everything on the set. Natasha walked slowly over to the group. *What am I going to say when I get there? He looks good. Why is he looking at me like that?*

"Hello, do we have anything special planned for today?"

"Hi Tasha, have you met Joe and Stella?" His smile lit up the studio, or that's how Natasha felt. She returned his smile.

"Joe, I have met. Hi Joe. Hello Stella. How did you get dragged into this?"

"Hello. I am being paid for this job. Don't tell anyone, but I would do it for free just to put this on my CV." Joe looked up from his cards.

"Why didn't someone tell me that?"

"I see from the show list we don't have the new product yet."

"No. We're still working on that." Natasha should have been looking at Joe. He was the client. Her eyes hadn't left Daniel since she opened the studio door.

"Sorry, Daniel, could you lift me up again? I want to rotate that box some more."

"Wouldn't it be easier for Daniel to just move the box?" Natasha bit her lip as all eyes turned to her. No one spoke until Paul saved her.

"We have steps for that job. Here, let me show you where I keep all my cool tools."

Stella followed Paul to the shelving by the studio door. Joe looked down at the cards and Daniel smiled. Natasha wasn't sure what to do. She was fairly sure she was going red.

Daniel walked over to her.

"That's a different outfit."

"The boss wants me to wear something we sell. I'll have to give out the numbers for it but don't worry, any sales count for you." Joe's attention had been roused again.

"You mean you will be selling other products in our hour?"

"You aren't paying for this hour, but there is a way you can do that. Your buyer probably explained that."

"No, she didn't."

"I am sure she can explain all the different options if you ask. I wouldn't worry too much; I can't see this selling too much today. That's probably why they asked me to wear it."

"Can I just show Natasha the exercises we wanted to do this morning?" Joe frowned and passed the cards to Daniel.

"Do you know how many demos Emma will want today? It is Em, isn't it? Not that guy?"

"It's Em. three or four is usually good, but it's best if we have five ready. Maybe we should see if Em can come down?"

"Could I just show you first? I have one I think would look good if you do it." They were interrupted by Stella.

"Daniel, where will you be standing? Are you doing anything on the floor? I want to get this right." Natasha frowned. Stella sounded excited and seemed to spend too much time looking at Daniel.

"I'm hoping I can get Tasha on the floor." His impish grin was back.

"Daniel, do you ever meet a girl and leave her alone?" Joe growled.

"It's OK, Joe. He told me he doesn't flirt with married women. He told Tilly that's why he doesn't flirt with her." Daniel's eyes met Natasha's. She looked away.

"I'll go find Emma." She walked away, trying hard not to break into a run. As she got to the door, she saw Paul watching her, amused.

She flew up the stairs and into her own dressing room. Inside, she leaned against the door, her heart pounding. This was going to be hard. She had been worrying about not showing her feelings today, but she hadn't considered she would feel jealous. It was a new emotion for her. One she had to get used to since Matthew had fallen for Jack. She wasn't even sure which one she was jealous of! Jack had taken her heart when he walked into their lives. Why was she so jealous around Daniel?

She closed her eyes and tried to slow down her breathing. It was 55 minutes, and she could do it. She did it every week.

Natasha had been planning to tell Daniel she would go up to see him at the farm. She was tired and her dad had been urging her to take a break. Avoiding being at home meant she had been working as many days as she could, and now they were pushing her to take her holidays or lose them.

Seeing Daniel with Stella had made her rethink.

DW: Are you OK?

TASHA: Fine

DW: I didn't realise it was that bad

TASHA: ?

DW: I don't know a lot about women, but I know when they say fine you are in trouble.

DW: I'm sorry.

TASHA: Daniel you have done nothing wrong.

DW: I've missed you.

TASHA: Can we just get through today?

DW: Is it Stella?

TASHA: No.

DW: I thought it would stop people looking at us.

TASHA: It's fine.

DW: Have you thought about coming up to Yorkshire?

TASHA: Can we please just get through today?

DW: Sorry.

Natasha sighed. Why are men so difficult? They make noises to suggest they are trying, but they do the stupidest things. She was going to say yes to going to the farm. Why couldn't she just say yes when he asked? *Because you want to be independent after this last relationship.*

She brushed her hair, and as she looked into the mirror she saw the door ajar to her bathroom. Her imagination brought Daniel back through that door with his tiny towel. *I am fantasising about the first man I've seen naked. Is this just a fling? Is this my ego checking out if I'm still attractive?*

She smiled at her reflection and offered herself some sound advice.

"For now, just go do this show and then the next one. Today is not a day for making decisions. God, now I'm talking to myself again. Is that why I miss Mikey?"

"Grrr!" She stood and adjusted the edges of the Lycra suit.

A slow deep breath was needed to take her calmly back down the stairs to studio one.

Paul swung open the huge studio door in front of her.

"You ready now?"

"I'm ready."

She took her place on the set next to Daniel. She reached out her hand and pulled him closer. He smiled down at her. With that smile, everything else fell into place. Daniel stood at her side, and the warmth flowed through her, and it all seemed clearer to her.

Emma, in her ear, seemed happy too.

"Tash, keep him closer if you can." Natasha was doing her best, but today Daniel seemed to find it hard to stand still.

Paul started the countdown.

5   I can do this.

4   What is this feeling?

3   Maybe I should go to Yorkshire?

2   Well, here we go.

1   Smile Natasha.

"God, he is talking so fast. I am putting up the product slide for you to do the numbers whilst Paul tries to get him to calm down."

Natasha fell into professional mode.

"981 751 is the product code. Online, on the phone or on the app. And just like everything you buy from More.U TV, your Gym Away is covered with our 30-day money-back guarantee. Place your order today and you will have this fabulous exercise product at home by the weekend." From the corner of her eye, she could see Paul talking to Daniel. Both men were smiling and looking at her. She smiled back.

Daniel demonstrated the first exercise from the mat on the floor. Natasha watched from the side.

"Hmm, Ms Poole can you take your eyes off the guest? And focus on the job."

Natasha straightened the smile on her face and looked at her notes.

"I want you to do the next exercise, Tash. It's women watching. Let them see this is for them. When you do the numbers again, I'll put up the product slide. I think we need some of that famous chemistry. I would like to get a few more units through the checkout. I'll put the card up for your outfit once you are on the floor."

"Thank you, Daniel. Can you show me something I could do next?"

"I certainly can." Daniel's eyes lit up and a smile spread across his face. He picked up the resistance bands and adjusted them.

"We have had some questions about my new suit, so I am going to give you the details of that whilst you get that ready Daniel."

When the product card was on the screen, Natasha made her way over to Daniel and placed her hand over his. She tried to squeeze him, to reassure him. They still needed him to calm down. She looked into his eyes to try to get the message over without speaking. Daniel placed his large hand over both their hands and offered her a soft smile.

The demonstration went well if the comments Emma was making in her ear were a good guide.

"Brilliant Tash. They are sitting in baskets though; we need to check them out if we get them to count in this hour."

"If you want to make sure you get your Gym Away for this weekend, please remember to check out your baskets." Natasha stood up and Daniel held out his hand to help her. She took it and instantly regretted the move. Emma was coughing in her ear.

"We've sold out every time we have had this product here. We don't know when the guys from Gym Away are due back. If you have been thinking about this, if you missed out last time, if you want to tighten those spare inches, then check out now."

"Well done, Tash. Let Daniel do one more."

"Daniel, can you show us one more example of what we can do with this fabulous bit of kit? Something that is stretching, perhaps."

When Daniel bent over to show her the next stretch, she was left looking at the rear view of him. His shorts looked to be straining but much more sensible than the fabled pair that left nothing to the imagination. Natasha felt her face flush at the idea.

They finished the show with Daniel doing the packing away demonstration. The overhead camera was focusing on his hands, and Natasha found herself doing the same. She was transfixed.

"One last set of numbers Tash, please, and we are there." Natasha went into reeling off the numbers on automatic pilot.

"That's it. I'll count you out whilst you thank the guest."

"Thank you, Daniel. Sadly, that is all we have time for in this show. But you are back on the air at 2 o'clock, so you have time for a break."

"6, 5."

"Daniel will be back with Alex Dunn at 2 pm."

"2, 1 and we are out."

Paul pulled the camera across to the next set and Natasha relaxed. Daniel lifted her into the air, and the panic returned. He seemed to realise his mistake and slowly lowered her to the floor.

"Sorry, Tasha, but that was wonderful. It's so much easier when I work with you."

"Good luck with this afternoon."

"Could we have lunch together?"

"Oh, Daniel, I wish I could, really I do, but it's not a good idea here."

Chapter 30

Natasha had spirited away, probably upstairs to her changing room. A massive part of him wanted to ask her to use her shower, but he didn't want to cause any problems for her. He knew she was going through so much already.

He made his way to the green room, where he found a smug-looking Joe and a bouncing Stella.

"I need to move some things before the next show. Do you think I can go to the studio?"

"You would need to ask Paul."

"How do I find Paul?" The door opened and Paul floated in.

"You were looking for me?"

"Yes but how…" Paul smiled and removed Daniel's mic pack.

"Oh, the mic!"

"Just a coincidence, we are short of mic packs today and there are three guests on the show in an hour, and two guests on now." Paul slowly looked up and down Joe Cookson.

"Are you going to join Dan this afternoon?"

"God no! I'm hoping the girls are fit to come back next time, I'm nervous just watching in here."

"Where are the fabulous duo today?"

"Tilly is having our first baby. She keeps telling me the next phase will be better, and she is due a burst of energy any day."

"And India?"

"India is still struggling to stop being sick. I think it's sympathy for Tilly, but Dan here thinks she might be pregnant too." Stella's face ran through a full range of emotions from joy to distress when she finally said. "Fudging heck, I hope not."

"Charlie is hoping I'm right. Is it really a problem?"

"It'll be the final straw for Maria Barrington Jones - India's mother- she can't cope with them living together without being married as it is."

"I better get this mic back."

"Right then, Joe, where's my lunch?"

"Lunch?"

India and Tilly usually have sandwiches and stuff."

"And stuff?"

"Salad, and cakes. There's always cakes."

"Sorry."

"Well, we have two hours, we can get some." Stella was on her phone looking at a map and Daniel looked at his phone. He was about to call Natasha when Emma walked into the green room.

"I came to say thank you, Daniel, that was a good show. The buyer will be in soon and will go through the numbers with you, Joe."

"I was just going to dash out to buy the team sandwiches or something. I wasn't told it was part of my job. But if I need to talk to the buyer..." Joe looked at Daniel.

"We are in your car, mate."

"Ah yes."

"I'm just heading out; I can take you to the supermarket if you like."

"You go, Daniel, I want to find Paul and change some things, now I have seen all his kit."

Daniel followed Emma out to the car park. As they drove past the gate, Emma laughed.

"Well, this will give them all something to talk about."

"Really?"

"I don't know. At least Nick knows you're with Tash so that's OK." Daniel sat silently looking ahead. He didn't know how to respond. *So, Nick thinks I'm 'with' Tasha, does that mean Emma believes I'm with her?*

"You are awfully quiet over there Mr Woods. Something wrong?"

"It's just what you said, that 'Nick knows I'm with Tasha'. Has she said something?"

Emma sighed. "She doesn't say anything. She plays everything so close to her chest. But we both saw you that night and I've seen her reaction today."

She looked across at Daniel. He didn't want to look at her. What could he say? He got the impression that Emma knew everything, but he couldn't be sure.

"Has she forgiven you for telling Nick and me about her husband?"

"She says so. I think she wanted you to know, to understand, but she is so loyal to Matt, she couldn't tell you herself."

"Well, I'm glad I know a bit more. I have been trying to persuade her to come out to the farm for a few days so we can spend some time together."

"Daniel, that's a wonderful idea. She seriously needs a break. She wasn't good before, but since they lost that dog, well she really is struggling if you ask me."

"Do you think so? What can I do to persuade her to say yes."

"That's a hard one. Don't push too hard. It might be easier if it's her own idea."

"I don't think I'll ever understand this relationship stuff."

"A relationship? Is that what you are looking for?" Daniel sat quiet, looking out the window. That was the question. Was he ready for a real relationship?

"It's OK. I don't think Tash knows the answer to that herself. What I think she needs is to see what life will look like on the other side of this divorce." Emma stopped talking to focus on turning right into the supermarket car park. When she finally parked up she turned to look at Daniel. "But Daniel this has been hard on her. Maybe I don't know what she needs right now, but I do know she doesn't need to be messed around."

"Emma, I promise you I have no plans to do anything to upset Natasha."

"Promise?"

"I promise."

Presenting with Daniel

The afternoon show went well. Stella was excited and Joe was happy with the sales figures. He spent a full hour talking to the buyer about what they would do next, showing them new products, and talking about the plans for the next six months.

Daniel was feeling confident with how things were going at last. No one could dispute that he was doing well presenting and not just with Natasha. He was doing a good job, and the product was selling.

"Daniel, I know the girls asked you to do three sets of shows. I hope you'll consider doing some more. If things go according to plan, we might look at adding more things after the end of the season. Will that work for you?"

"I don't see why not. Things are quieter on the farm during the colder months."

Daniel smiled inwardly. If he kept coming to More.U TV, then he would still keep bumping into Natasha. That meant more opportunities to build on getting her to take him seriously.

He wanted to see her, to say goodbye and maybe a little more. While Stella was talking to Paul and Joe was talking to Tilly back home, he slipped out of the green room and made his way upstairs.

With mixed emotions, he knocked quietly on her door. Every time he did that, it was with some fear of what would happen next. He was relieved when Natasha opened her door before anyone else came along the corridor.

"Hi, I just came to thank you for this morning and say goodbye."

"Come in Daniel." Daniel strode through the door and closed it firmly behind him.

"I thought you might never ask. Now as I was saying..." he gripped Natasha's arms and pulled her close. Dipping his head, he kissed her. Without hesitating, Natasha kissed him back. They seemed to have found a rhythm to kissing. There was no awkwardness. Daniel's arms dropped to encircle her and pull her closer to him.

"There, that's how I like to say thank you. I really don't want to say goodbye, I want to say, 'see you soon'."

He bent down again to kiss her. Natasha returned the kiss and hugged him back, too.

"Oh, Daniel, this is so hard."

"Come up to the farm, come to another match?" Natasha smiled at his eagerness.

"I'll think about it."

"In that case, I need to say goodbye, so where was I?" He pulled her back into his body and made sure this was a kiss she would not forget.

Chapter 31

DW: How are you today? I see you're working again.

Tasha: Just covering for people who are away. It's a busy time.

DW: When are you taking time off?

Tasha: I don't like being at home at the moment.

DW: Then come up sooner.

Tasha: I'm still thinking about that.

DW: Everyone needs a break. I'll be working. You can recharge.

Tasha: I'll see.

Natasha was so frustrated with herself as much as anyone else. *Why am I resisting? Everything seems so much harder without Mikey*. Was that her only problem? Was this feeling of being lost and alone, simply because of the breakdown of her marriage or was the loss of her constant companion the problem?

She couldn't keep hanging out at Emma's flat so much. But tonight, they were enjoying a night in with a bottle of red wine and a movie. When they hit the scene where the lovers broke up, she got up and went to the kitchen and put on the kettle.

"Are you alright?"

"Yes. Just fancied a drink."

"So, it's not because this guy looks decidedly like Matthew Poole?"

"No."

"Liar. Time to get it off your chest. What has been dragging you down?"

"And drag you down too. I'll pass."

"Seeing you so unhappy and not knowing what to do about it is pretty shitty anyway. Come on, tell me what is going on in your head."

"It's nothing. I probably need to stop filling up your spare room."

"And?"

"I've been feeling guilty." She looked in the cupboard to find cups.

"Guilty?"

"For abandoning Mikey to my dad for half the week."

"Is that all?"

"And for abandoning Matthew to do more days at the studio."

"You can forget both of those. You were made for more than that."

"Guilt is a funny emotion, though. And without Mikey, the house is so lonely."

"You haven't booked your holidays in yet."

"What would I do?"

"Relax, enjoy some time off."

"Emma, you know how much I hate being home these days."

"Don't you have an invitation to go to Yorkshire?"

"Do I need any more complications in my life?"

"Tasha, just go and relax."

"You were the one who said don't get serious about a farmer."

"It's a few days. You are not moving in. Anyway, time on a farm might just show you it isn't the life for you. Better to find out now."

"Why now?"

"So, when Matthew finally says you can start that divorce, you'll know whether you want to take things further with Mr Woods." Natasha didn't respond, instead she studied the cup in her hand.

"Just say yes Tash. You need a break." Natasha put the cup back.

"Pass the wine."

The girls enjoyed the rest of the film and spent the rest of the evening talking about work and those things they never got to finish. When Natasha settled down in her bed, she spotted a recent text from Daniel.

DW: How about next Thursday?

Tasha: Yes.

DW: Brilliant.

Chapter 32

Tasha: My Train is delayed.

DW: Don't worry, I'll wait.

Tasha: Still the same place?

DW: I'll be there.

Natasha checked her watch. At least thirty minutes more and then three whole days with Daniel. She tugged her sleeve down and looked around at her travelling companions. No one was looking up from their phones, but somehow, she still kept expecting someone to recognise her. The tension rising through her body had come from realising this was like a 'first date', something she had not experienced before.

She already knew Matthew well before they ever went anywhere alone. And here she was about to start a 'date' that was going to last three days. Nick had assured her that Daniel was 'one of the good guys'. Emma had said, 'Just enjoy it. It doesn't have to go further'. It was just a long weekend after all, wasn't it? *It feels so much more important. Is that me? Am I making this into something it's not? This has to be more than a few stolen moments.*

She took another sip of water; her mouth was so dry. She picked up her book once more, but the words just sat there. Single words that didn't make sentences, no matter how many times she re-read them.

Closing her eyes, she tried to remember the layout of the station in Leeds. Hopefully, she could get lost in the crowd. Her eyes flashed open to check her sunglasses and a baseball cap were waiting at the top of her tote bag. She wasn't sure what to wear on the farm and hoped that trainers and jeans would work. He had said she could go running.

"This is recharge time for you, so read, run and relax." He had warned her he would be working, but she was there to take a break. He had challenged her about how many days she was working now. When she admitted it was because she didn't want to be at home, he had urged her just to come up as soon as she wanted. She had insisted she could wait. But right now, as the train got closer to the end of the line, she didn't think she could cope with any extra delays. The house had felt empty. Matt was spending more time in London, and now, without Mikey, she had never felt so alone. Just thinking about that brought back the hollow feeling that was eating away inside her. The texts she had exchanged with Daniel had been a lifeline.

The scenery outside the window changed, telling Natasha she was back in Leeds. It was a huge city compared to the town she lived in. She hoped that meant she could be invisible. As the train slowed, she pulled on her hat and sunglasses. She held her large tote and her wheeled case close in the crowds as they spilt onto the platform and out into the main concourse of the station. Her head down, she walked as swiftly as she could out of the exit and around the corner towards a waiting Daniel. A quick turn down a side street, her head still down. She could see what she thought was his car. Her stomach somersaulted. She kept her eyes down and tried to slow her breathing.

The plan was for her to just slip into the passenger seat, so she was shocked when the driver's door opened, and Daniel stepped out. Already on edge, she didn't know how to react when he strode toward her. She turned to look around. Finding the street empty, she began to relax and let the smile spread across her face. When Daniel reached her, he took the case and slung a long arm across her shoulders.

"Welcome back to Yorkshire."

"It's good to be here." It came out with the breath she had been holding. Daniel pulled off her cap and kissed the top of her head. Once they were in the car and moving, Daniel looked across at her.

"You can stop hiding now."

"What if …"

"You're here having a break, a much needed one, with a friend from work."

"And that's what you told your family?" She pulled off her sunglasses, watching for Daniel's response. She needed to see his face.

"Yes, everyone," he cringed, "but the people who know you already probably suspect it's more. Although most people seemed to agree you need a rest."

"Thanks for that. Boost a girl's confidence."

"Tasha, you're here now, so relax. I know being here hasn't changed the situation, but maybe it can help you see what life could be like."

"Have you been talking to Emma?" In less than twenty minutes together, she was already putting up the barriers.

"Sorry, it was only something she said when I was down with Joe. We were talking about Tilly and India. And she said you not only needed rest, but you also needed to see a future."

With a long sigh, Natasha looked out of the window. The hard part of that conversation was it was all true. She knew she was looking tired. And Emma had been right, she needed to start her new life, whatever that was. Her friend was always ready to remind her that Matthew had already moved on. But Emma was also quick to suggest that what this was with Daniel wasn't her long-term future.

Natasha was worried that she was the only one who wanted it to be more. Daniel was talking, and she listened. She was listening for clues to the man that was taking all her attention. As they approached Malton, Daniel got more animated. He kept up running commentary of who lived where, the schools he went to, and a million other stories. Each one telling Natasha a little more about the man who was starting to fill the hole in her life.

The rough track that led to the farmhouse rattled her against the side of the car. On both sides, she could see field after field. Daniel was still pointing things out to her, full of pride for this part of the world, this part of who he was. Eventually, when the Range Rover came to a stop it was in front of a large barn with a blue door.

As Natasha navigated a way to climb out of the high doorway with dignity, the wide door of the barn swung open, revealing a woman she recognised as Rebecca Woods. Tall with hair a touch lighter than Daniel's, she was accompanied by a collection of dogs.

"You're here at last. Maybe this one will relax now," she indicated, a black and white border collie running up to Daniel. He opened his arms, and the dog jumped up onto his chest to be held close by him. Natasha's heart melted. The unconditional love of this dog for this man was clear. She realised someone else was talking.

"Put the kettle on, I'll show her to her room."

Rebecca was clearly in charge as she took Natasha's case and carried it toward the house. "And Daniel put some water in it this time."

"Very funny!" The face Daniel pulled at his sister made Tilly wonder what it would be like to have siblings to tease.

Natasha followed Rebecca up two flights of stairs. They were broad, bare wood that looked to have seen better days.

"I have put you up here with me. I don't think you sharing a bathroom with Dad is a great idea." Rebecca took Natasha's case into a room on the right of the stairs. The room was large, with a few older pieces of furniture. A huge brass bedstead covered with a simple quilt, which looked homemade, dominated the room. The large dressing table looked Victorian and matched the battered chest of drawers under the window. Heavy faded curtains pooled onto the floor. It felt like a sanctuary to Natasha.

"Thank you, Rebecca. I hope it wasn't too much trouble."

"Don't worry, I've made him work for it. Now, let's see if he has made a decent pot of tea."

Back downstairs, Natasha was stunned by the size of the kitchen. A large, scrubbed table sat in the middle, surrounded by eight mismatched but sturdy-looking chairs. At one end of the room was a large traditional cream range, in front of which was a collection of dogs.

"Take a seat, Natasha." When Daniel poured out the tea and placed it in front of Natasha, with no milk or sugar, she found herself smiling. She couldn't help but notice the way Rebecca raised an eyebrow at her brother. Daniel took the seat next to hers and she felt safe as a gentle heat radiated off his body to hers. She was having to resist the urge to touch him. Judging by the way he was drumming his fingers on the table; Daniel was having a similar problem.

As soon as Natasha put down her mug, Daniel jumped up.

"We might be late. Don't wait up." He didn't waste any time in getting Natasha back in his car and racing towards the road.

"I want you to see the sea, then you know you're on holiday, right?" He looked at her, a hundred questions in his eyes.

"Daniel, I'm just happy to be here with you, some time out from all that I need to tackle at some point."

"Now you are here, it's time for you to relax." He kept reaching over to take her hand and squeezing it. "I can't believe I have you here. I want to show you so much."

The drive towards the coast involved villages and open farmland. The sky was so big and blue that Natasha didn't know where to look first. She caught herself looking at Daniel more and more. He had always seemed happy and relaxed, but now he seemed to bounce with energy. It was wonderful that it was a result of her simply taking some time out to spend with him.

Eventually, Daniel parked up outside a café that was closing for the day. The tide was out as he led her down a steep slope towards a pebble-covered beach. With her hand firmly encased in his, she followed him step by step, downwards. Families were packing up and trailing back up the hill to their cars.

Finally, on the beach, Daniel smiled down at Natasha. Her trainers were making their height difference more pronounced. The air was fresh and clean, and Natasha was glad she agreed to this time together. The wind was whipping her hair across her face. Natasha was transported back to the seaside holidays when her mum was still alive. She would have insisted Natasha kept her hair under a hat. She was sure she would regret this next week but right now, she didn't care.

Daniel stopped to pull a strand of hair away from her mouth, then with one finger, he lifted her chin and kissed her.

"I've been thinking about that for weeks. Kissing you on this beach. Now I have you here, I don't want to let go."

"Oh!"

"Will you come to the match instead of going straight home?"

"Wouldn't that be a bit public?"

"Joe and Tilly aren't going, so you can sit with India in the stands." Natasha didn't say no, but she didn't say yes either. She didn't know what to say.

"It would mean I can have an extra night with you. Plus, you get to see me in action." When she still didn't speak, he started to backpedal.

"Forget I asked. I'm just being greedy."

"Sorry. I'll have to think about it. When do you need to know?"

"I'm not sure. I guess I need to let India know you're not interested. It's OK, she'll understand."

"It's not forever, Daniel. Things must change at some point. I will get divorced. It's not in question." Daniel turned to look at the horizon.

"Tasha, do you mind if we try not to talk about that for now? Not forever, but for now, let's work on keeping it simple." Natasha looked out in the same direction as him.

"I guess I can do that." His smile was back, and he took her hand and led her over to the rock pools. They danced across the stones, showing each other the next find and laughing. Natasha had forgotten what it could feel like to laugh and not worry about how she looked.

They were in constant contact with each other. If Daniel didn't have his arm around her shoulders, he held her hand. He would lift her down from the higher rocks, holding on that little bit longer. Natasha was enjoying the views.

"You can see so far out there. Look at the size of that boat. I wonder where it is going."

"Come on, I'll show you a better view." His hand firmly gripping hers, he led her back up the long, steep slope to the grassy headland.

"Sorry, am I going too fast?"

"It's those long legs. I have to do two strides to cover the same distance."

"Sorry!" The word hit a nerve. Matthew said 'sorry' a lot, generally when he didn't mean it. With Daniel, though, he used it for many things that weren't his fault, and she was pretty sure he did mean it. The difference between the two men was becoming more and more apparent. *Stop comparing them, Natasha. That is not what this is about.*

Daniel had steadied his pace but still held her hand. Over a stile, onto a path. The coastline turned back on itself, and they stopped, looking seaward. Daniel had been right; you could see further now.

Natasha shivered in the biting wind. It had been a warm day and as the sun sank slowly in the sky, the temperature had dropped. Daniel pulled her gently to stand in front of him, his arms wrapped protectively around her. He lowered his face to sit next to hers. Then he pointed. "Look over there, dolphins," he spoke softly in her ear. She could see five or six breaking the surface. They were moving south at speed, and around them, gulls were swooping.

"Oh wow! They look so happy. So free."

"There is so much sea life out there. Ben's kids want me to take them whale watching, but it will have to wait a few years."

"They are lovely kids; do you spend much time with them?"

"Not that much. Ben doesn't bring them out here often. They do love to see the horses and, of course, the pony. Becca keeps inviting them, but I guess Ben's busy. When he does come, it's when we need extra hands to work."

"It's amazing up here. The wind is taking my breath away. It's such a long way down, though. It's quite scary."

"Sorry. Are you OK?" *Sorry again.*

"Yes, I'm fine. I just feel so free up here."

"That's why I brought you. I want you to have the sense of escape I feel when I come here."

"I'll admit I do need to reset. I wasn't really ready for him to fall in love with someone else. It's silly because I am happy for him. For them even, but I won't pretend it doesn't hurt."

Daniel led her back the way they came, always keeping contact with her. It felt good. Finally, at the car, he gave her one last hug.

"Hungry?" he stroked the hair from her face.

"Sure, what did you have in mind?"

"Trip into Bridlington for fish? Or Filey?"

"I don't know either, so you decide. Somewhere we won't be seen."

"What about a pub?"

"I'm not sure, just the two of us in a pub? It wouldn't look good."

"That's OK. I'll stop and pick something up and we can park, watch the sea, and eat in the car?"

"I'm sorry, but I thought we were just going to be on the farm."

"I would rather not share you on your first night."

Daniel started the car and was driving towards Bridlington.

"So, take-away, fish and chips?"

"Just a fish for me."

"You won't regret it!" and she didn't. It felt naughty to be eating fried food. She had intended to eat enough to keep Daniel happy. In the end, she ate most of her fish.

The smile was back, and an ecstatic Daniel shared those smiles with Natasha. "I'm glad you came, Tasha. Now you can start and enjoy yourself."

"I'm going to have to run extra hard in the morning."

"Will you try to relax a bit for a few days?" The concern in his eyes made Natasha squirm. Emma had been nagging her to take things easier, but at the moment, her job and staying ready for it was all she had been able to focus on.

After they ate, Daniel took her for a walk along the beach. It was a busy seaside town, but as darkness fell, most people were walking on the front, exploring the brightly lit arcades. The beach was dark, and Natasha felt unseen. The combination of the waves lapping up the shore and Daniel at her side holding her hand made her enjoy this calm, content feeling. The neon lights and music from the arcades brought back memories of a simpler life when she lived with her parents.

On the ride home in darkness, the relaxation seeped further into her. Finally settled into the large bed on the top floor of the farmhouse she could reflect on her day. Mostly, she focused on that first kiss on the beach. The tingle it left on her lips. It was a new beginning for both of them. A kiss with a promise of new chances. A kiss to start a new life.

Chapter 33

The bed was so soft it wrapped around her in a hug. Natasha felt so rested and safe as she woke to the sounds of people outside.

She tiptoed across the wooden floor to the window in time to see a tractor disappearing out of the yard and Rebecca leading a grey horse over to the rail. Leaning forward to see what Rebecca was doing, she was startled when the door behind her creaked open. It was just Daniel. Of course, it was. He carried a steaming mug of tea and the thickest slice of toast she had ever seen.

"Oh, I was bringing you breakfast in bed."

"I can get back in."

"Good. Did you sleep well?"

"Yes, I did. This bed is so soft."

"Good, because you are here to recharge, and that bed is soft because it is so old." She smiled, pleased to be here with this man. It felt so normal. "Now, Dad has gone off to mow a field we call Rams Meadow, and I have to go down and turn where he mowed yesterday. But I couldn't go without seeing you."

Natasha sipped her black tea and eyed up the toast. It looked deliciously tempting in an evil sort of way. She wasn't sure how she could possibly eat it without wearing most of it across her face. Her mother's mocking voice was in her ear.

"That toast looks lovely; will you share it with me?" Daniel perched on the edge of the bed and took her hand.

"I don't know how I managed to stay out of this room all night. You do realise my bed is directly under yours."

"Oh, well, I do now. How did you sleep?"

"Terrible. It's like being fifteen again."

"That's a very specific time."

"Yes, and it's a terrible story that I'm not about to tell you. Look, I'll be back by lunchtime, then we can go for a walk on the farm this time so that you can relax a bit more. In fact, I'm going to make you stay on this farm all day, and then tomorrow, you will be begging me to take you somewhere else."

"So that's your plan, is it, Mr Woods? Was it wise to reveal that to me?"

"Hmm, not sure, but I have to get to work before Dad finds me."

"OK."

"That's not the right answer, Ms Poole. You are supposed to beg me to stay or at least kiss you before I leave you."

"Daniel, please kiss me before you leave me."

"Always Natasha. From now on, our goodbyes will always involve kissing." *How wonderful, if only that was possible.*

Daniel took her mug and the plate and stood them on the bedside table. Then so gently held her face, his palm cupping her cheek, and started a long, slow kiss. It was a kiss that could lead to so much more. Natasha's eyes were closed and as he pulled away, they stayed closed for just a while longer.

"Sorry. I better go, or I'll be boarding the door up and keeping you here and everyone else out." He stole a massive bite out of her toast and smiled down at her.

When he left her, the serenity she had been feeling before left with him. She did what she always did, she got ready for her run.

Downstairs, she found a large pan of porridge waiting on the ancient cream range. Remembering the toast she had just eaten, she made some mint tea with a bag from her handbag and slowly ate an apple.

She had decided that the long track back up to the road would be somewhere she could find her way back from. She wanted to work hard, so she revelled in the challenge of the land rising in front of her. When she eventually reached the road, she rested with her arms over the top of the traditional gate. Her breath was starting to regulate when a large SUV pulled up. Along its side in ornate writing were the words Pritchett and Inkle. Natasha was trying to decide if it was supposed to be a copper colour or if it was just a very expensive orange when the driver lowered his window and smiled at her.

"Are you my welcoming committee?"

"I'm sorry?"

"I'm the vet, Rebecca doesn't usually send someone to open the gate for me, but I have to say, I could get used to it." Natasha wasn't quite sure what this guy wanted but the word 'vet' made her think something could be urgent, so she opened the gate and held it open for the man to drive through.

"Could I offer you a lift back down?"

"That's OK, this is my daily run. I'll run back, thank you."

"I'm wounded! You mean you aren't here waiting for me?" Natasha shook her head. This man certainly was good-looking, but she got the impression he knew that. His slick dark hair was cut short but styled. He was dressed in a checked shirt that she knew cost a lot more than the plaid shirt Daniel had on that morning.

"Well, my name is Patrick Pritchett. I am sure we are going to be very good friends." Natasha cringed at the way he rolled his tongue around the words 'very good'. And then she registered the name. Pritchett, there was an MP from this part of the country she had met with Matthew. This man looked like a younger version of him. Natasha hadn't liked him either, but his wife, Sarah, was something else. She always seemed so full on whenever Natasha saw her. She didn't like the way Sarah touched Matthew. The last thought made a snort escape from Natasha. It made her think of all the women she had been jealous of where Matthew was concerned. And to add to the joke of it all, Natasha had found Jack incredibly attractive when she met him too. Shaking her head, she jogged back down towards the farmhouse.

This realisation that she could laugh cheered Natasha. The tranquillity of the farm and Daniel's easy-going nature were helping her to feel like Natasha again. He had no expectations of her and seemed to just want her to be happy.

Back in the yard, Rebecca and the vet were looking at the grey mare with the foot problem. Natasha went into the house to avoid any more conversation.

She went to the kitchen to get a glass of water. Rebecca was quick to follow her in.

"Has the vet gone?"

"His office called with an emergency, thank goodness. Means he didn't linger." Natasha smiled. *So, Rebecca isn't keen on Patrick Pritchett.*

"Have you eaten? Did you see the porridge? I can fry you some bacon and eggs."

"I had an apple; I hope that was OK. Please don't think I'm rude, but I don't eat that much."

"Well, I'm not going to force-feed you. But Dad might make a comment or two. Take no notice of him."

"I think Daniel will be back in time for lunch. Is it OK if I have a bath?"

"Sure."

The roll-top bath looked original to the house. It took a long time to fill, and the water was a peaty brown colour. Daniel had warned her life would be more primitive. The water dribbling out of the tap gave her time to rethink what to do. She clutched the towel tightly to her chest when she heard feet pounding up the stairs. *What if it's his dad?*

A gentle knock on the door, followed by Rebecca's voice, was a relief.

"Don't panic Natasha, the water's always that colour. Here, try this." A hand pushed through the door, holding a green bottle of bath foam.

"The water is soft, so you don't need a lot. I hide it, though or Dan pinches it."

Still a little stunned, Natasha managed a small "Thank you" as she took the bottle from Rebecca's hand.

"The others will be back for lunch about 1 o'clock. I'll be in the red barn if you need me."

"Thank you, Rebecca." Her normal voice returned with the realisation that Rebecca was an ally. She was still relieved when she heard the footsteps descending back down the stairs.

Although she took her time to enjoy the bath, she still had over an hour before she was expecting Daniel to return to the farmhouse. She went down to the kitchen, made a cup of mint tea, and looked out the window. She could see why Daniel liked it here.

The kitchen was a vast room. She loved the warmth of the old range and the scrubbed oak table.

The million small things that littered its shelves camouflaged the dresser at the far end. One thing stood out to Natasha, a small, tarnished frame which contained a faded photograph of three children. The older two each with an arm across the shoulders of a much smaller boy who stood in the middle. As a man, Daniel was so much taller than his siblings. That one photo showed her just how much he had been protected by his brother and sister. It explained the jibes they made. However much they thought they were only teasing him, those comments kept him the small, helpless boy who looks so worried as he looked toward her from out of the frame.

The sad look in his eyes pulled at Natasha's gut. She wanted to wrap her arms around him to protect him, too. Studying the room more, she could see that the essential areas were kept clean and clear whilst, in the corners, chaos had been allowed to spill over from boxes and shelves. From what Daniel had shared with her, Rebecca had been running the kitchen since she was twelve. It looked like running the farm occupied most of her time now. Natasha wondered what she could do to help. She resolved to ask at lunchtime.

She hadn't seen any other rooms other than the kitchen and her bedroom, and it didn't feel right to go exploring on her own. She developed a fear of Daniel's father based on everyone's comments. Suddenly, even standing in the kitchen, she felt like she was invading their privacy, so she took her tea back to her bedroom to read.

Propped up on the pillows of her bed, she could see the gate that the tractors had left through, and she felt sure she would see them return. She hadn't factored in how sleepy reading might make her.

Chapter 34

Running and laughing through fields as Daniel chased her created a deep sense of freedom. She ran through fields of tall grass bejewelled with wildflowers. Butterflies danced around her head as a herd of puppies and tiny sheep ran at her heels. Daniel was getting closer and would catch her at any moment. His breath was on her neck, and she could smell him closing in on her.

It was the soft kiss on her forehead that woke her again.

"Now then, sleepy head, what have you been reading?" Natasha blushed as Daniel picked up her book from where it had fallen and studied the cover.

"Sagan? Do you like her stuff?"

"Well, I…" Natasha was trying to wake up, but Daniel was still studying her book.

"A Certain Smile. She was incredibly young when she wrote it, wasn't she? Have you read anything else?" Natasha closed her eyes; Daniel didn't wait for her to reply. He continued talking about the book.

"I like her early work the best, but she was an amazing woman."

Natasha sat up on the bed, pushing her hair back and trying to smooth it out.

"Every little girl knows about love. It is only her capacity to suffer because of it that increases. She said that when they pushed her about how she could write so passionately when she was so young." Daniel pulled her hand away from her hair.

"It's the first time I have seen you asleep. You look fabulous. I just wanted to climb in behind you and hold you." Natasha finally found her voice.

"Sagan?"

"Ah, you are shocked I have read her work. The reading for my course at university was so boring, I read things that the other guys in my flat were reading for their courses. Anyway, I'm glad you had a sleep, but it's time for lunch and you get to meet my dad." Natasha's hand went back to her hair. She pushed Daniel away and moved to the dressing table to find a brush.

"I can't believe I fell asleep; I mean, I slept well last night. I never sleep during the day." The words tumbled from her mouth as panic filled her stomach. She recalled all the things Daniel and Rebecca had said about Mr Woods. *Why do you even care? It is not as if you are going to see him again.* The realisation that this could be the first and only time she would visit the farm, Daniel's home, changed the emotions in her body to sadness. Daniel seemed to see the change, and he walked up behind her, looking over her shoulder into the mirror.

"Tasha, it's OK. He's a miserable old bugger, so take no notice of him. No one else does." Natasha stopped brushing her hair.

"Perhaps that's why he's miserable?" she suggested, and Daniel laughed.

"Come on. I want you to meet him. And I want him to see Ben is not the only one who can find a wonderful woman."

"He doesn't think …"

"My dad has been told you are here to rest. He is unlikely to think anything could happen between us as you are a married woman, and in this family, such things don't happen. Obviously, they do because my mother left him for another man."

"Your mum remarried?"

"No, the new relationship didn't last long, but it helped her leave the farm and her family."

"Is that why you don't flirt with married women?" Daniel stared out of the window as Natasha watched him in the mirror. It took a long time for him to answer.

"Mum … and in some ways, dad, are a part of it. I don't want to talk about the rest. Not yet, anyway." He turned to look at Natasha.

"Ah, the magic yet. So, one day, maybe."

"One day, Tash."

"That's good then." They smiled, each enjoying being with the other.

"We'd better go down. I'm hungry." He pulled her up and towards the door. Natasha relaxed.

In the kitchen, they found Rebecca ladling soup into bowls. Daniel's father was taking off his boots.

"Dad, this is Natasha Poole. Tash, this is my dad."

"I reckon I'm supposed to say pleased to meet you."

"Thank you for letting me stay, Mr Woods." The older man studied her briefly and then sniffed.

"Well, it looks like Daniel was right. Looks like you do need some good sleep and some decent food." And he walked off, his boots in his hand.

Tasha smiled at Daniel, who was bright red.

"I'm sorry. I did warn you."

"You did," she laughed.

"I'm sorry, and now you know why I took you out last night."

"Daniel, you are not your dad. Why do you keep saying sorry for something that is not your fault?" Natasha watched his face.

"Do I?"

They all sat at the table with bowls of vegetable soup. Despite her reservations, Natasha enjoyed the bread, too. It looked like a plain white loaf, but it tasted divine. Rebecca was telling them about a mare that was about to foal. It sounded exciting.

"Have you shown Natasha what's in the red barn?"

"I'm saving it until after lunch."

"We have plenty of eggs."

"Good idea."

Natasha was intrigued but tried to watch this family as a spectator. She said very little during lunch, and after the others went back to work, she watched some more as Daniel moved around the kitchen.

As she sipped her tea, he boiled some eggs, then cleared and washed the dishes. She couldn't imagine Matt ever being this comfortable.

"What are you looking at, little lady?"

"You."

"I like the sound of that. Come here." Daniel took her hand and pulled her up from her chair. Sitting down himself, he pulled Natasha down to sit on his knee.

"Now, what were you saying?"

"I was saying I like the way you move." She kissed him just lightly on the lips, her arms around his neck.

"Hmm, I like this. Anything else?"

"I like that you brought me breakfast." She gave him another peck. He wrapped his arms around her.

"Anything else you like?"

"I liked that you knew the book I was reading." Again, she punctuated her sentences with a tiny kiss on his lips. Daniel pulled her closer and whispered in her ear.

"You are teasing me. Did I do anything that deserves a longer kiss than that?" Natasha smiled and held his face.

"You did." She kissed him again, a full kiss.

"What did I do to deserve that?"

"You were just you. You are so wonderful, Daniel. All of you." Daniel's eyes softened as he started the next kiss. It began a series of kisses that grew deeper and longer. Natasha began to squirm on his lap and as she shifted, she knew she wasn't alone in feeling more than a little excited by this exchange.

"Right, before this goes any further, I have things to do."

"Like?"

"Don't worry, you are coming with me. Bring those eggs."

Daniel collected a plastic box and a large bottle from Rebecca's pantry. He filled the bottle with water.

"Hmm, if we are going to the barns, you are going to need some boots. Let's have a look."

He took her into a room lined with hooks holding coats and jackets of all shapes and sizes. Under them stood boots. Lace-up boots, knee-length boots, and wellingtons.

"What size?"

"Four."

"So tiny."

She could see a row of what looked like Rebecca's boots, mainly the type she associated with riding. Jodhpur boots, yard boots, and tall brown boots.

"I think Becca wears eights, but try these."

Daniel laughed as she tried on a pair of Rebecca's boots and roared when she tried to walk in them.

"Hang on, we have kids wellingtons somewhere." He pulled out a brown cardboard box covered in dust. "Don't worry, they will wash."

The only pair of wellingtons that would fit were green with frogs' eyes and mouths at the front.

"I don't think I can wear them."

"No one is going to see you in them, Tash, besides they once belonged to Prince Harry."

"Really?"

"I don't think so, but it's what my mum told me to get me to wear them after Ben grew out of them." The very idea of Prince Harry, Ben and then Daniel Woods wearing the same frog wellies she was wearing made her smile. Daniel wiped the wellies and passed them back to her.

"Just for today, Tash, I'll buy you some boots for later." His smile was so wide she couldn't say no, and she did want to know what was so special in the red barn.

"I'm not even going to try looking for a coat for you. It's a good job it's not raining. I love this place, but the rain comes in horizontally."

In her 'new' boots, she followed Daniel carrying the eggs he had boiled earlier. His strides were so long she had to do two steps to his one. Natasha stopped for just a moment as she found herself in the yard at Woodhill Farm. It comprised of two brick-built barns with a couple of rows of stables and hay stacked up under corrugated iron roofs. She presumed the 'red' barn was the one with a large red door. Although the paint was peeling, underneath, she could see green paint.

Daniel opened a small door that was set in the larger one and stepped through. It was a high threshold, and Natasha had to concentrate to get her leg up and over it. Daniel came back and held out a hand to steady her. He held his finger up to his lips to tell her to be quiet as he walked softly towards a row of pallets at the end of the barn. Natasha followed him, and as she looked over the top of the pallets, she could see they were holding in Meg and a set of six puppies.

"Oh, Daniel, they are wonderful. Oh, I don't have my phone. I could have taken a photo."

"I haven't seen you with your phone much, I'm pleased about that."

"Why?"

"You're here to rest."

"Oh." She looked away from Daniel and back at the puppies. "Can I get a photo later? They do look so heavenly."

"Dad doesn't think so. Seems Meg has disgraced herself by fraternising with a Jack Russell rather than being mated with a decent border collie."

"Does that matter?"

"Well, to Dad, it is the difference between some pups he can sell rather than some he might just have to give away. He threatened to drown them." Natasha froze; she had lunch with this man. Daniel didn't notice he was too busy wiping out bowls. "He wouldn't. Some farmers like this cross, though. It gives them a nice-sized dog. Don't worry, Becca will make sure they go to suitable homes."

Daniel climbed into the pen. "Can you sit on that bale of straw and put this towel on your knee? Whilst she eats, I want to check them over. If you can hold them on your lap after I have checked them, I'll know I have looked at all of them."

"Sure, I can do that." Daniel filled one bowl with water and the other with food, including a couple of the boiled eggs. He placed the other eggs into the plastic box and secured the lid.

"For later," Daniel murmured. She didn't know if it was to her or Meg. Then, one by one, he picked up the puppies, turning them upside down and checking around their mouths. He placed each puppy carefully on the towel over Natasha's knee. By the time she had three, she was struggling to keep them in place. They were all wriggling and moving, searching for something on the towel.

"The towel smells of their mum. They are looking for her. It's a good sign." The last puppy was different. She was not moving as much and was limp in Daniel's hand. She looked smaller than the other five puppies.

"This is the one I am worried about. She isn't thriving as well as the others."

"Do you know why?"

"It's nothing obvious. We'll start weighing them tomorrow. I might let her have some time feeding with her mum whilst the others are busy being weighed. For now, we need to leave these little ones to sleep until Meg has finished eating, and then they can go back to be fed, too. Come on, frog feet, let's go check out the rest of the stock."

Daniel led her down the row of stables and introduced her to Rebecca's horses. In the 'blue' barn, they found six young horses corralled in half of the space.

"These are going out into the field later today. Rebecca just wanted them in to groom them and check each one of them over. They are all last year's foals, and she'll start to look at selling them."

"So, what's the history of the farm?"

"It's been in Dad's family for years. His dad did brilliantly well with sheep and bought extra land to make it the size it is today. But markets change, and when Ben and I didn't want to stay on the farm, he had to listen to Rebecca's ideas."

"So, the horse breeding was her idea?"

"To be perfectly honest, I think horses were Mum's passion. She was the one who brought the first stock with her when she married Dad. She already owned a few."

"No sheep at all now?"

"Dad keeps a small herd. I reckon it's what keeps him sane. Focusing on quality these days."

"Do you think he will retire?"

"Dad will leave this farm in a wooden box." He wiped his hands on the back of his jeans. "Right, one last job, then I am all yours."

"That sounds good. Have I got time to fetch my phone?"

"I guess." Daniel scratched his head. He didn't look happy.

"I just want to take some photos to send to Em. She will probably be worrying about me."

Daniel nodded and smiled. "Meet me in the blue barn."

Natasha found Daniel carrying two nets stuffed full of hay. It smelt divine. She could see small dry flowers poking out of the nets.

"Why do they look so pretty?"

"We grow different hays here. This one has red clover and a few other flowers in it. If you have a spare hour whilst you're here, ask Becca all the questions. I just drive the tractor."

"Can I take photos of the horses?"

"Knock yourself out. I've found another job I need to do."

Natasha took photo after photo to send to Emma. The horses, the puppies, and the views.

EM: That looks amazing. Are you enjoying it?

She was so busy looking through her phone that she tripped as she tried to get an ideal view of the driveway. She took a final photo of her muddy legs and frog boots.

EM: Who are you, and what have you done with my friend?

TASH: I'm fine. It is lovely here.

EM: So, I see. What about your host?

TASH: Equally lovely.

EM: I hope you are at least getting some rest.

TASH: I am.

EM: I expect more photos.

TASH: OK.

Chapter 35

Natasha lay asleep in the old bed in the room above his. He had brought her some breakfast, but he didn't have the heart to wake her. *She is here to rest. She should sleep.* He knew he was lying to himself, and the pulse in his groin told him to wait just a few seconds more. It was too late, she was waking now. *Act normal.*

"Good morning, sleepy head."

"What time is it?"

"It's only half-past eight. But this is a farm in summer. We tend to get up early."

"I'm sorry."

"Don't be. You're here to rest. I was just going to leave this tray for you. Then, when I saw you asleep in this bed, well, I just had to stand and watch." He put the tray down on the floor.

"And now I sound creepy." Natasha didn't speak, instead, she peered at the tray. Her soft smile made him believe there was a chance she didn't find that too creepy. After all, he was simply being honest.

"What have you brought me today? No toast?"

"I thought you might prefer muesli today. Rebecca makes some. It's quite nice if you like that sort of thing." He wanted her to eat well, and he was very aware of her face when she saw the toast he had brought the day before. Daniel knew she was far too polite to say what she truly felt, but mealtimes were beginning to worry him. He had a plan for today, though. Still, he was relieved to see her smile broaden.

"That sounds wonderful. Did you say Rebecca makes it? How does she find the time?" Daniel had never thought about it.

"Good question. I guess she hardly has a social life. So, in the evening she bakes and batch cooks. Dad likes simple food. So, we get lots of soups and stews, and when you don't know what time lunch will actually be, that works."

Natasha sat up in the bed and smoothed down the covers over her lap. Daniel leaned forward.

"I was wondering if this merited a kiss?" He couldn't tell what she was feeling, but he was pleased with the gentle good morning kiss she offered him, and he passed her the tray.

"So, I have muesli, but what's in the mug?"

"I thought you might like mint tea." Mint grew in abundance in his mum's old kitchen garden, and Rebecca seemed pleased he had picked some.

"Oh, I do." She took her first mouthful and instantly looked like she would finish the whole bowl.

"This is amazing."

"Becca says it's easy if you have good ingredients. Which, of course, we do because we grow it."

"This is made from things you grow?"

"Yes, mostly. We don't do honey, but we get some given from a beekeeper who has a lot of hives in our fields."

"But there are walnuts in this." He smiled. She had so much to learn.

"We have a pair of walnut trees. We get more than enough walnuts. Becca is always looking for ways to use them."

"It tastes amazing. Is there a plan for today?" Daniel swallowed. He hoped she was going to be OK with going into town.

"It's Saturday, and we don't work a full day. We look after the stock, of course. But generally, by lunchtime, we are taking a break. Becca goes into town, so I thought we could go with her and get you some boots."

"You don't have to do that."

"I want to. I presume you'll want to go for a run after breakfast. So, I'm going to do my chores. Keep Dad happy."

"Can I do anything to help? Can I get lunch ready?"

"Don't worry about it. You're a guest."

"I'd rather help." Daniel smiled. Even her offering to help made him hope she was happy on the farm with his family.

"I want you to rest. So, enjoy your breakfast and have a great run. Don't do too much. I have plans."

"Is there a shower?"

"Sure. It's downstairs, though."

Daniel went about the jobs he needed to do in the yard. He knew what needed doing, and he got on with it with little input from his dad or Rebecca. That left his brain to wander to the woman he had left in bed. He tormented himself with visions of her using the rather rustic wet room downstairs and wondered if he could time it right to catch her dashing back upstairs in a towel. Somehow, he couldn't imagine her with a towel as small as the one he had been stuck with in her changing room.

Remembering that time made him smile, and Debbie nudged him to remind him that he was checking her hooves. Brought back to earth, he recalled Paul knocking on her door and that he had turned his back on her, thinking she was a married mother. How could he imagine Natasha could be as heartless as his own mother? Debbie nudged him again, and he hugged the mare's neck. His mother had not only left him, she had also left Debbie. It was something he had never understood.

Mikey. The day of the impossibly small towel had been the day she lost her dog. Daniel moved more quickly with the horses and then made his way to the other barn to see Meg and her litter.

He settled the pups under a lamp so that Meg could eat in peace and he could take the time to check her over. Whilst the young bitch ate, he settled himself down on the floor and picked up the smallest puppy. Maybe some massage will help.

He gently rubbed her sides, repeating something he could vaguely remember his mum doing with a puppy he had fallen in love with. His dad had scoffed that if he didn't learn to pick healthy stock, he would never make a farmer. Daniel didn't remember the exact words he used, but he'd suggested the dog wouldn't make it into the next week. He had been so determined to prove him wrong, and his mum had helped him all she could.

It was a painful life lesson because although the dog had survived for three weeks, it did, in the end, die one day whilst he had been at school. His dad had left the puppy for him to find and bury when he came home. Life as a child on a farm wasn't all ponies and hayrides.

The door to the barn opened, and Daniel knew it would be Natasha, fresh from her shower. He looked up as she walked in. A soft smile licked across his face.

"Hey, there, pretty girl. Can I show you some puppies?" His grin was so broad, and Natasha laughed at him.

"Is that the small one? How's he doing?"

"She, she is doing OK. I'm a little worried. I might ask the vet to take a look."

"What are you doing with her?"

"Just a little gentle massage."

"Will it help?"

"I think it will. Maybe it just makes me feel better that I am doing something."

"Meg seems happy that you are doing it."

"I hope so."

"Anything I can do to help?"

"No, I'm coming now to start lunch."

He took her hand as they left the barn and smiled down at her. He had been right, here on the farm, they could be together even if they slept in separate beds. Seeing her relax and let him do a simple thing like holding her hand warmed his heart, and he hoped it meant they had a future. From what she said, her marriage was over. She was just stuck waiting to make that official.

He knew she was watching him as he moved around the kitchen. It was a large room, but she stayed close to him. Daniel smiled when he noticed her leaning into the range. It wasn't a chilly day, but something about the solid warmth was comforting. He passed her another mint tea.

"Oh, you made this with mint?"

"How else do you make it?"

"Tea bags?"

"I thought you said you were a country girl."

"I guess there are degrees of everything," she grinned over her mug.

He made omelettes for lunch. His father had brought home mushrooms, and there were still plenty of eggs. It was a meal that got him through university. Somehow, he had persuaded his father to let him live in the city for that. The fact that Ben was already there, plus the mention of cricket training, probably helped.

Remembering her face when she saw the toast the day before, he cut a thinner slice of bread for her. He buttered it carefully before passing it to Natasha, hoping she would eat it. Rebecca and his dad had joined them, and he noticed she had plastered on her professional smile and spoke only when they spoke to her.

Hoping she would enjoy this simple meal, he watched for a reaction. He noticed her face relax into a natural smile when she tasted the bread. Rebecca stopped him from staring at their guest.

"What time are we going to Malton, brother?"

"Straight after lunch, I guess. Have you got much to get?"

"I want to go to the chemists, the deli, and Partridges for some hoof oil."

"I'm taking Tash to Partridges so we can get you hoof oil if …"

"Thank you, brother. Oh wait, did you want me to do something for you? There's a novelty."

"Could you pick up something I ordered from the deli? It's paid for."

"OK, as I'm going to the deli, I guess I can do that."

When he unlocked the Range Rover, he was disappointed that Natasha climbed in the back, insisting that Rebecca sat in the front. His stomach sank as in his mirror, he could see her pulling up her collar and pulling down her hat. It hurt that she felt the need to hide.

"Are you ready for the dizzy heights of market day?" he teased, hoping to lift the mood.

"Where are we going?"

"We are going to get you some boots that don't have eyes on them."

Rebecca and Natasha both smiled, but the conversation ended. Silence filled the Range Rover as he focused on the drive into the nearest town. It was his town, and he tried not to think about her not wanting to be seen with him there.

He parked in a side street as close to their destination as he could. Daniel spotted the look in his sister's eye, and he hoped she didn't voice the thoughts he felt sure she was having.

He led the way to the shop he knew would have the perfect boots for Natasha. Painted dark blue and set back from the road, it was a shop both his sister and his mother loved. Above the door, in gold lettering, a sign proclaimed it to be 'Partridge & Daughters'.

Chloe Giles greeted them the moment they stepped through the door. Her long blonde hair and matching long legs had once been of great interest to Daniel. Now he was rather embarrassed about those times. But Chloe was an old friend, and he trusted her to help them get what they needed.

"Chloe, we need boots for my friend here." Daniel was surprised when she gripped his arm and tried to remember if she had always been that physical with him. He wanted to take Natasha's hand as Chloe led the way through a second room and into a third. He didn't like the way it made him feel when he realised she wouldn't like that.

The room was full of boots of all kinds, and he knew it was a place that excited his sister. He hoped it had the same effect on Natasha. He encouraged her to explore and try on as many styles as she wanted. *Girls like shopping, don't they? Hell, I enjoy shopping for myself. Hmm, she would look stunning in those knee-length boots with the stacked heels. Shit*

"Socks!" he said in an effort to distract his thoughts, "she needs boot socks." Daniel followed Chloe back to the socks.

"Daniel Woods, I do believe you are blushing," Chloe giggled, and Daniel remembered that was one of the many reasons he stopped going out with her.

He picked up three pairs and took them back to Natasha. The look of joy on her face when he saw her again took away all thoughts of the giggling Chloe.

"Here, put these on whilst you are trying on boots."

In the end, Daniel helped her choose a pair of sensible ankle boots. He made a mental note of which longer boots he would buy her on her next visit.

Chloe asked another girl to pack the boots as she went to fetch hoof oil. Before she left, she touched Daniel's arm for just a moment too long and Daniel was surprised at the change in Natasha's face. It was just a brief frown before the professional smile was back.

The new girl carefully packed the boots into a cotton bag and then into a smart blue box with gold lettering. The box and the socks were finally put in a classic ribboned carrier bag with Partridge & Daughters embossed on the side.

Daniel took Natasha to another room where he persuaded her to try on long waxed coats too. He had plans.

"It isn't all sunshine on a farm, Tasha. When it rains, you know about it." Natasha tried them on but insisted that it was something for another day. The idea that Natasha too was thinking there would be another day put a spring in his step as they left the shop.

Outside, they found Rebecca. When his sister dashed over and threw her arms across Natasha's shoulder and pulled her into a hug he was confused.

"Here she is. Did my brother look after my best friend?" Daniel was just about to say something when he saw the vet.

"You remember Patrick."

"Hello again." Natasha tried to smile, but Daniel was sure he couldn't hide the look on his own face.

"Hello, pretty lady. Oh, have you been buying boots? Has Daniel been using his influence on the lovely Chloe to get you a better deal? When are you just going to marry the girl, Daniel? Hasn't she waited long enough?"

"Patrick, fancy seeing you here," Daniel coughed. "Are you due out at the farm?"

"I'm coming Tuesday to look at the mare."

"Can you check out Meg's litter when you are there?"

"Of course, your dad didn't say she was expecting."

"That will be because this isn't one of Dad's projects. Meg has done this all on her own, which is why I'm going to ask you not to put it on the farm account. Could you bill me for it?"

"And will you be there to open the gate for me on Tuesday, Natasha?"

"No. I'm sorry, you will have to handle it on your own. I'll be back home by then."

"Oh! Where is home?"

"I'm sorry, Patrick, I have to drag Tasha home now." Rebecca linked her arm through Natasha's and moved her back towards the car park.

"That man is a huge prick," Daniel growled.

"Surely, given his name, he is a little prick," Natasha offered. Daniel frowned. He didn't like the man, he didn't like the way he spoke to Natasha, and he certainly wasn't happy about the Chloe reference.

"When did you meet him?"

"The first morning I was here."

"Will you two just get out of here before he catches up? He might be a prick, but he's the best horse vet for miles. You can thank me later."

They all walked quickly, and he was aware that Natasha was almost running to keep up. No one spoke on the way back to the car. In fact, they were almost back at the farm before Daniel broke the silence.

"Becca, I'm sorry I should have said thank you for protecting Tasha like that. And, Tasha, I'm sorry the man just pushes all my buttons."

"It's fine, brother. I'm pretty sure the man pushes plenty of people's buttons."

Natasha was in the front of the car for the return journey, and she was studying Daniel. *I don't want her to think I'm moody like that. And she must be wondering about those comments about Chloe.*

Daniel's frown was back when she twisted in her seat to look at Rebecca.

"Is Patrick any relation to an MP called Michael Pritchett?"

"Yes, he's his younger brother."

"I thought he might be. That's why I made the comment about little prick. It's what Matt calls Michael. It's his wife, Sarah, who I think is a piece of work."

Daniel's grip tightened on the steering wheel. He wasn't sure what upset him the most, her talking about Matt or the mention of Sarah's name. He glanced at Rebecca in his mirror, hoping his sister wouldn't betray him.

Rebecca was laughing in the back of the car. "Sarah Pritchett is a complete cow. I don't know anyone who likes her."

"Can we change the subject?"

"Sorry, Dan. I forgot." Daniel didn't like the puzzled look on Natasha's face. He hoped she wouldn't start asking questions he wasn't ready for.

Back at the farm, Natasha seemed ready for a change of subject, too.

"Do we need to check on Meg and her family?"

"I guess showing you my puppies worked after all. Come on."

Natasha followed Daniel quietly through the small door in the large one. Meg was pleased to see her friend. Daniel passed the smallest puppy to Natasha to hold whilst he fed Meg. Natasha cradled the puppy in her lap, and he could see her trying to massage it like she had seen him doing.

"You're still worried about her, aren't you? That's why you want the vet to check them."

"Just wanted to be safe, that's all."

"She has such pretty markings. Will she always be smaller than the rest?"

"She will probably catch up."

Natasha reluctantly passed the puppy back to Daniel.

"Come on. It's time for another meal with Dad. Then I'm taking you out."

"Out?"

"Well, up to the coast again. I'm taking you star gazing. We might even see some meteors."

Back in the kitchen, Natasha proudly showed her new boots to Rebecca, who seemed impressed.

"A great investment. I presume that means you are going to be coming back for more visits." Daniel smiled at his sister. But Natasha wasn't ready to agree.

"I don't know about that," she sighed, looking out of the window. "It's lovely, though, and I'm enjoying being here."

"Tomorrow," Rebecca paused to look at Daniel. "I'm taking Dad to chapel. I guess you are staying here."

"Yes, we are going on a picnic."

"Could you take some oats up to the top barn for me? I've moved the retired herd up there this morning. If you could drop off ten sacks of oats and just check they are OK for me?"

"Well, I could …"

"If you do that, I can take Dad earlier, and he can go visit his sister."

"For Aunty Margaret, I can do that."

"We might not be back until late. There is a tea at the chapel."

After dinner, Daniel fought to hide his excitement as he persuaded her to wrap up warmly and charge her phone. She pulled her baseball cap down again as they drove out through the gate onto the road. There was very little traffic. He wanted her to relax, but years of paranoia seemed to have taken their toll.

Daniel reached over and squeezed her hand.

"I thought I understood. About the press thing, I mean. I have to be careful, but I can go out, and I have my teammates. You seem so alone in all this. How do you cope?"

"It's all happened so slowly. When we were first married, Matthew wasn't particularly important. The more success he had, the better jobs he got, the more people who would like to see him fall." She tried to offer him a smile.

"Then, of course, being on people's TV three days a week makes me more recognisable than most MPs' wives. That makes it harder." She looked out of the side window. "I have Emma. I'm not alone."

"And you have me now."

"I do, and I am very grateful."

By the time Daniel parked, they were on a cliff top looking out across the North Sea. There were no streetlights, and the darkness seemed to extend out into infinity.

Daniel was relieved when Natasha let him hold her hand. He worried she would not be accustomed to such darkness. The way she held on told him he was right. He stroked her hand with his thumb. He told himself it was to reassure her, but it probably helped him too. This was all so new. For some reason, tonight was so important to him.

"There is a bench just over here, and we can sit for a while."

"Do you come here often?"

"If I'm on my own, I usually just take Meg for a good walk." He looked at Natasha and let out a small, soft laugh. "She's a superb listener." The smile she gave him and the darkness made him braver as he continued. "I must admit, I've brought a few dates up here. Once, I could drive and before I dare go to a pub."

"Oh."

"It was a very long time ago, Tasha." He wanted to reassure her.

"I realise there have been girls before me. I'm presuming quite a few."

"Well, one or two."

"That girl today, what was her name, Chloe?"

"Ha, yes, Chloe Giles. We were at school together. I was oblivious to the fact she liked me. I took her out a few times. Then I realised she was far too serious about it all. I did like her, but more as a friend who happened to be a pretty girl. It was all a bit embarrassing when I realised she 'had plans'." It was Natasha's turn to squeeze his hand. "Of course, everyone else knew before I did. I felt such a fool."

"Did you bring Chloe here?"

"No."

"I'm not sure I believe you."

"We said we were going to be honest. I meant that, Tasha. There hasn't been anyone else since …"

"Since when?"

"Since before I met you. I had decided, you see, that it was time to take life a bit more seriously. Then, almost as soon as I decided that I met ..."

"Look!" Natasha pointed out as a light flashed across the sky.

"If we're lucky, we could see a few more. I checked, and the weather is right for us to catch this meteor shower. The stars are wonderful up here, but with the extra show, well, I didn't want you to miss it."

"I've never seen one before."

"There is probably too much light pollution where you live."

"I've never seen so many stars at once. It makes it harder to recognise the constellations."

"Do you know many?"

"Is that Cassiopeia?"

"Well, yes." Daniel stopped and turned her towards him. He stroked the hair from her face.

"You are very clever Ms Poole; I think that deserves a kiss."

"I won't be much longer."

"What clever?"

"No. Ms Poole."

"Will you change your name? What with work and stuff?"

"I'm not sure."

"What was your name?"

"Webb."

"Natasha Webb."

They saw several more meteors that night, but Daniel thought he had his eyes closed kissing Natasha Webb so much he probably missed hundreds of them. He couldn't remember when he last felt this happy.

Chapter 36

On Sunday, Natasha lay in bed listening to the noises of people moving. She was expecting Daniel to bring her tea like every other morning. When she heard a car driving off, she tip-toed to the window to see the car leave and set off up the long drive to the main road. They were alone.

As the excitement grew about being alone with him, she went to look for Daniel. When she didn't find him downstairs, she went up a floor. She hadn't stopped on this floor before. The thought of bumping into Mr Woods still left her feeling anxious. Every door stood open, and the rooms empty, except for the one nearest the stairs. She remembered that Daniel had said his bed was directly under hers, so she felt certain that this must be his room.

She opened the door quietly to discover Daniel sprawled out on the bed asleep. He had one leg tucked up and one arm above his head. She crept quietly round to the empty side of the bed and crawled in beside him. She laid her head on his chest as his arm dropped around her, pulling her close.

"What kept you?" he growled.

"I'm sorry," she laughed softly.

"You won't believe how long I have been imagining having you at my side in this bed."

"Since I arrived here?

"Longer," he laughed.

"Since we spent the night in the hotel?"

"That was special, but longer than that."

"You only met me in May. It can't be much longer."

"I think I have been imagining you curled into me like this, in this bed, since I was fifteen."

"Fifteen, again. It's that significant. Why fifteen?"

"I'll tell you someday."

"Tell me, have you had many women in this bed, Mr Woods?"

"No, I mean none. I'm the baby brother. Very few women have even been to the farm."

"But there have been other women."

"I can't lie. Yes, there have been. But we are not going to talk about that today." He leaned up and kissed her, a brief kiss. "After breakfast, I'm taking you out across the farm." Another kiss.

"We have that job to do for Rebecca." Another kiss.

"We do."

"What about my run?"

"You are going to be walking a lot, so why not give it a miss for today?"

"I thought you might run with me today."

"My knee can't manage with that. It's the match tomorrow." He popped another kiss onto the tip of her nose. That always made her want to melt.

"So, breakfast first – the oats – then our walk."

"We can start our walk from the top barn, but you got one thing wrong."

"OK?"

"Breakfast is not first."

"OK?"

"First, we have to do this." His mouth met hers. This wasn't a small kiss. Daniel made this one count. It was a deep, passionate kiss, and Natasha surrendered to enjoying it. When the kiss stopped, she took a big breath to refill her lungs. Daniel reached for the hem of the long T-shirt she had been sleeping in. In one swift move, he pulled the shirt clear of her body and dropped it to the floor. He studied her body as the morning light beamed through a tiny gap in his curtains. With a single finger, he traced the outline of her breast.

"So beautiful." He kissed first one nipple and then the other.

"Natasha, I could wake to this every day."

"I can't promise you that, not yet."

"Our magic word."

He slid his hands down to her buttocks and lifted her to sit on him. Their underwear was still in place, but Natasha could feel his desire.

"Daniel, I don't want …" He froze, watching, waiting for her to finish the sentence. "That's a lie. I do want this and more. I wish every day could start like this." Daniel smiled.

"But …" Daniel put his finger to her lips.

"Shh. Just for today, we are going to believe everything is possible." He took his finger from her lips and kissed her again. His tongue danced with hers. As the kiss deepened, his hips lifted towards her. Natasha could feel the urgency in him, and her own body was responding. The dampness between her legs heightened the sensation of his hardness. Daniel reached between them to touch her through her knickers. She could feel his fingers rubbing slowly against her, raising her arousal.

"Daniel, I want …"

"Shh." He slipped the material away from her so that his fingers were rubbing directly onto her.

"Do you think we could lose these?" He pulled at the side of the elastic. She nodded, lying back on the bed, and slipped them off. She reached for his boxers and pulled them down, too.

"Let me help you there." Once he, too, was naked, he rolled over to lie over her. He held himself up off her body, all the time smiling down at her flushed face. He reached over to his bedside and found a condom.

"I think you are ready for this, but I want to hear you say it." Natasha's mouth went dry as she licked her lips. She wanted more, and he was right. She was ready. She nodded, and when he didn't move, she managed a husky, "I'm ready." His face softened.

Daniel's hands trembled as he tried to put on the condom. Natasha's hand covered his to still him as she took over the job. Daniel once again held himself over her, looking down into her eyes.

"Are you sure?" She nodded, and this time it was enough. He began to enter her, slowly, watching her face. She smiled at his concern, and his own smile broadened. He moved forward, filling her. He stopped, and watching her closely, he pulled back. As he pushed forward again, he filled her more, and her eyes widened. Daniel's eyes danced across her face. She stroked the side of his cheek as he leaned into her and kissed her with a passion that made her skin flush.

Daniel continued to thrust, again and again. Natasha lifted her hips to make more space for him. She needed this. She needed Daniel to make love on this gentle Sunday morning. She needed to know that this man could claim her.

As she lay in his arms in the euphoria following their mutual climax, she felt loved. It was a feeling she had forgotten. That sensation of home that followed orgasm. But this was something more. More than the hurried release she had found with Matt. *Is this what love feels like?*

"Round two or breakfast?" She opened her mouth, but no words came out. "Just teasing, breakfast now, but I warn you, I have plans for later." He sat on the edge of the bed and pulled on clean boxer shorts. He leaned back and kissed her.

"Thank you."

"Why?"

"For helping me christen this bed. Although I'll find it even harder to sleep here tonight."

For breakfast, he persuaded her to try the porridge.

"You are going to need the energy," he grinned. Putting on some eggs to boil, he explained. "Some for Meg and some for the picnic. You do like eggs?"

"Yes, I do. What can I do to help?"

"You just sit there and save your energy for later." She smiled at him.

"I have ten bags of oats for you to shift." She hit his arm.

Chapter 37

In the yard, Daniel opened an old Land Rover and threw a rucksack in the cab. It took no time at all for him to load the sacks of oats in the back. Natasha followed him when she realised he was going to feed Meg. She couldn't wait to check on the tiny one again. For some reason, she didn't understand the survival of the pup was important. In her head, she had equated this dog's survival to the survival of their relationship. That if this tiny dog could survive, it would somehow make up for Mikey not making it. She knew it wasn't real.

She watched as Daniel moved around in the pen, clearing it up and checking each of the puppies.

"Here, I know you want to see this little girl." He passed the tiniest puppy to her, and she sat down on the bale, gently rubbing her as she had seen Daniel doing before.

Natasha was wearing denim shorts and a white cotton embroidered vest with her new boots and socks. She threw a blue shirt onto the back seat with the rucksack. The drive up to the barn took them through fields she hadn't seen before. Daniel was explaining what they grew and why. He explained again about clover and herbs and went into great detail about ryegrass. He seemed proud of what Rebecca had done.

"It was a change that had to come. With me and Ben both off the farm for so much of the time, they had to find things that were less labour-intensive and crops that fetch a higher price. Becca's talking about taking on someone else, though Dad's not keen."

"Why not?"

"It's been a family working this farm for years. Employing others is something 'posh folk' do. He isn't very trusting either." It made Natasha smile to hear these stories about his family. Now she had met them, she understood so much more.

"My dad's the same. He struggles to trust 'these youngsters'. He seems to employ people over forty all the time."

The barn was more a set of buildings centred around a barn with a curved roof and two sides. There were two lean-to stores and one side opened onto the railed paddock. Six horses grazed peacefully in the paddock. Daniel took the time to introduce Natasha to each of the horses. One was particularly friendly, and she nuzzled into Daniel's shoulder.

"This is Debbie."

"She's beautiful."

"Debbie was my mum's horse; she was the first horse she bred here. Mum rode her every day."

"And she left her here?"

"Yes, just like she left her kids."

"I'm sorry, Daniel. Have you spoken to her about it?"

"About what?"

"About why she left you."

"Do you think I care?" He didn't wait for a reply. He made himself busy unloading the Land Rover.

"I'm sorry. Now, where are we going for this picnic?"

"I thought we would head up to the highest point on our land. You can smell the sea and look down on the farm." Daniel hoisted the rucksack, insisting he didn't need any help.

"You're squinting!"

"I forgot my sunglasses." Daniel passed her a battered ball cap.

"Here, try this."

Together, they set off walking, holding hands. His thumb brushed her knuckles. As they walked, Daniel continued to point things out. It felt so normal to be hand in hand with this giant of a man.

"You do love it here."

"I do, but only because I also have the cricket. I couldn't stay here day in and day out. I enjoy the work. I love the space, but only because it's a contrast to the rest of my life." He squeezed her hand. "Are you glad you came?"

Natasha looked at the wildflowers that danced through the grass as they walked. Overhead, a bird was hovering, singing a wonderful song.

"I have loved it. Thank you for persuading me to come."

"I had my reasons," he smiled. "Do you feel rested?"

"I do," she looked up at the bird again. "What's that?"

"Oh, that's a skylark. She has young at the moment. They nest on the ground, you know."

"It is beautiful here, Daniel."

"You're welcome back anytime, although it's not so pretty on a wet day in November. Ready for lunch?"

"I can't wait to see what you have in that bag other than the eggs."

"I brought some crisps as well," he laughed. Natasha started to panic. "I also have that bag from the deli. They sent some tasty things that even you with your London tastes should enjoy."

Daniel laid the blanket on the soft grass under the hedge. Putting the rucksack to one side, he sat down next to Natasha. He lowered his lips to her sun-kissed shoulder.

"Hmm, my favourite first course. Tasha, please say you will come back. Soon. This can't be our last day together."

"It might have to be until I sort things out with …" his index finger pressed against her lips. "I know. I can't spoil today."

"Can we agree that we would like there to be more days like these?"

"Yes. I would love more days like these. And we still have today."

"Today, another magic word." He kissed her mouth as she laid back on the blanket to enjoy his lips on hers. He blocked the sun from her eyes. Daniel removed her cap and kissed her hair. She didn't care. Her whole focus was on Daniel. He lifted his head and looked down at her.

"You're beautiful, Natasha." He stroked her breasts, his finger tracing the valley between them. He hooked his finger into the neck of her vest and pulled it down, revealing her bra. He shook his head.

"I can't believe that you are here." He kissed down her throat to her chest. With a move that was far too smooth, he unhooked her bra.

"You won't be needing that for a while."

"Interesting point of view." Natasha lifted his T-shirt and kissed his tight stomach. "You look pretty good to me." She pulled his T-shirt off as she kissed his chest again. Her hands worked like an advanced guard, seeking out new places for her to kiss. Daniel's smile widened, and he put a single finger on the bottom of her shorts.

"I'm trying to decide if I can talk you out of these shorts."

"That would leave me rather exposed."

"I know. Exciting, isn't it? But who would see you? I'm not sure the skylark will tell anyone."

"I'm not sure."

"I was thinking it might be time for round two." He kissed her, and she responded. The kiss was everything she had dreamed of. Daniel's tongue excited her and in response, her hips lifted towards him. Daniel's hand lifted her towards him more. Grinding against her. When his fingers wandered to her waistband, she stopped and removed her own shorts. Daniel pushed down his jeans, and they lay together. Lying still at first, then Daniel started to kiss her again. His hands explored her as she clung to him, desperate to keep him on her.

When they finally surrendered to sex, it was wonderful. Daniel watched her face as he took her to the edge, time after time. Until they laid back, spent and soaking in the sun. Natasha laid her head on his chest and held him.

"Would you like to eat now?"

"Is that your way of saying you are hungry? Or did you have something else in mind?" She laughed.

"Well, as interesting as that sounds, I am hungry."

"Do you mind if I get dressed first?"

"I could live with that." He zipped his jeans with care.

"Maybe you could leave your shirt off?" She teased.

"Would you like that?"

Natasha nodded. "Tell me, what's in this picnic?"

A grinning Daniel produced the boiled eggs and a bag of crisps, then laughed as he pulled out the bag from the deli. It contained chicken salad and sourdough, cheese and crackers, skewers of roasted vegetables, and relish.

He laid everything out on a cloth on the blanket. As he passed her a drink, he kissed her. The picnic was tasty, and Natasha let herself enjoy it. Daniel delighted in feeding her different things to taste. The salad had a fruity dressing, the cheeses tanged with the relish. Each mouthful enhanced by the sunlight.

When Daniel pulled out jars with screw top lids that looked like jelly and fruit, Natasha was eager to taste them.

"What flavour is this?"

"It's from the deli. They said it had Pimm's in it."

"Well, it's gorgeous!" Daniel reached over to wipe a piece of jelly from her cheek.

"You look like you are enjoying it." And then he kissed her. She had started to kiss him back when large splodges of summer rain hit them.

"Was this part of your plan?"

"Nope. Let's get back. It'll be quicker going downhill."

They packed the remains of the picnic quickly into the rucksack and set off down the hill towards the barn. The rain was splashing down, bringing up mud as it hit the dry earth. As soon as Natasha moved down the footpath, she could feel the new boots rubbing on her heels. She knew it was her own mistake, and she didn't want to complain.

Daniel helped her down from the style into the next field. As she walked ahead of him, he spotted her limping.

"What's wrong?"

"It's nothing."

"Tash babe, tell me."

"New boots. It was stupid, my own fault."

"Here, let me help you."

"No, I'll be fine." Daniel swapped shoulders with the rucksack and walked on but made a point of watching her carefully.

"Right, I've seen enough boots off."

"It'll ruin my socks."

"I'll buy you more socks. Now put the rucksack on and get up. I'll give you a piggyback." The rain was driving from their backs. Natasha's hair and clothes were plastered to her. The skin on her heels throbbed. She had run out of fight. She picked up the bag.

"Honestly, Daniel. I can manage."

"I'm too wet to argue with you. Just climb on."

He crouched in front of her, and she threw her arm around his neck. As he stood up, her legs went around his waist. As Daniel steadily walked down the hill, she noticed his stride had lengthened. *Poor Daniel. He has been walking slowly for me.* Natasha's head fell onto his back. They were both soaked now.

As they manoeuvred through the last gate before the barn, Daniel lost his footing in the deeply rutted mud. His body lurched forward, and Natasha fell over his shoulder. They ended up in a heap on the ground, amidst the mud that filled the gateway. They sat on the ground, rain streaming down their faces, and laughed.

"Thank goodness we're back at the barn. We can drive down from here." Daniel stood up and held out a hand to help her up. One step forward and he winced.

"Shit, this bloody knee, can you get to the Land Rover." Natasha looked at her feet. "Will you stop worrying about those bloody socks?"

"Sorry," Natasha shrugged and tiptoed her way across to the passenger's door. Now out of the rain, the drive back to the farm was uneventful, apart from them exchanging glances with each other and laughing.

Back in the yard, wet and muddy, they both limped into the boot room. Daniel checked the clock ticking away on the wall.

"We have an hour, maybe two. I think it's time for a bath. If we leave our clothes down here, I can get them washed."

"Are you sure?"

"I can be domesticated, well, when I try. Here, let me help you." Daniel peeled her wet clothes off her body. They clung to every inch, and Natasha began to shiver.

"I do love you. Now dive upstairs and start that bath. I'll get these in the washer." Natasha ran naked upstairs to the bathroom. The sight of herself in the mirror was a shock. She was a complete mess. Her hair was tangled and plastered to her mud-splashed face. And yet Daniel said he loved her. She wasn't neatly dressed or even clean, and he said he loved her. *He loves me when I look like this.*

She started the bath and wrapped herself in a large towel.

When Daniel joined her, he stopped and frowned at her.

"What?"

"What's this thing for?" he pointed at the towel.

"It takes a while for this bath to fill. I was just keeping warm." Daniel pulled the towel away from her.

"You don't need that. I'll keep you warm. Come here." He pulled her into his arms and wrapped her close.

"Is that any better?"

"A bit.

"Will this warm you a little more?" he gently lifted her chin and started a soft kiss. When Natasha responded, he deepened the kiss.

Sharing a bath with him was a delight. At home, she rarely even went in the bathroom if Matt was in there. They gave each other space. She had spent so much of her life being careful about her appearance. It was her heritage from her mother. To hide everything. To only always be on show. Daniel seemed to love her, blisters, and all.

"Let me check your heels."

Daniel caressed her foot gently, holding her slim ankle he wiped the sole of her foot with the flannel. As he dried her foot, he lifted her toes into his mouth and gently, so very gently, he sucked each individual toe, one at a time, pulling it out of his mouth with a gentle pop.

Under his kisses, her skin was so sensitive Natasha didn't think she could stand this feeling much longer. If Matt touched her toes, she screamed in agony, but this agony with Daniel with something even more intense and deliciously tempting.

"I have an idea. About your name," he kissed her toes. "How would you like to be called ..."

"Please, Daniel. Stop."

"You don't like it?" he looked crestfallen.

"No, I love it, but I can hear someone downstairs."

"Shit!" He pulled his hand down his face. "Well, that's the end of that. I'll go down and talk to them. You take your time and come down when you are ready."

Chapter 38

Natasha carried her bag downstairs. She had worried for so long about coming to Yorkshire, and now she really wasn't ready to go home. Her time here had been magical and not just the clifftop walk beneath the stars. It made her feel so small and insignificant. It had given her lightness that lifted her need to control how she looked every moment of every day. Life on the farm brought her joy. How do you add up all that love from the horses and puppies and mostly from Daniel?

These few days had also made her feel that with Daniel beside her, she could finally face her impending divorce with the idea that life afterwards could be better than before. That was a thought that had never entered her head before she came north.

She had wasted far too much energy thinking about how painful it would be and how she could endure what was to come. Now she could see that there could be magic in her life again. Daniel had shown her she could be loved again and, in doing so, had awakened something inside her. She found Daniel's smile infectious. The smile on her face was there now, like it or not. It wasn't a professional smile she wore with care. As her mouth curled up, she felt her whole body glow. She felt suddenly alive.

Rebecca was waiting in the kitchen. She had a bag of muesli for her to take home, and half a dozen eggs. Natasha tucked them carefully into her case.

"Are you going to be bored at the match?"

"I don't think so. I'm going to be with India."

"She'll keep you entertained."

"I'm hoping she'll explain a few things to me."

"Enjoy it, anyway. Thank you for coming Natasha. It's good to see him happy."

"Thank you for letting me come to stay."

"It's Daniel's home. He should be able to have visitors. Glad you understood he still had to work."

"Of course. Bye, Rebecca. Thanks again. Find good homes for Meg's puppies."

"Of course. I'm sure you'll be back. I hope you will."

Now she just had to say goodbye to Mr Woods. They hadn't spoken much but her mother would have been horrified if Natasha hadn't taken the time to thank him for her stay. She found him in the room with the boots.

"Mr Woods, I wanted to thank you."

"Oh!"

"I had a lovely time. Thank you."

"Well, I must say, you look a bit better at least. Did you sleep in that old bed?"

"I did. Thank you."

"I didn't do nought. You should thank the others."

"They are your children, Mr Woods. If they have made me welcome, then I think that means you have brought them up well."

"Is that what you think?"

"I do."

"Well, if you need a bed again, you know where we are."

"Thank you."

The drive to a match usually had him thinking about the day ahead. Daniel had packed his bag last night and checked it twice this morning. He had everything he needed and Natasha at his side was a bonus.

He couldn't stop looking across at her. She was smiling, and he was pleased she looked far more relaxed than when she arrived. Yesterday had been fantastic until his family came home early. But all of it had been special, and he hoped she now could see that his feelings for her were real. It wasn't something that was going to change.

"Thank you for doing this."

"Going to the match?"

"Giving me an extra day." He lifted her hand and kissed her knuckles.

"I have to say thank you for persuading me to come out here. I do feel so much better."

"I was being selfish."

"No, you weren't." She offered him a smile. Daniel was so happy that she had spent time in his space. He loved sharing his part of the world with her and seeing her fit in so well.

"You even won Dad over. That's a first." He saw the disbelief on Natasha's face. "Honestly. I couldn't be happier right now." He kissed her hand again. "Well, maybe if I didn't have to say goodbye to you later. I don't suppose you want to stay another night?"

"I need to go home. I had a wonderful time, Daniel. You were right, I could relax at the farm, and just be me."

"OK, different question. Would you come back again?"

"I would like that."

"You would? When?"

"I don't know. Let me get back to work and look at shifts. I need to talk to Matt, too."

Hearing her say her husband's name took the wind out of his sails. It set his brain whirling. *You know she is married. She isn't hiding that. You know the marriage was over before you met her. You said you could wait.*

"Are you OK?"

"Sure." He offered her a smile, but it didn't reach his eyes.

"I try not to talk about him, but he is still a factor in my life, Daniel. I don't want to lie to you."

"I know. I don't like it, but I know. I'm glad you can talk to me about it."

"Don't let this spoil today."

"No, I want to enjoy this last day. It's going to be a great match. I'll drop you at India's place. We can say goodbye there."

A bright sun was shining directly into the back of the car. The green fields and tree-lined hills gave way to more buildings and traffic. They talked less the closer they got to Leeds. Daniel was anxious not to spoil these last moments alone by saying something stupid.

Eventually, a very quiet Daniel parked carefully in front of a Victorian Villa. He reached over and squeezed her hand before getting out. Natasha reluctantly joined him as he lifted her case out of the car. He decided he needed to be the upbeat one. He tilted her chin and smiled down.

"Thank you for the best four days. I have enjoyed every moment of having you up here. And now I want you to enjoy watching me all day. Don't be sneaking cheeky looks at those other blokes."

Charlie pulled open the front door, looking harassed.

"At last, come on Dan mate." He was carrying a bag with three bats strapped to the outside and walked towards the back of Daniel's car. Zach followed him out of the house.

"I wanted to kiss you goodbye."

"It's OK, Daniel."

"I promised you all goodbyes would be with kisses. Proper kisses."

"Then this isn't goodbye."

Zach and Charlie were climbing into the car, and Daniel still looked into Natasha's eyes. He gently stroked the hair off her face and softly held his hand against her cheek.

"See you soon, Tash. Your boots will be waiting for you. And remember who you are watching today."

Chapter 39

India had come equipped for a day at the match. Natasha was wearing the white Yorkshire cricket hat that Daniel had bought for her and her sunglasses. They were sitting about eight rows from the front.

"I think you're pretty safe here, Natasha, and anyway, you have every reason to be sitting with me watching the match."

"How is Tilly?"

"She's fine, getting uncomfortable, which is making her grumpy, but she is having a wonderful time decorating the nursery and shopping. I'm fairly sure this baby won't need much before it starts school."

"I had a cousin who had twins. She got huge."

"Tilly is not that large; she just has high expectations of herself. But she's the strongest woman I know, so if anyone can do this, she can."

"You'll tell me everything I need to know about cricket, won't you?"

"With all the rain we had overnight, there might be a question about it even starting." And as if he had heard her, the announcer boomed out.

"Ladies and Gentlemen. Today's match will have a delayed start. We hope to begin play at 11 o'clock."

"Great. Time for us to go look around the food stands."

"I thought you had brought food?"

"I did, but there is something about fried onions at outdoor events like this."

"Daniel said you didn't come to the studio because you've been ill."

"I know, I get the point and that's why I bought food today." India looked down at the bag, and to Natasha's relief, she had second thoughts. "Damn it, woman, I hope you aren't going to spoil all my fun. Charlie hasn't got to you, has he?"

"No, but Daniel is worried about you, so Charlie must be."

"Daniel? Worried about me? About anyone?"

"He is quite a sensitive soul."

"Charlie says that. I haven't seen it myself. So, this thing between you and him. Is it serious?" Natasha didn't answer. What could she say? She still worried that this seemed important simply because Daniel was the first person who had shown any interest in her. In her head, she could hear Emma telling her to have fun, but her whole body ached just being apart from him for the hour or so since he left her at Charlie's house.

"I'm sorry, I'll shut up. I know how complicated life can get. It's just Tilly wants to know."

"Tilly?"

"She's got a nose for these things. I lost count of how many times I asked her to drop it before Charlie and I got together."

Natasha managed to change the subject by asking India lots of questions about her business and, of course, about cricket. With fifteen minutes to go to the proposed new start time, the umpires came out to the pitch with both captains. They looked around the surface, prodding and poking.

"Charlie was saying there were some areas that weren't draining as well as they should. I hope you are going to see some cricket."

"My train is at four. I have to be home tonight."

"I'm sure by then you'll have had enough," India laughed softly. "But I thought you said you weren't at work for the rest of the week."

"Yes, but I am needed at home."

It took until 11:15 for play to start. Yorkshire were fielding. Both Charlie and Daniel had their backs to where she was sitting with India. Natasha was struggling to watch the play and not to stare at Daniel's broad back. She watched as he started to swing his arms and shoulders, twisting at the waist as if he was warming up for something strenuous. Seeing him move like this did nothing to stop that ache she was feeling, knowing she was going home.

At the end of the next over, his brother, Ben, came over to speak to him. He handed Daniel the ball and together they walked back to the centre.

"Now you get to see him in action." Natasha didn't reply. She couldn't, she was transfixed in studying his body. Daniel walked away from the wicket. He seemed to start much further back than the bowler before him. He turned the ball in his hand, examining the surface and rubbing it against the back of his thigh. It pulled the fabric tight on his leg, highlighting the contours of his backside. When he finally turned to face the batsman, he stopped, staring at his target. Natasha thought he was steadying his breath. She was.

When he exploded forward, his long legs moved swiftly as his arm came back. His left leg hit the ground, and he released the ball, spinning towards the wicket. The batsman hardly seemed to see the ball. He ducked out of the way and the ball landed with a thud into the gloves of the wicketkeeper.

Ball after ball, he produced enough speed to keep the batsman from scoring. Both Natasha and India let out a long breath when he finally handed the ball back to Ben. As he walked back to field near the boundary to Natasha's right, she leaned forward to watch him. Was his knee causing him a problem? She couldn't tell.

When Daniel came back to bowl again, Natasha was sure his knee was a problem. He seemed to have eased up his run, and the batsman was able to hit a couple of balls out of the six that Daniel delivered. This time as he walked back to the boundary, his shoulders hunched just a little, but Natasha noticed the difference.

"I think it's his knee."

"He was having trouble with it last year. But I thought they had done some work on it."

"It was swollen yesterday after we had to walk back to the farm. He told me it was fine this morning."

"Well, yes, he would say that wouldn't he? He desperately wanted you to see him play again."

"Why?"

"I'm not sure I understand all of it. Charlie was the same with me. I have to say some players can be a bit moody, depending on if they win or lose. Charlie tries to hide it most of the time."

"And Daniel?"

"Daniel is just Daniel. Win or lose. He always seems so ..."

"So?"

"I was going to say childlike. But I don't think I can say that anymore. I have to admit when he asked about the Gym Away job, I wasn't keen. Don't get me wrong, I like Daniel, but this was an important job for me."

"So why?"

"Charlie persuaded me to give him a try, and the other candidate withdrew, so…"

"Other candidate?"

"Yes. One of the other players was keen to start with but changed his mind. And to be honest, Daniel has done so well."

"He certainly has some great ideas at the studio. As a professional presenter, he is easy to work with." India looked at Natasha, scanning her face. Natasha felt the need to say more. "And I'm not just saying that because … well, you know. It's his voice, his instructions are clear, and he is so persuasive. I know it's an excellent product, but that doesn't always translate to sales."

The batsman took a swing at the next ball, and it ran along the ground towards Natasha and India. Both Charlie and Daniel moved towards it. Daniel's long legs moved him faster, but he had to reach out with his left arm as he slid across the grass, desperate to stop the ball from crossing the boundary.

He stopped the ball and continued to slide into the wall in front of the seats. Charlie picked up the ball and threw it back to the wicket, then walked over to Daniel, who was still lying on the floor.

Natasha's heart stopped when he didn't move. India sprang to her feet to see what was happening, but Natasha felt glued to her seat.

"Is he OK?"

"He will be. Don't worry. Charlie is there. He looks like he is talking to him."

Charlie stood up from where he was crouched next to Daniel and signalled over to the player's balcony. The umpire and Ben walked over to them. Ben started waving over to the area where the rest of the team was waiting. Eventually, a young man walked over with a large rucksack, and he crouched down to talk to Daniel.

Charlie walked away and India held up her arms to him, wanting to know what was happening. Charlie just shrugged and walked over to Zach, who was standing near what looked to be a wetter patch of grass where Daniel had been doing his approach run. The second umpire joined them and bent down to poke at the grass.

Daniel was still laid out below the wall. The man with the rucksack started waving again, and India sat down. She gripped Natasha's arm.

"Look, they are calling for a stretcher."

"I can't look."

"Here, have a drink." India pushed a bottle of water into her hand. But Natasha didn't move.

"What is taking so long?"

A tall dark-haired man walked down from the away team's area towards the group on the floor. They all bent over Daniel; his face contorted.

"That's their physio going for a look. Fudging Heck, where is our guy?"

"Where's the stretcher?"

"Ben looks worried."

"I feel sick."

The crowd around them were getting restless. To their right, a group of men stood and started singing. Three older men in front of them tutted and passed around a bottle.

"I have no idea why Tilly likes to sit over this side."

"Does she come with Joe?"

"Yes, you're right. I believe he sees this as the opposite of how his family watches cricket."

"Where is that stretcher?"

"Don't look now, but the St John's volunteers are racing to the rescue." Natasha lifted her head to see two portly old men walking slowly around the ground toward the group that was surrounding Daniel.

"I can't believe this. Where will they take him?"

"To the physio room, I guess."

"It's just I don't think I can watch this any longer. But what can I do?"

"Do you want to ring his sister?"

"And say what? I don't have her number, anyway."

"Oh, it looks like they are immobilising his leg with one of those blow-up thingies."

Natasha stood up to try to see what was happening. What did it matter? Most of the spectators were watching, and they hadn't been in bed with this man just hours ago. She caught a glimpse of his face. It was now clear that the man was in severe pain. The colour had drained from his face and happy Daniel was gone. If only Natasha realised that Happy Daniel was gone for good.

It was nearly fifteen minutes before they brought a stretcher over to collect him. Charlie and Zach ran over to help lift him carefully onto the board. Charlie caught India's eye and indicated that the girls should go towards the emergency room.

"Come on, Natasha, it's time for us to go."

"What?"

"Charlie. I think he wants us to go out to see him."

"But?"

"Come on." India pushed everything back into the bags and stood. Natasha looked up at her, uncertain of what to do. She pulled on her hat and sunglasses as India walked off, squeezing her way past the legs of the people sitting between them and the aisle.

"Excuse me … excuse me." India kept going and people swung their legs to the side. Natasha looked down at her feet, picking her way through the bags and avoiding looking anyone in the eye.

"I hope he's alright love."

"That was a good old bang."

As they hurried up the steps and out, then back down under the stand, India stopped for Natasha to catch up.

"Look, I can't be certain, but I thought Charlie was telling me to go up this way. Let's walk slowly up here and see if we can find him."

"But what about …?"

"Just leave it to me to do the talking." India held her arm. "Look I've been there. Madly in love with Charlie and not able to tell anyone. Denying it at work." Panic hit Natasha. How did she answer that? She was pretty sure neither Charlie nor India had been married. She said nothing and looked away.

India stopped walking, and turning to her, murmured. "I'm sorry, but I know you care enough about Daniel to want to know he is OK."

Natasha nodded. She swallowed hard, but she couldn't find the words to explain just how she was feeling. She followed India down a tunnel until they heard voices behind them.

"Can you move to one side, please? Keep to the left, please."

Behind them came a group with Daniel on a stretcher. They had encased his knee and lower leg in an inflatable splint. Ben Woods was in the group behind the stretcher. Daniel's eyes were closed, but Ben spotted them and looked relieved.

"India, can you go ask Charlie to get my phone out of my bag and ask him to get Dan's stuff?" India nodded and looked at Natasha. She wanted to follow India as she turned to head back towards the locker rooms. Ben stopped her.

"Can you come with me, Natasha? I might have to go back to the team, and I don't want him to be alone." Daniel opened his eyes at the sound of her name. He reached out his hand to her, and she held it. Dropping into step with the group as they headed out of the tunnel and around the edge of the car park.

When they reached a green door, an older man who had been leading the way said, "You folks will have to wait out here for a bit whilst we check things out. Don't worry, you can see him again real soon."

Ben looked down at the floor, studying his feet. Natasha felt totally lost and did not know what to say. The bright sun that started the morning had disappeared.

"I feel so useless. What can I do?"

"When India comes back, we can ring the farm and let them know. Rebecca knows all the details of the specialist he has been seeing. I have no idea, and I doubt Dan does too."

"If you know the number, you can use my phone. It's lunchtime they might be in the house." She pushed her phone at Ben, eager to do something useful.

"Worth a try, I guess," and Ben punched in some numbers and walked away from her to make the call.

Natasha swapped between watching the green door that they had taken Dan through, Ben pacing with her phone, and looking for India's return.

The umpires had suspended play and called for an early lunch break. India came half running towards her with two carrier bags and Ben's phone.

"Where's Ben?"

"He's calling the farm with my phone."

"Charlie said it looked bad. I'm guessing he'll be off for an x-ray if nothing else."

Natasha pushed back her head, looking up at the sky. It was her attempt to push back the tears that were threatening to descend at any moment.

"Come on, Tasha, you have to be brave for him. Don't let him see you upset. Do you know why you are out here and not in with him?" Natasha shrugged, but Ben re-joined them and explained. "It's a tiny room. What with Daniel and the medical team, I guess they need space."

"Anyway, I caught Rebecca, and she is going to ring the specialist and call back. It might be on your phone, Tasha, because I ought to go back to the team. He might be my brother, but if the game restarts, I have to sort out what we're going to do."

He passed back her phone and started to walk away. He turned to look at Natasha.

"Look after him for me, will you?"

India put her arm around Natasha's shoulders, and the tears started to fall.

"I can't do this. I have to catch my train." India hugged her tighter. "I don't want to leave him, though."

"Your case is in Charlie's car. It can stay there. There are two spare rooms at the house. You can stay any time you want to."

The guy that seemed to be in charge came out of the green door and walked over to them.

"They're taking him to get it checked. Is that his gear?"

"Yeah, we've hung on to his bats and stuff. We'll take it to the house. It's got some clean clothes and his wash bag things." India passed over the bags and pulled Daniel's phone out of her pocket. The screen saver was a picture of him standing next to Natasha on the studio set. "Can you give him his phone?"

"Sure. He's a big boy, don't worry."

Despite the crowd that was spilling out of the stands now, Natasha had never felt so alone.

"I still don't know what I'm doing."

"You're coming home with me whilst we wait for news."

"Won't we get more news here?"

"Unlikely."

Chapter 40

When Natasha woke the next day, it took a moment or two to remember where she was. India had kept her busy talking and drinking wine and then insisted she stay with them rather than look for a hotel.

When Charlie and Zach got back, the whisky bottle came out. They had talked into the early hours. Natasha wasn't sure she had said much herself, but she was glad she wasn't alone. When she found her phone, she had one text reply to the many messages she had left for Daniel.

DW: Got to stay here 2 or 3 days until they know what to do.

The message felt cold. She tried to reason that out, but she felt something was wrong. She went downstairs, hoping to find more news beyond the message she received from Rebecca late last night.

"Morning Zach." She was trying to sound upbeat.

"What?"

"I just said morning."

"Sorry, princess, I'm as rough as guts this morning. I need some coffee. My mouth's like the bottom of a parrot's cage."

"Here, let me make it."

"I can't do that. Sit down. Have you heard anything about Dan?"

"They kept him in last night, probably going to be there for a day or two whilst they sort out a plan."

"Yeah, do they go in, you know, with a knife and make him all bionic, or do they see if he can heal, OK?"

"But if the swelling goes down, they won't have to operate?"

"I don't know, it's a hard call. Glad it's not me having to decide." Natasha bit her lip and looked at Zach. She could see everything he wasn't saying written on his face. She was quite sure an injury like this would have a more significant impact when the sport was your life.

"You once told me this is what Daniel was born to do. What will happen if he can't play again?"

"Gezz I don't know. But keep smiling that's what the guy needs now, smiles. Would you like a lift to the hospital?"

"I would love one, but I'm not sure it's a good idea. If the Press are hanging around ... They were there yesterday."

"Ha, you're forgetting what a ninja I am. I know ways into that hospital even some of the staff don't know."

"I don't like to ask why."

"Couple of reasons, but let's just say I don't always want the Press to see what I am doing either."

Charlie grunted a laugh as he joined them. "And a few husbands."

"Geez, mate, give a guy a bad name, why don't you."

"I'm not sure Daniel is going to want to see you." Natasha's stomach clenched, and she gripped her coffee to try to steady herself. Charlie looked up from filling a bowl with cereals. "Not today anyway."

"Nonsense, the guy is batty about her. Seeing her will give him something to think about."

"Best to check first."

"He hasn't answered my text."

"He might not have access to his phone. From what Ben was saying last night, he's pretty much stuck in his bed."

"I'd like to see him." Her voice was almost a whisper.

"Then I shall take you ..."

"You better not drive just yet mate, you drank enough last night."

"I wasn't on my own."

"We all had a bit of a shock yesterday. I was the first one there."

"That bloody outfield was lethal. I reckon his knee took a hit during that first over he bowled."

"You and me both, mate."

"He was struggling with it on Sunday," Natasha said quietly.

"Shit!" her companions said together. *I shouldn't have told them.*

"So why didn't he have it strapped?"

"The daft bugger."

"Probably didn't want to admit he had done something stupid."

"I shouldn't have told you." Natasha closed her eyes.

"We won't say anything, but it's best you don't mention it again."

"Not even to him," Zach said with a sigh.

"Especially to him!" Charlie shook his head and stood up. "Well, I'm going to take India a cup of tea. Zach, can you sort some breakfast? Maybe we can get some news about Dan and then decide what we do."

When he had left the room, Zach heaved himself out of his seat and started opening the cupboards. The morning dragged on, and Natasha got fidgety. She was rearranging the salt and peppers and the sugar bowl on the breakfast bar when Zach's hand covered hers.

"Go and make yourself beautiful. I'm taking you to the hospital."

Natasha looked at Charlie, he didn't speak but she could tell he didn't think it was a great idea. She looked up at Zach, who was smiling down at her. He seemed in no doubt, so she left to go to her room.

Dressing the part was something Natasha Poole did every day of her life, however, this morning she had zero ideas of what to wear. She decided to forget the one dress she had with her and pulled on a pair of jeans with a T-shirt and trainers. She took more care with her hair and make-up and hoped for the best.

Downstairs, she found India washing up the breakfast things.

"Sorry, I should have helped." Her brain wasn't functioning.

"Nonsense. You have more important things to do."

"Am I doing the right thing?"

"Sorry, Tasha, I don't know what the right thing is."

"Charlie doesn't think I am."

"Did he say that?"

"No, but I am pretty sure he doesn't."

"Charlie is a big believer in not pushing. On letting them make their own mind up. That is who he is, but not everyone is the same."

"I have to go home at some point, and I need to see him before I go."

"That's understandable." India's smile was soft.

"You ready, sweetheart?" Zach turned the keys in his hand.

"I guess so."

Chapter 41

Daniel tried to turn over. The pain in his leg was gnawing through him. Sadly, the pain relief they gave him only worked for so long but when it did kick in, he felt so groggy he could hardly focus. His elbow hurt where he had grazed it against the wall. It was nothing compared to his leg, but it still made it harder for him to get comfortable.

He couldn't believe how much his life had changed in a few short hours. Driving into Leeds with Natasha at his side, he felt he had conquered all those old fears. Fear of not being good enough. Of not being as good as his siblings. Knowing that his father hated his lifestyle and would gladly pretend he wasn't his son.

On Sunday, after the picnic, he could see a future. The work for Gym Away was going well and people seemed impressed with him as a presenter. Natasha had seemed happier, relaxed even. Just being in her company had felt right. If Rebecca had not brought their father home early from chapel, he was about to suggest she changed her name to Woods after the divorce. Looking down at his left leg, caged and strapped, that bright future had disappeared with one missed step to stop a ball from reaching the boundary rope.

He didn't like any of the options they had been discussing for his leg. Daniel certainly didn't like the way it had all been discussed over his head. He felt like one of his sister's prized mares. *They'll be suggesting putting me out to stud next. Not that anyone would want me.*

It all added up to him sleeping fitfully through the night, and he lay waiting for the next dose of pain medication each time. Praying the pain would get easier. It didn't.

Ben and Rebecca kept mentioning Natasha, but he couldn't face seeing her. She was supposed to be going home to see her husband. Why was she still here? He couldn't ask her to stay. He didn't know what he could offer her now. They seemed to think she was staying at Charlie's, which probably meant she was with Zach bloody Mitchell.

"Good morning, Daniel. My name's Jane. How are you feeling?"

"It still bloody hurts if that's what you're asking."

"I want you up soon, but I am going to give you this, and when it's had a chance to work, I'll come back, and we can go for a little walk."

"Does that mean I can go home?"

"I believe there is a team meeting with all the staff this afternoon. I want to see how you do this morning before I tell you what I think."

"Am I invited to this meeting?"

"Let's give you this first, then I'll see you in half an hour."

Those thirty minutes were the longest he could remember. He was determined that when Jane came back he was going to show her he could walk just fine as he was.

Getting out of bed was a laborious process, and Jane made sure he took the time to do it slowly and carefully.

"Can I go to the toilet, then?"

"That's a bit further than I would like."

"I can do it." His face didn't hide his pain.

Daniel's determination wouldn't let him show how hard this was. He had his arm around her shoulder as they took slow steps back down the corridor. Under his arm, he could feel how strong she was. He found himself comparing her to his Natasha. He loved pulling Natasha into his side, it gave him the feeling of protecting her. A lead weight settled on his stomach, as he knew he wouldn't be there to protect her now.

As if he had conjured her up by thinking about her, he heard her laugh. He stopped watching his feet and lifted his head to see Natasha sitting in a side room laughing with Zach, who had hold of her hand.

That heaviness inside him turned to ice in an instant. Bloody Zach!

"Ha, there you are, Daniel. You have some visitors. They have been waiting for you to come back. I have told them it isn't visiting hours, but I have been persuaded to let one of them in for just five minutes."

"I'm sorry this has wiped me out. Can you ask them to go? I want to sleep."

"Are you sure you can't manage a few minutes?"

"I said no, and I mean no." He limped on toward his door.

He stopped after three painful steps and without around turning added. "And tell them not to bother coming back."

Chapter 42

Daniel looked again at the photograph in the newspaper as it lay on the floor where he had thrown it. Bloody Zach Mitchell, he just couldn't leave her alone, could he? He suspected something when he saw them laughing at the first event.

Seeing them together in the hospital had made him feel sick. Watching Zach holding her hand was too much. Now seeing him hug her like that. The whole world seeing him hug her like that when she had made him sneak around. *How stupid could he be? Another Married woman! They are all the same. Use me, and then drop me for another sucker. Well, Zach is welcome to her. I hope she makes him happy.*

He tried to roll over in bed, but the brace stopped him. It only served to make him angrier. A small knock on the door announced a nurse coming back in.

"You have a guest. Let's make you presentable."

"How many times have I told you? I don't want any 'guests'."

Charlie walked in and picked up the newspaper from the floor.

"Well, tough, because this is the third time I've trekked across here, and this time, I'm going to see you."

"Oh, it's you."

"I'll take that as 'a nice to see you', Charlie. Here, India sent you this." Charlie placed a gift bag on the bed next to his good leg. He folded the newspaper carefully and put it in the cupboard. Then sat down all without saying another word.

They sat without speaking for some time before Daniel gave in.

"I have a right not to see anybody if I don't want to."

"Quite right, you do. The better question is, why don't you want to see people?"

"Seeing people won't change it. It'll just remind me of what I have lost."

Charlie didn't reply. The stoic Scot sat and waited it out.

"Ben and Rebecca have had to look after me all my life. They don't need me holding them back again." Daniel looked at Charlie for a response, but he didn't get one.

"My dad will only rant on about what I can't help with this summer, how he'll have to finish getting the hay in by himself. He can't afford time off from the farm just to sit here trying to make conversation with me. He doesn't know how to talk to me without moaning." Charlie sat still, not responding at all to Daniel.

"The lads from the team just want to talk about cricket, and who knows if I'll get to play again." Silence descended once more until, finally, Charlie spoke.

"And what about Natasha?"

"What about her? I won't be going to the studio anytime soon."

"Are you trying to tell me you only see Natasha at the studio? Because you're many things, Daniel Woods, but a liar isn't one of them." It was Daniel's turn to stay quiet.

"Have you any idea what it was like for her to watch that happen to you? How much shock it caused all of us?"

"I am the one lying in this bed in pain, not knowing what is happening next. Surely, they should be thinking about me."

"Do you seriously think Natasha or everybody else isn't thinking and worrying about you? Don't you think they want to do anything to try to make it better? You haven't even looked in that bag India sent you. She must have spent most of yesterday trying to work out what to send, buying stuff, packing that bag and writing the note."

Daniel picked up the bag and sheepishly peered inside.

"Put the bloody thing down and look at it when I've gone. Now, back to my question. Natasha?"

"What do you want me to say, Charlie?"

"Maybe you could explain why you think pushing her away was a good idea?"

"It worked for you, didn't it?"

"Daniel, just because it worked for me, doesn't mean it is the right thing to do for you. Natasha is in a very different place to India."

"It looks like Zach has stepped in quickly enough. Holding her hand, the next day. Maybe he had been seeing her all along."

"So, this is about what was in the paper. Surely, you know Zach better than that. And the bloody Press."

"Are you going to tell me that picture was photoshopped?"

"No. But maybe if you stop and think about what happened. Natasha saw your accident and was powerless to do anything about it. They wouldn't let her come to the hospital with you. She stayed with us overnight to see you the next day. Zach offered to bring her because, according to him, he had ninja routes to get into this place without being seen. The girl was a mess, so yes, he might have held her hand." Daniel looked away. Charlie continued.

"They get to the hospital, and you start with your 'I want to be alone' trip and send her away. She wasn't fit to get the train home. India was worried, saying she had too many changes to make. So, her husband's office arranged for a car to collect her and drive her home. India and I came here to try to see you, and Zach was left to put her in the car. So, the daft lummox that he is hugged her before she left." Charlie shook his head and laughed.

"Maybe you're right, and she was just using you. Now, you'll never know, but at least you're safe, and if you're happy, then that's OK, I guess. One thing I know is, the Natasha that I saw wasn't happy."

Daniel wiped his hand down his face and sighed.

"Do you really think I know anything right now?"

"I know that India sent biscuits. Shall I go see if we can get a cup of tea?"

Chapter 43

Natasha still had three long days ahead of her before she had to go back to the studio and to the solace of work. She was sitting at the table in the kitchen, looking at the newspaper that held the photo of her being hugged by Zach. It made little sense. Ash Road was a quiet enough street, and even if a photographer was there, why would they have taken her photograph? She was wearing her sunglasses and jeans. She hardly looked like an MP's wife or a TV presenter.

The photograph was the least of her worries. She was most concerned about Daniel and the way he was refusing to see her. India had told her he was refusing to see anyone, but somehow, it still hurt. She felt hollow, just as she had started to feel more herself, this happened.

Every day, she hoped that would be the day Daniel would get back to being himself. She checked her phone again, but still no reply to her last two messages. She had tried telling herself that he might not be able to use his phone in the ward, and she felt sure he wouldn't be out of bed much.

She rubbed her eyes and checked the time: ten a.m., and she wasn't dressed. This was the third day she hadn't been for a run. Sighing, she stood up to go upstairs when the kitchen door flew open and in stormed Jack Wilson.

Whenever he entered a room, Natasha found herself holding her breath. This tall, good-looking man had come into their lives to make them easier. He had taken over organising Matt's diary; he dealt with the emails and phone calls. He could organise a constituency event with one hand tied behind his back, and he still took her breath away every time she saw him.

Today, he carried the largest bunch of cream freesias she had ever seen. He always knew which flowers to send anyone. The scent of the bouquet filled the air, and Jack set about putting the kettle on.

Natasha was still stunned when he pulled a box of chocolates out of his bag. Only when he placed a cup of coffee in front of her did he speak.

He picked up the newspaper and put it to one side.

"Natasha, darling, I am so sorry. I knew you would be upset. But I didn't expect this. My God! Look at you. Here, have some chocolate, it cures most things."

"Thank you. How is Matt taking it? Is he mad at me?"

"Well, he can't really be mad if you have found someone else, can he? And what a hunk. I have to say you have amazing taste in men. Can I have this one too? When you have finished with him, of course."

"Zach? I am not seeing Zach. He is just a friend."

"Tasha, baby, this is me. You don't have to lie to me."

"I am not lying, Jack. Nothing is going on with Zach."

"But I thought you had found someone else. Was that just to make Matt feel better about us?"

"No. There is someone."

"And this someone is a cricketer?"

"Yes." Natasha tried to sip her coffee to hide her face from Jack.

"So, why were you staying with this gorgeous guy? And why is he hugging you? Just look at those arms."

"I was staying the night in Leeds with India, a friend from work. Zach lives in the same house."

"And the hug?"

"I was upset," she sighed. "When I was at the cricket with India, there was an accident, and my friend was badly injured. I stayed over because I wanted to see him before I came home. Zach gave me a lift to the hospital, but he wouldn't see us."

"OK."

"He has stopped replying to my texts. And after this photo …"

"Shit! I'm sorry. Here, have more chocolate."

"Thanks, Jack. What would I do without you? Thank you for arranging a car for me." The look on Jack's face made her stop talking. When he looked away, she knew.

"Why, Jack?"

"Because it's driving me bonkers. And I know you aren't happy. Matt's not happy. But we could be Tasha. We should be happy."

Natasha stared at Jack. The tears were back. She thought she was happy. Daniel had made her more than happy.

"I just thought if the press found out about your other person, then it would get everything moving in the right direction." He gripped her hands. "Matthew is furious with me."

"Did you tell him?"

"I had to because he was so mad at you."

"At me? After ..."

"I know. You don't need to tell me. I keep telling him, he isn't being fair."

"Is that why you're here?"

"I had to tell you it was me. I'm sorry, I didn't realise I would be causing so much trouble. What can I do?"

"I'm not sure even you can fix this Jack."

Natasha stood. "I am going for my run. I have to process this."

Chapter 44

Natasha was trying to pack. Everything she picked up was a difficult decision. Matt probably thought he was being kind when he said she could take whatever she wanted, but it wasn't helping. He was just shifting all the decision-making onto her. It was typical of Matthew.

She hadn't heard from Daniel for over a month, but that didn't stop her from looking at her phone far more than was necessary. She had messaged him after Jack's confession, but the only reply he sent simply said OK. Natasha was anything but OK.

George Webb let himself into her kitchen.

"Natasha love? Are you there?"

"In here, Dad. Sorry, I haven't managed to pack much yet. I am so glad you are here, though. I'm finding this so hard."

"Sorry, love. I can't stop. A machine has broken down on that new site at the far side of Longborough. It's stopped the entire job. I've brought the van. Max is going to pick me up from here."

"Dad! How am I going to do this? Matt will be here tomorrow."

"Great, then he and that other bloke can help you. It's time he did something useful."

"I want to be gone before they get here."

"Well, you've got the van now. You can do as much as you can, and I'll be back as soon as possible. If I can get this job back working, I can probably bring a couple of the lads with me. There is usually someone who wants a few extra hours."

"Dad!"

"Here's the key to the van. And the keys to your new house."

"Thanks, Dad. Sorry for sounding so ungrateful."

"I know it's been a tough time for you. You should have told me sooner, and we could have been moving you a bit more slowly."

Alone again, she pulled out three more boxes. With the van parked on the drive, she could do this box by box. It seemed like a plan. Coffee in hand, she started again. The first two boxes were easy. But with each box, the decisions got harder.

She pulled out a drawer and revealed photographs. It hit her hard as she started to sift through them. She became lost in this drawer full of memories. The doorbell ringing took her by surprise. She missed Mikey he was always her advanced warning system. By the time anyone rang her doorbell, she had time to do a check in the mirror and smooth a hand over her hair, make sure it was all firmly in place.

She was angry with herself for not being on top of things. Her hair was in a ponytail. It hid the fact that she hadn't washed it in days. Her shower followed her run every day and for four solid days, she had not been for a run and no shower. She had nothing to look special for.

Natasha Poole opened the door to a courier carrying a small parcel.

"Mrs Poole?" Natasha racked her brain; she had ordered nothing, and she had no clue what this box could contain.

"Yes?" *It must be something for Matt. I won't live here tomorrow.*

"Sign here." Robotically, she signed the electronic pad. This man thrust the parcel at her before she was ready.

"Thank you," she whispered.

She carried the box into the kitchen and placed it on the table. The label read Mr & Mrs Poole.

The Mrs: Just had a box delivered. Any idea what it is?

MP: No idea. Does it have my name on it?

The Mrs: It has both, Mr and Mrs Poole.

MP: No Idea.

The Mrs: OK I'll just open it.

MP: NO, you never know, I'll get Jack on it.

She made a coffee and examined the box some more. She found a tiny label with a web address. Mountwood Fields. It took less than a minute to find the website.

Mountwood Fields Pet Crematorium. This box contained little Mikey. Tears fell from her tired eyes again. She had never felt so helpless and alone.

Chapter 45

Zach squeezed past Daniel, who, even with an aisle seat, was struggling to get comfortable. Having the brace over his knee stopped him from doing so many simple things. The World Cup match they were trying to enjoy wasn't going so well. Daniel couldn't help but wonder why they had come. He suspected it was his brother's attempt to get him off the farm. Rebecca had tried several times.

He really wasn't ready to watch cricket. His career was over. He hoped he would be able to enjoy watching it again at some point, but he was pretty sure this wasn't the day. Zach had been the one to call him. It felt like a challenge, but all the way down to Edgbaston in the car, sitting in the back with his leg up, he wondered how it was going to feel. He was right; he felt crap.

Things between him and Zach had been awkward since the photographs of him with Natasha. They had both assured him it was one hug after he sent her away. He had messages from them both to let him know her husband's P.A had set the whole thing up.

Just as Zach returned and was squeezing back past him and his leg, Daniel's phone started to vibrate. In his haste to pull it out of his jeans pocket, he extended his leg some more and caught Zach with his brace.

"Just wait a minute, Danno."

Ben laughed. "No, watch this. He has to rush to check if it's Natasha. If it is, he sends it straight to voice mail. Watch."

Damn, if Ben wasn't right. It was Natasha. He sent it to voice mail.

"Now he needs to listen to it immediately."

Scowling, Daniel stood up.

"I better move my leg. I'll just go get a drink."

"We have drinks, Danno."

"I'll get some water."

As soon as he found a quiet spot, he checked his voicemail. Today, she sounded a mess, and Daniel couldn't make sense of her call.

Something about a new house and her dog being settled there. Daniel listened to the message three times, then saved it like all her others.

But it wasn't like her other messages. Her voice seemed small, broken even. As he walked back to his seat, he replayed it again in his head. He walked past the steps to his seat. He just kept walking. He couldn't help thinking about Natasha and her message. Why was this one so different? Hearing her upset didn't sit right with him.

He found an empty bench in a quiet spot and sat down to call her, a knot in his stomach. They hadn't spoken since they said goodbye outside Charlie's house that fateful morning. When she answered, he stood up and began to pace, limping with every step.

"Tasha, is that you?"

"Daniel, I'm sorry. I don't know what I was doing."

Daniel's heart melted. He felt guilty for shutting her out. How could he not help her, whatever the problem was? He wanted to know what had upset her, and he needed to solve it. He walked faster.

"Tasha, just take a breath. I'm here. Start from the beginning. Tell me what happened."

"It was such a shock. I'm trying to pack. I wasn't expecting it. I think it was Jack."

"Tasha, sweetie, I am still lost. Did you say you were packing?"

"Yes, I want to be out of here before they come this weekend. But I just can't."

"Tell me about the shock. What was a shock?"

"The doorbell went. It was Mikey's ashes. What am I going to do with them? I can't take them with me. He won't know the new house; how will he settle? I can't leave him here."

"Well, I'm not sure, Tasha."

"I think Jack must have arranged it. It's a lovely casket."

"I'm sorry, Tasha, who is Jack?"

"My husband's P.A."

"Tasha, is that who your husband is having an affair with, Jack?"

"Yes."

"And Jack is a man?"

"Daniel, you can't tell anyone. Promise me."

"Tasha, you really haven't googled divorce, have you?"

"I told you about that. What do I do with the ashes? How can I pack and move out by tomorrow? I just don't know where to start. Dad was going to help, but he had an emergency. He left me his van."

"Tasha, just a minute. Are you alone? Do you want some help?"

"Daniel, your knee … I couldn't ask you …"

"I'm with Ben and Zach. They can do the lifting. I can sit in a corner and pack stuff." He sighed. "You shouldn't be alone today."

"I couldn't ask you to come all this way because I'm having a bad day."

"It might feel like a bad day, but you're in luck. We're watching a match at Edgbaston. Put the kettle on and text me the address."

Daniel made his way back to his seat. As he walked, he was trying to work out how he could get the others to agree and go with him.

"Ben, I hate to ask, but could you drive me over to Natasha's place? She needs some help." Both Zach and Ben cheered and were standing up before he'd finished his sentence.

"About bloody time, mate." Zack slapped him on his back. Ben just smiled and pulled out his keys.

"Does this mean you have finally come to your senses?"

"Nothing's changed. But today, she needs help."

"So, we're going to help her and not for you to make a move?"

"You catch on fast, Zach."

"Well, I don't get it. But let's go."

In the time it took them to drive to the rescue, Daniel tried to explain what he understood about the problem at Natasha's. He focused on telling them about moving house and the arrival of her dog's ashes.

Eventually, they pulled up outside a rather splendid cream stone house with a sweeping drive. The boys exchanged looks.

"Help me get out, and I'll go see what we're dealing with. She sounded so upset on the phone." He leaned into the front of the car.

"And Zach, keep your head down. We don't need anyone seeing you after your last photo call."

"Shit Dan!"

"Just keep your head down. I'll get you inside as soon as I can."

Daniel knocked quietly, desperate not to spook her any more with the doorbell. Natasha was quick to open the door and pull him inside.

"Are you on your own?" She looked puzzled.

"I left the others outside. I wanted to talk to you first, with no one else listening."

"Daniel?"

"It's what you said earlier. You told me that for a quicker divorce, Matt was OK with you divorcing him on the grounds of his adultery."

"Yes, I thought I explained."

"But then, on the phone today, you said that the P.A. was a guy."

"Well, yes, don't tell me you have a problem with them being homosexual because …"

"Oh no. I don't have a problem, but I am afraid you do, Tasha."

"What do you mean? I love them both. They are a great couple."

"No, you don't understand. I mean the divorce. Matt having sex with his P.A. If he is a guy, it isn't adultery."

Natasha looked at Daniel, stunned at this news, and then sank onto a kitchen chair. It was a second shock.

"You seriously haven't looked."

"Matt said not to."

"I bet he did."

"Daniel, I know you haven't met him – them both – they are lovely people. I know you think I am naïve. My marriage has been over for a long time, Daniel. I love Jack, and Matt is always going to be my friend. I am happy for them both." She paused to watch Daniel's reaction.

"I just want to be happy myself. I want to move on as fast as we can. I've already waited a long time. There still isn't a date for the election, but I just want this to be over."

"Is that why you're moving out? Won't that start gossip?"

"Maybe, if I used an estate agent and a removal firm. This is Dad's house and Matt is staying in it with Jack. I'm moving into another of Dad's houses. I might move again anyway to be closer to the studio." Daniel smiled when he heard she was thinking of moving again.

"I'm so pleased you're thinking of a future."

"Have you started to think about your future, Daniel?" He didn't answer, just looked around the room.

"So, are you moving furniture or just personal stuff?"

"Oh, Daniel. I just don't know."

"Are we going to be useful? I just don't want to leave them out there long." Natasha smiled, and he realised how much he missed her.

"Get them in. I'll put the kettle on."

"Good Idea. We can see what we can do." When he returned with Zach and his brother, Natasha was on the phone.

"Dad, don't worry. I have some help."

"Yes, three of the cricketers."

"Well. Ben and Daniel Woods. Yes, both and Zach Mitchell."

"Dad, I've told you I am not seeing Zach. He's just a friend."

"OK, see you later."

"Right, first job tea or coffee?" Natasha smiled.

"Dan, will you please sit down? Stay off that leg," Ben growled.

"Oh! Daniel, I'm so sorry." Daniel gave his brother a stern look.

"I'm OK, honestly."

"Just sit down, mate. It's not a pissing contest. Ben, you help Tasha and I'll get him sat down. Tash, can we pull some blinds? Some bloke is coming up the drive."

"It's just the mail guy. But yes, I'll close the front blinds, and then no one will see us moving furniture."

Over coffee, they made a plan. Zach and Ben carried the large pieces out to the van. They were family pieces from Natasha's grandparents. Natasha packed clothes, which left Daniel sitting at the table. He packed the breakables that Tasha kept finding and put on the table.

The kitchen door opened, and George Webb walked into his daughter's house, ready to meet her new friends. Daniel greeted him from the table.

"Hello."

"Hello, I'm Natasha's dad. You must be Daniel. Thanks for this."

"She sounded like she needed a friend."

"She needs a friend all the time at the moment."

"I'm sorry, I haven't …" The guilt rose to choke his next words.

"Dad, you're back."

"Yep. What do you want me to do?"

"Can you get the van loaded? Then get it over to the new house."

"You haven't taken anything yet?" He looked disappointed with her; it made Daniel want to hug her. He knew too well how it felt when your dad couldn't see you were trying. He had to speak up.

"I think there is just a bit too much emotion involved in this today. She hasn't stopped."

"Well, it's not like you can't come back for things, sweetie."

"I just want this over, Dad."

"She has had a couple of shocks today, too."

"Shocks?"

"They delivered Mikey's ashes today, Dad."

"God, I'm sorry. I don't think I can ever say sorry enough for that."

"But what do I do with them, Dad? Where can I put him?"

"Why don't I take him home with me for now?"

"Thanks, Dad."

"What else?"

"Not something I want to talk about today. Can we just focus on getting me to the new place?"

"Sure, love, just tell me what to do."

Chapter 46

With the help of her dad and the cricketers, Natasha was soon in her new home, surrounded by her possessions.

"Get the kettle on Natasha."

"I haven't got a kettle – yet." She saw that bring a smile to Daniel's face. It made her smile, too. 'Yet' it was their magical word.

"I do have a brand-new coffee machine. It's on the front seat of my car. I'll get it."

Life was starting to feel better, and the unloading was quick. Too quick. As people went home, the sadness returned.

The rest seemed to have conspired for Daniel to be alone with Natasha in the kitchen. She was scared he was going to say goodbye again.

"Tash, can I have a word? I know this is hard, and you've got to process what I've told you about divorce. But there is another way. You could divorce him, or he could divorce you. If you need someone. I mean, I could … you can use my name. I will sign a statement for you. That's all it takes."

"Daniel, I don't know. I've still got to get my head around what you told me. So far, all Matt and I have ever said is I would divorce him. I honestly don't think he knows."

"It won't be like this forever, Tash. There's going to come a point when even the UK has no-fault divorce. Zach was absolutely amazed when I tried to explain it to him. Australia is light years ahead of us. What do you think about it, Tash? I only want you to be happy. From what I've seen, you've needed to move on for a long time. And then when you finally decide, you find out just how archaic British law is."

"Right now, I'm going to focus on this move. Hopefully, over the weekend, I'll talk to Matt, and we can come up with a new plan."

"The offer's there. If you need it, you've got it." Natasha stroked Daniel's face.

"You're a good man, Daniel. I miss you."

"I'm sorry, Tash. We need to go, but I just don't like leaving you like this." At that point, Ben and Zach came back into the room. They looked tired.

"Well, that's done, Tasha. Time to get this one home. He gets kind of tired and grumpy. And he probably should take more meds soon. Rebecca will have my guts for garters if I don't look after him." They each hugged Natasha and made their way to the car.

Daniel stood up carefully, holding the table as he struggled to look at Natasha's face.

"So that's me they were talking about. I must admit I have been a bit grumpy since this," gesturing to his leg. "I'm going to have to go with them and for what it's worth, I do miss you too, Tasha."

"Could I have a hug?" Daniel wrapped his long arms around her. It was a comfort, but Natasha knew there would be no kiss to end this hug.

"I'm sorry Natasha, I just can't do this at the moment. I don't …" He adjusted how he was standing. "This damn leg, the pain, messes with my brain. I don't know anything anymore. I know I don't want to drag you down. You've been through so much already. I don't want you to get through it and then take on my mess. I have no idea what I'm going to do now."

"Yet. You don't know what you're going to do yet."

"This is your time to live, sweetheart. You are a beautiful woman. Go spread your wings."

"Daniel, please don't say that."

"I'm sorry. I can't do this to you. You deserve a whole man."

He didn't turn round as he limped out the door and got into the waiting car.

Her life with Matthew was finally over. She had been waiting so long for this, and now it was finally here, she wanted to rewind the clock.

She missed Daniel. She missed his texts. She missed his hugs, and most of all, she missed those kisses. The house was silent, not even the persistent ticking clock of the old house.

Natasha trailed up the stairs to her new bedroom. The new bed was roughly made, but at the top of her list tomorrow was new bedding and, of course, a new kettle. But at four a.m. she awoke to silence. It felt very strange. Since losing poor Mikey, she had been alone in the old house plenty of times, but this was new.

Natasha felt so alone. The loneliness weighed down her body and held her pinned to the mattress. With great effort, she pulled herself up to a sitting position and reached for her phone. She looked at the photographs from her time at Woodhill Farm. She stopped flicking through them when she came to one with Daniel holding the smallest puppy. Suddenly, she needed to know if the puppy made it. She immediately sent a text to Daniel asking about the puppy. She didn't expect an instant reply or any reply at all. It was a wonderful surprise when Daniel quickly assured her the puppy was fine. She was relieved that Daniel felt he could reply. It was a beginning. For some reason, Natasha felt she wanted to see the puppy for herself.

She rolled over in bed and tried to close her eyes. The only problem being with her eyes closed, all she saw was Daniel and how forlorn he looked with that cage on his leg. Why couldn't she help him see that he, too, had a future? It might not be the one he expected to have. That didn't mean he couldn't have a great life. Natasha realised that she had to sort out her own mess first. If she could overcome her own issues and find a new future for herself, then maybe she could help Daniel.

Chapter 47

Daniel was still avoiding his old life out at the farm. Rebecca had picked up much of the slack and was out driving the tractor. Daniel couldn't watch her without feeling guilty. His pain was hard to take, but the pain he felt from his guilt was something else. He couldn't see how it could end.

The team, his local mates, and Natasha all sent him messages most days. He knew they meant well, but he couldn't find the words to reply. Hearing their news only made his new confined life seem dead. He had sent Natasha photos of the puppies, especially the one she seemed the most interested in.

The doctors had rebuilt his leg, but they couldn't rebuild his life. The pain was still very real despite the number of pills he popped. Sleep was only available thanks to yet another pack of pills. The medication gave him vivid dreams that he could remember as clear as day the next morning.

In those dreams, he played the perfect game, night after night. Even his batting had improved. Each perfect match saw him receive a hero's welcome from Natasha. He kept her pillow in his room. When he held it, her perfume surrounded him. It reminded him of his mother's roses and something else he couldn't name. He knew her work schedule and watched her shows online via his phone. He wasn't ready to let the rest of the world into his fantasy life with her.

Sitting on a straw bale in the red barn with Meg and her puppies had been one thing he could do. Every day, he weighed them and checked them over. They were all growing well. Rebecca had made an excellent job of finding homes for most of them, and they were due to be going to their new owners over the next week. He wasn't sure if it was part of the plan, but the tiniest puppy that Natasha had taken a shine to had not been re-homed. More than once, the puppy had found a place in his dreams of a life with Natasha. He couldn't bring himself to name the puppy as he felt that Natasha would want to do that herself.

With the cage finally off his knee, he had taken to riding again. Debbie would take him across the farm towards the coast. Meg would come with him some days now the puppies could be left. It was another of the ways he employed to avoid other people. Today, as he rode back into the yard again, he spotted his mother's car. It annoyed Daniel that she thought she could just turn up at the farm uninvited.

He could see that Rebecca was back with the tractor, and he thought she would be in the house entertaining his mum. He took Debbie into the blue barn. He managed to drag the saddle off her back and stand to one side. Daniel picked up some straw and wove it to use in rubbing down Debbie's back and legs. His knee ached more today, so he leaned against her shoulder to take some of the weight off his leg. As he rubbed his mother's old horse, he thought he had conjured her up. He could smell her perfume, old roses.

"Hello Daniel." They hadn't spoken since she left, but he knew the voice.

"What are you doing here?"

"I came because Rebecca asked me to. She sounded like she was struggling."

"And whose fault is that?"

"Is this you blaming yourself? Or are you still blaming me for this?" Daniel didn't answer.

"I realise I must take some of the blame, Daniel. Do you think I don't know she has had to step up more since I left? And, of course, your father expecting her and Ben to do so much when that happened has nothing to do with it." Daniel leaned into Debbie and threw his arms around her neck.

"If you're in pain, sit down. Stop being a martyr. I hope you aren't turning into your father, hiding away up here on this bloody farm."

"I hope not, too. Why are you really here, Mum?"

"Rebecca needed to talk to somebody who understood just how stubborn the Woods men can be. Someone who understands how hard life can be on this farm. On any farm."

"She has been doing a great job with the horses." As Daniel sat down on the bale, Debbie shuffled over towards his mum.

"Hello, Debbie, old girl. Still looking after my kids for me. I've missed you."

"That was the one thing that kept me sane when you left. That you didn't just leave us, but you left Debbie. I could believe you didn't love me, but I could never believe you didn't love her. Is that warped?"

"Daniel, you were young. And you wouldn't speak to me, so I couldn't tell you how much I still love you. I do, you know; I love you very much, and I know you are going through a rough time at the moment, so I wanted to be here for you. It was Rebecca who asked for help, and I want to help her as much as I can. I brought some dinners to lift some of the burden." Daniel's eyes lit up. He remembered his mum's cooking. It was part of what he missed when she left.

"Shepherd's pie?"

"Yes, I brought shepherd's pie and as many other of your favourites as I could think of. Daniel, I'm glad I could help Rebecca with some cooking, but what I came here for is to try to help her with her biggest problem."

"What's that?"

"You. She loves you, and seeing you in so much pain is killing her."

"My knee is getting better. The brace came off this week." What he didn't say was how scared he felt without the security of the brace. It had made him more cautious.

"I am guessing that she'll be relieved to hear that. Daniel, I'm sorry to say this, but I don't think it's the pain from your leg that is upsetting your sister the most."

"If you're referring to my cricket career disappearing with the surgery. Then that is going to take a bit longer."

"Well, it will take forever if you don't make a start!"

"What do you know about it?"

"What do I know about having to change my life? About letting go of all my plans and starting again. Of having to leave my home and my loved ones? About having to find another way to earn a living?"

"Sorry Mum, it was a rubbish thing to say. I didn't have any choice, though."

"I see. So, you think that makes it harder?"

"If you have come here for me to feel sorry for you, Mum, you picked the wrong week."

"I'm sorry I haven't come here to argue with you, Daniel, or to make you feel bad. I wanted to talk to you to say you can change your life. You can build a new one. It could even be one you haven't even considered before."

"Mum, I was trying to say not now."

"Shall I come back next week, then?"

"Mum, please."

"Daniel, this has happened. You said yourself that the leg is healing. I think it's time to start doing something. I am not saying make a big decision today. I am saying start thinking about it, start talking about it and check out your options. Maybe you want to go back to studying law?"

Daniel sighed and pulled at the straw at the side of him.

"Let's try a different question. What could you do to help out at home a bit more?"

"The brace has been holding me back a lot. I can't drive the tractors. I can't muck out."

"The question was, what can you do?" Daniel stared at his mum.

"What do you want me to say, Mum?"

"I want you to say you'll try. I want you to try helping Rebecca."

"I'll talk to Becca tonight."

"And you'll start and talk about what you want to do next. Don't shut them out."

"Yes, Mum,"

"Now, can I get a hug?" Daniel didn't move.

"Too much too soon, I guess. What about these puppies I have been hearing about?"

"They are in the other barn."

They spent twenty minutes together talking about the puppies. It was the first time he had had a real conversation with his mother in fifteen years. Eventually, he walked to her car before his dad came back to the yard. None of them was ready for that conversation.

When they reached her car, Daniel gave her a hug goodbye. It felt so natural.

"Thank you, Daniel. I do love you and miss you. If I could have found another way, I would have. Rebecca and Ben have my phone number. If you want someone to talk to, I hope you will try me."

Daniel knew that if he were going to talk to anyone, he would want it to be Natasha. He wouldn't do that to her. He didn't want to weigh her down with his problems now she was finally free.

Instead, he called the one person he trusted to tell him straight and without judgment. He picked up his phone and sent a text to Charlie.

Dan: Are you around?

CWR: Just on my way back to the house. Ten minutes.

Dan: OK. I'll call later.

Daniel could see Rebecca was busy in the kitchen, so he took his phone round to his mum's vegetable garden. Maybe this was a place he could start to do something useful. He needed to talk to his sister about what would make the most difference to her.

Chapter 48

Natasha Poole was at the table in her new kitchen. She looked at the list of jobs she wrote when she moved in last month. She crossed off the very last job.

So, what to do this week? It was Monday morning, and she wasn't back at the studio until the weekend. Her fingers stretched out, and she picked up the envelope that had arrived the previous week. It was from Daniel and contained a statement for her to use for the divorce.

Reading it had created a myriad of emotions for her. It was a cold and clear statement, with dates and details of their time together. She knew why he sent it, but she really wished she hadn't read it. It took all their magic moments and made them very matter of fact. She hadn't told Matthew about it yet because she didn't want to share it with anyone.

The kitchen door opened as her dad stepped through, and she pushed the envelope firmly under a pile of papers on the table.

"You're looking very pensive? What's up?"

"Nothing. Sorry, I must look a mess." She stood up and put the kettle on to boil, which put her back to her father. She wasn't ready to look at him until she had found some composure again.

"Cup of tea, Dad?"

"Yes, I just popped around to see if you need any jobs done. And Natasha, you look wonderful, as always."

"I bet Mum wouldn't think so."

"Natasha Webb, your mother was a wonderful woman who I loved very much. If she was hard on you, she was even harder on herself. But think about it, that was how she was raised. Now, do you have any jobs for me?"

"No, all done. You did most things before I moved in."

"You usually still find something. What about the garden?"

"I'm not sure I am going to do too much outside."

"I get the feeling you aren't telling me something Natasha love."

"I tell you everything, Dad."

"You were a bit slow telling me about your marriage."

"Sorry Dad, I didn't know where to start, and it happened so gradually."

"How do you feel now you're settled in here?"

"I don't know." She exchanged a glance with her father. "I'm not sure I am settled. I don't think I want to be."

"I was right then. What with not wanting to decorate or do much with the garden. It doesn't feel you are here for the long haul."

"You could be right. I hadn't actually realised that. Now you've said it, well, it makes sense."

"Is that because you haven't moved on from Matthew? You keep saying you'll always be friends. Is there a part of you that doesn't want the divorce? Do you want him to come back to you?"

"Heavens, no. Matthew and I are friends and I think we love each other in a way. I eventually realised we were never in love with each other." She handed her dad his tea and sat down next to him.

"What makes you say that?"

"I suspected it when I first saw him with Jack. He was never like that with me."

"And what made you sure?"

"When I met Daniel."

"So, you think you're in love with Daniel Woods?"

"Sadly, yes." Natasha looked down into her tea.

"Why sadly?" George Webb squeezed his daughter's hand.

"I guess it's such a mess. He is up in Yorkshire on the farm. And I am stuck between here and London. I think that is why I'm not settled in the house. It would make more sense to be in London. But I would miss you."

"But if you love Daniel, and he is in Yorkshire, wouldn't London be even further away?"

"I could get a train from London to Leeds much easier than getting there from here."

"So, you have thought about that?"

"Yes, I'm not sure why, because he wants nothing to do with me."

"What makes you say that?"

"He doesn't reply to my calls or my texts. He told me to 'Spread my wings'."

"So, he doesn't hate you?"

"No, he is worried that he doesn't know what he is doing. The injury to his knee means he may have to quit cricket. I think he is in a bad place."

"The man I saw packing for you and helping you that day had a purpose. He was there to help you. I can't believe he wouldn't want to talk to you now."

"That's the reality of it, Dad. He hasn't responded to my messages. Well, just once."

"Once?"

"I asked about the puppy that had been struggling when I was at the farm. He replied straight away to that message, then the next day he sent me a photo of the puppy."

"How did he end up at your house that day?"

"I rang him."

"And he answered?"

"No, he didn't. I left a message, and he rang me back."

"Why? Why did he ring you back that day?"

"I was in a mess; it was the move and Mikey's ashes came. Then he found out Matt was sleeping with Jack."

"He didn't know before?"

"He knew Matt was having an affair. Emma blurted it out, but he didn't know Jack was a guy. It complicates the divorce you see. Apparently, because Matt is sleeping with another guy, it isn't technically adultery. Daniel studied law. He wanted to explain it to me."

"Natasha love, you realise that guys don't run around telling girls they love them. I am guessing that is especially true for Yorkshire farmers."

"Well, yes."

"And you said he is in a bad place, doesn't know what he is going to do? What did Daniel do when you were in a similar place?"

"He turned up to help. But I can't just turn up at the farm."

"Do you think his family would mind? Would they object to you turning up to help? You've been before, haven't you?"

"I know if I ask, he will say no."

"Then don't ask. Look, if you don't need me I am going to the site, there is plenty to do there. Stop being so hard on yourself. Just think about it. If you go, at least you will know, won't you?"

Natasha washed the cups after her father had gone. Then she vacuumed through downstairs and then took the cleaner upstairs and went through every room up there and changed the bed. She took the dirty bedding down and put it in the washer.

Whilst that whirled away, she went out into the garden and watered all the decorative planters she had around the front door. She was just stepping back into the kitchen when her phone started ringing.

"Hello Matt."

"Natasha, can we talk?"

"Sure, on the phone, or did you want to come over here?"

"Oh, I was thinking you could come here. We have some mail for you."

"Well, you could bring it with you." Matthew didn't answer her very quickly and Natasha clenched her fists. This was typical of him, everything on his terms. She had nothing left to do that day, but it annoyed her he simply assumed he could call her, and she would dash over.

"What is this about, Matthew? Does this have to be today?" She was feeling stubborn. She just didn't want to do what he wanted. She wanted to stand up for herself.

"Jack and I are going back to London tonight; I would like to get this sorted because I'm guessing you'll be working next weekend."

"What do you want to talk about?"

"The bloody divorce what else?" *What else indeed?* Matthew's voice was sharp. Natasha's fingers touched the envelope. Did she give it to Matthew and get the divorce finally sorted?

Divorce. It felt like a failure. Her husband didn't love her anymore, he loved someone else. It wasn't something she was happy about. But when she was honest with herself, she knew it wasn't her fault, or Matthew's for that matter. It was a mistake. If she gave him the statement from Daniel, this could be over, and she could move on with her life. The problem was she didn't see where she was moving on to.

"Are you still there, Tash?" Natasha looked around the kitchen. She only had the washing to sort; she could do this.

"Yes, I'm sorry. I'll be there in an hour or so."

Natasha ended the call. If she was going back to her old house and seeing Matthew with Jack, she was going to do it looking her best. Anxiety filled her stomach as she tried to work out what she would say. She knew the letter from Daniel was the answer, but she was still reluctant. She sat on the bed and replayed the conversation with her father. The things he had said about Daniel turning up to help her and how it was Daniel that needed help now, even if he wouldn't admit it. She thought about her time at the farm and how physical the work he did there was. She understood Daniel enjoyed living there, but being a farmer wasn't his long-term goal. She knew the plan was for Rebecca to take over the farm. If Daniel couldn't play cricket, what was he going to do? It was a question she had asked Zach when the accident happened.

She made an effort to look good, she wanted to hold her head up when she saw Matt and Jack.

Back downstairs, her phone bounced in a message. She opened it to see a new photo from Daniel. He had the puppy on his knees, and she could see the brace was gone. It was only a photo, but it meant he was thinking of her.

It felt strange parking her car on the drive back at her old house. It felt even more weird when she walked in to find that they had decorated. She suspected that was down to Jack, as Matthew never seemed to notice such things. It looked nice, and she told them.

"I like the new wallpaper. And you bought new sofas." She stroked the fabric on the seat at her side. The room looked vastly different. A small part of her was a little niggled as she had left the sofas for them, but she checked herself. She loved her own new sofa, so why was she cross about an old sofa? *Stop this Natasha, they are just things. You are here to move on.*

"I'll make the coffee." Jack left them alone. He was good at that.

"So, the divorce. It seems we might have to wait two years." Matthew Poole looked down at the carpet. *When did it get so bad he can't look at me?*

"Well, we could. Or you could divorce me."

"That is not what we agreed."

"I know, but that was when we knew nothing about divorce. Now we do, so we know we have to change the plan."

Matthew was clearly not happy. Natasha knew Matthew liked his life planned out. He wouldn't be pleased when she talked to him about Daniel's suggestion.

"Daniel said ..."

"Daniel who?"

"My friend, Daniel Woods, the cricketer. He was saying ..."

"What does this have to do with him?"

"If you are going to keep interrupting me, Matthew Poole, we'll not get very far." Matthew lifted his eyebrow at her change of tone. Jack took that moment to come into the room carrying a tray with coffee and a neat plate of biscuits.

"Did I hear raised voices? I know having to wait isn't ideal, Tasha baby, but ..." Natasha threw up her arms.

"Good heavens, will you two ever just shut up and listen?"

"Certainly." Jack passed her a mug of coffee and she refused the biscuits. When they were all sitting down and drinking their coffee, Natasha tried again.

"When Daniel found out about the situation, well … it was him that told me we had a problem." She sipped her coffee. *They have even changed the coffee! Damn, and it tastes wonderful.*

"I like the new coffee." Her eyes bounced about the room. It just felt so strange.

"I can send you the address of the shop in London. Or I could bring some back next week."

"Thanks, Jack."

"So, when did you find out?" Matthew was clearly struggling with not being in control.

"It was only the day I was moving out of here. The day they delivered Mikey's ashes. Daniel found out about Jack being a guy and he came to explain to me. And help me move, of course."

"How did he find out?"

"Can we focus on moving forward, please?"

"Sorry, Tash baby, Matt is going to shut up now, aren't you, Mr Grumpy?"

"So, what Daniel said was, the other alternative is you sue me for adultery. It will mean we can get this cleared up quickly, as we hoped. It should be easier on your reputation and will probably only enhance mine."

"Is that what you want to do?"

"I admit it isn't ideal, and if we do this, I want you to promise not to read this." She pulled the envelope out of her bag.

Matthew reached for it, and she pulled it back.

"Not before you both promise you won't read this. You will give it to your solicitor in the envelope still sealed."

"What is it?"

"It's a statement about the dates and times I have been with Daniel."

"I don't think a letter from you is going to cut it, Natasha."

"Daniel knows the law; this is a signed and witnessed statement. It uses all the right words."

"I thought this was the cricketer or have you been with someone else?"

"There is no reason someone who studied law can't be a cricketer."

"Well, I guess not."

"So go see your solicitor, give him the letter and hopefully we can take it from there." There was no response. Jack silently reached out and took Matthew's other hand and Natasha realised it didn't hurt her anymore.

"Now, did you want to talk about anything else?" Natasha wriggled in her seat. Her eyes kept spotting more changes to her old home. Matthew had moved on in more ways than she had imagined, and Emma was right, it was time for her to move on too. Why had she worried so much about the changes that would need to happen? If she went home now, maybe she could go to Daniel today.

Jack and Matthew looked at each other but didn't speak. She stood up and gripped her handbag to her side. Matthew stared at the envelope in his hand.

"If you're sure?"

"It's time Matthew." And finally, she believed what everyone else had been telling her. It was time for the next stage of her life. The question was, would she be facing it alone? There was only one way to find out.

Chapter 49

Back home, Natasha was on a mission to get to Daniel. She pulled out a bag and packed it quickly. A life of shifting backwards and forwards to work meant she had a bag that remained ready with everything but clothes.

It took very little time for her to put clothes into her bag. Her jeans from her trip to meet up with Matthew would be fine for the journey. She didn't rush, she just didn't waste any time.

She would ring her father on the drive. With her case safely in the boot of her car, Natasha drove north. It took an hour for Natasha to pull onto the M1. She finally felt she was on her way to her future. She asked her phone to call her dad.

"Dad?"

"Speak up, love, I'm on the site. It's noisy."

"I just wanted to tell you I'm on my way. I talked to Matt and I'm driving up north."

"Good. You spoke to Dan?"

"No, Matt rang. I spoke to him about the divorce."

"I thought that was all to cock."

"I told him he could divorce me. I gave him a statement from Daniel. And now I am going to see him. Daniel, that is."

"Did you call him?"

"No! He would only say don't come. But if I'm there, he won't send me away... well, he might, but this way I get to talk to him first." Her dad didn't reply.

"I have to try, Dad. I need to try to help."

"Even if what he needs doesn't include you?"

"Daniel has helped me to see a new future. I have to help him do the same."

"Drive carefully, Natasha, love."

By the time she was passing Nottingham, the traffic was starting to slow. All three lanes were full of cars. There was nowhere to go, and eventually, the traffic stopped.

She thought about her coffee that morning when she crossed off that last job. That feeling of having everything sorted. She was a long way from that now. Here she was, miles from home and going nowhere fast. She turned on the radio, something she could control.

They had been at a standstill for a full ten minutes when the emergency services started to make their way through the traffic. Natasha tried to find a local radio station for more information. She began to worry about the end of her journey. She hadn't been able to find the farm on a map to put it in the Sat Nav. If it got dark, she didn't know if she would find the entrance.

She sent Daniel a text asking him to call her. He hadn't, of course. It made her nervous. Sitting in a traffic jam on the M1 didn't help to calm her nerves. It was well over an hour before they moved. The police were filtering vehicles into one lane, so movement was slow. As she reached the exit for Sheffield, she was two and a half hours behind time. It was getting dark, and the traffic was building up again. She was struggling with what to do now. If she arrived at the farm at night and Daniel wasn't there, what would she do? If he was there and sent her away. What then? Better to go in the morning.

So, what to do now? She pulled into the service station to call the hotel she had stayed in previously. It was a small hotel, and it was full. *There must be another hotel in Leeds.* Natasha was struggling with not being in control. A sense of panic was rising through her. She rang India for advice on where to stay. India immediately insisted she stayed with them. That is why she was now parked outside their house, a little embarrassed and feeling like she had invited herself.

"Hello Natasha. Come on in."

"I am sorry about this, India. There was a major accident on the motorway."

"It's fine. Happy to help. And another girl in the house balances the odds a bit."

"I have to say you're looking better."

"Yes, well, they suggested I come off the pill. It seems to have done the trick. A certain person is thrilled."

Natasha was glad to stretch her legs. Inside, she was pleased to see the three faces of her cricket world.

"Hello, mate. It's good to see you, but what brings you up here?" Typical Zach, always straight to the point.

"I was aiming for Malton. Then I got stuck on the motorway. I'm not sure I could find the farm in the dark." Charlie handed her a cup of tea.

"Have you let him know you're not going to get there?"

"He doesn't know I'm going."

"Oh!"

"I sent him a text and asked him to ring me." Charlie raised an eyebrow.

"He didn't, well, he hasn't yet."

"No, Danno is a bit of a bugger about that these days. We all message and text him, but he doesn't get back to folks. Ben says the messages are helping, so we all keep doing it. I hope he's right." It was the first time Natasha had ever seen Zach look sad.

India reached over and touched her arm. "We're all hoping he can find himself again. Physically, he is on the mend."

"I saw he had the brace off." Charlie lifted his head.

"You saw?"

"He sent a photo this morning of the puppy. It was on his knee."

"Hmm … That's a good sign."

"So, you're on the way to see him? Is that another good sign?"

"Well, I am hopeful. I just have hope he'll listen to me. I need to at least try."

Chapter 50

The sun was shining happily on the house on Ash Road. Natasha could hear Zach in the shower singing something she couldn't recognise. As she lay in bed listening to his upbeat tones, she resolved to be brave and ask the one person who she really needed to ask about this next part of her life.

Daniel had been withdrawn since his accident and she had been frustrated when he stopped responding to her texts. But the others had reassured her that he did that with everyone and that he has finding the idea of not playing cricket again difficult to handle. Maybe they could explore finding a new life and new roles together.

Once the bathroom was free, she showered slowly, enjoying the freedom of no tight time scale. The sun peeking around the blind was intense. Natasha loved the sun. She pulled on a favourite sundress she had loved for years. It was made for summer walks in the country. Layers of cotton softened over the years, tied with knots on her freckled shoulders.

This was going to be an important day, a day she would ask Daniel to build his new life with her. She took the time to apply her makeup carefully. Not the quick whizz of her workday on-screen defined look. Today she was aiming for the barely there look that they spoke about in magazines. She combed her blonde hair down onto her shoulders and just for today she didn't try to tame it or hold it back. Pushing her clothes, makeup, and phone into her bag, she set off down the two flights of stairs and into the great room where the others were scattered around the big table.

India's smile greeted her, and Zach winked. Charlie looked surprised as he glanced up from his paper. Zach jumped to organise some toast for her, and she took a seat next to India.

"By the look of the bag, you're ready to leave us." India smiled some more. "I hope that is another good sign. Do you know what's next?"

"Well, I guess that depends on Daniel."

"If you're looking for a response from Daniel, I was going to suggest you try a cattle prod," Charlie grumbled from behind his paper.

"But on second thoughts, that dress might just do it."

Along the drive, Natasha practised her speech. But what was the best approach for Daniel Woods? He could be stubborn, as Charlie had suggested. Maybe she could try asking him questions, but if Zach was right, he didn't know what he wanted to do. That was his problem. The life he had planned in his head was probably based on what he had seen his brother do. Marry his childhood sweetheart and captain Yorkshire. Rumour had said that Ben would do the same for England. Poor Dan, he had a lot to live up to. If only he could see he didn't have to do the same thing as his brother had done all the time. What could she do or say to help him realise that?

As the road left Leeds and moved towards York, Natasha was confident that what they felt for each other was enough. Everyone she had spoken to yesterday thought she was doing the right thing, but it wasn't their lives. This was about her and Daniel. This was about getting it right forever. Something she believed she'd had with Matthew. Could anyone do that? Start a relationship and know for sure it would last forever, that they wouldn't grow apart and lead separate lives like had happened in her marriage?

After York, the scenery changed, and every horizon was covered with trees. With the change in the environment came a shift in Natasha's thinking. Daniel had been so stubborn in the first place how could she hope to change that? What if being home on the farm had him considering staying on there and marrying that girl in the shop? What was her name? Chloe, Chloe Giles.

The sign read.

MALTON

The food capital of Yorkshire

To Natasha, it said:

MALTON

The start of your new life.

The weather had changed to rain and the rhythm of the windscreen wipers was persistent. The reality of what she was about to do hit her straight in her solar plexus and doubt shattered her earlier confidence. A light flashing on her dashboard said she was running out of fuel as well as bravado. She saw a sign for fuel at a supermarket and pulled in.

As she filled up with petrol, the voices in her head were telling her she could do this and the rain that lashed down tried to wash that away. The days and nights of trying to work this all out had taken their toll and tiredness hit her again.

The lights from a small café lit up the street despite the dark clouds that hung in the sky. Natasha was attracted to its old-fashioned net curtains and the neon open sign beamed out a welcome through the driving rain.

As she pushed open the door, the ding of a bell was loud in the almost empty café. A young woman behind the counter nodded a greeting as she wrestled with an impressive-looking coffee machine for three young women she was serving. As they left with their coffees, Natasha ordered a pot of tea and a scone and tucked herself into a corner table.

It was time for some serious thinking. She pulled out her phone to check the map app for the farm. Natasha wasn't sure just how far outside Malton it was. Worried, she checked how far it was back to the Cotswolds and how long the drive would be to her new house. She was even more upset with herself when she realised she had put in the postcode for her old home first.

A portly man in his 50s delivered her food on a neat tray as her phone announced a text.

EMMA: Where have you got to?

TASHA: The Food Capital of Yorkshire

EMMA: ??

TASHA: Malton

EMMA: How's the food? If that is what you are there for.

Tasha snapped a photo of her scone and pot of tea and sent it to her friend.

EMMA: Looks delicious. Tea for one?

Tasha didn't reply.

EMMA: Are you on your own?

TASHA: Yep!

EMMA: Care to explain what you are doing on your own? And don't tell me you dropped in for a scone.

TASHA: I thought I would talk to Dan.

EMMA: And?

TASHA: I stopped for fuel.

TASHA: I wanted time to think.

TASHA: The heavens opened & I look like a drowned rat.

Natasha grabbed a selfie and sent it to her friend.

EMMA: I am pretty sure that won't bother Daniel Woods!

Natasha's smile broke out across her face at the realisation her friend was right. Daniel had seen her looking much worse and looks were not what was stopping him. It was her marriage, and what a joke that was in so many ways.

The tingling of the doorbell announced the arrival of two well-dressed women. They looked out of place in the local café. It made Natasha study them more closely. Sarah Pritchett the wife of another MP. The smile left her face as she looked down into her tea.

"Natasha Poole! I nearly didn't recognise you. What are you doing in Yorkshire? Is Matthew with you?"

Natasha went into professional mode and was thinking fast for an excuse to explain her presence in Malton. As she looked around the tiny space with its cheery curtains and simple menu, her phone pinged.

EMMA: GO FOR IT! What is stopping you?

Natasha Poole flicked back her hair as she straightened her back and crossed her legs.

"Matt isn't with me."

"Oh?"

"We are getting divorced." WOW, I said that to someone other than Dad and Matt. I am really doing this. The world will know before I tell Daniel. I better get there soon.

"So, why are you here? Oh! You're here to see my brother-in-law! Patrick hasn't stopped talking about you."

Natasha's smile was back. Let her think that for a while. It might give her a little time. She picked up her bag and prepared to leave her solitary scone.

Back in her car, she found the road out of Malton towards the coast and, hopefully, her future with Daniel. She just had to find the farm.

As if to challenge her intentions, the rain seemed to come down harder. It was difficult to see the road ahead. She tried to remember the landmarks from her last visit. The summer rain was bouncing off the road as her windscreen wipers picked up the pace. Natasha had to brake suddenly as a Pritchett and Inkle branded car pulled out of a driveway. In slowing down, she realised this was the turning she was looking for.

The radio was throwing out Michael Bublé. He was signing Me and Mrs Jones. The words sent tears slipping down Tasha's face as she peered out to follow the narrow track. In the distance, lightning flashed over the farmhouse, lighting up her destination. She tried to sing along, but singing and crying at the same time wasn't working for her, so she started to hum, and the tears began to fade away.

At last, she knew what she wanted. She just had to hope that she could convince Daniel that he had not broken up her marriage and that he wasn't a broken man.

Her car bounced against a large rut in the driveway. She didn't remember it as being such a tough drive down. *That's because you were in big four-wheeled drive vehicles, not a silly mini. I really am stupid some days.*

If only she could persuade Daniel that he had a future beyond playing cricket. She had taken long enough for herself to see a different future. What could she do to get him to listen to her?

Finally, the drive ended at the yard. First, she had to navigate the gate into the yard and today that was firmly closed. In the battle to open the latch, she tore her dress. It just wouldn't shift.

Getting wetter by the second she switched off her car and climbed over the damn gate, which created another tear in her much-loved sundress. The summer sandals that displayed her glossy coral nails this morning was not the right choice now. *Oh, Daniel! You better be here.*

With a few more strides, she realised the gate was closed to keep the chickens in the yard. They seemed to imagine that Natasha had food for them, and they crowded her. Natasha felt the need to tiptoe past them as she made her path to the door.

As she lifted her hand to knock, the door flew open to reveal Rebecca bundled up in a long-waxed coat and holding a flask. Behind her was Mr Woods.

"Natasha? What the hell? Well, come in. Come in."

"Is Daniel here?"

"He's never where he's needed." Mr Woods moved to push past her. "Excuse me, Mrs Poole."

Natasha slumped defeated onto the nearest chair. "I'm sorry." Mrs Poole. Two words from his father had put her firmly in her place. Maybe she had more to do than persuade Daniel.

"Hey, don't look so downhearted. He is only in the barns with a mare that's about to foal. The vet's just been, and it looks like being a long time yet."

Natasha jumped back to her feet. "Just tell me where he is."

"Are you sure?" Rebecca looked her up and down. "I mean, are you definitely sure about you and Daniel?"

"I'm sure. I've spent a lot of time thinking about this, questioning it."

"I get that, but Daniel is still processing things. I believe if he can figure out whatever is bothering him about you, then the rest will fall into place." She stopped to look hard at Natasha. "So, I am going to ask you again, are you sure you want to do this with him because I don't think he could take another loss in his life right now?"

A worried Natasha sat down again and looked at Rebecca.

"How is he?" she asked, her voice subdued.

"Physically, I believe he is doing well. He is probably overdoing it this week to convince Dad he is still valuable." Rebecca sat down next to Natasha. "Mentally he is a mess. If he could let go of this need to compete with Ben. I've tried talking to Dad, and he makes fewer comments to Dan, but his body still gives away his feeling. And the silence is eating away at Dan, who is quiet too. Mum even came up to speak to him. That kicked him out of hiding in his room, but now he is overdoing it instead. He still isn't talking about it. I tell you; the silence is deafening these last few weeks." Rebecca reached out to touch Natasha's arm.

"Natasha, can you take him away for a few days? He needs to get off this farm." Natasha squeezed Rebecca's arm.

"First, I have to speak to him and pray he will listen."

"He's in the red barn. Your boots are still in the boot room. There's a coat there he had delivered too." Natasha stood up.

"Natasha, if you don't get the answer you expect, please know he isn't in the best place. Don't give up on him. He's worth fighting for." Natasha smiled.

"Thanks for the warning. I do know he is worth fighting for."

"I'll go make up a bed for you." Rebecca got up to leave, "and make sure there is enough hot water for a bath."

"Thank you."

"That flask is for him if you want to take it with you."

Chapter 51

Natasha peeled off her sandals and pushed her bare feet into the boots. A long blue waxed coat hung above 'her' boots waiting for her, as if he knew she would come back to the farm. The coat was like the one she tried on in the shop the day they bought the boots. Daniel had said she should have a blue one.

In the boots and coat, she pulled up the hood and went outside. She hugged the flask to her body as she hurried across the yard to the red barn. At the huge door, she paused briefly to remember the barn contained some valuable horses, one of whom was in labour. Natasha stopped to take a much-needed calming breath. She had to think of this as a first step. Daniel's injury was a big issue for him. The end of his cricket career. She just had to take it one step at a time.

Quietly opening the small door set in the large one, she stepped quietly inside; Debbie lifted her head and whinnied hello and Daniel turned. The shock of seeing her written across his face. Silence. He frowned and then turned back to the stall he was leaning on. Still focused on the mare.

"So, she's fetched you in now."

"Sorry?"

"Rebecca, last week she had mum come, now you."

"Sorry to disappoint you, but no one asked me to come."

"So why are you here, then?"

"I came to see you." Daniel hitched his weight onto his other leg he didn't look at her, he kept his focus on the mare. Natasha walked over to stand next to him. Not as close as she would have liked, but she was afraid of spooking the horse, or maybe she was afraid of spooking him.

"I wanted to talk to you." Her voice was soft, still afraid.

"I thought we had said everything we needed to say. You got my letter?"

"I did, and I gave it to Matthew."

"So, what more do you need from me? Have you forgotten about my leg? I am not the man you met, Tasha. You don't want to marry a second dud."

"Marry?"

"Tasha, there is no way you can be a few dates and then move on. I can't do that with you."

"Marry?" repeated Natasha.

"I wanted to ask you to marry me. I knew that day we had the picnic, but they came home early before I could find the words to ask you. How can I ask anyone to marry me now? My career is over."

"Your cricket career might be over, Daniel. I don't know enough to argue about that, but we can face that when you have explored all the options. But Daniel I didn't fall in love with a cricketer. I fell for you, Daniel. The tall, funny, caring, lovable Daniel Woods. The man who made my skin dance and kissed me like the world was about to end. The fact you played cricket is just one thing about you. It's not the reason I love you. You fool." She slapped his arm.

"Ouch. You love me? Are you sure?" She hit him harder this time.

"Of course, you big twerp." In her stall, Debbie whinnied again.

Daniel grinned down at Natasha as he rubbed his arm. His long arms swung around her, lifting her from the floor. Hugging her to him, flask, and all. One of her boots fell off as Daniel covered her face in a hundred tiny kisses.

"Daniel, your leg!"

"It's getting stronger every day. I doubt I'll turn out for Yorkshire again. I might make the Malton first XI in a year or so." Daniel stood her back down on the floor and gently helped her put her boot back on.

"Dad is convinced I won't be any use as a farmer or a cricketer." Daniel shrugged, "because he always thought I wouldn't be any good. This knee is just him being proved right."

Natasha walked over to Debbie and stroked her muzzle. She turned to look squarely at Daniel.

"I know cricket is important to you, and I know you love the farm. Do you want to be a farmer?"

"Would it matter if I did?"

"No," she grinned, shaking her head. "I'm pretty much stuck with loving you, whatever you decide to do." She turned back to Debbie, stroking her nose and feeling the velvet of her mouth.

"Have you been looking after him for me?"

"She has, but I reckon she was doing it for my mum."

"Did you say she came to see you?"

"Yeah, last week." There was a ghost of a smile on his face.

"How did that go?" She looked sideways at Daniel.

"Not so good to start with, but by the time she left, I guess we were at least talking. She told me I needed to pull my weight. Not fair to Becca and all that. I have been trying more, doing stuff for her in the house. Washing … cooking …"

"I know you can do the washing, but you've been cooking?" she looked at him more carefully now.

"Yes, I have." He nodded, the smile widening.

"Does that offer of marriage still stand? Because it's sounding good right now." Daniel threw his arm around and hugged her to his chest.

"It might not be pretty. I have been difficult to live with."

"So, I've heard." She laughed and Daniel laughed too.

"How's this going to work?"

"We'll have to take this one step at a time. Matthew has gone to see a solicitor this morning. I guess I need to find one, too." She looked down at her boots, the ones he bought for her. She lifted her eyes to his. "What's the next step with the knee?"

"I have scans again in two weeks. So, we have a couple of weeks to wait before …"

"Two weeks. Do you want to wait that long?"

"Natasha, I don't want to wait for another two minutes, but after all this time, I think I can wait until we get away from this farm."

"Oh!" Natasha moved back.

Daniel pulled her back into his arms and kissed her, a long, slow kiss that explored her soul.

Chapter 52

"I am not letting you out of this bed," Daniel huffed, as Natasha tried to get ready. "Besides, I can't go anywhere until Dad is out of this house. If he knew I was here..." Natasha smiled back at Daniel.

"Much as I hate to leave you, I only have today to get home and then get down to London tomorrow. The traffic on the way up was awful, which is why I ended up at India's."

"And that is why my phone is buzzing with texts."

"Don't you think it's time to start answering them?"

"I've been waiting until I knew for sure. You know when the scan results were in."

"Why are you waiting?"

"I guess I wanted to be able to say what was happening rather than I still don't know."

"From what you said yesterday, you have made some decisions that don't involve the results of the scan."

"You are right. It's all going to take some time, whatever the scans say. I was thinking during my recovery I could explore what I can do if I can't play first-class cricket again."

"I thought the doctors were hopeful."

"Oh, they are. But for how long? No one plays professional sport all their working life. You need to have some idea what to do after cricket."

"So, you have been planning this from the start?"

"God, no! You see, the Daniel Woods that you met was a guy who didn't think past the next match. No, that's not true. By the time I came down to the studios, I guess I had started to change. I certainly knew I wanted to change."

"Did you want to come back with me?" Daniel curled his body around hers. His arms holding on to her.

"I'm stuck here until I get the results. There are physio appointments and stuff. Anyway, wouldn't that defeat the object? I thought we were keeping this quiet."

"Ah well, yesterday I told the world, so maybe that might have changed now."

"You told the world?"

"Well, I told Sarah Pritchett, and that is probably the same thing." Daniel rolled away from her, his face like ice. She had seen this reaction before. Then she'd thought it was the mention of Matthew's name, but now she had to ask.

"Daniel, Sarah Pritchett, do you know her?"

"I'm not sure I'm ready for this conversation."

"Daniel, please."

"Tasha, you have to understand this is something I haven't spoken about ever. It was years ago, but ..."

"Daniel, I just want to understand. I feel sad that I didn't trust you earlier. It was all so much easier when you knew."

"Trust? You trust me?"

"It wasn't anything about you, I just ... I had promised Matthew."

"I see." His voice was still quiet, and it worried her.

"But once you knew, how did you feel? Was it easier for you to understand?"

"So, if I explain this, it's just between us." She could see this was hard for him. She touched his arm, hoping her could see he could trust her.

"I promise. I just want to understand."

"You know I have always been adamant about married women; you know, not flirting even. And everyone assumes it's about my mum leaving my dad and us kids."

"Sarah Pritchett?"

"Yes. I was only eighteen and she, well, she ate me up and spat me out."

"Daniel, I am so sorry. Who knows?" Natasha rolled to lay her head on his chest and comfort him.

"No one. You can't tell anyone, Tasha. It began long before, though. I was fifteen when I noticed her. Then she started being nice to me, just saying things, you know. I guess I was lost after Mum left. Ben was away in India for the summer. Rebecca had some guy she liked from over near North Allerton. School was over. I was alone with Dad so much. I couldn't do anything right as far as he was concerned, and I just … I wanted someone to love me."

"Daniel. I'm so sorry. Did no one notice if she started when you were fifteen?"

"The secrecy of it all made it more exciting. She didn't need to pressure me. Everything I did, I wanted to do. My hormones were flooding my body more each day. It was only a problem for me when she stopped seeing me."

Natasha's heart broke for him. He was still so young in many ways. She couldn't imagine how he felt as a teenager. How he missed his mum.

"And she was married?"

"Please Tasha, I want to forget it." He lifted her chin and kissed her. He kissed her with a passion that stirred her to relax back into the bed and him. She felt the kiss was as much to stop her talking as to keep her there, but she hoped she understood both emotions.

"Tasha, are you sure you can't stay?"

"I'm working four days, then I'll have four days off. Do you want me to come back? Then we can talk and make plans."

"Can I phone you?"

"Yes, Daniel, don't you understand? I gave Matthew your letter. Being seen with you is not a problem anymore."

A loud rumble rattled the windows as a tractor left the yard.

"That's dad off for the morning. Time to get up." He swung his long legs out of the bed and left Natasha lying there, a little bemused.

"Can I tell Becca?"

"I think she might know already, Daniel."

"I know, but I want to tell someone. I want to say it out loud."

"Well, maybe you can ring Charlie and the team and tell them that bit of news even if you can't say much about your knee. They want to know you are OK, Daniel. Yes, they are worried about your injury, but mostly they need to know how you are."

"I'll send a text. I'm not ready for questions. It's a start." He smiled down at her in just his jeans. Natasha was settling back down into the mattress.

"Do you want to see your puppy before you go?"

"My puppy?"

"Yes, the little one. I kept her for you. I know how much you miss Mikey."

That was just the motivation Natasha needed. She was dressed quickly and ready to see the puppy before breakfast.

In the barn, Daniel put the puppy into her waiting hands. He laid one arm across her shoulders, and he took a selfie of the three of them on his phone.

"Can you send me that photo?"

Daniel smiled as he pressed SEND TO ALL.

Epilogue

A party, Daniel loved a party. It was his happy place. It always had been. This was the first party he had given himself. Excited wasn't a strong enough word.

They were renting India's old flat in London as the first place to live together whilst they found where they wanted to settle. He loved the tall ceilings and good proportions in the few rooms they had. They were both working in London. It all made sense.

It was small compared to the Yorkshire farmhouse that had been his home so far. Not that he cared. Being anywhere with Natasha was better than a palace without her. If he had a comfortable bed that would fit him and her, he was happy.

Tonight, was a flat warming party where his old life could meet his new one. An alert on his phone made him step up a gear. Time to get this show on the road. Pulling on a T-shirt, he left the bedroom to find Natasha in the main room, systematically moving things and putting them in cupboards and drawers.

"What are you doing?"

"Just clearing a few breakables."

"What sort of party do you think we are having? Who have you invited?"

"Just Em and a few others from work. But …"

"But what, Tasha?"

"Who have you invited?"

"Same as you, folks from work and Becca, of course. The whole reason for doing this today is because she is down for the show."

"Is that cricket work? Or the radio? Or the agency?"

"So, you think a few guys from the BBC mean we need to hide the good stuff?"

"Not that so much, as it's a small space and a lot of people. I've just got the flat looking like it belongs to us, thanks to help from Stella."

"It is small, Tasha. Are you sure you are OK with us living here?"

"I'm just happy to wake up with you every day." He hugged her.

"Right answer!" He kept her locked in his arms. Looking down he kissed the tip of her nose so gently. "I better get busy in the kitchen."

"If you've finished in the bathroom, I'll go clean up in there now."

"Will you relax? I hope you don't feel the need to be hiding stuff in there, too." He hugged her again.

"Dan, much as I love you, and your hugs, people will be here soon."

"Oh yes, Becca is coming early."

"I can live with that."

"Music, then food," he announced.

"Music, what are we doing about music?"

"I've got a playlist." His grin was so vast. There was no doubt he was happy now.

"When did you have the time for that?"

"It's the one from Ben's party, so you know when it's time to come and dance with me."

Music was on, and Natasha was busy clearing the bathroom and the hall. Daniel was humming to the music. It helped him focus on organising his pizza-making. The dough was ready, so he was slicing toppings whilst intermittently stirring the sauce.

When he looked across at the table, he felt a moment of pride as he admired the stack of boxes filled with snacks he had spent the morning preparing. This might be his first party, but he was determined that wouldn't show. He knew what a great party needed, and he had been planning and shopping all week.

Over the noise, he heard the door buzzer.

"It's Becca, I'll let her in."

Daniel wiped his hands as he walked over to open the flat door to welcome his sister. Rebecca was clutching two carrier bags, which she pushed towards Daniel.

"What?"

"Mum sent food. I take it you told her."

"Tasha sent her a new address card."

"I think it made her happy."

"Really?" His eyebrow raised in question.

"I don't think you understand how much she was hurt by you freezing her out."

"I'm sorry." Daniel walked away with the food bags, anything but look at his sister. Rebecca pulled his arm to turn him around.

"Dan, she doesn't blame you! She blames herself."

"Come through, Becca. Can I get you a drink? Do you know why she sent food?" Daniel struggled to find where to put the newly arrived bags. In the end, he put them on the floor under the table. "Drink?"

"Hi, Becca."

"Hi, Tash. The flat looks nice."

"Thank you. I can't take the credit. I had help from Stella."

Before long, the small flat was bursting at the seams with friends. Daniel was ecstatically happy. He grinned wildly at Natasha, who was pouring a drink and handing it to Charlie.

"This place brings back memories. I spent a night here. That's when I knew I loved her."

"So, this … this is where …" Daniel couldn't hide his surprise.

"Oh no. It was all very proper. But that night was when I knew for sure. I had been watching her with Nick. It was when I was convinced they were a couple. I was lost."

"Em had the same problem." Daniel shook his head.

"Em was wrong, Tasha. They were always just mates."

"But Nick's with girls all day and every day. They've split up now." Daniel knew Natasha, like Nick, thought it was for the best. Charlie didn't seem to get it.

"But that was his job. He took photos of me and Dan, but I hope she didn't think he was having a relationship with us."

"Emma knows it's her problem. They're still friends. They're both coming tonight."

India joined the group and was looking around the room.

"It feels weird. It looks different, but you haven't even decorated it. Or have you?"

"We've moved some things about, changed the curtains and added some different art. Stella helped."

"Where is Stella? She is coming, isn't she?"

"She said she would be here, but she's been working stupid hours."

"I think I'll pop up there."

Daniel had started making another round of pizzas when India returned with Stella.

"Ha, you found her." Daniel frowned when he saw Stella's face. "Is she OK? She looks like she's been crying."

"She will be. Tasha, you will not believe what I've just worked out."

"Go on." Natasha encouraged. Daniel's ears were alert. What was this piece of gossip?

"Her boss. It's Jackson Wilde. Or should I say it was Jackson Wilde? She quit this afternoon."

"I'm sorry she loved that job, but Jackson Wilde, I can't help but think it's for the best. It explains a lot, though. The big money spends and the silly demands on her time. He hasn't…?"

"She isn't saying," Daniel watched as Natasha and India shivered.

"Do I know him?"

"You might do. He was that creep in the car park in Leeds."

"Has she reported him?"

"Who to her boss? What can she say? He is always so careful." Daniel could see how angry Natasha seemed about this man.

"Tilly is the only one I know who got the better of Jackson Wilde from the start. She is very much her father's daughter."

"Probably because he found out she's Maxwell Sykes's daughter."

"How is Tilly?"

"Fed-up. They're pretty sure she'll have this baby by Christmas."

Daniel was putting more snacks into the bowls on the table and collecting the plates for the next round of pizza. He was concerned when he saw Stella arguing with someone on her phone. He assumed it was her boss. He marched over and stood beside her, poised to take the phone from her and give this man a piece of his mind. He quickly realised his mistake. Stella seemed to be trying to persuade a friend she was fine and at a party. Daniel touched her arm and whispered to her.

"Your friend can come if it helps."

"Thanks, Dan." She walked out onto the landing to get enough quiet to finish the call. Daniel saw her return, and he smiled at her. He didn't understand how he hadn't known this guy was a problem before today. Stella offered him a thumbs up.

Daniel found Natasha still chatting with India. It sounded like they were talking about upcoming shows at the studio.

"Hey, no talking shop. This is a party."

"I'm pretty sure there will be some cricket discussed tonight."

"Ah yes, you've got me there."

Stella came over and kissed Daniel on the cheek. "Thanks, Dan, my friend's coming. Her name's Sarah."

"I hope she isn't a troublemaker." Daniel teased her.

"She is a lovely girl, but sorry to tell you, but when we get together, we are known for causing trouble."

"Not that Sarah!" India said in all seriousness. At least that is what Daniel thought until he saw the smile emerge on India's face. "I haven't seen her since school. Is she living far away?"

"Her brother is in the US. She's staying in his flat for a few weeks."

"I don't think I ever met her brother. Is he older than you guys?"

"Four school years older than us but didn't go to our school. A long streak of nerd. He wasn't one for coming down the pub."

"Tasha, watch those pizzas whilst I go make room on the table."

India looked into the oven. "Do you want me to make some more?"

"No!"

"OK."

"You're a guest, India. I've got it all under control." Rebecca walked over and whispered in her brother's ear.

"Careful, brother, you wouldn't want to upset someone."

"Shit India. I didn't mean to be so harsh."

"Oh! I get it. I'm a bit like that at my house."

"See Dan." Rebecca nudged him. He was still puzzling about the conversation when he found Nick rearranging the food on the table.

"Making patterns?" Stella teased Nick.

"Hi Stella, I was just thinking if I photographed food, I might not have as much trouble keeping a girlfriend."

"I should introduce you to Sarah. She'll be here soon; I've been trying to talk her into writing a cookbook. She uses being crap at photography as her excuse not to do it."

"There she is. Sarah, come and meet Nick."

The party was getting busy, and now it was in full swing, Daniel felt he could relax. He took the pizzas out of the oven and sliced them before putting them on the table. He glanced over when he heard Natasha's laugh. She was talking to Charlie and Zach. His stomach tightened. Always Zach. But when she looked up and smiled at him, he knew he had nothing to worry about.

Daniel returned her smile and walked over to stand behind her. Wrapping his arms around her waist and pulled her close. He kissed the top of her head.

"I've come to claim that dance."

Daniel danced with Natasha without having to think about who could be watching them. In fact, he hoped everyone was watching and could see how much he loved her. They danced, and he kissed her. He kissed her more because he could. He looked at Charlie dancing with India, too. Last Christmas, he couldn't begin to believe that he would ever find himself in a relationship.

As the party began to wind down, Daniel found he had more food than he could fit in the fridge.

"Stella, have you any room in your fridge or freezer?"

"Sure, bring it downstairs."

"Stella, this thing with your boss? Are you OK?"

"I am now I've quit. I had a long talk with Sarah tonight. I was debating going back home for a while. Hurst's Bridge to see my dad. I've decided to go see my mum instead."

"Where's your mum live then?"

"New York. So here, take the spare key and you can get the food when I've gone."

"When are you going?"

"As soon as I can get a flight."

By the time Daniel was back in his own flat, Natasha was saying goodbye to Nick.

"I'm sorry Em didn't turn up for your party, Tasha. She keeps saying she doesn't mind, and we're still friends, but she isn't, is she?"

"She says the same to me, Nick, and for what it's worth, I think she was right to end it. I love you both."

"Good night, Dan, I'm going."

"Everyone gone?"

"Yes. It's just you and me now."

"In that case, shall we dance, or would you like a drink first?"

"I would love a dance and then maybe a coffee whilst we clear up."

Daniel cued the music to Me and Mrs Jones. It was their song, and it marked the end of their first party. Daniel kissed Natasha softly on the lips as they carried on moving to their song.

"Thank you." He kissed her once more. "Thank you for all this, for being with me."

"Have we got to 'Yet' now?"

"What do you think?"

"I think we have."

"In that case, come with me." He bent and scooped her into his arms and carried her to their bedroom.

A Note from the Author.

I have loved writing Daniel and Natasha's story and I have many more such stories to tell you.

I promise you that my stories will be full of strong women who have their problems to solve and brave men who will join them on their journey. Most of all, I promise you many, many happy ever afters.

As I send you this book, I must thank those who have helped me. The ones who have encouraged me, the ones who have written alongside me at silly times of the day and the ones who have helped me lick the story into shape. I have listed them here in alphabetical order. Ben, Christine, Christine, Elaine, Helena, Katie, Joanne B, Joanne P, Linda, Martin, Rebecca,

Come and find me on social media. Cheer me along as I write more.

If you haven't read the story of Charlie and India, you can find it here Books2read.com/CWRW

And if you would like to know what happened When Joe Met Matilda (Tilly) then that is available for free from my website.

BEE

Find Belinda online at www.booksbybelinda.com

Facebook @BelindaEdwardsAuthor
Instagram @booksbybelinda
Twitter @BooksByBelinda

Printed in Great Britain
by Amazon

42199709R00169